Hugh Ewing

The Black List

A Tale of early California

Hugh Ewing

The Black List
A Tale of early California

ISBN/EAN: 9783743348837

Manufactured in Europe, USA, Canada, Australia, Japa

Cover: Foto ©Andreas Hilbeck / pixelio.de

Manufactured and distributed by brebook publishing software (www.brebook.com)

Hugh Ewing

The Black List

THE BLACK LIST.

TALE OF EARLY CALIFORNIA.

BY

GENERAL HUGH EWING,

(Ex-Minister to The Hague.)

Author of " A Castle in the Air."

———— ————

NEW YORK:

PETER FENELON COLLIER, PUBLISHER.

1893.

(Copyright, 1893, by the Author.)

THE BLACK LIST.

CHAPTER I

OPENS WITH A DREAM OF LOVE AND GLORY.

"'So listen to me, good people, for thus it begins."—DON QUIXOTE.

THE royal road, or King's Highway, that leads from Durango to the sea at Mazatlan begins the ascent of the Cordillera on leaving Durango, and, after a sinuous course of two hundred and eighty miles, descends to the coast almost in sight of the latter city. It was laid out, or rather traced, by the conquistadores three hundred years ago ; and, though in name a royal road, is in fact a mule path. It passes at one point over a mountain of obsidian, which furnished spear and arrow-heads to the armies of Montezuma and his predecessors. At another, it looks down a thousand feet upon the summit of mountains piled upon each other without order and without end, animated alone by flocks of parrots that scream and tumble somersaults in the air as they fly from peak to peak across the chasm. At times, it leads along the edge of a sheer precipice, with a perpendicular wall on the one hand reaching up into the blue ether, and on the other sinking down into the abyss, with only width enough for the careful mountain mule to make his footing sure. At points where this appalling pathway turns a crag, and is especially narrow, the laden mule steps out along the very verge to avoid a contact of his pack with the wall. One touch, ever so slight, and he is overbalanced, and falls, literally, from the temperate region into the tropics, crushing in his arrest the banana and the orange. At one point it winds high over the rushing waters of the Agua Caliente— deceptive stream ! that has lured many a wayfarer from the narrow path, and offered him, **after a long** toil to its banks, a scalding draught.

The Cordillera cannot be crossed in safety by the m
and horses reared on the plains of Matamoras. The adve
turous American who sets out from the Rio Grande to cro
the continent must halt at Durango to dispose of his sto
and superfluous baggage, and place himself in the hands
a carrier.

On the receipt of the first authentic intelligence fr
California of the discovery of gold, a party of Floridia
took passage on a lumber schooner from Santa Rosa to Ne
Orleans, and thence made their way by water to Braz
Santiago, in Texas, and by land via Matamoras and Montere
to Durango. Here they found their progress arrested by th
Cordillera. In this party rode Peter Hayward, with tw
retainers reared as drivers in the swamps and pine fores
of a Florida cattle range. They were of about his own age
young men, tried and true.

An American merchant, living in the city, advised h
countrymen to sell their impedimenta and engage a chi
of train to transport them to the sea. In reply to the inqui
for a reliable man, the merchant said :

"Take any. They are all honest, and the terms are fix
and never vary. The time occupied is the same by all
fourteen days from city to city. Six dollars for a ridin
mule, which they attend and feed on the route, and sixteen
for a cargo of two hundred and twenty-five pounds. Yo
may safely load their mules with gold, if you chance to hav
it, and they will account for it at the end of the journey t
the last ounce—accidents, of course, by falling over prec
pices, excepted. They have been reared to act in a fiducia
capacity, as their fathers before them. They are honest
instinct and inheritance ; besides, their business could n
exist without perfect integrity."

In compliance with this advice, the party sold their effec
from day to day as they found a purchaser, and engaged
chief of train. During this enforced idleness the Floridia
visited the churches famed for their magnitude and deco
tions ; the Alamada, or Park, in which they saw carriag
in fashion in the days of Gil Blas, drawn by white mul
along the margin of artificial channels through which r
water clear and cold from the mountains, bordered by lof

trees with spreading arms, the pride and shelter of the Park. But in this pleasant time, these hours of dalliance, a trial overtook Hayward—one of his retainers fell dangerously ill and was carried to the hospital.

The early adventurers, one and all, were eager to reach the gold fields at the earliest possible moment. They had an impression that the gold lay about in heaps in particular spots, and that the first comers would pre-empt them and leave only gleanings to the laggards. A few weeks lost en route might make a difference of millions—a difference between the riches of a king and the poverty of a courtier. So strong was this belief that every nerve was strained to reach the goal. Hayward was torn by conflicting feelings. He resolved, at last, to leave what money he could spare with his retainers and go on with the party; but, when the chief of train came to weigh the baggage and adjust it into cargoes, he withdrew his from the heap with a heavy sigh and re-resolved to remain. Charity had prevailed over his thirst for gold. He stood by in a discontented mood and saw the muleteers weigh the cargoes, balance them on the mules, tugging and tieing till they finally got them fastened to their mind, after much tribulation, shouting and kicking. He bade adieu to his comrades, and watched the long train file off to the west and disappear.

Months passed before his comrade left the hospital, and in the meantime Hayward took lodgings with a gentle but decayed family whose possessions consisted of a large house and garden, partly vegetable and partly fruit—pineapple, orange, and banana—with a courtyard and corral, surrounded by a high whitewashed wall. It was a secluded and meditative spot, and the widow and her children were hardly heard as they pursued their daily routine of duty. But one of them, a daughter—Catalina—was seen and watched by Hayward, who soon fell into the toils of love. To acquire language in which to express his admiration he beset the various members of the household, speaking, listening, and repeating with such assiduity that he soon managed the language sufficiently for ordinary conversation. He made himself useful to the widow in as many ways as he could devise, became popular with the children, and was winning his way in the esteem of his inamorata, when an event occurred which hurried on the current of his courtship and made him famous.

A vaquero from a hacienda some miles to the south galloped one day into the city, and announced a raid of the Apaches, with the murder of several of the ranchmen and women. A call was made for volunteers to assemble in the plaza. Forty or fifty men soon came together and set out on a gallop for the hacienda. Half as many more offered to go if furnished horses, and the two Americans, who had been drawn to the scene by the excitement displayed around them, joined this company. The horses were soon furnished, and, as they mounted and were moving off, Senor Armendaris, an old, white - haired gentleman, whose people had been slain, stood up on the wall of the fountain, and, waving his sombrero excitedly, called after them :

"Two hundred dollars a head for each Apache ! "

The horsemen, as they galloped off, returned his salute and answered, half turning in their saddles,

" Woe to the Apache ! "

The excitement, terror and hatred caused by an Apache raid must be witnessed to be understood. They are so bloodthirsty and unsparing, and, at the same time, so cunning and audacious, they mutilate their victims in so horrible a manner, that they seem to the "old Christians," who still believe in evil spirits, to be the incarnation of the lowest and most debased of the Satanic kingdom.

From his gallant bearing and his character of "Americano," Hayward, or Don Pedro, as they styled him, was supposed to possess exceptional qualities for strategy and war. and at once assumed command of the party. The more dashing caballeros of the city, moreover, had gone off with the advance party. He had seen something of the Indians in the everglades of Florida, and was by nature a strategist. On clearing the city, under the guidance of one who knew the country he deviated from the direct road to the hacienda, and bore toward the mountains. His sagacity was rewarded. As he issued from a chaparral through which they had been compelled to ride at a slow gait on to a long but narrow glade, he struck the flank and rear of the retreating

Indians. The Mexicans evinced a momentary disposition to draw rein and fight from the cover, but Hayward dashed spurs into his steed and rushed on the Apaches with a yell. His company, inspired by his brilliant exhibition of courage, followed close at his heels. The head of the robbers pushed on with their stolen stock : the rear faced about and met the charge. Hayward rode to close quarters before delivering his fire, and emptied two saddles in quick succession, receiving an arrow through his arm and his horse a lance thrust which brought him to the ground. The Indians fled in the trail of their party, leaving five dead on the field, while the Mexicans had several wounded. The affair was a dash, over in a few minutes. Great was the exultation over the slain Apaches. They were seldom brought to bay, or punished. Coming down upon the defenseless ranchos by surprise, they committed their atrocities, rounded up the stock and gained the defiles of the mountains before pursuit could overtake them.

The victorious party returned in triumph to the city, with the bodies of the slain Indians, which they laid out in a row at the base of the fountain in the Grand Plaza, thronged with excited people—men, women and children. Senor Armendaris again mounted the wall of the basin. Several servants placed on the wall beside him five large checked cotton handkerchiefs, each containing two hundred silver dollars. Three of these were awarded to the men entitled to them, and then followed a pause. Several women of the lower class, widows perhaps—made so by some former Apache raid—pressed through the crowd that was gazing on the dead Indians, and, with exclamations and tears of excitement, cut off each a piece of an Indian's ear and carried it off through the crowd that opened to let them pass.

Hayward now rode into the plaza, with the barbed arrow still in his arm, and was received with deafening shouts. His fame had preceded him. He had been shaken by his fall, and had ridden back slowly. Way was made as he rode to the fountain, took off his sombrero to the senor, and looked down on the bodies of the Indians. The two remaining handkerchiefs of silver were carried to him, but he declined to receive them, saying to the senor, with a bow, that he

had fought for honor. The enthusiasm at this announce.
ment knew no bounds. He turned and rode out of the plaza
to his lodgings, accompanied by a throng of people, the
senor himself following in his carriage with a surgeon to
remove the arrow and dress the wound. As Hayward rode
into the courtyard of the widow, amid the plaudits of her
countrymen, he made the senorita, who was looking down
from her balcony, a courtly obeisance. Her heart was won.
The brave deserve the fair.

"Catalina," he said to his bride, as they were sitting, some
months thereafter, in the shade of an orange, "I had a dream
last night of California."

"Relate it, Pedro," she replied with animation; "tell me,
did the country look like this? did you come to a mountain
of gold?"

"It seemed to me more like Florida than Durango," he
answered, "and yet it was unlike my native land too; for,
beside an everglade, on the bank of which I seemed to be
standing, there rose a lofty mountain capped with snow."

"There are no mountains in Florida, Pedro, only sand-
hills."

"Only sandhills," he responded, "and no snow."

"On with your dream," she said. "Did a band of Indians descend the mountain and attack you? did you conquer them, as you did the dread Apaches that murdered the
rancheros at the hacienda of Don Philipo Armendaris?"

"No," he answered, "but a man approached me whom I
knew; he said the mountain was California, that the gold
was all gone, and I had better go back home. I inquired
what had become of the remainder of our company. He said
the Indians had stolen their gold and shot them to death
with arrows, and he alone was left alive to tell the tale."

"What a dreadful catastrophe," exclaimed Catalina,
throwing up her hands in affected dismay; "how glad I am
it is only a dream; and then what happened?"

"Then I said I would go up the mountain and see for myself, maybe there was some gold left; but he stood in my way
and ordered me back. Then a scuffle ensued and I threw him
into the everglade. He swam to an island and stood on the
shore threatening me. I saw his arms move but could not

hear him; then he turned and disappeared. The next thing I can recall, I was looking in at the mouth of a cavern. I saw piles of bags, filled with gold, leaning one against another, as I remembered them in the picture of Ala Baba and the forty thieves. Here, I thought, is the accumulated treasure of California; it will make Catalina a queen, and the plains of Durango a garden. I entered, seized a bag and was dragging it to the door, when suddenly the cave became dark. Then I thought I was in the cavern of the forty thieves, shut in like the brother of Ala Baba, and let go the bag and stood erect, trying to recall the magical words that caused the door to swing open to Ala. Presently they came to my mind, and I called aloud, 'Open, Sesame,' and awoke. Did you not hear me?"

"No," she answered, "I heard you not. But did the cave open at your command, or did the dream terminate, leaving you in darkness?"

"In darkness."

"Then it was a warning," she said, "to stay with Catalina, and not go up into the desert in search of death, for the darkness meant death."

"Catalina will go with me," he replied; "we will court fortune in company. Death flies before the young and strong in purpose. Here comes the senora; tell her we are going. You will go with me, will you not?"

"To the end of the world," she answered.

The senora stood before the lovers, under the shade of the orange, and her daughter informed her of their purpose. She was not unprepared for the announcement and received it in mournful silence, looking from one to the other. Presently she spoke:

"Why, my son," she said, addressing Hayward, "do you wish to quit this peaceful spot, to wander in search of bread whiter than wheaten, which does not exist? You have now a home and honorable employment. This world has nothing to offer beyond this; not all the gold of California can buy more. Stay."

"We can make a new home in California. Catalina and I. We will return soon, and buy back the old hacienda of the Morales, and restore the family to its ancient grandeur.

Would it not please you, senora, to see Catalina the queen of La Vina?"

"It would bring cares upon her," answered the senora; "she is happier here. La Vina is gone; it exists for the Morales only as a dream. If you will go, my son, leave Catalina. What," she said, plucking an orange from the tree and offering it to him, " will you find in California superior to this in beauty and taste?"

" An orange of solid gold," he answered smiling, " would please me better."

" It will not satisfy hunger or thirst," she replied. " It is merely one means of procuring the real orange that possesses that power, and which you already hold in your hand. But I see you are going; you will leave Catalina with her mother."

"If she so wills," he replied. " It is to enrich Catalina that I go."

"When you cross the Cordillera and enter Mazatlan," said the senora, " dismount at the door of my brother; he will entertain you and attend to your embarkation. He is a merchant, striving to get the means by trade to reinstate the family. He is a wise man, and will give you good a d vice. Follow it, and fortune may favor you."

" I would like to go with Pedro over the Cordillera," said Catalina; "to see him on board the ship and to visit my uncle. Pedro might fall sick on the way and need my help."

"It is needless," replied the senora, " and dangerous. Stay with your mother, child. And when do you think of setting out, son Pedro?"

" In ten days or so," he answered. " The sooner I start the sooner I will return to this heaven on earth, this garden of Eden and its Eve."

" Eve will be desolate without Adam," responded Catalina: " when he departs the garden will become a solitude to her. Come back soon, Pedro. I will wait for you on this seat under the orange."

Soon after Hayward entered the mountains, on his way to Mazatlan, he was taken sick; and before he reached the waters of the Agua Caliente became so weak that he was unable to retain his seat in the saddle and fell from time to time to the ground, but happily never at a dangerous point. Where the path led along the verge of a precipice he seemed to rally his strength and passed in safety. At noon one day, at a turn of the narrow path he was pursuing, he saw, a thousand feet beneath him, a mountain torrent rushing over its rocky bed. The water in his canteen had long been exhausted, he was parched with thirst and slightly delirious from fever. He turned his mule from the path and began to descend.

" Senor !" exclaimed the mulero who rode behind, and the only one who was in a position to witness his departure from the path, " the river is the Agua Caliente; the water is hot."

" No es caliente," replied Hayward, partly in Spanish, partly in American ; " it is a mountain torrent, it is cold as ice."

" Hold on !" called out the mulero in expostulation, looking down on him as he continued to descend ; "you cannot drink, the hot water will burn your mouth."

" I will drink," he answered doggedly ; " it will cool my mouth."

" Never ! you will never regain the train," replied the mulero, slipping from his saddle and running forward to notify the comrades of Hayward.

" Go on with your train," he answered ; " I want water."

Nerved to accomplish his purpose Hayward kept his seat in the saddle until he reached the sandy beach and the mule stopped, when his system relaxed and he fell to the ground ; but crawling to the river, he bent hurriedly down and dipped in his face. He drew back as hurriedly—the water was caliente, the river was truly named. He crawled away from the delusive stream, unable to mount or walk, stretched himself at length on the burning sand, shading his face from the hot sun with his hat, and became unconscious. In this state he was found, his mule cropping the grass near where he lay, by his Floridian friends, who rode down to his rescue.

" He is dead," said one, as they dismounted.

" He is not," replied the other, thrusting his hand under his coat. " His heart beats."

" Hold up his head," responded the first, "while I pour

some water from my canteen down his throat. See, he is reviving ; let us lift him on his mule and be off."

" He can't sit his mule," replied the other.

"He must," said the first speaker. "Come, help lift him up."

When they got him in the saddle and steadied him, Hayward, roused from his lethargy, took the reins in his hand feebly, and set out, with a comrade on either side supporting him, to regain the trail, and, if possible, to overtake the train. They could not follow up the track they had taken in coming down, but entered a gorge in the mountain that promised an easier ascent ; but it led them away from the trail. At dusk they reached a plateau, on which they discovered an Indian hut, up to which they rode and dismounted. This was a stroke of fortune, as they had no food, but not a matter of special wonder. But one occurred soon after that was, and seemed to Hayward, as he thought of it long after, as providential—it was so unlooked-for and so extremely unlikely to have happened in that wilderness of mountains, almost absolutely unpeopled ; but it did happen.

A frame covered with an ox hide stood in front of the hut. This the Indian woman offered to the sick man, and he was lifted from his mule and laid on it. He sunk at once into an unconscious state, unable to take the water offered him, and his comrades left him to care. for their mules. While so engaged the Indian woman came out of her hut with a lighted torch in her hand, crossed over to the couch and held the light to the face of Hayward, stooping down and examining the features closely. Then, rising, she approached the Floridians and said, holding the torch in position to cast the light on their faces, which she watched anxiously as she spoke:

" Your friend will die to-night."

" We fear so," replied one.

" We hope not," said the other.

"Yes," she continued, " he will die to-night; he will never see the sun rise again : he will quit the world at midnight."

" How do you know he will die, and at that hour?" inquired one of the men. " He may take a turn for the better when he gets rested. I have known men as ill as he is recover. He has a chance."

" No," replied the woman, shaking her head slowly and mournfully to and fro, " he has no chance. Take the torch and go look in his face. His spirit is struggling now to get away from the body. Pray that the good God may receive it with favor, and not with a frown."

" I hear the tramp of a mule," said the man, looking in the direction from whence the sound came ; and in a few moments there emerged from the gloom of the pine forest, and approached the light, a small thin man mounted on a mule. He politely saluted the company as he dismounted, and, taking from the saddle a pair of fair leather bags, he stripped the animal and turned it loose to graze. Then, turning to the woman, he said :

" Can you give me supper?"

" Corncake and goat milk," she answered.

"Good !" he exclaimed. " Goat milk and cornbread is a feast fit for a hungry French king, to say nothing of a poor French doctor. Get it ready, woman, at once."

" Are you a physician?" eagerly inquired one of the Floridians.

" And botanist," answered the Frenchman, with a bow; "a jack of two trades and master of neither, at your service."

" We have a friend here who we fear is dying. Will you step over and see him ? "

" The dying are incurable," replied the doctor ; " but I will see him at once. Woman, bring the light. What is the matter with your friend ? "

" He has a fever ; he has eaten nothing for a week ; he seems to be sinking rapidly. The woman says he is dying."

" That is bad," said the doctor, " for the Indian women are sharp observers in such cases ; but we will see."

Hayward was roused from his lethargy, and the doctor gave him a rapid but anxious examination, putting to him several questions which he answered. He then walked to the hut, with his saddle bags on his arm, followed by the two Floridians.

" What do you think, doctor ? " inquired one of them.

"He will die to-night," he answered, "unless a reaction sets in soon. If we had a bottle of porter or other strong ale here, and he relished it as I think he would, it would save him. But where is the ale? in Mazatlan, a hundred miles off."

"Have you no medicine in your bag that will cause reaction?"

"I have medicine in my bag that would hasten his death if he could retain it, which he could not, even if he could swallow it. He must have a grateful stimulant, or sink and die to-night; he is sinking fast now."

"Do you give him up, doctor? Can nothing be done for our poor comrade?"

"A wise physician never gives up his patient, until *he* gives up the ghost," replied the doctor with irritation, as he opened his bag and drew some hot couls out on the hearth. "The good doctor and the ghost quit in company. Yes, something can be done for your friend. One of you go sit by him, ready to answer if he speaks, and the other build a small fire near him. It is growing cold ; you are both wasting time talking to me."

The men did as directed : one rolled a stone to the bedside, and sat down ; the other carried out hot coals from the hut on a piece of bark and built a fire at the foot of the couch. The dictum of the doctor had banished hope ; they sat in mournful silence awaiting the end. The flame of the fire illuminated the face of the declining man, and glittered in the branches of the pine under which he lay. His heart beat feebly, and the blood crept in sluggish currents through his flaccid veins : his spirit was struggling to be free ; already it was beginning to reach out its tentacles into the unknown. The doctor emerged from the hut. carrying in his hand a vessel filled with. steaming tea ; as he drew near the couch the fragrance reached the sick man, he rose up unaided. took the vessel in his hands, and drained it to the last drop. Presently the blood began to tingle in his veins, his heart beat more rapidly, over him there stole a feeling of pleasure, and he sunk to repose : reaction had set in.

CHAPTER II.

THE DREAMER IS ENTERED ON THE BLACK LIST.

THE city of Mazatlan is situated in the tropics, on the shore of the Pacific Ocean, at the mouth of the Gulf of California. The residence and offices of Morales in this city inclosed a courtyard, in the center of which was a fountain shaded by palm trees, from the lower branches of which hung jars of porous clay, filled with water cooling by the process of evaporation. A cardinal bird was suspended in a cage from one tree and a songster from another. Members of the family sat in the shade engaged in their occupations, and servants crossed the court from time to time, giving to the seclusion some life and animation. From his couch, looking down on the scene, lay Hayward slowly recovering. A report reached him that a ship bound for San Francisco had put into the port for water. The following morning he appeared in the courtyard, and announced his intention to take passage on it. Animated were the protests of the ladies against his quitting his chamber, and they threw up their hands in dismay at the mention of his purpose to embark.

" But you will perish, Pedro ! " exclaimed his aunt. " Run quickly, Pepita, and bring your father to reason with this mad youth. He will restrain you, child, you will see. You must abandon this wild thought. It is self-destruction ; it is a mortal sin."

" I can keep my bed on shipboard as well as on land," replied Hayward coaxingly ; " and the salt air is wholesome."

" You cannot keep your bed, as you call it ; which is not a bed, but a narrow berth, out of which the storms will toss you to the floor. And the motion of the vessel, even in calm weather, will sicken you to death. Wait, my son, for the next ship ; there will soon be another in."

" I must go on this one," replied he ; " another may not be in for a month. They seldom put in here for water ; they take on enough at Panama to last them to California."

"Then see the improvidence of this one," said the senora. "He runs short of water. A good captain does not run short of water above all things. This man is dangerous. Take advice, do not put your foot on his deck."

"As to that," replied Hayward, "the captain may have taken in a sufficient supply and been delayed by a storm."

"Then he is a man of ill luck, and that is worse yet. I have often heard it said," retorted the senora, "that it is better to remain on land than to go to sea with a luckless officer."

"What will Cousin Catalina say, and how will the poor girl feel," said Pepita, returning to the fountain, "when she hears that her Pedro has gone to sea, sick, with a fated captain? She will speak no more, I think; she will die."

"Catalina will never hear of it," answered Hayward; "no one will be cruel enough to inform her, and I will write a cheerful letter the day I go aboard. Fear not, all will end well."

"How is this, Don Pedro," said Morales, joining the party; "the senora sends me word you have lost your wits."

"I have determined to sail, senor," he replied, "on the ship that is now taking in water."

"On the bark *Celina!* She is a tub, in the slang of you Americans; she will not reach her destination in forty days."

"And what is the average trip?"

"Three weeks," answered Morales.

"Still, I will go. I long to be in motion, however slow."

"Sick as you are?"

"Sick as I am."

"Go, then, with God! Don Quixote. Willful men will have their way."

At the end of a week the bark *Celina*, having on board a supply of water sufficient to last her eighty passengers twenty-four days, put to sea, sailing due west to double Cape San Lucas and get offing. On the following day, having crossed the mouth of the Gulf of California, Hayward, sitting on the quarter-deck, caught sight of the cape and inquired of the ship's mate what land it was.

"The southernmost point of Lower California," he answered.

"Then the bark will soon turn her head to the north."

"No ; the wind comes down the coast," replied the mate. "We keep on west a hundred miles or so till we get the wind on our quarter before heading up."

"Does the ship sail well ? "

"Before the wind, yes ; close to the wind, no," he answered.

"Will she make it in three weeks ? "

"In about that time, with luck," he answered, as he walked away. "If not, look out for short allowance of water."

"I am sorry we ever boarded this concern," said one of Hayward's comrades to him. "I know enough about the sea to know that this hulk has no sailing qualities ; it will be many a long day after twenty-one before she runs into port, as we will find to our cost."

"Too late now," replied Hayward, looking serious. "We must make the best of a bad bargain. Senor Morales told me she was a tub."

"She will run when the wind is chasing her," said the other ; "but when her head is turned toward it she will fall off and make no headway. Yes, the senor told you the solemn truth, the *Celina* is a tub."

After making due westing the vessel was headed north, with a fair wind on the quarter, and beat to and fro, losing by drifting a part of the little progress she was making. The passengers were put on a pint of water a day. Then a storm set in from the north and drove her down into the equatorial regions, and the allowance of water was further diminished. Food fell short, and the discontent on board rose to the point of mutiny. The captain secluded himself in his cabin. A calm followed, and the ship lay on the water for days, motionless. A shark and a dolphin played about in the forlorn hope of picking up something to eat, and were themselves caught and eaten. The dying dolphin, as he lay gasping on the deck, duly changed the color of his scales.

"How beautiful !" exclaimed with enthusiasm one of the

lookers-on, who, having a private store of claret in his trunk,
felt comfortable, "each particular scale is momentarily turning from one brilliant tint to another."

"I would rather have a quart of cold water," said Hayward, "than to witness the death of all the dolphins in the
sea."

"Still it must look very fine," said a thirsty Irishman, in
a philosophic tone, "to a gentleman with his stomach full of
claret."

This sally caused a laugh, and the aristocrat withdrew
from the circle.

A faint and fitful breeze began to play here and there
over the surface of the water ; it grew steady and stronger,
the sails slowly filled, and the *Celina*, with the wind abaft,
entered on a career of glory, her speed satisfying the most
critical. On the seventy-fourth day after leaving Mazatlan
she ran in to the harbor of Santa Barbara, to take in water.
The admiration of the passengers at the beauty of the view
was unbounded, their joy at getting within reach of food and
water was undisturbed by the memory of the past ; they experienced unalloyed content.

"We will go up the coast by land," said Hayward to his
comrades. "It is only a few hundred miles. I will buy
mules, and we will ride up."

"And forfeit our passage money to San Francisco," replied one of the men.

"Yes, the *Celina* may not find the wind abaft when she
puts to sea again ; in which event, as like as not, she would
land us at the South Pole. Pack up our effects, and we will
go ashore in the next load. The senora was right, dry land is
better than the ocean in a dubious boat."

After a few days' rest the mules were purchased, and the
Floridians set out for the north, intending to halt at Monterey and go from thence into the southern mines. But when
they reached that town the mining season was over, the
snows had driven down from the sierra the miners and the
population that lived upon them ; and they had taken refuge
in the foothills and valleys, and in the cities and towns on
the rivers and coast. The earnings of the industrious were
diminished, as the lower waters yielded but a comparatively

small return, and they had neither the power nor desire to further support the numerous parasites that had fastened on them during the Summer harvest. The gamesters, therefore, passed on to the cities, already well supplied with men of their craft, and spent the Winter in idleness or in preying on one another. Many gentlemen gamesters, fastidious and careful of their health and comfort, congregated in Monterey to pass the Winter and were followed by the low-caste gamblers who hang about them as the jackal hangs about the lion. They cast disrepute upon the nobler animal, but it is one of the punishments of those who seek gain by dubious pursuits to be so followed and afflicted, and they find it impossible to shake them off. Those of the better class who had rendez-voused in that city to enjoy its delightful Winter climate pursued their occupation in quiet, and gave no public of-fense ; but the lower order was not so circumspect, and often overstepped the limits of the law.

One day as a gentleman named Wayne, and called Don Antonio by native and American alike, was out riding some miles down the coast, he saw a well-known gambler seize the bridle-rein of a young lady who was riding toward him. He had come in view of them suddenly at a turn of the road, and, hearing the cry of alarm, and being a 'gentleman of courage and gallantry, he put spurs to his horse and gal-loped to the rescue. As he approached he was fired upon, but before the assailant could deliver a second shot he re-ceived a reply which terminated his career ; and the rescuer, after quieting the fears of the distressed damsel, and seeing her to her home near at hand, like a true knight, rode into the city and delivered himself up to the alcalde. The officer who held that honorable position had lately been notified by General Riley, the military governor of the territory, that, in the trial of certain cases, he must thenceforth summon to his assistance a jury—a body heretofore unknown in his juris-diction. Manslaughter coming within this class, a jury was called on the following morning to try Don Antonio's case. It was composed of native Californians, with the exception of Hayward, recently arrived in Monterey from Santa Bar-bara, and a Hibernian-Mexican. It assembled at the private residence of the alcalde, where he was accustomed to administer justice, and was duly sworn in—the first jury impaneled in Monterey.

Don Antonio pleaded not guilty and stated the facts in justification. No witnesses were called. Being well known, and his standing and character high, his word was accepted as sufficient. His friends took it for granted the trial was a mere form, and the case went to the jury without argument. The alcalde, with many apologies, conducted the jurors to his wineroom, as the only spare apartment in the house, and, much to the surprise of the natives, locked them in. By Hayward's advice, a foreman was elected, who proceeded to address his companions in Spanish. He said that, while he had great respect for the prisoner, and fully approved his action, he was under the impression that it was the duty of the jury to find him guilty, as in point of fact he was, of the killing, and leave the rest to the governor, who had the power of pardon. He thought the governor expected this. Theirs was the first jury : they should set an example. Hayward replied, with some indignation, that it made no sort of difference what the governor or any one else expected. It was their duty to decide the case according to the law and evidence, and that, according to it, the prisoner was completely justified. A vote was taken which resulted in nine for a verdict of guilty and three for acquittal.

It was now the dinner hour and the jury became impatient to be off. The alcalde was summoned and a request preferred that the jury be permitted to retire to their homes for dinner. He replied that he had been advised by a gentleman learned in American law that he must keep them under lock and key, without food or water, during the first twenty-four hours of their deliberations ; and that, however much he regretted so to treat his old friends and neighbors, his duty in this novel and trying case must be done. He then retired and locked the door, and an urgent appeal was made to the minority to yield. It was represented as their bounden duty to do so, as it was preposterous to expect that nine should go over to three. This discussion resulted in a loss of one to the obstinate minority, and the jury stood ten to two.

In the meantime, the party having become thirsty with

their labors, the Hibernian-Mexican proposed to break open a case of wine, and this proposition was carried, nem. con. Other cases were opened from time to time to suit the varied taste, and the jury room soon assumed a highly unprofessional aspect.

The Hibernian, who had the honor of forming one of the minority, had made himself very busy in the vain attempt to bring over the majority, but finally gave it up as hopeless, and turned his attention to his family affairs. He indited and forwarded a letter to his Spanish wife, in which he explained his situation and endeavored to make her appreciate that it was not for any crime committed by himself that he found himself in the lock-up for the night. But he woefully stated to the jury that he had no hope that his wife would believe him ; that she could never be made to comprehend it, and would die in the conviction that he had been incarcerated for some offense against the laws. He implored the majority to come over to his views ; and, failing in this, he finally went over to theirs and begged Hayward to follow. He took him aside, and, over a bottle of wine, explained to him that in old Mexico they had juries of seven, and the majority of four gave the verdict. Then how unreasonable it was in him to stand out against eleven. He said his wife was of a suspicious temper, and the consideration of his case, a peculiar and very hard one, ought of itself to induce Hayward to abandon his stubborn attitude, go over and make the thing unanimous, and allow everybody to go comfortably home. However, he got in reply only reproaches for his desertion, and the solitary juror was given over to his hardness of heart ; and one by one the indignant eleven dropped off to sleep. When the fatal twenty-four hours had elapsed, the jury was discharged and a new one empaneled, which, warned by the fate of its predecessor, promptly brought in a verdict of acquittal.

Some days after this, as Hayward was seated reading in his room overlooking the bay, Don Antonio entered, with a shotgun on his shoulder, and informed him that the man he had killed was a Mormon ; and a gambler of Monterey, who was said also to be a Mormon, had just sent him notice that he would shoot him on sight. The gambler dealt monte in a long room on the ground floor of an adobe house on the outskirt of the town. His game was much frequented, and he was perhaps the most influential of the lower class, and noted as a dead shot.

In the border country the unpolished do not object to the arrest and trial of one of their number for the crime of murder, provided he has not given previous notice to his victim of his intention to kill him. But if he has sent him formal notice of his determination to "shoot him on sight," they deem the killing fair and lawful, and resist the arrest of one who has thus slain a notified man ; and the law is powerless in the face of their united opposition. But this unwritten border law is limited in one particular—the shooting must take place *on sight ;* that is to say, on the first meeting. And if, as it sometimes happens, the notified party should see his opponent first, and "get the drop on him," but refrain from shooting, and the other does not, while so covered, draw and fire, the feud is forever at an end, and the threatened man may rest secure that he will never be disturbed thereafter. This is the tribute they pay to the moderation of the man who has the life of his enemy in his power and refrains from taking it.

Don Antonio had in him the blood of "Mad Anthony," who never awaited the attack of an enemy. Giving his friend a few directions as to his affairs, he cocked both barrels of his gun and, placing it under his arm, marched to the gambler's room, up to the table, and halted in front of him. The crowd fell back and left them face to face. The gambler read his doom in case he moved. There was no escape from a shot-gun at close quarters. The discharge which was sure to come before he could draw his pistol and fire would have torn him to pieces. Don Antonio looked his opponent in the eye, and he returned the look steadily, without stirring a muscle. They stood thus confronted perhaps ten seconds, when Don Antonio inquired if he had anything to say to him, and, receiving the answer that he had not, and seeing that the abandonment of the purpose to take his life was complete, he uncocked his gun, threw it carelessly over his shoulder, and walked out. The entire fraternity of gamesters united in expressions of admiration and commendation of the brilliant manner in which Don Antonio "had played his game," and henceforth looked upon him with great respect.

But his antagonist, while restrained from pursuing the feud in person by the code, wrote a highly colored account of the "murder" of his brother Mormon to a relative named Corby, a high official of the Mormon secret council, that held its sittings in San Francisco; in which report he made it appear that Don Antonio had martyred their co-religionist for opinion's sake, and escaped by having a confederate on the jury; and urged the placing of his name on the "black list." At the first meeting of the council after his receipt of this letter Corby laid it before them, and, having vouched for the veracity of his kinsman, the inscription was ordered, and Don Antonio became a marked man. In a postscript the writer added that an attempt had been made by Don Antonio, instigated by the juryman Hayward, to assassinate him; and the latter name was also entered, but noted "Held under advisement."

This note appended to the sentence of Hayward was a surprise to Corby, and angered him. His large and prominent pale-blue eyes rested with an open stare on the member of the council who had proposed it, and his light-red eyebrows contracted to a frown. He rose and pushed back his chair.

"Why hold this name under advisement?" he said, addressing Stubbs, the president, who sat at the head of the table. "Am I to understand that my word or the letter of my kinsman is doubted?" casting, as he concluded, a glance of defiance at the members who sat across the table, and giving his mustache, which was sufficiently belligerent already, an additional twist.

"Assuredly not, Brother Corby," said Stubbs, in a soothing tone, leaning back in his chair; "but we are in the country of the Gentiles and must move with caution. We are not in the valley of the Great Salt Lake, remember."

"I voted death to the malignant Don Antonio," said the member who had suggested the note, irritated by the insolent tone of Corby, "because he had bathed his hands in the blood of the saints; but the man Hayward is simply accused of talking, and I enter my protest against swelling the black list with such cases."

"We must move with caution, brother," interposed a wealthy councilor. "We will have the mob down on us if our acts should perchance come to light."

"Swelling the black list," sneered Corby, looking at the chief offender. "Does the brother know how many men are on it, unexecuted?"

"Seven," he replied.

"Six," returned Corby, triumphantly.

"One then has been destroyed since our last sitting," said Stubbs.

"I have removed one since my last report," replied Corby.

"What number?" inquired the president, opening a book and referring to the list, while expectation and curiosity was displayed at the board.

"Number Nine."

"'Number Nine,' said Stubbs, reading from the ledger of death, 'the order for his removal came from the Great Salt Lake, marked "peremptory and immediate," no cause assigned.'"

"If it is in order," said a member, who with his associates seemed disappointed at the brevity of the record in the case, "I move the chief now make his report of the execution."

"The report is in order," replied Stubbs; "the secretary will take notes of the narrative for transmittal to the lake."

"I attended to Number Nine in person," responded Corby, lighting a cigar and leaning back in his chair with his thumbs in the armholes of his vest, "because time had been lost in finding him, and his case was marked immediate. I had sent his name and description to our friends in the upper towns and to the mining centers, but got no hint from them; when, ten days ago, I saw my man come out of the office of the *Alta California*, followed him to his boarding-house, and back, got his name and shadowed him from that hour till eleven last night. Number Nine was on the staff of the paper. His case was difficult, because his habits were regular. After tea he went down to the plaza. and passed the evening with his friends, spending most of the time in the El Dorado; returning to his lodging with a companion between ten and eleven. Night before last, when they left the saloon, instead of going to their boarding-house the two men turned down to the water, and walked out to the end of the long wharf.

Last night when they left the saloon they walked together to the corner of the plaza, where they separated, the friend going home, and Number Nine turning down again to the water. I knew what was taking him there from a conversation I had overheard in the evening. I took a short cut through an alley, reached the wharf in advance of him, and walked rapidly down to the end. The moon was shining, and I saw him coming down, walking leisurely. As he approached, I stepped up on the top of the corner pile, that rises some three feet above the level of the wharf, and shading my eyes with my hands, looked out to sea.

" ' Looking for the steamer?' he inquired.

" ' She is days overdue,' I answered. ' I am expecting an uncle on her. I fear she has met with disaster.'

" ' My brother is on her,' said he ; ' I came down to take a lookout before going to bed. I thought I saw her head-light last night, but it turned out to be the glitter of the moon on the waves.'

" ' There she is now,' said I. 'Yes, it is the head-light of a steamer; I can catch a glimpse of it as the waves rise and fall; step up here and look,' and as I said so I jumped down on the wharf and made way for him.

" ' It's a ticklish post to stand on, friend,' he answered, ' with the ebb tide running to sea like a mill race. I haven't got the nerve that you seem to have.'

" ' Nonsense,' said I, ' there's no danger. Give me your hand and I'll help you up.'

" ' If you'll hold on to my hand after I get up,' he answered, after hesitating a bit, ' I believe I'll venture a glimpse.' "

" He stood erect on the pile a few seconds looking out to sea, and then plunged headlong into the water."

" Did he rise to the surface ? " inquired Stubbs.

" Once," replied Corby. " I stepped in his place on the pile when he left it and watched. I saw him rise some forty or fifty yards below and struggle fiercely in the moonlight, but the tide was too strong for him and carried him under."

" Did he call out ? "

" He called for help," answered Corby.

" Did you answer ? "

" I laughed."

" Brother Corby," said a fanatical looking member, raising his hands and eyes, " is a veritable destroying angel, he
will meet high reward in a better life; would it were in our
power to recompense him here."

" You can recompense him here if you like," replied
Corby, flipping the ashes from the end of his cigar and giving
it several vigorous puffs to keep it from going out.

" And how? in what manner?" inquired his fanatical
brother, laying his clasped hands on the table before him
and stretching forward his neck.

" By striking out the words ' Held under advisement ' in
the entry of Hayward in the black list."

" I will vote for it, friend Corby, I will vote for it," earnestly but anxiously replied the member. " Naught that
you ask in reason should be denied you."

A discussion now ensued in which Corby, leaning back in
his chair and puffing his cigar, disdained to take part ; followed soon after by a vote by which, but one dissenting,
Hayward was handed over to the tender mercies of Corby,
" Chief of the Avenging Angels," and was entered in the
register as Number Twenty-one.

CHAPTER III.

A SERPENT LURKS IN A GARDEN OF EDEN.

ON the sea coast, some miles below Monterey, stood the hacienda of San Pablo. The estate comprised the one-half of an old Spanish grant, and was used for the rearing of cattle and horses, small bands of which were scattered over its feeding grounds, each confining itself to its own water and pasture, and dividing up the territory by a law of their own institution. Sometimes, however, a band would take alarm from some sight or sound, and stampede, break over the imaginary line that had hitherto confined it, and run for many miles, often crossing the boundary of the estate ; and finally, when exhausted, settle down on some strange pasture. It was the duty of the vaqueros, or mounted herdsmen, to ride by each band at stated intervals, and, in case one had quitted its accustomed range, to take the trail, pursue, and bring it back. It was a part of their duty also to kill and hang up to the limb of a tree near the quarters two or three fat cattle, at intervals of a few days, for the use of the family. the peons, and the dogs ; and to " round up " the stock yearly and brand the increase. These men led a half-wild life, galloping over the country, visiting their herds, lassoing cattle and horses, bears and wolves, and lounging in their hours of idleness about the peon quarters of the hacienda. They were exceedingly expert horsemen and faithful servitors.

The quinta, or residence, was situated on a bluff with a level lawn in front which broke off and sloped to the sea, down which ran a winding road and pathway. It was built of adobe, whitewashed, and had an extensive front, covered in its entire length by a broad arcade, supported by white columns. The view from this open apartment—for it was much used as such and for promenading, especially in wet weather—was extensive and beautiful, reaching up and down the coast for miles, and bounded in front by the ocean horizon. To the rear were quarters for the peons and house servants, and to the left front a pathway led to a cliff that

overhung the ocean, on which stood an ancient chapel with
a belfry showing white and glittering from the sea. A
flower-garden adjoined it, from which the altar and statues
within were daily decorated with fresh flowers ; and behind
it, inclosed by a low, whitewashed adobe wall, was a diminutive graveyard—God's acre.

The proprietor of this estate was the Senor Don Manuel
Velasco, an old Castilian by descent, in whose veins ran no
admixture of the blood of Indian or Moor. He was of medium
height and size, wore no beard, dressed well, and was a gentleman in manners, appearance and fact. He was quiet and
affectionate in his intercourse with his family and depend-
ents, was a student of Spanish literature, overlooked his
estate, and passed a life of joint activity and contemplation.

The only other gentleman in the family was the Senor
Don Gregorio, a superannuated Franciscan friar, a relative
of Don Manuel, who officiated at the chapel and attended to
the spiritual wants of the family and people of the hacienda
and adjoining estates. He was tall, ascetic in appearance,
a student, and habitually wore the brown habit of his order.
One day, before the Mexican government broke down the old
missionary establishments, he was superintending the Indians at work at the tanning vats at the mission of Santa
Barbara, when a party of wild Indians came down from the
mountains. They approached him, and, after some conversation, the chief brought out from under his blanket a lump
of pure gold weighing several pounds. Handing it to the
friar, he said :

" Is it good ? "

The Franciscan held it in his hand, weighed it, and
thought.

" Here," he said to himself, " is a minister of evil. I see
the rush of the adventurer, the end of conversion, the cor-
ruption of the Christian Indian, the destruction of the mission. No," he answered aloud, tossing the gold lump into
the vat before him, in which it sunk with a splash to the
bottom, " no es bueno " (it is not good). He told this tale to
Sherman.

The Senora Dona Theresa, the spouse of Don Manuel, was
a lady of good presence, of amiability and character, and

managed her household quietly and well. The daughter of
the house, the Senorita Maria de los Dolores, an only child,
was a Spanish beauty, bright and graceful, and as sweet as
the honey of Hibla. She had captured the heart of the gallant knight who had ridden to her rescue, and who dreamed
day and night of his distressed damsel.

While Don Antonio was yet in the flush of his popularity
with the orderly class for his gallant defense of the beautiful
Dolores, and with the disorderly for so bravely "getting the
drop" on the gentleman who had condemned him to death
on sight, there rode up to his door a vaquero from San
Pablo, leading a splendid horse, richly accoutered. He inquired for Don Antonio, and presented him a letter from
Don Manuel thanking him for his service to the family, and
begging him to accept the horse and furniture, and an invitation to dinner, to give the ladies an opportunity of pre-
senting their thanks in person.

Don Antonio, as he rode out to San Pablo on his new
steed, presented a fine appearance. He was tall and young,
of large frame, fair hair, clean-shaved, as was the custom of
the time, and quiet and self-possessed in manner. The moderate sum of money he had brought with him from his home
on the lower Potomac had been more than half engulfed in
San Francisco in some small ventures, and he had dropped
down to the quiet and inexpensive port of Monterey, in hope
of meeting with less competition and more honesty. He had
purchased several suburban blocks of ground and laid them
out in lots, and was in wait for the slow-coming purchaser ;
for the real estate pool had not yet moved in this sluggish
town, which, leaving out the stir made by the military, very
much resembled a deserted village. The prospect was dis-
couraging, and he was ruing his investment, and settling
into a state of despair, when the late excitement awoke him
to fresh life. Still the town, though so quiet, was a pleasant
place of Winter residence. Many old Spanish or California
families, who lived in their " casas de campo " in the Summer, had their town houses and passed their Winters in
Monterey. Tertulias, or informal evening parties, were held
every night ; riding parties were frequent, and the sound of
the guitar and the song of the lover were heard in the moon-

light under the balconies of the fair. The military governor
of the Territory, residing here with his staff, was General
Riley, a tall, thin, war-scarred veteran, who vowed when he
sprung from the boat on the sands of Vera Cruz to " win a
yellow sash, or seven feet of ground," and who won his
" star " at the storming of the Molino del Rey, nearly at the
cost of his life, making a narrow escape from the alternative
seven feet. Artillery was stationed at the Monterey fort
overlooking and commanding the town and harbor, and in-
fantry under the commandant of the post. The firing of the
morning and evening gun, the parade of the troops, the mu-
sic of the military bands, the visits of officers to the resident
families, and the courtship and rivalry of the younger sons
of Mars—all tended to make the Winter pass pleasantly.
But there was little business, and no fortunes to be made.

Don Antonio was received at San Pablo with marks of
distinguished consideration. His bridle and stirrup were
held as he dismounted, and he was received at the door by
Don Manuel and the old Franciscan with a Spanish embrace,
the hacienda being placed at his disposal. The Franciscan
complimented him in stately phrase and was pleased with
his manly appearance. Don Manuel and the ladies expressed
their gratitude and thanks in polite and earnest terms, and
made him feel at ease and at home at once—a great art possessed by the few. The Franciscan displayed several very
ancient books in dead letter, that lay near his heart, and
Don Antonio expressed great interest and admiration, as in
duty bound, though his thoughts were on the living Dolores.
Points of beauty in view from the arcade were called to his
attention, and the flower garden and chapel visited. A walk
was taken down the winding path to the sea, and along the
beach, where the lover contrived to separate his inamorata
from the elders, spoke softly to her, and gathered and presented her shells. In the evening Dolores played the guitar
and sang old Spanish melodies till the hour came for Don
Antonio to take his departure, and the day of enchantment
to close. Don Manuel rode with him to the limit of his estate, and a vaquero followed him to the door of his lodgings.

In compliance with pressing invitations from her father
and mother, and a gentle one from the senorita, Don Antonio

repeated his visit, and soon fell into the habit of spending the Sunday at San Pablo ; coming to breakfast and attending the ladies to chapel. The theology of the Franciscan and the explanations of the senorita softened his prejudices, and by the aid of a Spanish prayer-book, from the pages of which, it is true, he threw an occasional side glance, he passed muster in the rural congregation as a promising neophyte.

The days passed here were full of peace and quiet and growing love. It was a household, indeed, in which peace reigned, only disturbed from without, at long intervals, by a midnight raid upon the cattle. The hereditary servants were docile and content, ruled over and swayed by a mild and paternal authority. The ladies passed their time in superintending the household and garden, and in visits to their neighbors ; the Franciscan in meditation, and reading the " Ascetico Mistico," and other old Spanish works of similar import which delighted his solitary soul, though possessing for the general reader little of interest beyond the pure Castilian in which they were written. Don Antonio dipped into them to improve his Spanish, and caught a glimpse of an interior world of thought. the existence of which had been up to that time unknown and unsuspected by him.

Spring had come and the land was literally carpeted with flowers. Bands of small wolves swept over the plains at night, howling regardless of melody. Wild geese fed on the rolling prairies in droves that fairly covered the face of the earth. Wild fowl in the lagoon. deer in the mountain, antelope and wild cattle on the plain, with the village of the as-sociated marmot and owl, animated the landscape ; and the country, not yet defaced by cultivation, surpassed in beauty the fabled Utopia of the venerable More.

But the serpent lurked even in the garden of Eden, and Corby, impatient at the procrastination of his agent, came down to Monterey. He sat in a low garret over the play-room of his kinsman, reading a voluminous report, in which the figures twenty and twenty-one frequently occurred. The gables of this dismal apartment had each a small aperture to admit the light, the shutters of which were closed and bolted ; on its sides the roof came down to the floor. One could stand erect only in the center. The trap-door that closed the stairway at the western gable was down and fastened ; near the eastern gable, at a low table, on which burned two tallow candles, his kinsman sat opposite to the chief, studying the backs of a pack of new cards, and slowly smoking. The pattering of the rain falling on the tiles overhead filled the garret with a gentle and pleasing murmur. It was past midnight ; the two men were whiling away the time—they were waiting.

" Marcus says in his report," said Corby, laying the document on the table and lighting a cigar, " that he has lost all trace of Twenty-One, and I want Twenty-One especially ; I had a wrangle to get him, and don't relish losing him a bit."

" Marcus tried hard enough to track him, I know that," replied the kinsman, laying down his cards and leaning back in his chair. " He followed him two months ; yes, let me see, over two months, before he came back to look after Number Twenty."

" I hope he will bag Twenty, at any rate," said Corby, lying down on a cot near the table, " and I think he will. I never set a better trap in my life, and there couldn't be a better night to spring it in. Twenty will have to walk his horse every foot of the way, and our folks can bring him here without meeting a soul ; but I wish I could have gone with them, then a failure would have been impossible."

" Why didn't you ? " inquired the kinsman.

" Because I had a dream last night that unmanned me," answered Corby, assuming a sitting posture, with his elbow on his knee and chin in his hand, gazing at the floor.

" What did you dream about ? " inquired the kinsman, with a look of surprise.

" I dreamed," he replied after a pause, with his eyes still fixed on the floor, " that I saw your aunt."

" Your mother ? "

" Yes, my mother. You remember before going to bed last night I told you of the removal of Number Nine. I take pride in that execution, because it was bloodless and secret and left no trace. Well, I dreamed the scene over in the night with a variation. All went on in the dream as it actually occurred, until the body rose to the surface—not forty yards below, but precisely where it took the plunge—and disclosed, with the moon shining brightly on it, the face of my mother."

"What a shocking circumstance," exclaimed the kinsman. "I don't wonder you're unfit for business to-day."

"I will be fit for nothing for ten days to come," replied Corby, rising and pacing the floor. "This has happened before—not once, but many times. Now and again she appears to me smiling : but nearly always mourning, or in tears. I disregarded the warning on one occasion, and came within an ace of losing my life, and made a deplorable failure. It's dreadful ; she seems to haunt me."

"If I was you, Corby," said his kinsman in a compassionate tone, moved by the agitation of the dreamer, "I would go to bed now and get some sleep."

"And dream, perhaps," he answered. "No! no sleep for me to-night. Listen ! there's a knock ; that's Marcus."

"No," said the kinsman, after a lengthened pause, during which they both listened intently ; "it was not a knock."

"I have but few distinct memories of my mother," continued Corby, resuming his walk with his hands clasped behind his back. "I recall her once, standing between my father and me in tears, protecting me. Then her face looked as it did last night. My father was a stern man. I never see *him* in my dreams. I remember well the two men bringing his body into our cabin the night the mob attacked us in Missouri. His breast and shirt was bloody. The sight made me sick."

"I was not born then," replied the kinsman, moving uneasily in his chair.

"I have a picture in my mind," resumed Corby. "of my mother leading me by the hand one day down a hill, going to the spring for water. The sun was shining, and the birds singing in the bushes. Before dipping her bucket in, she lifted me up and held me over, and looked at my face in the water. I looked at her reflection—a pale face lit up with a smile, blue eyes, fair hair. I see it now as distinctly as I did then. It comes to me in my dreams. but not often."

"You have no recollection of her death ?" inquired the kinsman.

"None," he replied, "and I am glad of it. All after the scene at the spring is a blank."

Corby lay down on the cot and turned his face from the light ; the kinsman resumed his study of the backs of the cards. After a lapse of ten or fifteen minutes a distinct rap was heard at the door below. The kinsman threw his cards on the table, raised the trap door and descended the stairs. Corby rose to a sitting posture on the cot. In a few minutes the kinsman returned, followed by a tall, powerfully built man in a faded blue army overcoat and slouch hat, dripping wet. He took off his hat and shook the rain from it, disclosing the features of a man of forty-five or fifty, with a small head, gray eye, and sallow, pointed face, on which he wore a thin, light-colored mustache and imperial, then just coming into fashion. Corby returned his salutation with a nod and pointed to a seat, and Marcus his lieutenant, second in command in the band of Angels, hung his wet hat on the back of the chair, smiled benignly on his chief, and sat down quite at his ease, with all the appearance of having dropped in to make a friendly call.

"Well !" exclaimed Corby impatiently.

"Well !" repeated Marcus, "we failed."

"So I see," said Corby, with increased irritation ; "but how ?"

"Simply because Number Twenty had sense enough to keep in out of the wet ; that's the why and the wherefore. Twenty was snugly tucked up in bed while we were waiting for him in the dark and rain at the point of rocks. As we couldn't go up to the hacienda and pull him out of bed we naturally failed to bag him ; no fault of ours."

"He couldn't have passed you in the dark ?" inquired the kinsman.

"Not to any alarming extext," replied Marcus with a smile, "as we had a rope stretched across the road breast high to his horse, and stood beside it."

"He couldn't have come back by any other road, could he ?" inquired the kinsman.

"He was obligged to pass up through the break in the clifft," replied Marcus, drawing a candle toward him and lighting a cigar.

" It's plain you'll never get him," said Corby impatiently.
" Then try your own hand on him, chief, if you think that," retorted Marcus, smiling. " He's living here ; he'll not run away."

" I have to leave for the upper country in the morning," gloomily replied the chief ; " you may stay and try on, if you think you can do anything."

" I'll tell you what I can do, Chief Corby," retorted Marcus eagerly, knocking the ashes from his cigar and pulling at his imperial, " and I'm willing to stake my rank in the band on it. I can remove Number Twenty inside of a week from to-night, if you'll give up your singular prejudice against bloodshed, and let me use the knife."

" I will have no bloodshed ! " exclaimed Corby fiercely, getting up from the cot with a dazed, wild look, and taking off his coat preparatory to going to bed. " It's against the moral law, and brings retribution. Blood will have blood ; ' he that liveth by the sword shall die by it.' "

" I daresay you're right," said Marcus, rising and throwing his overcoat over his shoulders and putting on his hat ; " it's sound Scriptur' doctrine, anyway. Good-night."

" Wait a moment," said Corby, drawing off his boots and stretching out at full length on the cot. " You say in your report you had some reason to think Twenty-One took dinner at the cabin of Dutch Charley. What led you to think so ? "

" I'd rather go over the report with you in the morning, when we have more time," replied Marcus, " if it will suit as well."

" Answer me now," said Corby, peremptorily. " I get into the saddle at daybreak."

" Indeed ! then I will not see you again," exclaimed Marcus with surprise, resuming his seat. " Well, I have the word of those four brigands for it, whatever that's worth. You see I dined at Dutch Charley's myself, partly because I was hungry, partly to make inquiry ; and they told me a man answering the description of Twenty-One, with two companions, had put up there some days before. Whether they told the truth or not, I couldn't make up my mind ; for four more unmitigated scoundrels don't walk the earth than those four landlords. Do you know I hadn't got half through dinner before I was convinced they were scheming to knock me on the head. When I got down the mountain, I found the valley overflowed, and it took me half an hour to force my horse into the water ; and we were very near being swept down with the current when we did get in. Now it struck me at the time that if Twenty-One and his friends did pass Dutch Charley's, and tried to swim over, that they were most likely drowned ; either that, or the landlords pistoled them. Beyond the river there was no sign of them. I think they're dead."

"It may be," replied Corby, after a thoughtful pause. "Those men at the cabin are capable of anything."

"Is that all?" said Marcus, rising.

"That's all ; good-night."

"Shall I set the trap again at the point of rocks?" inquired Marcus.

"No," replied Corby decisively. "Never set a trap twice at the same spot ; it's unprofessional."

CHAPTER IV.

THE DREAMER IS CONVERTED INTO A GRAND LADRON.

SOLOMON SAMPSON STUBBS, so named at an early period of his existence by an alliterative and ambitious parent, was a Mormon millionaire, and chief of the Vigilantes of San Francisco. He was the head of the great Mormon house of Solomon Stubbs & Co., wholesale importers, and president of the bank of Utah, at which the California Saints did business and deposited their accumulations. He possessed the only fire-proof building in the city, an enormous sheet-iron warehouse imported from London, in a rear and private room of which the Mormon council of which he was the head held their secret sessions and directed the affairs of the sect in California. He came from Salt Lake with a company of his co-sectarians, and washed gold on the American River. He removed thence to Sacramento City, and became one of the many bosom friends of Suttor, on whose great ranch the city was laid out, and grew rich in the ratio that his benefactor grew poor. Here the little polygamist "cut a wide swathe," in the role of leading merchant and sensational gambler, having been known to approach a table in a crowded saloon and lay down a bag of gold-dust, containing ten thousand dollars, on a single card. When he had gathered in the harvest at Sacramento he sought new fields to conquer ; descended the river to San Francisco, and pushed to the front in all popular movements. He was a man of medium height, light-built, active and "smart."

Stubbs was standing one evening at the bar of a brilliantly lighted saloon on the plaza when Hayward entered. Several men who had taken their drink walked away at this moment, leaving room next to Stubbs, and Hayward stepped up. As he took his station a party who were aiming at the vacant place pressed in and gave him a shove. This pushed him against Stubbs, who was raising a glass of champagne to his lips and nodding to the friends who were drinking with him, and the wine spilled over his hand and cuff. He turned angrily on Hayward, and threw the remainder of the contents of the glass in his face.

"You Mormon dog," exclaimed Hayward, seizing him by the collar and throwing him by a dexterous turn of the wrist, and trip, to the floor. Men scattered in all directions as the Mormon rose, expecting the usual firing that followed such affrays. But he was mastered by the steady look and bearing of Dom Pedro, and walked out of the saloon, followed by a derisive laugh from the crowd.

Late the next night a man turned with a quick, active step into a dark alley that led to the secret council door of the iron warehouse. He was admitted on giving a signal knock, and disclosed as he entered the lighted room a figure, not tall, but powerfully built, with red, coarse hair ; heavy red beard and mustache, brushed out from the mouth and chin, giving him a fierce aspect ; face broad and complexion mingled red and leprous white ; long arms, terminating in large sinewy hands, and a long body with legs slightly bowed. His movements were quick and confident ; his voice and tone peremptory. He was the chief of the "Avenging Angels."

"Brother Solomon," said he impressively, as the door was closed and locked, seating himself with an air of importance, "your assailant is found."

"Where !" eagerly exclaimed Solomon.

"I met him coming in as I was riding out to the mission this evening."

"Who is he? what is his name?"

"He is known to the Gentiles by the name of Hayward," slowly answered Corby, willing to prolong the pleasure the communication gave him. "He figures on the death-roll as Number Twenty-One."

"Heavens !" exclaimed Solomon in amazement. "What a dispensation ! what a wonder ! that the brute should have run into the toil open-eyed. Execute him friend Corby, forthwith. I want the villain's blood !" He was pale with aroused passion, and trembled with excitement.

"Hold !" exclaimed Corby in turn, raising his hand in deprecation. "No blood !"

"Deal with him as you like," replied Solomon, pacing the floor. "By poison, by the rope, by water, any way so you remove him from the face of the earth before next Sabaoth. He shall not live to see the coming Sabaoth sun. By Heaven he shall die the death by midnight Saturday. Yes, by the Prophet, he shall."

"Friend Solomon," said Corby, in a judicial tone, "set down and listen to reason."

"I'll not give you another day, Corby," said Solomon, seating himself with a determined look, "not another hour."

"What," replied Corby solemnly, "has the city talked about all day but the open shame put upon Solomon Stubbs last night? Nothing! It rung in my ears wherever I went, • from the rising to the setting sun. What will the city ring with Sabaoth morning, if this man's friends proclaim his murder in the night? Whose name will be coupled with that of the assassinated Peter Hayward? The name of Solomon; Stubbs; none other."

"You are right, brother," responded Solomon, his passion checked by this view of the case. "You are quite right; we must proceed with caution, and take time."

"We must take time," replied Corby, "and we must take space. The deed must not be done within a hundred miles of this city—the further off the better. In the meantime he will not be lost sight of ; he will not slip away from here as he did from Monterey."

"Where is he now?" inquired Solomon.

"I tracked him and his friends to a boarding-house on Broad Alley. You have noticed the house, perhaps—south side, midway."

"Yes, I know the place. I owned the block once."

"It seems to me you own half the city," said Corby.

"Not quite that proportion, but I own a fair share of it."

"Making money is not in my line of business," replied Corby. "If it was, I'd make it, and fast enough ; but I've other fish to fry. Well, as I was saying, I tracked them to Broad Alley and watched the house until the last light was put out, and then hurried here to report. While I was watching I laid my plans. We will lure Number Twenty-One from the city, or, failing that, follow when he leaves of his own accord, and deal with him at a distance."

"Is any one watching the house now?" inquired Solomon.

"Yes; Sim. I intend to take boarding at the house in the morning. Well, that's all for the present," he said, walking quickly to the door. "Good-night."

"The Prophet is growing old," said Solomon, in a low, mysterious tone, as he slowly unlocked the door, looking Corby meaningly in the face. "You have the executive ability. Who knows?"

"Nonsense!" exclaimed Corby, as he disappeared in the dark.

But the suggestion dwelt in his mind nevertheless, and spurred him—if he needed a spur—to increased exertion. Several nights thereafter he again walked rapidly up the dark alley and was admitted to the secret chamber of the iron warehouse.

"Brother Solomon," he said, as he picked out a cigar from the box on the table, and, lighting it, seated himself, "I have called to say adieu. Simeon has gone to Monterey: I follow in the morning at daybreak. We are going into the stock business; there's money in it."

"Indeed!" replied Solomon in surprise and pleased expectancy; "and who rides with you? You hardly intend to face the dangers of the road alone."

"Three gentlemen, reared among cattle, ride with me," answered Corby, with a grim smile. "I made their acquaintance on Broad Alley, and, finding they had come down from the mines, out of money and seeking employment, and were skilled in cattle, I employed them at high wages in money and an interest in the sales. Indeed, as I told them, I wouldn't have a man in my employ unless he took a personal interest in my ventures; and they have a deep interest in this one, I assure you. And this reminds me; I promised to make them an advance, and need a handful of gold."

"Well," said Solomon anxiously, "go on."

"I have sent word to Marcus by Simeon," continued Corby, "to note the sleeping-place of an outlying herd of horses on the San Pablo hacienda—he knows it well—and to meet us at a tavern on the north road. A conversation will occur. showing that the horses were purchased. We will drive through the Pacheco Pass, cross the San Joaquin, and manage to be captured on the Mariposa, where death by lynching will be swift and certain."

" Death of the three, you dropping out when the chase grows hot. You will take care to run no risk, I hope."

" We will take especial care to be absent at the moment of the capture," replied Corby. " My determination on that point is quite fixed. There is a spice of danger in this plan. It will require delicate handling, but it will divert from your name the slightest breath of suspicion."

" Lynched by the people on the Mariposa ! " exclaimed Solomon with enthusiasm, rubbing his hands together and bending toward Corby with a smile of admiration. " Excellent ! You have a head for strategy ; you are the Napoleon of the Saints."

" Hayward will be sent to the hacienda before we start," said Corby, elated by this praise, " that they may know him when they ketch him."

" Better and better," responded Solomon ; " and about where on the Mariposa will you spring your trap ? "

" As near the mines as possible. That will depend on the speed of the pursuit somewhat. In the mines they make short work. I will press as fast as I can without exciting his suspicion. Well," he continued, rising, " this is all, I suppose ? "

" All," answered Solomon, going to his safe and handing him a small pile of gold coin, which Corby put carelessly into his pocket without counting, and took his departure.

Several days after this conversation, Corby and Hayward, followed by his two adherents, rode up to an abode tavern within a few miles of Monterey, and were met at the hitching post by a man whom Corby addressed as Sim.

" Well, have you made a trade, yet ? " inquired Corby.

" I bought a drove of thirty this morning," answered Sim, " at fifty."

" Pretty high," said Corby. " I thought we could have got them at forty-five down here."

" It was the best I could do. I tried four or five ranches, and some wanted as high as fifty-five. These Spaniards will not jew at all. You must give their price, or go without. The Lowrys, by the way, are down. They bought a drove yesterday, and leave in the morning for the Mariposa. They gave the same that I did, fifty all round."

" By Heaven !" said Corby. ''They will spoil our market unless we leave to-night and drive through express. Is your bill of sale all right? Let me see it."

Sim handed him a paper, which he read and handed back.

"All right," he said ; " but I think you might have jewed them down at least a hundred. How far off are the horses?"

" Three miles or so south," answered Sim.

" If we can pick up ten more to fill out our number we ought to be off to-night. Where can we get them? From the same ranch ? "

" No," replied Sim ; " they will not break a drove. I tried them. There is a hacienda to the southwest about five miles, called San Pablo, where we may get a few. A cross-road a half-mile below leads by the house."

" Take these two young men with you," said Corby, " and get your horses into the road. Hayward and I will ride to San Pablo and see what we can do. If we can pick up ten or a dozen there we will follow with them in the morning ; if not, we will overtake you to-night. We must try to reach the mines two days in advance of the Lowrys. Horses are in good condition at this season, and can stand a sharp drive without spoiling their looks."

With this the parties separated, Corby and Hayward taking the road to San Pablo. They reached the hacienda at dusk, and Corby, dismounting under an oak out of sight of the entrance, requested Hayward, as he spoke Spanish, to go in and make the inquiry. Hayward dismounted and, handing the rein of his bridle to Corby, passed on. In a few minutes Corby tied the horses to a limb of the tree and approached the house. No one was in sight and the hall door stood open. Moved by curiosity or suspicion he cautiously entered and listened. From the dining-room door, which opened into the hall, a dim light shone, and a murmur of voices came through from the arcade beyond. Peering into the room, and finding it deserted, he stepped in to overhear the conversation, and as he did so his eye fell on a small buckskin bag that lay on the table near him, and his face lit up with a smile. A cautious step or two brought him within reach of it, and he took it from the table, and, on tiptoe, passed back into the hall and out of the house, reaching the horses unobserved. He untied them, and mounting, waited for his companion. Soon after Hayward joined him and reported no horses for sale. As they rode off Corby held him in conversation and their horses at a walk until they were out of hearing, when they broke into a fast gallop.

In the meantime, the party on the arcade were discussing their late visitor, little thinking, as they criticised his failure to give his name, that they were about to bestow upon him one by which he would be known in times to come. He appeared to them in the interview as above the middle height, of handsome form, and proportions expressing strength and activity; his complexion olive, eyes dark and melancholy, lit up when speaking with humor and kind feeling. Hair black and fine, tending to curl or wave, worn long behind the ear, reaching the shoulder; feet small, and hands thin and delicate, but powerful. He was dressed in Spanish riding costume of fine material, with heavy silver spurs.

A dim lamp, brought in with the wine to light their cigars and husk-covered cigarettes, shone on the dining-room table in the dark now settling rapidly. The senor entered, and in a moment returned and announced that the buckskin bag of gold-dust had disappeared. He had spoken at the close of dinner of the extreme fineness and freedom from black sand of a sum he had received in part payment for cattle he had lately sold, and had brought it from his strong box to exhibit. The bag was stamped with the initials "P. B. & Co." of the bank from which it had come ; was soft and well made, and was further marked in a fine clerkly hand " 32oz." After pouring the gold into a plate for examination, he had returned it to the bag, tied it up and tossed it aside on the table. The servants were above suspicion, and the conclusion was unanimous and irresistible that the stranger had taken it on his way out.

" The Grand Ladron ! " (great robber) was the general exclamation.

" He must be an old offender," said the senora. " He will never let himself be caught."

" He is bold and dangerous," added the senorita. " Pray do not follow him."

" Welcome the misfortune that comes alone ! " said the Franciscan. " You are not through with him, Don Manuel. Let the vaqueros look to the cattle. O, opportunity ! " he added, glancing at Don Manuel, " thy guilt is great ! "

While these and other remarks were following each other in rapid succession, the vaqueros were mounting and receiving their instructions. They were to visit each herd, and to arrest the Ladron if found in their rounds. In the day the vaquero, when on a tour of inspection, rides to the elevated points from which he can look down upon the herds and assure himself they are intact and in place ; but in the dark it is a different matter. Hence it was past midnight before they returned and reported a drove of horses gone. Two vaqueros had been left to hunt the trail, while the others returned to report and prepare for pursuit. They had seen nothing of the ladron, or of any party or campfire, or the remains of any, to indicate the presence of strangers on the estate.

Soon after the break of day, a pursuing party was on the pasturage of the missing drove and took up the trail. Prayers, and even tears, were employed by the ladies to prevent Don Manuel going. but in vain. Old Domingo was added to the party. He was a good cook, and watchful, but so taciturn that, unless he had something important to say, he seldom spoke except in answer. His judgment was highly valued, and he was charged by the ladies to speak out when occasion required. He knew the country, having visited from time to time his wild Indian relatives, who roamed the foothills of the sierra beyond the San Joaquin. His alforjas were well stuffed with provisions, and he carried the branding iron of the hacienda. Taken all in all, he was an important member of the expedition.

On the Salinas plains they called a halt to bait and change horses and interview an old acquaintance of Don Manuel, a thin, small Spaniard, whom they found seated in the middle of the room, with his feet to the brazier, and cloak and hat on, playing the guitar. He received them with great suavity, and said that during the night the dogs had feróciously signaled a passing party which was doubtless the one sought for. Resisting his earnest entreaties to stay for refreshments, they galloped on, and soon after lost the trail in the flooded valley, the Salinas having risen in the night, a cold rain still coming down. The general opinion was that the marauders were making their way to San Francisco via San Jose, and that, abandoning any attempt to pick up the trail, they should push straight for the latter place.

But Domingo demurred to this proposition dogmatically, and, speaking for the first time since he left home, said :

" The Ladrone will dispose of his plunder at the mines, and to reach them will go through the Pacheco pass of the Diablo Mountains, and cross the San Joaquin, depending on the flood to cover his trail."

This seemed so sagacious a course to pursue that Don Manuel, believing in the astuteness of the wily Ladrone, concluded he had followed it, and the party deflected to the right and crossed the Coast Range. They struck the trail in the pass and heard of the troop at the cabin of Dutch Charley, where they halted to feed. As they descended into the valley of the Joaquin and approached the river they found it flooded for miles out. The animals plunged from one hidden trench into another, making the route both fatiguing and anxious. At length they reached a low bluff on the river bank standing out of the water, and welcomed it as drifting sailors the longed-for land. Here again the trail of the ladron was struck, and pronounced by Domingo and the vaqueros to be about six hours old. There was but one point on the opposite side of the river, where the bank shelved so as to admit of the landing of horses. Domingo swam his horse over, and, dismounting, held him by the bridle. The extra stock, which had been driven to the bank, and had watched the passage of Domingo, had their attention fixed on him by his shouts and the waving of his sombrero. They shook their heads, and plainly expressed their disinclination to accept his invitation to cross, but were forced over the bank and plunged in, heading up to breast the current. The river was over, half a mile wide, but all made the landing in safety. They understood as well, when shown Domingo and his horse on the other side, that they must emerge at that point and could not get up the bank elsewhere, as the vaqueros that explained it to them. On the landing of the loose stock, the remainder of the party swam over, and in the evening reached solid ground and went into camp.

———

CHAPTER V.

THE LADRONE IS PURSUED BY THE PEOPLE OF THE PLUNDERED HACIENDA.

THE Manley Rancho on the left bank of the Mariposa, a stream that rises in the Sierra Nevada and flows west into the San Joaquin, was rather a trading post, or store, though starved and brokendown stock—mules, horses and cattle— were fatted on the surrounding rolling plains and re-sold at a great advance. Not a vestige of a fence, save that which formed the corral or cattle-pen, was to be seen from the old adobe building, of one low story, that stood on the bluff above the river. Dust and mud, in their respective seasons, looked in at the doorway and invaded the interior from time to time, on the boots of the traveler and ranchero and the feet of vagrant dogs. The floor was of beaten clay, and the transient lodger spread his blanket on it, and had the shelter of the roof in bad weather, or slept without in good. No one thought of finding either bedstead or bed-clothing in these primitive caravansaries, and the table groaned only under the weight of salt pork, beans and cakes. Though the charge for meals was high, it is but fair to say the lodging was free, being furnished, in fact, generally by the sky. The river banks were clothed with trees, as was also the intervening land, where it occurred between the river and the rolling plain, which in some places came to the water and in others stopped short. Here and there a solitary tree, or clump of trees, dotted the plain, but far apart ; and as its clayey soil was seamed with wide cracks in Summer, the trail, except where great bends occurred, kept the river bank.

Four partners, three of whom were brothers, or relatives bearing the same name, "kept the ranch." They were active men and prosperous, full of business, and thought no time ill-spent in the pursuit of horse-thieves and their summary punishment. The terror of their name was felt far and wide among evil-doers, and so pertinacious and determined a pursuit was made when their ranch was invaded that they enjoyed comparative immunity from wrong. Cattle could not be brought in at night, but were necessarily left out on the range, and were thus exposed in the hours of darkness to be " lifted " by rogues that infested all parts of the country. There was a quick sale for them in the mining centers, and but for the rapid pursuit and sudden and unsparing infliction of death on the captive marauder, the plains would have been swept clean of cattle in a month. Public opinion sanctioned the vindictive and unlawful procedure of the cattle men, and only here and there a law-abiding man was found to lift up his voice in favor of turning over the captured to the sheriff; and when a chance one was carried off to jail by him, the indignation of the community was aroused to a high pitch. But notwithstanding all this, reckless men were found to incur the risk. The cattle once sold, the captor vanished with his ill-gotten gains, and that section of the country knew him no more.

On the morning following the passage of the San Joaquin by the men of San Pablo, a man rode over from the Merced to summon the Manleys to the trial of a horse-thief. He had been arrested far up that stream, at a mining-camp, with the horse in his possession; but he denied his guilt. Friends were standing by him, and the ranchmen required re-enforce ment. Indignant at this attempt to frustrate the ends of justice, the Manleys in full force galloped off for the Merced, leaving the post in charge of a Mexican retainer, and their stock unguarded. They intended to return down their own bank of the Mariposa and reach home some time in the night. The day proved a dull one at the rancho, and the sun beat down on their adobe and its forlorn surroundings with great force. The dogs, too much debilitated to keep watch, slunk about hunting cool spots in the shade, and the Mexican fell asleep in his chair at the door. The murmur of the stream alone broke the stillness of the afternoon, and the snow-capped peaks of the sierra looked down from afar on the death-like scene.

After a time the dogs, one by one, left their lairs and assumed a position of expectancy. There was a sound of an approaching troop, and low growls, followed by a chorus of

barks, woke the Mexican as Corby and Hayward, the Grand
Ladrone, came in sight, followed by the squadron of horse
driven by the three men. The Mexican scrutinized them
closely as they approached; and, finding he was passing
without halt or salutation, called after the Ladrone in a significant tone :

" Vaya con Dios, amigo " (Go with God, friend). To
which the Ladrone replied :

" Queda con Dios, hermano " (Remain with God, brother),
and passed on.

The Mexican resumed his seat, meditated, and shrugged
his shoulders, until, in the accomplishment of his last shrug,
he again fell asleep. The dogs, dissatisfied that nothing had
come of the late excitement, also dropped off, and quiet was
restored.

The sun was sinking behind the Coast Range ; the dogs
and the Mexican had finished their siesta and were strolling
about enjoying the cool of the evening, when two Americans on mules rode up and dismounted. The Mexican noticed at a glance that the men were new to the country and
unaccustomed to riding, but, though this was a highly dis-
paraging circumstance, he kept his thoughts to himself and
served them with the refreshments they called for with as
much politeness as he could bring to bear in behalf of men
so wofully deficient. However, they paid their score and
put many questions concerning the road and country, and
learned that the men of the ranch were absent on the
Merced, but did not learn of their purpose to return that
night down the bank of the Mariposa. Taking a final drink
they rode off, and the disproportion in their height, the one
being very tall and the other quite short, together with their
awkward horsemanship, made the Mexican, who was watching them, laugh ; for which involuntary compromise of his
dignity he reproached himself a moment after.

Night fell. An open lard lamp burned on the counter
and shed a dubious light through the doorway, when the
dogs signaled the San Pablo party which a moment after
appeared on the scene. The Mexican removed his sombrero
and bowed to Don Manuel, of whose caballeria there could
be no doubt. He recognized the hidalgo by his seat in the

saddle alone. He held his stirrup as he dismounted, and invited him to enter.

"En adelante, senor," he said as he stood aside to let him
precede him.

"Friend," said Don Manuel, addressing him in Spanish
when they had entered, "what parties have passed your
house to-day?"

"Senor," replied the Mexican, "two parties have passed.
One led by an American in Spanish dress, with four followers and thirty horses, that had passed through the flood of
the San Joaquin and bore the brand of the animal from
which your honor has just dismounted."

"How many men did you say were in the party?" inquired Don Manuel.

"Five, with the leader, senor; bad men all, in my opinion. They have made a raid upon your honor?" .

"Yes, they have made a raid."

"I said to myself as they passed," said the Mexican,
"those horses were reared together; they are fresh from the
pasture of a hacienda; there is no vente brand on them ;̈they
are stolen."

"Did the men speak as they passed?" inquired Don
Manuel.

"They did not, senor," answered the Mexican, "save the
leader, who answered my salutation in Spanish."

"Were they well armed?" asked Don Manuel.

"To the teeth, senor; and to attack them on the march
will cost life. Will the senor listen to me?"

"Speak," was the answer.

"These men," continued the Mexican, "will camp to-
night. They think themselves quite safe, that their trail
was lost in the flood. I read this in their faces as they
passed. Now comes a question—where will they camp? Let
us think. The senor does not know the country. It is for
me to decide. The senor will see in the end?"

"Yes," interrupted Don Manuel, with a smile, "al fin se
canta la gloria." (At the end one sings the gloria.)

"The gloria will be sung!" continued the Mexican.
"Listen. Here we are," making a point on the counter
with a piece of chalk. "There runs the road over the dry

plain to avoid the bend, for three leagues. The senor will admit," said he, looking up, " they will not camp until the trail again touches the water?"

" Admitted," said Don Manuel who was following the tracing in chalk on the counter.

" Good !" resumed the Mexican. " Now here, as they descend into the valley, is a small house of our next neighbor, and the road resumes its course, and also sends a branch over the stream which leads across to the Merced far below the mines. It is conceded the ladrones will not cross the stream but will take the road up ? "

" Yes," admitted Don Manuel, " if they know the country."

" All know that the up-river trail leads to the mines," returned the Mexican. " The ladrones will not take the trail across, if they know where it leads, nor will they fall into an unknown trail at such a critical juncture. They will therefore go up the river. No es eso, senor? " (Is it not so ?) he inquired, looking up with a smile.

" Eso es," answered Don Manuel, now much interested.

" The ladrones will not camp at the crossing," the Mexican went on. " nor between it and the house a short league up stream, for two reasons. First, because the grass at those places is all eaten away ; and second, because, beyond the house, they enter on a long stretch without a habitation, with plenty of grass, where their camp-fire will be unseen and themselves unnoticed. Therefore, here." said he, finishing the tracing with a cross mark, " one league beyond the second house, the senor will find them."

" Friend," said Don Manuel, drawing from his purse a large gold coin of Mexican mintage, called, in common parlance, " an ounce." " have the goodness to accept this for your information."

But the Mexican was not disposed to mar the glory of his triumph by the touch of gold.

" Many thanks, senor," he replied, declining it. " When your honor returns victorious we will sing the gloria."

The senor laughed at this retort and put up his gold piece, and the Mexican added :

" Besides, I have not yet finished. I have still to lay
down for your honor the plan of battle."

" Good ! " said Don Manuel, laughing. " You will in-
struct us in tactics, as well as strategy: teach us to find
the enemy, and then to whip him."

The conversation was here broken off by the senor order-
ing a collation for his men and barley for the horses. Precious barley ! that cost a dollar a pound, and for the lack of a
quart of which many a gallant horse, hard-pressed, had suc-
cumbed on the journey. It was decided to lie over an hour
or so for rest and then push on and beat up the Ladron in his
camp. After supper, Don Manuel lit his cigar and walked
out to the bank of the stream. Here the Mexican joined him
and resumed the conversation.

" The men of this rancho, senor," he said, " are on the
upper Merced, and will come down to-night on your road.
They will gladly join you, if you state your business. The
little house holds but one, a caballero, Senor Digby. His
vaquero is absent. The next house, two stalwart men. They
will help. With such a force you may close in and capture
the ladrones without a fight. This is the plan I spoke of. Is
it good ? "

" It is good," replied Don Manuel, " and I will follow it ;
but the general, it appears to me, when the battle begins,
should be less than five leagues away from his troops."

" The general, senor," he answered with mock gravity, " is
brave, but prudent. He would like to join you, but duty to
his absent employers holds him back. He will pray for you.
To pray for one, at such a moment, is not bad."

This remark brought to the mind of the senor the ladies
at San Pablo, then supplicating, he knew, for his safety ;
and he walked away, moved. Don Antonio joined him, and
they strolled out in company on the rolling plain, discussing
their plan of attack.

" If the Mexican is right as to where the robbers will go
into camp," said Don Manuel, " and I think he is, we will
come upon them after midnight, and find them asleep, and
more than likely without a watch set. Should we see their
camp-fire in time, my plan would be to dismount and quietly
close in on them, and capture them, perhaps without a fight,

as he suggested. He seems to me to be a very sensible man."

" Their fire will have burned low by that time," replied Don Antonio, " perhaps be a mere pile of coals and ashes, and we may not see it until close on it. The noise of our approach will have alarmed them in that event, and, once on foot, they will make fight ; for they know that to surrender would only prolong their lives a few hours at most."

" But we will hand them over to the authorities," said Don Manuel

" The allies we propose to pick up will never consent to that," replied he. " Never."

" Then let us make the capture alone," said Don Manuel, "and form no alliance. I will not be a party, even indirectly, to a breach of the law."

" Five desperate men, skilled in the prompt use of the pistol, and fighting for their lives," replied Antonio, " will make a slaughter before they succumb. We must get a re-enforcement, or face the probability of a heavy loss. It is our lives against theirs ; and that is not fair, either."

" No," responded Don Manuel with hesitation; " they are, after all, not entitled to a fair fight. Well, we will see."

" If we secure an addition of eight good men," continued Antonio, " and are fortunate enough to surprise the brigands, we can overpower and bind them without the loss of a man. It would be unwise, in my opinion, not to take all the help we can get, letting after events shape their own course."

As he spoke, they were approaching a solitary tree that stood out on the plain, and there rose from under it a large, yellow animal who faced them with an inquisitive look, exhibiting in its countenance neither fear nor anger, merely curiosity. The men stopped suddenly, and Antonio moved his hand toward his revolver.

" For Heaven's sake," whispered Don Manuel, " put your hand down and come slowly with me."

They turned a little to the left to avoid the animal, and walked by with apparent unconcern. When they got well out of reach they made a detour and retraced their steps to the ranch.

"What was it?" inquired Antonio, when they had reached a safe distance.

"A California lion," answered Don Manuel; "and if you had fired he would have torn you to death."

"But I was so near I could have hit him in the head."

"No matter where you might have struck him," replied Don Manuel, "even if in the heart, you would have perished at the moment he did."

"But there was danger of his springing on us."

"None, as long as we made no hostile demonstration. If he had construed the motion of your hand as one, which happily he did not, he would have sprung. He is the monarch of the plain; he will admit no trifling."

Meantime, a lively conversation was carried on at the ranch, between the Mexican and the vaqueros, in which Domingo, contrary to his custom, took a part.

"Who is your Grand Ladrone?" inquired the Mexican, as he heard one of the men use the title.

"It is the chief," replied Domingo; "the one who stole the gold from the table of the senor. I will tie him with this rope," throwing back his serape and displaying a cord wound about his waist. "Yes! I will kneel on the breast of the Grand Ladrone, and tie him. Then I will take the bag of gold from his pocket and return it to the senor."

"If Domingo ties him," said a young vaquero in a deferential tone, "he will be bound fast; he will not slip the knot."

"No," responded Domingo.

"It is so," responded several voices. "Domingo is adroit."

"Friends," said the Mexican, in a tone of admonition, "be not too confident. Unless you spring upon them in their sleep, the five robbers will fight. Then he will slay Domingo."

"He will not," retorted Domingo. "I will lasso him. I will drag him down."

"Take advice," returned the Mexican, raising his right forefinger to insure attention. "One of you help Domingo capture the chief, and three," holding up three fingers before them, "three, mind you, attack the robber with the red beard."

" Why?" exclaimed the vaqueros, in chorus."

" Because," replied the Mexican with decision, " he is a • tiger."

" And the others, how are they?" inquired the young vaquero.

" They are sheep," he replied, with contempt.

"Brother," said a middle-aged vaquero, leaning over the counter toward the Mexican, and blowing a cloud of smoke through his nostrils, " you think Domingo will not bind the Grand Ladrone?"

" Who knows," he replied, with a doubtful shrug of his shoulders.

" I will wager," returned the vaquero, taking from the folds of his sash a silver dollar, and laying it on the counter, " this peso that he does."

" Who shall hold the stakes," inquired the Mexican, producing a coin of the same value and laying it beside the other.

" Let Domingo hold them," said the young vaquero.

" No, Domingo shall not hold them," replied the Mexican with a quizzical smile. " The Grand Ladrone may overcome Domingo and rob him."

" Ha! ha! ha!" laughed the vaqueros, " a good joke ; to rob Domingo. He will not find it easy ; he will be the first. A grand idea."

" Easy, or not easy," said Domingo, abstracting, after some fumbling, a dollar from his sash and laying it on the counter, " I will also venture a peso on the event."

" Also I! also I!" exclaimed several in a breath, and each vaquero that found himself in funds sufficient put down his peso. The Mexican counted them carefully, drawing the coin toward him one at a time with his forefinger, pushing the one he had laid down off to itself, and then made up the deficit and drew them all together in a pile.

" Now hand it over to Domingo," said one with a laugh.

" Hide it, brother," said Domingo, addressing the Mexican, " in some good place, until we come back ; not in the ground, or your dogs will scratch it out."

"Friends! saddle up!" exclaimed Don Manuel, as he and Antonio neared the rancho, and the vaqueros poured out at the doorway and hurried to their horses. In a few minutes they were led to the front and the command to mount was given, and again the Mexican held the stirrup of Don Manuel.

"Go with God, brothers!" he called aloud, waving his sombrero, as the party set off at a gallop.

"Remain with God, friend!" came back the response, mingled with the clatter of the horses' hoofs.

CHAPTER VI.

HE IS CAUGHT IN THE NIGHT, AND TRIED BY THE LIGHT OF A CAMP-FIRE.

THE party, known to their pursuers as the party of the Grand Ladrone, when they reached the ford, drove the horses in to water, and Corby threw off his coat, saying he would take a bath, and directed Hayward to drive on and go into camp at the first good grass. He handed him the bag of gold to carry, saying, with a satanic smile, he feared to leave it on the bank while swimming. As soon as the party was out of sight, Corby and Sim, who had remained with him, resumed their clothing, crossed the ford and disappeared. Supper past and bed-time come, with Corby still absent, Hayward lay down by his camp-fire with his two companions, filled with forebodings. A vague suspicion crossed his mind concerning the bag of gold. He recalled seeing one like it on the table at San Pablo.

A few eccentric mules were to be found on every ranch who were in the habit, in couples or small parties, of quitting the rich pastures and strolling by the roadside, cropping the short and dusty grass. What induces them to this disreputable proceeding has long been a subject of inquiry among ranchmen, without elucidating a satisfactory solution. What motive he has in quitting clean, rich grass, to feed upon that which is dusty and poor, is perhaps a mystery to the vagrant mule himself. Be the attraction what it may, a group of three, and, further on, of five, such unreasoning quadrupeds so mysteriously drawn to the roadside, presented themselves to the view of the tall and short American as dusk fell on them, a short hour after leaving Manleys' ranch.

The devil, always busy with suggestions to the sinner, mounted, as well as to his humbler brother on foot, was not long in persuading these two adventurers that they had before them a chance for much gain with little risk. In an evil moment they yielded to the impulse, and drove the seven mules into the trail before them. As they descended the rolling prairie some hours after, and approached the little house, Digby, the occupant, who was a better student than ranchman, was deeply absorbed in his books. It was the custom to have at least one horse tied to a stake near the door all night, saddled and bridled for immediate use. One was so tied at the side of his house, and Digby was suddenly aroused from his studies by the stamping of the animal's feet. He opened the door and looked out. The night was dark, and he could just make out the figure of a man on muleback riding off. He thought it was one of the Allens who lived above on the river, and called out: "Bill, is that you?" The answer came back, "Yes," and Digby closed the door and resumed his reading. After the lapse of over an hour, he heard the gallop of a horse and a call from "Bill" who summoned him to go up and assist at a trial of horse-thieves. On looking for his horse, he found he had broken the hitching-strap and was missing. He saddled another from the pen and followed Allen, who had ridden back. On reaching their ranch he found there two men, prisoners, bound hand and foot, one of them exceptionally tall and the other notably short.

The Allens, like Digby, had heard the stamping of their tied horse, a white one, and one of them quickly opening the door observed the short prisoner give him a lash. He stepped out, drew his pistol, laid hold of the man's bridle-rein and demanded:

"What are you doing here?"

"Several of our animals," answered the man, "have strayed from the road, and I thought this horse was one of them."

"Not satisfactory," replied Allen; "dismount."

Under the influence of the cocked revolver pointed at his breast, the man complied, and as he did so his companion rode up from the trail, which was over fifty yards off and in the shade of the trees, and was immediately confronted by the second armed Allen, and also dismounted. A man was then called out with ropes, who bound them both securely. Bill then lit a lantern, walked down to the trail and ex-

amined the brand on the animals. This done, after com-
municating with his brother, he mounted the white horse
and rode off to collect a jury. On Digby's arrival, Ryder,
from across the river, was on the ground with two of his
men, and the prisoners were called on for their defense. The
short one, who acted as spokesman, said :

"We bought our stock in Monterey, and are driving them
to the mines for sale. Several strayed from the road in the
dark, and, looking for them, I mistook this white horse for
one of ours, and gave him a cut to head him back to the
drove."

"The animals never saw Monterey," said Allen. "They
all have the Manley brand, except one horse, which has the
brand of the ranche below—a circle with a curve in the center—and belongs to this gentleman. Perhaps you bought it
also in Monterey?"

"No," he answered. "That animal must have fallen in
as we came up the road. I had not noticed it."

Allen now proposed to string them up at once, and was
seconded by his brother and man. But Digby interposed,
and made the proposition to turn them over to the sheriff of
the county. He was a law-abiding man in the strictest
sense, and, though he had suffered heavy losses by marauders, yet looked with horror on the unlawful taking of life.
He had great pity in his composition for the unfortunate,
and no vindictiveness whatever when it came to action. He
took Ryder and his men aside and won them to his views,
and the prospect in favor of the prisoners was brightening,
when the proceedings were interrupted by the arrival of the
San Pablo party.

Through Digby, who understood some Spanish, Don Manuel explained his business, and requested aid. The passage
of the Ladrone by both ranches had been unnoticed. Digby,
close by whose door the road ran, was absorbed in reading,
and the Allens, back from the road on the river bank, had
not heard him go by. But all agreed they would be found
on the river road, when the Mexican's views were explained
to them, and readily volunteered their assistance. A bustle
now ensued. The prisoners were placed under guard, and
the remainder of the party saddled up and took the trail.

The combined force rode on quietly for several miles, when they came in sight of an expiring camp-fire, by a small lagoon to the right of the road, on the edge of the rolling prairie. They at once dismounted; and, after a consultation, sent Domingo forward to reconnoiter. In his absence the horses were tied, and the pistols drawn and prepared for action. Domingo, with his inherited Indian instincts, disappeared in the thicket with the silence of a snake, and in due time as noiselessly reappeared and reported. The Grand Ladrone and two men were sleeping by the fire. Other men, he said, though he did not see them, were no doubt lying down near the horses which he saw feeding out on the prairie. The vaqueros were sent to the prairie, and the remainder of the party closed in on the fire. Some one stepped on a dry stick, and it broke with a crack. The Ladrone sprang to his feet.

"Quien?" he called out sharply.

"Men of peace," answered Don Manuel. "It is death or surrender. Speak."

"Surrender," answered the Ladrone, uncocking his pistol and dropping it on the ground. In a moment the three men were seized, and the thoughtful Domingo produced his rope and proceeded to bind them.

"Senor," said Domingo in a low tone, as he finished tying the Grand Ladrone, "shall I search him for the bag of gold?"

"Not now," answered Don Manuel.

At these few words in Spanish the mind of the Ladrone flashed back over the late events to the scene in the saloon in which he had flung the Mormon leader to the floor, and he saw it all. He saw he was in a trap, with the evidence against him overwhelming, and explanation hopeless.

The prisoners were led out to the road and the party mounted, leaving the vaqueros to bring on the horses.

The Allen ranch faced the road, with an oak with low horizontal arms on the right and a stump and fallen tree on the left. On this stump the Ladrone took his seat when he alighted, while his companions in captivity lay down on the ground beside him. The moon had risen and lighted up the scene. The company sat on the log, or grouped themselves in the open space. Don Manuel, through Digby, announced that his party would have no hand in a violation of the law. The Allens, now in a woful minority, submitted under protest. They said, in effect though in more forcible terms, that things were coming to a pretty pass. The feeling among the prisoners was one of unspeakable relief ; but it was momentary, for at this favorable juncture there rode up to the house a dozen men on a full gallop, whooping and shouting. It was the Manley party on their way down the river from the trial of the suspected horse thief. The evidence against him had turned out to be so weak that the death penalty could not with propriety be administered. They had insisted, however, on a whipping, to which the friends of the man had assented in a spirit of compromise. They were one and all elated at their good fortune in happening by at such an opportune moment. They had been drinking, and turned into the Allens', with a shout, to " fire up." Their yell, as they dashed in, struck on the hearts of the prisoners like the sound of a death knell. The Grand Ladrone requested one of the newcomers, who walked up and drew his cigar close to his face to light it up for better inspection, to have the goodness to give him a cigar. The man broke off the end of one and put it in Hayward's mouth, his hands being tied behind him, and held up his own until he got a light. He then said, with an ominous laugh :

" You are a cool one."

"And an honest one, friend," answered the Ladrone. " The guilty are not cool."

The man turned and looked again at him, as though this answer struck him as containing originality and perhaps truth. Hayward had made an impression ; his spirits rose. Some conversation now took place between the Allens and the new arrivals, at the conclusion of which one of the latter, who conceived himself gifted oratorically, stood up on the log, and addressed the assembly.

" Boys," he began, " there are men here who have ;no right to vote."

" That's so," echoed a number of voices in the crowd.

" It is the right of every Englishman, I mean American." he continud, " wrung from the barons at Magna Charta, to be tried by his neighbors. Now there are men here from

Monterey who are not neighbors ; on the contrary, foreign-
ers. They can't vote in this crowd."

" Not much," came decisively from his adherents.

" Now, I propose," he resumed, " for a jury to try these
thieves, six men as follows : "—here he ran over the names.
" Now those in favor of these men say ' Ay.' " A loud
chorus of " Ayes " followed this appeal. " Those in favor of
a contrary opinion say ' No.' " The " Noes " responded.　٥

" The ' Ayes ' have it," he concluded. " The jury will
take their seats on this log."

The orator now stepped down, flushed with success, and
received the congratulations of his friends. The jury advanced from the crowd and sat down on the log. The two
Americans, the ill-assorted and misguided couple, were led
up and stood between the jury and the low-armed oak, an
ominous conjunction, and the trial began.

William Allen was the only witness. Digby declined to
testify. Allen related the circumstances of the arrest, and
the Manley mules and Digby's horse were driven up to the
fire which had been kindled and the brands examined by the
jury, who left the log and walked among them for the purpose. The prosecution here rested their case, and the prisoners were called on for their defense. The small man
repeated in effect the story told by him on his arrest, but
changed the location of the purchase to Manley's ranch.
The tall one had nothing to say.

Digby now stepped forward and made an appeal to the
jury to obey the law of the land and hand the prisoners
over to the sheriff. He was the hidalgo of the neighborhood, was held in high esteem, and listened to with attention. All that could be said in favor of the lawful course,
he said briefly and to the point.

After a few words among themselves the foreman of the
jury stood up and answered him. He said the jury fully admitted the truth of all he had said, but the jails were good
for nothing and the courts not much better. That the defenseless condition of the stock forced the community to
take the law into their own hands or give up the attempt to
hold property. This being so, the jury had decided, with all
due respect to him and the other gentlemen present holding

his views, to render a verdict and judgment ; and within five minutes thereafter, he announced the verdict :

"Guilty, and the sentence, death."

Thirty minutes were allowed the prisoners for preparation, and in which to make a confession or statement, if they wished to make 'one. No longer time, the foreman said in apology, could be given, as they had another case on hand and the night was advancing. Digby mounted his horse and rode home ; Ryder and his men did the same. The Allens treated the company freely and without charge. Some self-constituted executioners lariated the prisoners and led them under the oak. They were asked if they had anything to say. The tall one began a confession. The short one nudged him with his elbow, and said : "Hold your tongue !" But he went on and made a clean breast of it. He said :

"We are from Bangor in the State of Maine. We landed at Monterey a few days since. Some distance this side of the Manley ranch we came upon two bunches of mules, one after another, on the side of the road, and drove them before us. We are new to the country and had not the least idea of the risk we were running. We had heard the Manley men were away on another river, and felt confident we could dispose of the mules at the mines and get off before any pursuit could be made. We would never have touched them had we thought we were running any risk of our lives. At the Digby house my companion cut the tied horse several lashes ; he broke his halter and joined our pack. A man opened the door and spoke to us, but took us for friends. As we were passing this house we saw the white horse. But for his color we would not have seen him and got into trouble."

"Yes," interrupted a by-stander ; "the Manleys would have caught you all the same."

"It is true," he resumed with a shudder. "We were doomed. My companion rode up, against my advice, and cut the white horse with his whip. When I saw him dismounted and only one man out, I rode up to assist him and was caught myself. It looks like fate."

The short man, who had watched his companion during his confession with an expression of contempt on his face, was asked if he had anything to say, and answered scornfully :

" Nothing."

The lariats were thrown over the limb under which the condemned stood, and were manned. The foreman of the jury approached the fire and looked at his watch. A hush fell upon the crowd. He raised the watch above his head and called out:

"Time ! "

The men at the ropes ran back and drew the condemned off the ground. The short one called out, hurriedly:

" Remember what I tell you. I bought those mules."

The word " mules," the last he uttered, was only half-articulated as the Bangor men were summoned to final trial before a legal tribunal.

After an interval, a dropping of the curtain, as it were, between the acts, filled with a buzz of conversation and the partaking of refreshments, the jury resumed their seats upon the log and the second trial began.

Don Manuel and his men declined to testify. Domingo, under orders from the jury, surrendered the San Pablo branding-iron. The horses were driven up and examined. A juryman pressed the iron against the scar on the flank of one of the horses, giving an ocular and triumphant demonstration of the fit. The capture of the prisoners with the stock in their possession was notorious and needed no proof. The prosecution called on the prisoners for their defense.

The Grand Ladrone rose from the stump and stood before the jury. He asked as a favor that his hands be untied, and, while it was being done, he sharply scanned the faces of his triers. After a few moments' pause he began, in a tone calm and dignified :

" I am a citizen of Durango, in old Mexico. I came to San Francisco several months since, bringing with me a large sum of money, which I deposited with the banking firm of ' P. B. & Co.,' and engaged in the purchase and sale of horses, the only business with which I am familiar. I have made three transactions since my arrival. I bought two droves from old California ranches, on the Contra Costa, and sold them in the city. I got rid of the last venture ten days since, at a loss. Sales were dull and prices had fallen. I learned that prices were high in the lower mines, and set out several days since, taking with me these two men, who are in my employ, intending to buy in Monterey County and drive to the Mariposa and the Merced.

"We were taking our coffee the other morning on the Salinas plains, when a party came by with the drove of horses you have just examined. I invited the man in charge to take a cup of coffee, and he dismounted and we fell into conversation on the state of the stock market. He was driving to San Francisco. I discouraged him from going there, by giving the prices I had received for the last sales I had made, and recommended him to sell in the mines. He answered he had never been to the mines, and, from stories he had heard, was afraid to drive there. 'Besides,' he added, 'the Salinas is over its' banks, and no doubt the San Joaquin is likewise.' Then finishing his coffee thoughtfully, and setting down his cup, he said :

"'Friend, I am afraid to go to the mines and ashamed to drive back home. Buy my horses.'

"I answered, 'Good, if we can agree.'

"I appeal to the men beside me," he said, turning to his companions, "to say if I am not reproducing the conversation word for word."

The men modestly confirmed his statement.

"I examined the animals and made him an offer which, after some figuring in his note-book, he accepted. I paid him with a bag of gold-dust from the bank of P. B. & Co., and as the amount in it fell a trifle short, I produced another smaller bag from which to make up the deficit. But he said, pointing to the large bag from which I had paid him :

"'Throw in this handsome bag and we will call it a bargain.' I assented, and the transaction was closed.

"That I was indiscreet in purchasing upon the road the event has proved. To pay for that indiscretion, and at the same time to compensate the owner of this stock for his damage and outlay, I am willing to hand over to him what money I have remaining, and if he thinks it is not sufficient, to give him a check on my banker for a further amount to satisfy him."

At this he drew from his pocket a fine buckskin purse of gold-dust, and turned to approach Don Manuel, who stood to his left in the semicircle that surrounded him. But several of the jury reached out and called to see the purse, and he turned back and handed it to them with a bow. They scrutinized it carefully and read aloud as they did so :

"P. B. & Co., 32.oz."

" He has been telling the truth, by George !" whispered one of the jury in an astonished tone.

" Yes," answered the man next him, "and he is a gentleman to boot. He wants to do the square thing."

" This tells big for him," said the one on the other side ; " but, all the same, I think he is lying."

The Ladrone took the purse from the foreman, and approached Don Manuel.

" Senor," he said in Spanish, " I trust this sum will compensate you for the trouble my indiscretion has caused you. Only the thought of my young wife in Old Durango has nerved me through this tragic scene." He then handed him the purse with a bow and resumed his seat.

The buzz of conversation recommenced ; the jug and tin-cups were put in circulation ; the fire was replenished, and blazing up brought out in relief,the bearded group in slouch hats, red shirts, and corduroys thrust in boots from which protruded the handles of knives, and belts stuck with revolvers ; and it cast a diabolical glare upon the two figures slowly swinging under the oak.

Public opinion was expressed pro and con in hearing of the jury—that valuable institution " wrung from the barons," which was as far from unanimity as the crowd. The speech of the Ladrone had unsettled their conviction of his guilt. After a prolonged struggle of twenty minutes, the foreman announced it impossible to agree.

" Then compromise," called out a voice from the crowd. This struck him as a reasonable suggestion ; he sat down and the consultation was resumed. The individual who had illuminated the face of the prisoner with the coal of his cigar strongly favored acquittal. A compromise was at length effected and announced. Verdict—" Guilty." Sen-

tence—" The letter 'R' branded on the cheek." Ryder, over
the river, had an " R " branding iron, and the knowledge of
one being so convenient had suggested the sentence.

· Don Manuel ordered his party to horse. As they were
mounting he was notified that the Ladrone wished to see him.
He found him still seated on the stump, from which he rose
and begged him to accept his thanks for the kindness he had
displayed. Don Manuel said he was sorry for the indignity
awaiting him. The Ladrone replied:

" Sir, it is nothing to a man death has been staring in the
face for hours."

As he repassed the fire Don Manuel saw a man thrust a
branding iron into the glowing coals.

It was determined to ride back to the Manley ranch, which
they would reach soon after sunrise, and rest there during a
good part of the day. Don Manuel and Antonio rode in advance, followed by Domingo and the young vaquero; the re-
captured herd of horses came next, and the main body of the
vaqueros brought up the rear. Silence was unbroken until
they reached the ford and began the slight ascent that led
into the open plain, and saw before them the little house of
Digby.

" I would halt in passing," said Don Manuel, " and pay
my respects to this noble man—a soft heart is a patent of
nobility—but the house is dark."

" He said to me, as we were riding up the river," replied
Antonio, " that with our vote the safety of the prisoners
would be assured; that there was no danger whatever of their
being lynched. This made me feel perfectly easy until the
Manley party came riding in, like wolves on the fold; and
when the fellow made his speech and appointed the jury, I
saw, as I told you, all hope was gone. Who do you suppose
the Grand Ladrone turned out to be?"

" Who knows. He looked and acted like a gentleman,"
he replied. " Had he not called at the hacienda that night
and carried off the bag of gold dust I would have believed
his tale. It was artistically constructed."

" He was Hayward, the gentleman who stood out alone
for a verdict of not guilty in the jury at my trial; he left
Monterey soon after, but I called on him several times, and

in despite of my better judgment, and the overwhelming evidence against him, I cannot overcome a feeling that he is innocent. His tale to the jury was a lie, of course, and he was taken with the gold in his pockets; still I feel so."

"All things are possible," replied Don Manuel ; "and I hope it may be as you feel, and not as you think. Our feeling is often right when our thought is wrong. We know not if the poor soul is innocent ; but God knows. I did not see you speak to your friend Hayward."

"When he rose up at the fire, and disclosed the person of Hayward, I was dumbfounded," said Antonio. "He never looked toward me, and I saw plainly he did not wish me to accost him. Thinking he would be taken to town, I intended to ride with him, talk with him, and do all in my power to effect his release, by bail and the employment of an able attorney. Then came the rush of the Manley party, the speech, the jury, and I gave up in despair. I didn't have the heart to speak to him after the sentence, especially as he showed he didn't wish it."

"His management of his case was certainly admirable," said Don Manuel. "His dramatic production of the bag of gold, in part payment for the horses, was a stroke of genius and saved his life. I watched the faces of the jury as t..ey read the lettering on it. Several were deeply impressed. A death sentence from that moment was impossible."

"He took the chance of your silence. If you had exposed the theft his defense would have vanished."

"There again he showed his nerve and judgment," replied the don. "I caught him looking earnestly at me before his trial came on. He was studying me. On his right judgment of my character hung his life. I felt it a high compliment when he came up and offered me the gold. I would not have betrayed him for a myriad of horses."

"I wish now I had gone up and spoken to Hayward before we left," said Antonio. "I would feel better satisfied if I had. By the way, senor, what became of the robber with the red beard ? Domingo told me he was the desperado of the gang. His absence from the scene was very singular."

"Domingo !" said the don, turning in his saddle, "ride

up. What did you hear concerning the man of the red beard? Who told you?"

"The Mexicano, senor. He said the red beard was a tiger."

"Certainly, a very disreputable tiger," replied Don Manuel, "to fly the fight as he did. There was no sign on the plain, Domingo, of the two missing marauders?"

"None, senor. The vaqueros say they surrounded the herd and closed in. No robber seen—not even a wolf. Nothing but the horses."

"And what do you think had become of this eccentric tiger?"

"I think he was a cunning tiger, senor, and laid down to sleep far out on the plain."

"What was that bet you were talking to the young man about?"

"Did your honor overhear us?"

"I overheard you."

"We ventured a peso each against the Mexicano that I would capture the Grand Ladrone, that I would bind him. Which won, senor?"

"Give me the words of the bet."

"Well, senor, it was thus. Bernardo leaned over the counter and said to the Mexicano: 'Brother, you think Domingo will not bind the Grand Ladrone?' The Mexicano said: 'Who knows?' and then Bernardo said: 'I will lay a peso that he does,' and laid a peso. And we all laid pesoes, and he covered them. And then your honor called to horse, and we hurried out."

"Inasmuch, Domingo, as you did not capture the Ladrone," decided Don Manuel, "you lost. But inasmuch as you actually bound him, you won. Therefore let the adversary keep the stakes, and when we get home I will give you an equal sum to distribute on your side."

"A most equitable settlement," said Antonio, laughing.

"Yes, senor," responded Domingo, falling back to his place in the ranks smiling ; "it is not so bad."

CHAPTER VII.

HE PURSUES A BUBBLE OF GOLD TO THE SUMMIT OF THE HIGH SIERRA.

HIGH up in the northern mines, as near the summit of the sierra as fear of the wild Indians and lack of provisions had so far permitted the white man to push, was a camp on a plateau or bench which lay some fifty feet above the water, and ran back as many yards to the base of the mountain, which rose abruptly. The torrent that rushed by washed on either side the base of lofty and perpendicular mountains, leaving scarcely any room in low water to pitch a tent, and none in high, save on the plateau. Through this gorge lay the way into the mysterious and hitherto unexplored region of the High Sierra.

This exceptional plateau was the palatial residence of six young men who had little more than attained the age of man-hood. They had built themselves, in a spirit of pride, each a separate bush arbor of the boughs of pine, ranged in a mili-tary row against the mountain. In front of the doors were rustic stools, ranged also in a rigid line, surmounted by tin wash-basins, and the joint fireplace occupied the front cen-ter, with its pots and pans, when off duty, also ranged and clean. Altogether this camp presented a most unusual and aristocratic appearance.

The youths who occupied it had quitted the academic groves of a New England university in company, and made their way to this advance post of a new civilization in a spirit of joyous adventure. Their claims, duly staked off, began at high-water mark on the opposite side of the stream, crossed over and ran back over 'the plateau and indefinitely up the mountain. The bed of the stream and its adjacent banks were, however, alone considered of value. Their claims in width took in the entire plateau, and their wash-ings on the river were rich and yielded a good sum daily. Once a week they descended in a body to the village at the forks of the stream a mile below, and, after thoughtfully

laying in a stock of provisions, "fought the Tiger" as far
into the night as their ammunition held out. This combat,
unknown to the serious public, possesses a peculiar fascina-
tion for the assailant who returns to the struggle again and
again, though each time worsted. He believes that in a fair
fight he is more than a match for his adversary, and hopes
in each recurring encounter to meet him on equal terms.
But this he never does, for it is a law of the tiger's existence,
without which he would cease to be a tiger, to fight unfairly.

On the morning following one of these encounters, the
"Boston Boys," as they were familiarly and affectionately
termed by their neighbors, who held them in high esteem on
account of their gallantry, might be seen at a late hour at
their little wash-stands, indulging in prolonged ablutions of
cold water. Then a week of work rolled around, bringing in
a plentiful harvest of dust, followed by another night passed
in the tiger's den ; and so they played their part on the aristocratic Boston Flat.

It must not be supposed that all the claims on the river
were rich. Far from it. Many proved worthless and were
abandoned ; were tried over and over again by newcomers;
and again abandoned. Very many yielded scant returns,
barely procuring the miner his daily flour and bacon. Men
roamed about in great numbers looking for "pay dirt," and
not finding it, until, utterly discouraged and starving, they
hired out to the more fortunate, sometimes for wages, sometimes for bare food. Claims that were promising, or known
to be good, were sold and re-sold, and passed from hand to
hand, men who had accumulated a sum being everywhere on
the lookout to purchase, and the owner or owners, afraid to
risk the sudden giving out of their claims, if prudent men
would sell and return to their homes, or engage in other
pursuits.

There sprang up a low caste in the mines, a parasite on
the laboring community, detested of all men, sneaking about
under the scornful appellation of "hounds." The portrait
of one of these individuals is not prepossessing. He is slim
and gaunt, and slouches in his gait, looking aside, evasively,
when questioned ; sallow and unwholesome in complexion,
and is supposed never to sleep, and known never to work.

In the day time he lounges from group to group and place to place, listening, never speaking, and at night time eavesdrops. On the other hand, he has his virtues, or, perhaps more properly speaking, his avoidance of vice. He steals not, in the common sense of the term, so as to make himself amenable to punishment ; he is temperate and abstemious in his habits ; the pipe is foreign to him. The energies of his entire being, body and soul, are concentrated in *lurking*. That he is a coward goes without saying.

On what does the hound live ? He lives on secrets, gathering where he has not sown, on the " finds " of other men. The going out of every man that issues on a prospecting tour is noted by one or other of the confraternity of hounds. The prospector can carry with him over the steep mountains, besides his necessary tools, but a small amount of provisions, and is therefore compelled to return for a fresh supply after a certain absence ; when he is shadowed day and night until it becomes apparent that his search has been unsuccessful, or he sets back on his old trail—in which latter case he is dogged. The hounds work singly until the game is started, and then come together in packs, more or less numerous, and run it down. They are never seen by the men they follow and never lose the trail, and all attempts to throw them off by doubling or other devices have uniformly failed. The miner, as he goes to work on the morning after his return to his "find," has the mortification to see them walk up and call on him to select and mark off the four claims to which, as discoverer, he is entitled by custom. Each hound now measures and stakes off his individual claim. Some stay to hold possession, others go back for provisions and to spread the news ; for the hound relies for his gain on selling his claim in the excitement of the first rush.

In a village a long distance south of the camp of the merry Bostonians dwelt several men working in harmony a passable claim. All were content but one, whose dream of wealth was far from being realized by his modest income, and who finally announced his determination to " strike out." He made his little dispositions, shouldered his tools and sack of flour, and, promising to inform his friends if he

met with fortune and let them share it, went up the sierra—
his departure duly noted in the mental diary of an intelli-
gent hound. After a prolonged absence he appeared one
evening at the old camp-fire in a sorry condition, dilapidated
in apparel and woe-begone in looks, but with a mysterious
air, as though freighted with heavy tidings.

As soon as the neighbors had deserted their fires and
retired for the night, and silence had settled on the camps,
he related his adventures to his friends in a low, cautious
tone. He said he crossed a mountain and prospected up a
stream at its base, eight or ten miles. Finding but little, he
crossed a second mountain and ascended another stream
with like success, but followed its winding until it carried
him into the High Sierra. Here he lost his way on the summit, which was rolling and extensive, and became bewildered. He wandered for two days, during which he several
times crossed his own track, and, on the second night, was
alarmed by the light of an Indian camp-fire. He rose and
crept through the woods in an opposite direction, and
walked until sunrise, when he found himself overlooking a
lake several hundred feet beneath him, the shores of which
glittered like gold. It was oval in form, and several miles
in circumference, and seemed to him to have been the crater
of a volcano. He climbed down to the shore, which he found
strewn with bowlders of gold quartz, mingled about half and
half, and spats of pure gold weighing many pounds, that
looked as though they might have been cast up and dropped
in place in a half-molten state. He knelt down and took a
draught of water, as his throat was parched, and found it
sweet and refreshing, though tasting of sulphur. He then
built a fire, concealing it as well as he could for fear of
Indians, and cooked the last of his flour, ate his breakfast,
and lay down and slept many hours. When he woke up he
found himself refreshed, and his self-confidence returned.
He put into his empty flour bag a beautiful specimen of
pure gold, weighing about twenty pounds, reflecting that it
would not do to overload himself, ascended from the crater,
took his bearings by the sun, and "struck out" for the
mines.

As evening approached, he reached the summit of a long,

gentle ascent, and sat down on a rock to rest, facing the direction from which he had come. The forest was composed of great pine trees, but open, and he could see back a long way. Suddenly a band of Indians came into view on his trail. He sprung to his feet and darted behind a huge bowlder, of which many were scattered about, leaving his bag and blanket where they lay, and ran for his life. He soon reached a thicket and plunged into it, wandering there two nights and a day, living on berries and sleeping by snatches. Finally he came out into the open, his clothes in tatters, as they saw them, took his bearings, and finally reached a mining camp, worked a few days for food and then hurried home.

His story was listened to with profound attention, not alone by the inmates of the tent, but also by an inquisitive gentleman lying on the ground on the outside, who had noted the miner's return as he had previously noted his departure.

The excitement of the party was raised to white heat. To strengthen themselves against the Indians, they took into their council a company of trusted friends working an adjoining claim, and with profound caution made their secret preparations and decamped in the dead of night. The hounds in a body pursued them, and they, in turn, were tracked by a train that grew in numbers as it wound its sinuous course through contiguous defiles, until hundreds on hundreds were involved in its seemingly interminable convolutions. The passage of this miniature army over the plateau was watched by a disabled Bostonian, stretched out in his arbor, unfit for active duty, by reason of a late prolonged encounter with his enemy in the village.

About the middle of the forenoon, he saw a file of men pass in front of his arbor, bent with the weight of provisions, rifle in hand. This was the advance guard, led by the discoverer. After an interval of time there stole up the path the advance hound, tall and lank, with his eye on their trail. Then followed the pack off duty, marching at ease. After they had disappeared, the main body came, single file, and all the remainder of the day, and far into the night, they kept it up, their line unbroken. The next morning the weak, who had dropped to the rear, crossed over; the sick, leg-weary and footsore, singly, and in little gangs, dragging by their weary limbs; and, last of all, an old lame man, his long, white beard covered with dust, limped across, supporting his steps with a pilgrim's staff that reached above his head. His progress was impeded by the necessity he was under of swinging one leg in the arc of a circle at every step; but his eye was bright and fixed before him, and he evidently entertained high hopes of reaching the front before the spoil was all appropriated. He constituted the rear-guard.

The column reached the region of the High Sierra, passed over the mountain of bewilderment, was pointed out the stone on which the discoverer sat when he caught sight of the pursuing Indians, and at the foot of which he had abandoned, in his precipitate flight, the bag of gold. It was therefore near the oval lake, and pressed on in the hope of reaching it in time to see its golden shores illuminated by the rays of the setting sun. But night caught it in the forest, and by noon on the following day it became evident that the discoverer had lost his way. He acknowledged that he ought to have reached the lake, and had hoped to reach it the night before.

"But, come on, my friends," he said. "Follow me. I will lead you to it yet."

"No, John," answered one of his company. "We will go into camp and consult. Better prospect from here than wander further."

They accordingly halted where they were standing, by a pool of snow water, and went into camp. Some went to work to construct a shelter, others to bring in wood, and a fire was soon blazing. To the hounds, the halt at such an unusual hour, and the cumulative evidence that the advance was preparing a permanent camp, seemed proof positive that the vicinity of the oval lake was reached at last. They consequently threw off all reserve and came to the front. The main body followed their example, and, when night fell, the discoverer was the center of a host, and the forest blazed with fires.

The next morning the bubble burst. The discoverer, on

being requested to lead one of the prospecting parties it had
been arranged to send out, declined, with the alarming announcement that he was again bewildered. 'This spread
with the speed of electricity through the camps, and a
threatening croud surrounded him. To all the questions put
and denunciations launched at his head, his repeated answer
was :

"I am lost ! I am bewildered ! "

Cries of "Lynch him ! lynch him ! " now arose from all
quarters. The deluded crowd was ravenous for a scapegoat.
They sought to smother their sudden and bitter disappoint-
ment in the stronger emotion evoked by crime. They
thirsted for blood, and when a mob thus criminally inspired has its victim in its hands, to interpose may be
likened to stepping between the tiger and its prey, and
calls out the hero.

By a concerted movement, the friends of the discoverer
were pushed back and a ruffian seized him by the collar. A
lithe powerful man, with black close-cut hair and beard,
caught the scamp by the shoulder and said in a commanding tone :

"Let go your hold—the man is mad ! "

"He is not ! " replied the assassin fiercely. '"He is a
traitor ! "

"Let go, I say ! " said the Ladrone, forcing him back.
"Men," he added, raising his voice, "listen to common
sense. This poor fellow has lost his reason. We followed
him on our own motion, without his knowledge. Let us act
good-humoredly. I move that this crowd pack up and take
the back track. All in favor of this motion signify the same
by saying ' ay.' "

A vociferous affirmative was the response, followed by
loud laughter, shouts and yells, and the mob broke up.

The noise of the retreating column gradually died away,
and the smoke of the deserted fires rose in a still air and
mingled with the foliage of the pines. Of all the host that
lately peopled the forest but three remained, seated in silence
on the summit of the solitary mountain.

"If we fall too far behind," said one of the number at
length, "the Indians may catch us."

"The Indians will follow close on the rear of the column." replied Hayward smiling. "By waiting a while, we can fall on the rear of the Indians and catch them."

"There are the two men to bury," continued the first speaker; "that will take some time."

"I take it we will find more than two that died last night," said Hayward; "but we have plenty of time. I would rather take the chance of a fight with the Indians than to travel with that disorderly crowd. We would be plagued for food or water at every step. Besides, we don't want any one to follow us down the canyon when we leave the trail."

"It's a risky business to quit the trail and hang about in these mountains."

"I admit the risk, David," said Hayward, to the one carrying on the conversation with him, a small man with a pockmarked face acquired at Durango, and who did the talking for the two companions. "It is true the Indians may get us, but let us hope not; and we may pick up a fortune in that canyon, and that is what we came all the way from Florida for, knowing when we started we would run risk after risk; in short, risk nothing have nothing."

"If I had foreseen this confounded pockmark and the trial on the Mariposa," returned David, "I'd have stayed in Florida, sure. My folks won't know me when I get home: I'll have to get somebody to introduce me to my mother."

"Take back plenty of gold, David," said his chief, "and you'll be known."

"Well, Billy," said David, rising and addressing his companion, a large, solemn, silent man, "let us go and bury the dead. I suppose it will do to lay them between two rocks, and cover them with brush and stone."

"Yes," replied Hayward.

While the men were gone about their pious task, Hayward sat gazing in the fire, thinking of Catalina and the dream he had related to her under the orange tree, of the cave of Ala Baba in the mountain of gold, and longed to find that mythical cavern and get back to his lovely companion. In his left breastpocket, over his heart, he had a letter from her, read many times, which he took out and was reperusing when the men returned.

"We found this small bag of flour," said David, as they approached, " holding, I should think, some eight or nine pounds, under the head of one of the poor fellows. This will keep us from starving in the canyon, anyway."

Hayward made no reply, but put up his letter and resumed his gaze in the fire. The men sat down, showing signs of impatience to be off. After a time a drove of wolves invaded the camp, and on seeing the men set up a dismal howl of indignation. Hayward came out of his revery and rose to his feet.

"Come, boys," he said, "let us tramp and leave the camp to the wolves."

The following forenoon, as they neared the face of the canyon down which they intended to descend, they saw on the trail or near it the bodies of several men pierced by the arrow of the Indian. David entered a protest against going down, but Hayward was inflexible, and the little party slowly and cautiously made the perilous descent to the water. They were disappointed in getting at the bed of the stream, which ran full to its banks and with great velocity; but set vigorously to work at such points in the sides of the canyon as promised returns.

Having nothing but their pans to wash with they could accomplish but little, but the gold they found was coarse, and they hoped each hour to come upon a rich deposit. Thus sustained, they labored on, in constant apprehension and with little food, until the evening of the third day, when the patience of David gave out, and Hayward himself was compelled to succumb to approaching famine.

"Look at this bag, Mister Hayward," said David, acting cook, holding one up for inspection as they sat at supper that evening, "it's the flour of the dead man."

"Well," replied Hayward, " what of it?"

"It's the last!"

"Why, that will hardly see us out of the mountains," said Hayward, " even if we start in the morning."

"No," replied David, "it will not; and if we stay here

another day we'll starve, unless the Indians save us from it, which is more than likely."

" Well, men, we will climb out of the canyon in the morning," said Hayward, regretfully. " What a pity we couldn't stay a week longer."

" Yes," replied David, winking at his companion, " it's very trying; I feel it very much."

" There is a fortune in here for us," continued Hayward, "if we only had the time to look it up; the lump gold we have washed out shows it clearly, to my mind. If we could get at the bed of the river we could soon take shipping for Mazatlan, with all we came for."

Night had set in, and as they sat in conversation the silent man took up the basin and, stepping to the water's edge filled it to the brim. Returning, he splashed it over and put out the fire.

" Halloo. Billy !" exclaimed Hayward in amazement " Have you gone mad ? "

" Not quite," he answered. " Look ! "

Far up the canyon they saw the faint glimmer of an Indian camp-fire.

CHAPTER VIII.

THE MERRY BOSTONIANS FAVOR THE LADRONE, AND ROBBERS PURSUE HIM.

SOONER or later, in one form or another, punishment overtakes the man who, despising the day of small things, makes haste to get rich. Not every one came down again who went up the path into the High Sierra. Many died of prostration brought on by fatigue and hunger. Many wandered from the path to prospect, and were lost and starved— the wonderful sameness everywhere of the great pines and scattered rocks making even a slight deviation from the track extremely hazardous to any other than the accomplished woodsman. Many fell by the arrow of the Indian, who hung upon the flanks of the retreating column and picked off the incautious. The hounds, who in the ascent had enjoyed a temporary breeze of popular favor, on account of their sagacity in detecting and want of sagacity in failing to keep to themselves the brilliant secret of the gorgeous lake, were now cursed from one end of the line to the other with a fertility and variety of expression that approached the superhuman.

In a few days the multitude began to pass over the plateau in return, not with the hopeful, elastic step with which they had advanced, but lagging, downcast, and forlorn. The fascinating allusions to the "oval lake," which murmured along the line as they wound up, were now exchanged for sarcastic and bitter cuts at the "Goose and Fool's Lake" as they wound down. Men along their pathway who had not been drawn into the upward current, but had remained at their work, from motives of prudent suspicion or from whatever cause, uncharitably taunted the melancholy band on their return. Some received the jeers thrown at them bitterly, and retorted in the strongest phraseology at their command; others passed on in silence, already too badly wounded by the arrows of outrageous fortune to feel the smart ; while many, philosophers these, joined in the laugh against themselves and trudged good-humoredly on. From day to day, as they passed down, the various camps from which they had issued absorbed them. The deluded army, as an organization, vanished, and the famous expedition to the Oval Lake became a reminiscence.

It was the custom, where a company of miners had a common mess, to perform the menial office of water-carrier and cook, day or week about. The cook, as he was called during his incumbency, rose earlier than his comrades—even before the sun's rays touched the top of the mountain, and hours before they reached the camp—and went to the river for water.

The Bostonian cook one morning, in accordance with this laudable custom, had risen early, and was crossing the plateau with a bucket in each hand, when he met the Grand Ladrone with a light pick on his shoulder, followed by two men. They were the rear-guard of the disastrous expedition. After bidding the cook good-morning, the Ladrone said :

" Sir, I see you are not mining up on this flat. "

" No," answered the cook, with a laugh ; " excuse the pun, but we are not such *flats*. Gold does not grow this high above the river."

" On what terms will you permit me to sink a hole here ? " he inquired.

" You may sink as many holes here as you please, without terms," was the answer.

" But your comrades ; will they consent ? "

" Oh, my comrades will be all right," the cook replied ; and, as he started on, he called over his shoulder, " Come and take coffee and a flap-jack with us, and the comrades will confirm and quit claim ; but let me tell you, stranger, you will waste your time all the same."

" Many thanks," answered the Ladrone ; and as he spoke he threw the pick from his shoulder by a sleight of hand. It turned in the air in falling and stuck in the ground.

" Look up and down the river," he said to his companions, " and see how this flat juts out from the mountain. See how the river turns around it and returns to its course.

This is an ancient land slide, and the river once ran under that pick."

"It looks like it," said one of the men.

"One must dig as deep down as the river bed to get anything, and that is at least fifty or sixty feet," said the other. "It is impossible, of course, to go that deep."

"The present bed, yes," replied the Ladrone; "but the ancient bed, how deep down is it? High water passing over the slide, perhaps for ages, has washed it away and left only this flat. How near did it come to washing it all away before the new bed was deep enough to carry off the waters? My impression is it stopped but little short of it. In my opinion, we can strike the ancient bed-rock in fifteen or twenty feet."

"It must be rich when we strike it, to pay," said David.

"It must be rich when we strike it to pay," echoed the Ladrone. "If we strike smooth bottom, we shall have lost our labor; if we strike rough bottom, who knows how much gold we may find, caught there in past ages for our special benefit?"

"We will know when we get there," answered the other, dubiously.

"True," said the Ladrone, "and to get there we must go to work. Nothing venture, nothing win."

The cook, coming by with his water, said, nodding at the pick sticking in the ground:

"I see you have struck your first blow."

"The handle of that pick," answered the Ladrone, laughing, "is made of witch-hazel. I threw it at random in the air, and it stuck where you see. It is bewitched, and is now pointing to one of the mines of Plutus."

"May Plutus prosper you," laughed the cook as he passed on.

"Mark out a square, with the pick as a center," said the Ladrone, "and we will go to work."

The cook informed his friends, when they issued from their arbors, of the occurrence of the morning, and they laughed at the matter, discussing it as they made their toilets. When breakfast was ready, the cook called out in a theatrical tone:

" Come. stranger, the banquet is served—pork and beans, coffee and flap-jacks. Advance and fortify the inner man before descending into the realms of Pluto."

"I come!" answered he in a like tragic tone, dropping his shovel; and he and the young men sat down to breakfast in fine humor.

"Our new friend and guest," said the cook, with mock gravity, "has a fancy to mine the plateau. I have given him permission to dig it up. He seeks a confirmation of the grant from this honorable company. He has broken our bread—flap-jack, I should say, but the effect is the same—and his grant is thereby confirmed, nemine contradicente."

"Nem. con.," responded the others, with a laugh.

"But, gentlemen, let us be serious," said the Ladrone. "I have, as you see, already commenced work. Now is the time to settle our terms, before I strike 'pay dirt.'"

"You will never make a strike, my deluded friend," answered the cook. "No written terms are needed; base are the slaves that make them. Dig away, and pocket all you get."

"Stop your banter, cook," said a more serious member of the party. "The gentleman must be protected before he expends his time and labor. He is running risk enough in working up here at all."

He walked to the arbor, and brought out paper and pencil; resumed his seat, and began to write, reading aloud as he went on.

"This is to certify that we, the undersigned, forever quit claim to and transfer our interest in, that part of our claims commonly known as the Boston Flat, to—" here he paused and looked up at the stranger.

"Pedro," responded he. "I am known among my friends as Don Pedro."

"Don Pedro," continued the writer. "for no consideration, as the land is of no value."

"Hold," exclaimed the cook, reaching for the paper with feigned alarm. "The avaricious Don Pedro may undermine our fireplace, our line of wash-stands, and even penetrate to our tents. He must be restrained. I move that a line be drawn parallel to the wash-stands, through a point five

cubits in front of the fire, to the west of which he is not permitted to strike a pick."

"I move," said another, "to substitute the word yard
for cubit. The latter is indefinite, and ill-understood by the
common people, who may one day be called upon to construe
and adjudicate on this important paper."

"I accept the amendment," replied the cook. "It ex-
tends the reserve."

"Nonsense!" said the writer.

"Put it in," interposed the Ladrone. "Who knows what
may happen?"

The paper was accordingly amended by adding: "Excepting therefrom all west of a line drawn five yards in front
of the fireplace, and running parallel to the arbors." Each
Bostonian affixed his signature to the document, and it was
handed to the Ladrone by the cook with burlesque solemnity
and a gracious bow.

Several mornings after this event men were seen hurrying from all directions to the plateau. A crowd surrounded
the hole, looking down and uttering exclamations of surprise and wonder. Two of the three men at the bottom
were engaged in scooping gold out of a crevice into a bucket
already two-thirds full, and the third, Don Pedro, in attempting to pry out with his pickax a great, smooth, oval lump,
firmly wedged in between the layers of rock. Great was the
find and great the excitement. The Boston boys bent over
and gazed into the hole, paralyzed with wonder. Thirteen
feet beneath the surface the Ladrone had come upon the old
bed, seamed with deep, rough crevices opening up-stream
like mouths.

"What awful luck!" exclaimed an envious miner.

"There is no luck about it," returned a philosopher who
was enjoying the spectacle. "The man is smart; that is
where it is."

"Smart or no smart," said a third, "I wish I was in his
boots."

"So do we all," said another. "But what is the use of
wishing? I wish I had the half of it, and was safe back
home again."

"It was that confounded hazel pick-handle," said the

cook, "and no man living shall ever make me believe to the contrary. Boys," he said, addressing his fellow Bostonians, "we are beat by the superhuman. The devil is in it to a reduced certainty. I say, old fellow," he called down to the Ladrone, "I see you have found your old friend Plutus. Throw us up a chunk."

"I have found my old friend Plutus," answered Don Pedro, looking up with a laugh, "and I will bring you over a chunk this evening after supper."

"Gentlemen," said Don Pedro, as he walked up to their camp-fire after dark that evening, and found the Bostonians with their heads together in deep consult, "Fortune has become my friend."

"Say your slave, Don Pedro," said he who had drawn up the deed of gift, "and you will be nearer the mark. Whoever heard of the jade prostrating herself before a man in that groveling style before?"

"Fortune often gets credit where none is due," said another. "It is possible the don thought it out and is entitled to the credit himself."

The cook muttered something about the pick-handle, and the quick ear of the Ladrone caught it up.

"Let us call it the pick-handle," he said with a laugh. "And now, friends, let us come to business. What are your terms?"

"Terms!" exclaimed the writer. "We let the opportunity slip for dictating terms. The property is yours."

"Yes," he replied, "the property is now mine, but I again invite you to propose terms. It is true, as my friend the cook has darkly insinuated, I owe my wonderful fortune partly to the pick-handle, but I would be an ingrate if I forgot, in the hour of my triumph, that I also owe it to your merry and thoughtless and good-hearted concession. Very many would have roughly refused a wayfarer any, the slightest chance, and many more would have loaded it down with onerous conditions. Gentlemen," he continued, with emotion, "I have stumbled in my path often, once nearly unto death; but I have yet to incur the detestation of the gods by the sin of ingratitude."

After a short silence, which the company respected, he resumed:

"What proportion of the spoil shall I relinquish? What are your thoughts?"

"To be open with you," answered the writer, "we were discussing the subject when you came up. We agreed that, while we had no shadow of title, and would not think for a moment of asserting one, yet it would be a fitting thing in you to return to us one of the six claims, whichever you preferred, and the cook, who represents the face of the company, volunteered to suggest it to you."

"To modestly insinuate it to him?" corrected the cook.

"Yes, insinuate, I believe, was the word. And now, Don Pedro, what do you think of the insinuation?"

"I think it a modest one," he answered, "and propose to amend it. I will retain the half of the flat I am working on, and return to you the remainder."

This proposition was received with polite protestations but secret delight. The writer said it was more than generous, it was munificent; and the cook solemnly and publicly renounced his belief in the agency of Satan. A collection of tin cups was immediately made, and a bottle produced from a recess in an arbor, and the great act of renunciation was celebrated in a smiling bumper. Pipes were filled up and set to fuming violently, and the Boston boys determined to make a night of it. When comparative calm was restored, Don Pedro said:

"Chance, gentlemen, has thrown us together, and we are friends. I will confide to you my plans, and take the liberty to give you a little advice. I will work out, or at least, partly work out, the claim I am on, and then sell all three to the speculators and quit the mines forever. It may be the other claims are good; but, on the other hand, it may turn out that I am now working the only rough bottom claim on the flat. I will not take the chance, when I can sell out at a reasonable price to others who will gladly accept it. Great sums will be offered for every one of our claims as long as they remain unexplored. Sell yours, as they stand all together. Do not let yourselves be tempted to sink a hole, or even scratch the surface. You are acquainted, I am told,

with the phraseology of the green cloth ; you have listened
to the fascinating rattle of the bones ? "

" We have heard the chimes at midnight, Master Pedro,"
answered the cook.

" Very well, then," continued the Ladrone, " I can convey my advice to you in a single phrase. Watch my play."

With this, he rose to take his departure, pleading fatigue
from the excitement of the day; took a parting cup, and retired to his blankets.

The following morning the Ladrone set a number of hired
men to work to strip the earth from the claim, widening and
lengthening the hole. The enormous yield continued through
the week. The excitement increased and spread. Speculators came from a distance, and large offers were made
for single claims and parts of claims ; but Don Pedro replied to all that he was not a retail dealer. If a respectable offer was made, he would part with all ; otherwise,
he would work them out himself. The Bostonians assumed
a like attitude, and the speculators, their offers rejected
with contempt, were driven nearly frantic. The desire to
get   footing in the ancient bed was all-absorbing.

On Saturday night a syndicate was formed at the Forks,
composed of the heaviest men in that and the surrounding camps, and on Sunday evening, after an all-day negotiation, a sale was closed of the entire flat.

The roads leading from the upper mines to Sacramento
were infested by robbers, chiefly from the United States
and the English penal colonies of the South Seas. They
were merciless men, and almost invariably murdered their
victims. They chiefly fell upon persons going down suspected of carrying gold, and vigilance was required to get
through in safety. The lawless men from the States were
not less brutal than their convict rivals in crime, and the
solitary miner traveling down, or even up, if gifted with
any caution, would immediately stop, on being joined by
a countryman, and require him to go in advance or fall
back. In the mountains bands of wild Indians would cross
the trail and occasionally camp near it, and murder individuals or small parties coming under their notice. But the
white men made it a business, and were far more dreaded

than the Indians. A white man on horseback would often
overtake another while passing through the Indian country
and propose to ride in company for mutual defense. If the
proposition was entertained, as it sometimes was, the man
overtaken would usually say:

" I have no objection, if you let me ride on your left, and
behind you when the path is too narrow to ride abreast.".

"That is the position," the other would answer, "that I
propose to occupy, if we ride in company."

"Then," the first would reply, "as you have overtaken
me, and seem to be better mounted, you had better push
ahead."

And so the two fellow-citizens would part, and risk an
encounter with the Indians alone and unsupported.

This being the state of the public highways, it behooved
the late proprietors of the Boston Flat to move their treasure
down the mountains with caution. A Mexican arriero, who
commanded a pack train of mules, carrying provisions from
the city to the Forks, was engaged by Don Pedro ; and the
gold, well bagged and wrapped, was made into cargoes. The
Bostonians sold the portion of their claims lying in and on
the river banks, having resolved, under the advice and influence of the Ladrone, to return to their native heath and
abandon their unprofitable conflicts with the tiger. They,
the party of the Ladrone, and that of the arriero, made their
force too formidable to be attacked with any prospect of success, however alluring the cargoes. But, nevertheless, after
consultation with the arriero. Don Pedro and his party set
out in the middle of the night ; and, when the sun rose, the
time given out for their departure from the Forks, the train
had reached the mountain-top on the opposite side of the
river, and was winding along the summit under the giant
pines.

A band of outlaws, however, had organized the day
before, under a determined ruffian named Max, to follow the
convoy and make an attack, in case a favorable opportunity
offered. They were surprised and chagrined on finding the
train had set out in the night, and two by two they ascended
the mountain in the morning and assembled on its summit
at noon. After a short consultation they mounted and

filed into the trail, Max and his lieutenant, Toby, heading the troop.

An animated conversation took place between these worthy leaders as they rode along, in which the ways and means of effecting the end in view were carefully gone over. The men who rode behind discussed the subject also, and several of their number, possessed of decided views, did not hesitate to ride up to the chief and impart them, when the width of the trail permitted or the party halted at a snow pool to water their horses. A good deal of anxiety was felt and expressed—as they were inferior to the enemy in numbers—as to the result of an attack, unless they could succeed in taking them unawares and get a decided advantage at the start ; this they hoped for, and to this end they cabaled.

" This trail's no good," said Max, addressing his lieutenant. " I never see a meaner one ; never, no whar. The trees is so fur apart a feller can't git in shootin' distance afore he's spotted. I don't see what sich a woods was ever made fur."

" 'Twant made fur our bene*fit*, that's perfectly sartin," responded Lieutenant Toby with a sigh.

" It's the wust laid off trail I know of," reiterated the chief ; " 'taint got a ambush on it."

" Ef it oney runned through a chapperal now," replied Toby in a melancholy tone, " or a cactus thicket, like we had 'em on the Rio Grande ; why, 'twould be woth talkin' about."

" I've worked in them," responded the chief with enthusiasm ; " they're beautiful ; ef thur was cactus a growin' on this cussed mountin, instead of nothin',we could massacre every soul in that train and not get a scratch."

" And then these mountin sides is no good fur business," said Toby, in a complaining tone, " which they in most countries is considered prime. Thur so feerful straight up and down you can't work on 'em to no advantage. I wish I was back on the Grande."

" Well, I don't," returned the chief, " the travelers thar is too durned poor ; here thur harder to git, but they pan out better. Why, I've knocked over men in the cactus, likely looking men, too, that didn't have a red cent in thur pockets. It's disgustin' to be took in that away, that's wot it is."

"It happens here, too, Max," said the lieutenant. "You remember the man on the Calaverus. *That* was a disap'intment."

"That feller caught it from the wearin' of a white shirt and a shiney hat," replied the chief. "Wot right hes a man to dress up in a stove-pipe hat, and a white shirt and stand-up collar, lest he's got somethin' in his pocket to back it?"

"It's a deceivin' of the public," responded Toby with indignation, "fur sich a chap to go a roamin' round the country on a hoss, with his nose in the air, tryin' to make believe he's somebody. It makes my blood bile to look at 'em."

This delectable conversation was here broken off by the approach of a man mounted on a mule, clothed in irreproachable attire : a slouch hat much the worse for wear, a red flannel shirt open at the throat, and yellow corduroy breeches thrust in heavy cowskin bootlegs. The troop halted and the chief accosted him.

"You didn't see a train as you come along, did you?" he inquired, throwing his right leg over the pommel of the saddle and sitting sideways to rest.

"Yes," replied the traveler, with a look of apprehension. "I did."

"And how fur ahead mought it be?"

"I passed it about two hours ago," replied the traveler.

"Was they strung out much?" inquired Toby.

"No," he answered, "they were marching compact ; they minded me of a company of soldiers."

"Glad to hear it," replied Max, though with a look of displeasure ; "they belong to our party, and we was afeerd the Ingins mought attack 'em afore we caught up. Well, that's all."

"Wait a half a second," interposed Toby. fixing a penetrating glance on the traveler and leaning toward him from the saddle. "We seed a bad c'aracter back aways, alayin' in the bresh fur game. You better look out. You hain't a carryin' of no gold about your pussen, I hope?"

"Not an ounce!" replied the traveler fervently, turning

pale and trembling in his seat; "not the tenth part of one! I am going to the mines to try to get some."

"Hope you'll have good luck," said Toby, assuming an erect position in the saddle and giving his horse the spur. "By-by."

"Good-by," responded the traveler, hastily touching his mule with the spur and speeding on, quite reckless of the bad character laying in wait for him in the brush.

"What's to be done?" inquired the chief of Toby as they resumed their pursuit. "We'll not overtake that convoy afore dark. They'll pick out a strong camp, dead sure, and keep watch all night. The case begins to look tremendous bilious."

"We'll never make the riffle," responded Toby gloomily, giving the mouth of his horse a wrench to vent his humor. "Not without heavy loss—never."

"Whatever's done must be done to-night," said Max; "fur they'll camp nigh the edge of the mountain, and fust thing in the mornin' begin to go down, to cross at Goodyear's Bar. Now, here's my plan, and here's what's got to be done. We'll ride up to thur camp-fire, and talk sweet to them, and build our fire close to theirs, and rise on them in the night. Thur ain't no other way, and it's a good way."

A short distance before reaching the point at which the descent to Goodyear's Bar commenced, a chasm crossed the trail, filled, though it was midsummer, to the brim with snow. At the crossing it was beaten down and safe, but elsewhere treacherous. Pools of water were found on either side, and parties belated camped here for the night.

When the pursuing party reached the chasm after dark, headed by Max and Toby, they were commanded to halt, by an armed man who stood in the trail beyond, by a small fire. His voice was loud, and reached his comrades, who were seated at supper some distance farther on, and Hayward, followed by the "Boston boys," left his seat and walked down. When they reached the chasm, they found Toby pathetically remonstrating with the sentinel.

"You don't want the Ingins fur to git us, do you?" he inquired.

"I don't care a cuss whether they git you or not," replied the sentinel. "I've got orders to shoot the first man that attempts to cross this ditch, and I'll do it."

"Captain," said Toby, appealing to Hayward, "the Ingins is on our trail. We've ben a runnin' from them all evenin'. We want to camp nigh you fellers fur pertection. That's what we want, and this man says as how we shan't."

"What Indians?" inquired Hayward.

"The Feather Ingins," answered Toby. "They've ben over a fightin' of the Yubas, and tuck after us two hours sense. I suspicion thur can't be no objection to our campin' alongside of you, neighbor-like."

"Camp on your own side, friend," replied Hayward; "Indians never attack at night."

"We're afeered of them a pitchin' in to us at daybreak," returned Toby.

"We will be at our breakfast at that hour," said Hayward, "and can cross over and take the Feathers in the rear, if you will take the trouble to call us. What do you think of that for strategy, my friend?"

"It seems to me kind a hard-hearted," answered Toby.

"And it seems to me," broke in Max, with asperity in his voice and a determined look in his face. "that this here trail is public, and no man hasn't got no right to go a stoppin' of it up; that's about the size it looks to a man on this side of the ditch. We don't keer to camp alongside of men as ain't good-natered, and don't keer to keep thur company. We kin ride past your fire, captain, and go down to-night yit to Goodyear's Bar."

"No one can descend the mountain in the night," replied Hayward.

The Hayward men had one, by one, as they finished their supper, strolled down to the chasm; and now were all present, standing here and there, within hearing of the conversation. A movement now occurred among the robbers, who broke ranks and crowded about their chief in whispered conversation. The Bostonian cook and the arriero disposed their men to the best advantage, walking to and fro among them, quietly dropping a hint here and there. In front of them stood the sentry by the fire, with his "arms aport," ready to take aim, and near him on a rock stood Hayward, his hands clasped behind his back, close to the handle of his revolver. Presently the robbers moved apart, leaving their chief standing alone in front.

"I will give you men," he called out in a threatening tone, "two minutes to clear the track!"

"I will be more liberal with you cut-throats," responded Hayward firmly. "I will give you four minutes to clear out of my sight."

"You've lost the trick, Max," whispered Toby, mournfully. "The capt'in has seen your bluff and gone you two better. Take my advice and light out; the quicker the better. Minutes is precious. I'm off."

"We'll meet ag'in, my fine feller," threatened Max hoarsely, rising in his stirrups as he turned his horse about, and shaking his fist at Hayward, pale with rage, his eyes flashing. "And when we do, I'll cut your heart out."

"Ha! ha! ha!" laughed Hayward. "You're a barking dog."

CHAPTER IX.

HE MEETS HIS EVIL GENIUS IN THE ALLEY OF ASSASSINS.

MANY years prior to the events narrated in the last chapter, Morales had crossed the Cordillera and established a small commission house in the city of Mazatlan. He depended in the beginning entirely on shipments or consignments from Durango ; but, as his business grew, he added a banking bureau to his house, and engaged in a small way in the importation of French goods and the exportation to France of Lima-wood and copper.

After gold was discovered, and the old *Presidio* of San Francisco had become encompassed by canvas by land and sea, when ten thousand tents were pitched on her surrounding sand hills, and a thousand vessels rode at anchor in her bay, Morales, attracted by her far-reaching magnetism, that drew men from the remotest parts of the earth, changed the current of his exports and shipped to the north the products of the tropics.

In the midst of a profitable business his correspondent in San Francisco failed, and Morales took the first monthly steamer that passed up to save what he could from his last consignments. When the steamer was signaled and entered the Golden Gate, crowds poured down the long wharf to witness the landing of the passengers. From stem to stern the decks presented one mass of people, and as she rounded to, a shout of welcome went up, responded to by those on board by the waving of handkerchiefs. It was an animated spectacle, marked by special recognition of friends, and great enthusiasm. Very many disappointments could be noted as well, as thousands who were due were left at Panama to wait for passage in succeeding steamers.

The Ladrone was in the crowd on the wharf, and as Morales walked down the gangway met him with a Spanish embrace and escorted to his quarters in the city the uncle of the fair Catalina.

Some days were spent in settling the business which had brought Morales up, and, not understanding the American language, he would have been embarrassed in prosecuting it, but for the efficient help he received from Hayward, who displayed ability and tact in the affair, and brought it to as satisfactory a conclusion as could have been hoped for. The evening after the settlement, he invited Morales to his room and entered on a confidential relation of his affairs and of the Mormon trap into which he had fallen, and the invention by which he had saved himself.

He then advised Morales to establish a branch of his house in the city, offering to furnish all the capital needed, as against his uncle's experience and services, and asked him to name his cash price for a half interest in the Mazatlan establishment. Morales made some calculations, expressed a willingness to take him into partnership, and named his terms, which were at once accepted. It seemed so certain that a great business could be speedily established in the city, with a Spanish and French clientèle, that Morales, though conservative and cautious, fell in with the proposal, and the house of Hayward & Co., a branch of the house of Morales at Mazatlan, making dealings with the Spanish and French population a specialty, was duly established.

"There is some scheme being hatched," said Morales one day, "in the brain of your old enemy. He is revolving something to work us harm."

"What enemy?" inquired Hayward, looking up from his writing at the bank parlor table.

"Don Solomon," answered Morales, "the Mormon prince."

"Oh, Stubbs," exclaimed Hayward. "I have been keeping a sharp eye on the little polygamist. I don't fear him. What is he at now?"

"I think he is preparing to attack our title," replied Morales. "Dona Augusta stopped me on the street to-day and intimated he was at work in that direction. She said a man she was satisfied was an emissary of Solomon was busy among the old Spanish inhabitants, always after dark, hunting for a clew to the Gomez family. She said the Mormon was thus seeking satisfaction for his public overthrow in the saloon."

"Did the senora give any reason for thinking the inquirer connected with Stubbs?" asked Hayward.

"Yes; when Don Solomon first came to the city she says the man was much about him for a time, and then vanished. Putting two and two together, she said she divined the purpose while the man was questioning her."

"And who was the man—his name? Did she state?"

"He introduced himself as Mr. Lamb, but the senora says he didn't in the least resemble one. In fact, from the description, I took the dubious lamb to be your old friend Corby, who deserted you on the Mariposa."

"Ah!" exclaimed Hayward, brightening. "If Corby has taken the field we must spring in the saddle. Corby is not to be despised, as I know to my cost."

"The senora said," continued Morales, "that from the drift of the questions he put she was satisfied he intended to get up a forged conveyance, in case he failed to find a Gomez to buy one from."

"No doubt! no doubt!" said Hayward, rising. "I will set out forthwith in search of the Gomez that owns the title to the land we stand on, and will find him, if I am compelled to travel over all Spanish America and old Spain in the bargain. It will be a pleasure to cross swords with brother Corby with my eyes open."

When San Francisco was a Spanish village the alcalde, or mayor, gave grants of land within its boundary to settlers, and it was on these grants, duly recorded, that the titles in the city rested. A large and now very valuable grant, recorded in the name of Gomez, was apparently without an owner; and an enterprising gentleman, pitying its desolate and forsaken condition, induced the new American mayor to grant it to him in the old Mexican fashion. As soon as the paper was recorded he began selling lots, and asserted over the tract a most despotic sway. The prices given, however, were not large, and the buildings erected were cheap and small, as the shade of the departed Gomez hung threateningly over it. It was on a corner of this tract, where the main business street of the city entered it, that

Hayward & Co. built their bank, as the situation was favorable ; but they were from the first uneasy respecting the title, and now Don Pedro determined to ferret out the representatives of the old proprietor. Inquiry among the few old residents that had remained in the city developed the fact that several gentlemen besides his friend Corby had been before him in the investigation, and had evidently failed to trace the missing parties. It appeared that Gomez had died several years before the advent of the Americans, and that his widow, with several grown children, had left the village on a coasting vessel for Santa Barbara.

Hayward took it for granted that Santa Barbara, and, probably, the other ports in California, had been searched by preceding inquirers ; and, even if this were not so, if the parties were living anywhere in the Territory they would have learned of the value of their property and come forward and claimed it. He therefore decided that they had gone to Mexico, and would probably be heard of at Mazatlan, or a trace be obtained there of their whereabouts. Accordingly, he took the steamer for that port.

Arrived there, he found on inquiry a family of the name of Gomez; but, on learning his mission, they were sorry to say that none of their relations had ever, to their knowledge, gone to California ; and that certainly none had returned thence, or they would have known it. They informed him that inquiry had been made several times before, after which they had looked about and satisfied themselves that no such parties were in the city. Hayward now called at the Custom House, and, feeing the official, was permitted to examine the minutes taken of the manifests of vessels that had entered the port during the year in which the Gomez family had left San Francisco. On one of these abbreviated manifests he found noted, under the head of "Passengers"— "The Senora Navarrete and family."

It was an ancient custom in Spain and in Spanish countries, still in part kept up, for the wife to retain her maiden surname, or to resume it in widowhood. It seems the breach of this good custom had begun far back, for we find Teresa Panza complaining to Sancho, that "her father's name was Cascajo, and she being his wife was called Tersa Panza, though, indeed, by good right, she should have been called Teresa Cascajo." The children assumed the surname of either parent, as they pleased, and frequently of both, connecting them by the letter *y*.

This custom was unknown to the inquirers at the Custom House who preceded Don Pedro, and, on finding no Gomez on the lists of passengers of the few vessels that had entered the port from the north, they had retraced their steps and given up further pursuit to the south. But not so the Ladrone, who was better informed.

"My friend," said he to the official, on reading the name of the Senora Navarrete, "this is the family I am in search of. The Senora Navarrete and the Senora Gomez are one and the same. She has resumed her maiden surname. Did she land here?"

"She did not, or her landing would have been noted in the minutes. She passed on to the south."

"For what port did the vessel clear?" inquired Don Pedro.

"For Tecapan," was the answer, as the officer glanced at the record.

"It is not likely they disembarked at Tecapan," said the Ladrone. "There is no country behind it. A family would not be apt to return to Tecapan who had once left it. No, when they abandoned California they were going to a better country. San Blas, below Tecapan, is an important port. It must have a good country behind it."

"San Blas is a rock, surrounded on all sides but the sea by a swamp, but the interior is splendid," said the officer. "I have been back to Tepic. It is a fine city in a rich district, with a large population."

"Tepic be it," responded the Ladrone. "I will seek them there. Here, friend, are a couple of ounces. If any San Franciscan follows on my trail I shall expect you to say nothing of my whereabouts, and nothing of the change of Gomez into Navarrete."

"Vaya con Dios (Go with God), senor. I will be silent."

"Queda con Dios, amigo," he answered. "When I return successful I will make the two ounces ten."

When the Ladrone landed, in a high wind-storm that portended the commencement of the rainy season, the rock on which San Blas is perched was enveloped in dust and encircled by screaming sea-birds. The town was nearly deserted, the inhabitants having gone to the interior in anticipation of the rains. It poured down in torrents in the night, and the thunder and lightning were terrific. Hayward set out in the morning with a guide, and rode through the sultry air, over the steaming plain, to the hills. They nooned at the village of Fonsequa, and late in the evening looked down on Tepic, the beautiful, seated in a smiling valley, surrounded by mountains, the hoped-for home of the family of Gomez y Navarrete.

Gomez had talked of moving to Santa Barbara, and the family, after his death, when they proposed to leave San Francisco, fearful that some impediment might be thrown in their way, as the authorities were known to be averse to inhabitants returning to Mexico, left the report in circulation uncontradicted that they were shipping for Santa Barbara. This threw many an after investigator off their track.

Visions of her native land and old home had come to the widow in her desolation, and she had persuaded her children to return with her. They sold their movables and made a feeble and ineffectual attempt to sell their real estate. It was poor in proportion to its extent, consisting of a succession of sand-hills without value. It was a case for abandonment, and it was abandoned as unworthy of an afterthought. The day after they put to sea, the captain of the sloop came to her with the manifest, and she recorded her maiden name, which the children, in her honor, assumed also ; and the family reached their destination under the name of Navarrete. having begun their voyage under that of Gomez.

In an hour after leaving his fonda, on the morning following his arrival, Don Pedro entered the courtyard of the residence of the widow Navarrete. He found the senora and her daughter at work in the shade of a cluster of cocoa-trees that grew in the center and overhung the fountain.

" The Senora Gomez ? " said the Ladrone with a bow.

" And Navarrete," she answered with a look of surprise.

" Yes, senora," he responded. " I am from San Francisco,

where the former name is better known. I am come to treat with you for the land you possess in that city."

"We abandoned a sand-hill in that village when we sailed," she answered, "but we never attempted to deceive ourselves by calling it land."

"It is still sand, senora," he replied, "but it has acquired value. You have heard, no doubt, that the village has become a city—of tents, it is true, but still a city—and your sand has become valuable. I am surprised you have not sold it or re-assumed possession."

"We have heard that the Americans have seized the unoccupied lands, and even much of the occupied. How could I permit my sons to leave our home and plunge into a strife with those eager invaders over a sand-hill? No, not if it were of gold! Neither have we money to carry on a war. It would take money, senor, would it not, to make the American gold-hunter loosen his grasp?"

"It would require money, senora," he answered, "and a good deal of it."

"How much would you think?" inquired she.

"Perhaps thirty thousand dollars," he answered.

"Heavens! What a sum. And the land, as you call it; what is it worth?"

"Perhaps half a million," he answered, "or soon will be."

"You amaze me, senor. You speak of the riches of Peru. Surely those in possession will never give it up, and the American judge will favor the American side. It is a dream."

"I am ready to make it a reality, or attempt to do so," said the Ladrone. "I will undertake its recovery on shares, or I will give you cash for your claim, if you prefer it and we agree upon the price. Hold a family council, senora, and consult some trusted business friend, and summon me from the Fonda de Espana when you are ready to treat." With this he made his bow, comprehending both ladies, and returned to his fonda.

Early the following morning a messenger was sent for him, and, repairing to the widow's house, he found assembled under the cocoas, besides the family, the padre, a lawyer and a merchant. He was treated with great politeness, the gentlemen all rising to receive him, and the padre began the conversation by saying :

"Senor, we have heard from the senora of the candid conversation you held with her yesterday, and it made us believe we were called on to treat with a gentleman, which your presence confirms. We are glad to have the honor of making your acquaintance. Be seated."

The Ladrone bowed his thanks and took a proffered seat, when the lawyer opened the business of the meeting.

"We have advised the family," he said, "to accept a comparatively moderate sum for the sand-hill, as the senora jocosely styles it, and, as I term it, her immense estate. The decision of a court is uncertain in all countries, and our adversary is in possession, and has to be ousted, if at all, with expense and perhaps danger. We have advised the family to abstain from entering the arena, and to leave the battle to some adventurous caballero, like yourself, who is armed, and equal to the fray. What sum, senor, are you willing to offer the family for a quit-claim conveyance of their title ? "

" I would prefer," answered he, " that the family would announce their price."

" We think it more regular," replied the lawyer, "that with your superior knowledge of the value of the property—"

" Excuse me," the senora interrupted. " The gentleman has been open with us, let us be equally so with him. We have fixed our price, senor, at what is to us a great sum, thirty thousand dollars."

" I will respond to your avowal, senora," said the Ladrone, " in kind. I have brought with me a certified check of the house of Morales for forty thousand dollars, which is the amount beyond which I did not intend to go. I now make this proposition. I will indorse over the check to you, with the condition that if I fail to establish our title ten thousand shall be returned to me."

" I think the proposition a very generous one," said the senora, addressing the lawyer. " Do you not agree with me ? "

" I am of the opinion," he answered, " that you have settled the negotiation, and that, if you had left it for me to arrange, you would have got the forty thousand without condition. But the gentleman has certainly acted in a very liberal spirit, and I am content. Your terms, senor, are accepted."

During the day of the sale and the day after, the lawyers were busy in drawing the deed of conveyance, and having it attested by the Mexican officials and the United States consul, who had fled from San Blas to Tepic with the elite of the population of that weather-beaten rock. Hayward had brought with him accurate copies of both grants. The one to Gomez, being general in description, was helped out by the more particular one given by the American mayor, bounded by streets and alleys. He was also furnished by Mr. Benham, his attorney, with a carefully drawn deed containing the form and points required by the American law. Two recitals were made in the instrument to him, one in the Mexican form and the other in the American, and the utmost care taken to make it impregnable to the searching attack it was destined to undergo. On the exchange of the deed and check, and formal closing of the great transaction, Hayward was invited to a grand convite and entertained in royal style. .

Weeks elapsed before he could secure a passage from San Blas to Mazatlan, and in that city he was subject to a tedious waiting for a steamer to carry him north. But he passed the time not .idly, sending letters and bales of presents, by every train that crossed the mountains, to his Catalina, and studying the affairs of their Mazatlan house. He passed his leisure hours at the fountain in the court with his aunt and cousins, answering their many questions and describing the new city in the north, in which the family were now so deeply interested.

"Senor," said a servant, approaching the fountain, as they sat in conversation one moonlight night soon after dusk, "a man at the gate wishes to speak with you."

"Show him in, Mateo," replied the senora.

"He is not fit to appear before the ladies," rejoined Mateo.

"I will go to the gate and speak to him," said Hayward,

rising and crossing the court. Presently he returned with a scrap of paper in his hand, which he held to the light of a lamp that burned before a small group in ivory of the Holy Family, hanging on the body of one of the palm trees that overshadowed the fountain.

" Read it aloud," said the senora.

" It is in American," he replied. " I will translate it. The hand is trembling and scarcely legible. It reads thus :

" ' I am dying, will some kind American come and write a letter for me to my poor wife.' "

" Come where ? " inquired the senora.

" I don't know," answered Hayward. " I didn't ask. Mateo, bring out my hat."

" And tell the messenger to come in, Mateo," called the senora. " I wish to speak to him."

As he approached the fountain the bearer of the letter took from his head an old stained hat, and halting at a respectful distance from the company, saluted with a bow. He was an Indian, of the class that worked about the landing and did the servile labor of the city; was poorly dressed, had bright bead-like eyes, and black hair, matted and unkempt. He folded his hands before him, holding his hat in one of them, and stood to be interrogated.

" Where is this dying man ? " inquired the senora.

" On the floor in my room, senora," answered the Indian.

" And where is your room, man ? "

" To reach it, senora," he answered, " one must descend the street that winds to the old landing, and turn into an alley near the ocean. It is there, a few steps in the little alley."

" And how came the stranger in your room, in that out-of-the-way part of the city ? "

" It was thus, senora. Paquita and I were going into the alley. It was the hour of siesta ; the sun was hot. We saw the Americano coming down, staggering. We stood in the shade and watched him. Then he fell, and we ran and raised his head, and pulled him from the gutter. He had fallen over, senora, into the gutter. I said : ' It is the aguardiente, Paquita ; he is drunk.' But my wife said : 'No ; it is not the aguardiente ; it is the sun. Lift him, man, and I will hold up his legs, and we will lay him on the cold floor in our room and throw water on him.' I said : 'Lay him in the shade in the alley.' She said : 'No ; it is colder in the room. Carry him in.' So we did, and bathéd him, and did everything. And he came to and talked ; but we could not understand. Then he made signs, and Paquita said : 'Man, the stranger wishes to write. Go to the shop and bring paper and a pencil.'

"So I did as she said, senora, and the paper the senor holds in his hand the shopkeeper gave me, and I pledged a medio for the return of the pencil. Then we propped him up and he wrote, pointed to the door, and said : 'Americano !' And Paquita spoke and told me to take the paper to an Americano. And I asked what one, and she said : 'Any one, imbecile ; go!' So I went, and I knew of none but the senor, and I brought it here."

"You think the stranger will die to-night?" inquired the senora.

"He will die to-night, senora," answered the Indian; "it may be he is dead now. The sun of Mazatlan is cruel to the stranger."

"Come ! let us be off," interrupted Hayward impatiently, starting to the gate, followed by the Indian. "Run in, Mateo, and bring me paper and pencil."

Turning to the south on emerging from the courtyard, they walked rapidly for nearly a mile in the direction of the suburb, and turned into the winding street that led down to the old abandoned wharf, from which commerce had been driven by the shifting sand. The mind of Hayward was busy with compassionate thoughts; his unfortunate countryman might be parting forever from a Catalina—no, there was but one Catalina—but he was yearning to communicate with one he loved, and to dictate his will, and be soothed in his last moments by the sound of his native tongue.

"Hurry, man," he said to the Indian, under the impulse of these thoughts. "Step out."

"See," he replied, pointing a few yards in advance, "it is there, the mouth of the little alley. The senor will not mind its being dark, it sheltered your honor's compatriot from the burning sun. A few steps within and the walk will end. Enter."

As Hayward followed the Indian into the narrow alley the sudden transition from the bright moonlight to the gloom blinded him, and he stretched forth his hands mechanically and groped his way with hesitating step. In a moment he was seized, overpowered, and thrown to the ground. His cry for help was smothered and his hands firmly bound; he was then raised to his feet and hurried along in the dark.

In the meantime the birds that hung over the fountain in the Morales courtyard slept peacefully, with their heads buried under their wings ; but the mind of the senora was disturbed, as she sat, manual in hand, before the little shrine, reading the vesper hymns. Her eyes were on the book and her lips repeated the prayers ; bnt her thoughts were on the Indian who had led Don Pedro down the winding street to the lonesome neighborhood of the old wharf, What was it in the speech or manner of the Indian that, after he had quit her presence, aroused suspicion ? She could recall nothing. His tale was simple and at the time seemed truthful, and she accepted it without misgiving ; but now it was otherwise. In some mysterious way it was borne in upon her that the Indian was false. The quarter that he lived in was almost deserted, the abode of smugglers. How chanced a stranger to be walking there at the hour of siesta, in the burning sun ? She closed the book and rose to her feet as these thoughts crossed her mind, and called, in an agitated tone :

"Mateo ! come ! "

"What does the senora wish ? " said Mateo, crossing the courtyard from the servants' apartment, and as he neared the fountain, and noticed her disturbed countenance, he exclaimed : " Holy Mother ! what ails you ? "

"Follow Don Pedro quickly!" she replied rapidly. "Run ! take the watch you meet with you, and rescue him. He is in danger. The Indian is an assassin ! "

As Mateo ran down the street, he was joined by three watchmen, one after the other, carrying dim lanterns. But he was compelled to moderate his speed to a rapid walk, as

the policemen were old and indisposed to race, and felt and
expressed doubts as to the bad intent imputed to the Indian.
About an hour had elapsed since Hayward had gone into the
alley when the watchmen appeared at the entrance. High
walls, white and coped with broken glass, bounded the passage on either side, without a door or gateway throughout ;
and the habitation of the mythical Paquita was looked for
in vain. As the watch made the turn looking down on the
bay the light of their lanterns startled a party of men, who
were seated in the alley near its lower mouth. They rose and
hurried out, crossing the landing toward the old wharf. As
they emerged from the shadow of the buildings into the
moonlight, the watch observed them and gave chase. Midway on the wharf the fugitives halted. One of the number
sprang down into a boat that lay rocking in the water beneath. One of the remaining three cast off the rope, and
then followed a brief struggle, interrupted by the approach
of the watch. Two of the party followed their companion
into the boat, to which they gave a vigorous shove that sent
it out into the water, leaving Hayward standing on the
wharf blindfolded, and with his arms bound to his body.
The watch opened fire on the outlaws, the balls pattering the
moonlit water about them, and a coast-guard boat put out
from the shore in pursuit.

Hayward was released, and ran with the watch to the
end of the wharf to see the chase. The *Guardacosta* was
gaining rapidly on the flying boat, which pulled but two
oars, and had an idle man, the Indian, seated in the stern,
whose weight seriously impeded her passage through the
water. One of the oarsmen, looking back, perceived the
situation, and, passing the handle of his oar to his companion, seized the Indian under the armpits, lifted him from
the seat, and threw him overboard.

At this moment the moon went down and darkness
spread over the waters of the bay. The Indian rose to the
surface, but sunk before the coast-guard, which had backed
its oars to pick him up, could reach him. It paused, watching for his reappearance, but not coming up in due time, the
officer in command called out : " Forward ! the shark has got
him ; " and the pursuit was resumed ; but the fugitives, re-

lieved of the useless weight, and favored by the delay and night, effected their escape.

The senora knelt on a Prie-Dieu before the fountain shrine. reciting aloud from her prayer-book the "Litany of the Most Holy Name of Jesus," imploring the preservation of Don Pedro ; while her family, uniting in response, knelt behind her. A ring at the courtyard bell interrupted their devotions, and they rose to their feet, their faces beaming with hope and expectation. A servant ran to the gate and threw it open, and Hayward entered, followed by Mateo and the three watchmen swinging their feebly shining lanterns. When the excitement of the re-union had somewhat abated. the senora knelt again at her Prie-Dieu, requesting all to join in a prayer of thanksgiving. Hayward went down willingly on his knees on the hard flagstone beside his aunt ; the children and servants knelt in a group a little to their rear : the watchmen, with their lanterns on the ground before them. knelt apart ; and a bird, awakened by the noise. burst into song.

"The Indian you all saw," said Hayward in answer to an inquiry of his aunt, on seating themselves after the prayer, "he has gone to his account."

"May his poor soul rest in peace !" exclaimed the senora.

"Amen !" responded the three watchmen in a breath.

"The others I did not see," continued Hayward, "for my head was covered ; but I heard them speak, and they were Americans. One spoke broken Spanish to the Indian, and the voice of the other I am sure I had heard before ; but I cannot associate it with any person."

"You will recall the person after a time, child," interrupted his aunt.

"It may be," replied Hayward. "Well, they hurried me along to about the middle of the lane, and halted and sat down against the upper wall. After a time I heard one of them grit his teeth and curse the moon. Another pause ensued, when the Indian was called on to give an account of his expedition. and he repeated his conversation with the senora. On this their uneasiness increased, and they ordered him down to the mouth of the lane, to look out and report. He returned presently, and said the landing was deserted and the moon still a half-hour high. More curses ensued, and they rose and moved slowly on, the Indian remonstrating, telling them the coast-guards would surely capture them if they ventured out in the bay in the moonlight. Again they halted, and sat down against the wall, and did not move until they started to their feet on seeing the lanterns of the watch. I knew they were closely pursued, by their exclamations and their hurry, and when I felt the moment for action had come, I resisted and they abandoned me."

"A merciful Saviour was watching over you, child," said the senora, "and overturned the design of the unhappy men at the proper moment. Thank Him fervently in your chamber to-night, before you retire."

"It was by means of my good aunt that He accomplished His intervention," responded Don Pedro. "He inspired her to send the watch."

"Yes," replied the senora simply, "I was inspired." Then she added, humbly bowing, "There is no good in us but comes from Him."

The watchmen were munificently rewarded and dismissed with many thanks. The entire household, servants and children, then entered the little domestic chapel that opened on the court, said the customary night-prayers, and dispersed to their sleeping apartments.

"Senora," said Hayward at the breakfast-table the following morning, "I have called up the owner of the voice. He stands before me."

"Where?" exclaimed his cousin, looking behind her in alarm.

"In my mental vision, senorita," he replied, laughing. "He came into view suddenly, a moment ago. I know him well. I have reason to remember him."

"Have him arrested, Pedro, at once," said the senora, "before he can renew his machinations against you. It is your duty to society."

"I will go at once," he answered, rising. "Run in, cousin, and ask the cashier to send me eight ounces."

On his way to the police office he turned down to the bay and called at the Custom House. To the officer he had questioned concerning the widow, when on the way to Tepic, he said :

" Friend, I have called this morning for a double purpose, to hand you eight ounces and to ask a question.'

" Many thanks," replied the officer. " I congratulate you, senor, on your success. You found the widow ? "

" I found the widow, and am now on another hunt," said Hayward. " On the hunt of a man who has been hunting me. Has any one inquired for the widow since I left ? "

" Two Americans came down on the steamer following the one you came on," he answered, " and put questions concerning the whereabouts of the much sought for widow. One, who seemed the leader, made the inquiries in American, and the other translated them into indifferent Spanish. I told them the name of Gomez was not on our list of arrivals. They then asked if any member of the house of Morales had been looking for the widow. I answered, that, as far as I knew, the respectable house had not, as yet, adopted the avocation of chasing widows. On this the leader turned abruptly on his heel and walked out, and the interview terminated."

" Paint me a portrait of the leader," said Hayward, drawing a chair to the table, leaning on it and looking intently at the officer.

" Let me think a moment," he replied, assuming a like position opposite. " He stood there, by that desk," pointing and fixing his eyes on vacancy, " with his hat on; the other had removed his hat. I see him now plain, his hair is red, his eyebrows whitish, his eyes light blue, his face broad, thin and mottled, cheekbones prominent, red bushy beard, arms and body long, legs short and bowed."

" Enough," said Hayward rising. " It is him, the Devil of the Mariposa."

CHAPTER X.

THE GENIUS DRIFTS TO SEA IN AN OPEN BOAT IN THE TROPICS.

" I AM afraid that was bad policy," said his companion to Corby, as he resumed his seat after throwing the Indian overboard.

"It lightens the boat," returned Corby, bending with vigor to his oar.

"True, but the chase will pick him up," continued Marcus, "and get from him a description of our persons. We are both notable men, and personally I would prefer to be unknown at present ; a fancy, perhaps, but I would prefer it."

"I thought of that," replied Corby, "and hesitated, but I saw the fins of a shark in the water, and over he went. How swiftly we are forging through the water now, and how dark it has got. I can barely see the guard-boat. I think they must be waiting for the Indian to come up ; they saw him take the plunge, for the moon was shining when I flung him over."

"The moon and the victim to expediency sunk simultaneously," said Marcus, who affected fine words; "the moon will rise again, but the victim never."

"Never," responded Corby with decision.

"The Indian," continued Marcus, in a philosophical tone, "is now undergoing the pleasing process of digestion in the stomach of the shark who displayed his fin so opportunely. I think, on the whole, it is the best thing could have happened to him. He is the right Indian in the right place. Moved by a bad motive, tempted by lucre, he was luring a fellow-mortal to destruction, and fell into the very trap he had set—the mouth of a shark. It is a case of poetic justice. It reconciles one to life to witness such an exhibition of the eternal fitness of things."

" I would think it more eternally fit," said Corby sharply,

"if Number Twenty-One was in the Indian's place. Luck seems to dog that Gentile."

"It was the moon, friend Corby—the moon that saved him to-night—the moon and the old lady. And it served us a good turn in going down when it did. The enemy is out of sight ; we also are saved. Let us pull in to shore."

"No ; straight on out of the harbor. It is safer to drift on the ocean and take our chance of being picked up. If the Mexicans catch us they will shoot us before sundown."

"I wish we had some bread and water in the boat," replied Marcus gloomily. "I've got a flask of brandy in my pocket, but what's that for a sea voyage—not at all satisfactory."

"Don't begin to whine," said Corby roughly. "Pull on and trust to luck. Let to-morrow take care of itself. Sufficient for the night is the evil thereof."

"My arms are ready to drop off," said Marcus, after a long pause. "Don't you think we might rest a little?"

"Yes, the tide is with us now," replied Corby; "let us ship our oars and breathe awhile."

"Have you ever suffered from thirst, Corby?" inquired his companion.

"Often."

"But never in a boat at sea."

"Never, but it's likely I soon will; it looks that way just now."

"I am told," continued Marcus, "that it is very trying in a boat on the ocean in the tropics. We are in the tropics at present, are we not?"

"A little way in, not deep."

"Deep enough to make it unpleasant in an open boat without water," replied Marcus. "Why, I stood a minute in the yard at noon to-day, and my figure cast no shadow."

"Your figure is attenuated, friend," returned Corby, "and casts no great shadow at any time; perhaps you were standing in the shade."

"Perhaps I wasn't !" retorted Marcus; "and I grew so dizzy in a few seconds that I staggered walking back into the house. I would go mad before night if compelled to sit in the sun all day in an open boat."

"No one is compelling you, that I am aware of," returned Corby coolly. "You are your own master. You prefer a seat by a fountain, under the shade of a palm-tree, to the open boat. Very good, I enter no objection; hunt up your palm. Perhaps you would rather hang from one of its limbs than to float on the hot ocean; if so, speak the word."

"I would!" exclaimed Marcus earnestly. "I would rather hang in the shade, suspended over a cool fountain, than to drift out to sea. Let us land and take to the swamps."

"But I intend going to sea."

"Then put me ashore," demanded Marcus.

"Tell me where the shore is and I will do it," responded Corby, laughing. "See how dark it is getting. One can hardly see the end of the boat. The tide is running out like a mill-race. Put your hand in the water and feel it. Soon the rain will pour down in torrents, and we will not see our hands before us. Put the oars in the bottom of the boat and lay down in the bow. I will take the stern. We are adrift. By daylight we will be far out in the ocean, out of sight of land."

"Without a compass—without anything," replied Marcus bitterly.

"We will not be entirely destitute," rejoined Corby, laughing at the distress of his friend.

"How so?" he inquired sharply. "What do you mean?"

"I mean that you have a flask of brandy, to begin with, that will not be despised. I have in my pocket a cake of black Mexican sugar with a little nibbled off—not much, call it a pound, and a plug of strong tobacco. Just the thing to go to sea in an open boat with—it wards off thirst. Then the bottom of the boat will be covered with water, good to drink if the salt water doesn't break over the sides into it. And, last and best, we will have with us—what do you think? Guess, Brother Marcus."

"What?"

"Hope—that never deserts the brave!"

The Custom House and police departments of Mazatlan united in a vigorous but vain search for the fugitives; the keel of their drifting boat left no trace behind, and their feet had made no impress on the land. The Custom House officer passed his leisure moments in describing to his callers the persons of the two assassins and announcing the munificent reward offered by the city for their apprehension.

Carriage after carriage drew up on the following evenings at the gate of Morales, from which ladies and gentlemen descended, and entered the illuminated courtyard, to congratulate the family on the happy escape and compliment the senora on her inspiration. People on foot and horseback wound down the suburban street, passed through the "Alley of Assassins," and strolled out on the wharf, gazing out to sea with a dim expectation of catching a sight of the fugitive boat. Later on the plot was dramatized and brought out at the theater, drawing crowded houses.

Hayward, in his letters to Catalina, treated the affair lightly; and to divert her attention from the rumors that he knew would reach her, sent over a gold cross, wrought in filigree in the city of Mexico, studded with brilliants. Letters from Durango implored him to cross the Cordillera, and for a day he wavered; but the thought of the conflict of titles that awaited him in the north carried the day, and love, as usual, was sacrificed to ambition. Catalina was left under the shade of the orange tree to mourn.

A few days after the husband of the mythical Paquita had been thrown to the shark, the monthly steamer running from Panama to San Francisco put into the harbor of Mazatlan, and Hayward took passage for the north. On the day of his arrival he delivered his deed to his attorney, instructing him to spare no cost in a proper conduct of the case, and declaring he would empty the vault of the bank, if need be, in the fight.

When Mr. Benham filed the Gomez y Navarrete deed for record, and caused a writ of ejectment to be issued against an occupant of the tract, San Francisco shook to its center. The alarm was not confined to the party attacked, but spread over the city. It was believed that many other titles were defective, and few holders felt safe.

The inhabitants of the city, suddenly assembled from the four quarters of the globe, unknown to each other, and unrestrained by public opinion or custom, lived in a state of

social chaos. The strong hand ruled. Many men, notably
the rich, seized upon real estate, built their stores and resi-
dences, and defied the owner in terms of contempt and de-
rision. "Go to the courts," they would say, "or drive us
off if you think you are strong enough." The courts were
corrupt and the juries for sale. Here it was a question as
to who could bribe the highest and most skillfully. The in-
jured owner, unless he had money to expend and willingness to engage in this ignoble strife, was utterly helpless.
Many men, having no friends to assist them in expelling the
intruders, took private vengeance and shot them down, or
were shot down by them or their satellites in street encounters. Others collected their friends, or hired bravoes, and
bore down on the property in battle array, when bloody conflicts ensued. But many, too timid to appeal to arms, and
too poor to appeal to the courts, or too conscientious to appeal to either, were trodden down and disappeared as factors
in the rising city.

Ever since the scare which the inhabitants of Britain experienced during the gathering of the great Armada it has
been the custom of the writers of that illustrious but diminutive island to berate the Spaniard, especially for his thirst
for gold. It may be questioned whether the native of Spain
stands alone in his indulgence in this demoralizing appetite.
Especially would a denizen of San Francisco at this epoch be
led to doubt it ; for here people of all nationalities seemed
both to hunger and thirst for it. Gold was the first thought
on awaking and the last on falling asleep. It was the motive power that drove them in restless throngs through the
streets by day and dictated their visions by night.

Men who at home were models of propriety astonished
their friends by bursting out, on landing here, into the most
amazing iniquities. Fear of public opinion, that modern
substitute for the fear of the Lord, had heretofore made
them appear moral. There was no public opinion here ; and,
this all-pervading and masterful restraint removed, men with
unblushing effrontery displayed in their outward conduct
the inner man. They were not changed by the act of dis-
embarkation on the sand-hills ; they were simply set free.

What chance of success had the widow and the orphan

in a contest in this moral field? The Senora Navarrete showed wisdom in keeping her simple sons by her side, in the peaceful valley of the Santiago, shut in by surrounding mountains from the turbulent ·world, and appointing the well-equipped Ladrone her champion to ride into the press.

The battle opened by an assault in the morning papers on the original Gomez grant made by the California alcalde. An examination of the records by the attorneys of Julius Alfred McCauley, the defendant, and grantee under the American régime, satisfied them, and they so informed their client, that the Gomez title was unassailable in the courts. It was brief, clear, and conclusive, without a weak spot. They had hunted diligently for a crevice in the armor in which to plant an arrow, but could find none, and advised him, if possible, to effect a compromise. But Julius, like his great namesake, was of an uncompromising nature, and declared he would never relinquish a foot, but would fight to the end. He believed, or affected to believe, that his assailant was a scoundrel, and had forged the Tepic deed, and that the good citizens would not stand by and see him robbed, especially as it would threaten the stability of their own titles. He instructed his attorneys to go on and do the best they could, while he and his co-defendants would wage war before the mob, that great tribunal at whose voice the judge trembled and the jury rendered up the demanded verdict.

The Gomez grant, it was solemnly asserted in the editorial column, was a fraud. Men of veracity, old and highly reputable California residents, living here at the time of the so-called grant, and still residing here, in full mental vigor, were prepared to testify that the grant was really made by the alcalde to a relative, who, having one already, could not lawfully accept the second, and the name of Gomez had been used as a cover. One old Mexican gentleman was ready, when properly called upon, to take his oath that he was within earshot and overheard the said Gomez give his assent to the fraud, and saw him receive a Mexican ounce gold piece in payment for the use of his name. And now an American citizen is to be robbed of his hard earnings, deprived of a valuable estate in which he has sunk the fruits of a life's labor, and by whom? By a forger, who has been going about like a ghoul in the dark, resurrecting worse than dead claims that shock the sense of the community and make all men tremble for their titles.

After the changes had been rung in successive editorials on the grant, until the characters of the old alcalde and his mythical relative had been torn to tatters, and every turn and phase of their connection with this baleful transaction was exposed to the public gaze, and when they perceived that the mob began to tire a little of the original grant, they turned their batteries upon the Tepic deed.

" It is a well remembered fact," said the editors, in varying phrase, " which will be established before the court, if the adventurer who has brought this iniquitous suit has the temerity to force the property owners to trial—which he will hardly do if he has any regard for his life—that a few days after the departure of the sloop conveying the Gomez family from this port a tempest swept the coast and wrecked the few vessels then at sea. Neither this sloop nor any man or woman who went to sea in it has ever since been heard from. There can be no doubt of the fact that they all perished. And now, from the bottom of the ocean, is fished up a spurious deed to disturb titles and depress the value of real estate in this great city. The patience of the American people is great, and their respect for law and order a proverb, but it may be pushed too far. We do not counsel violence, but we warn a certain partner of a foreign banking firm in this city, once known as the ' Grand Ladrone,' that he is parading our streets with his life in his hand."

On the return of an agent sent by McCauley to Tepic, and the approach of the day of trial, the papers blazed out anew.

" We are in receipt of quite recent intelligence from the so-called city of Tepic. If the accounts of our correspondent possess a tithe of truth. it is a wonder that the surrounding mountains do not fall in and cruch that devoted spot. Bull and chicken fights and gambling are the innocent recreations of the inhabitants ; their serious occupations we will not wound the public ear by reproducing in print. Suffice it to say, and we are pleased to be able to say it, we have no parallel to it throughout the length and breadth of our happy land. It is a spot from which we are not surprised to find emanate the hopeful Gomez deed. We drop a veil over our correspondent's description of the so-called Gomez family. Perhaps that veil will be lifted at the trial. We shall see."

In the meantime the party of the Ladrone was silent. Nothing was said in favor of his claim or character in the public prints by him or for him. But, a day or two before the trial commenced, the most influential paper faced about, and, in a well-considered editorial, in large type, the editor acknowledged that he had been misled. A patient investigation which he had set on foot at considerable expense, which he did not begrudge, as he owed it to the public to discover and make known the truth, had led him to the irresistible conclusion that the Gomez title was perfect in all its parts. He regretted that *The Trumpet of Truth* had been the innocent channel to convey to the public false impressions regarding this important cause. He would say nothing now concerning the persons who gave him the information on which he had based his earlier editorials. Statements he had then conscientiously believed to be true he now knew to be false. It was a bitter thing for one occupying the position of a public instructor to be deceived and made to deceive others by artful and designing men ; but it was a consolation and a duty to cast them off and lay the truth before an honest people when it came to light.

This opportune article gave rise to universal comment and criticism. Some captious individuals among the " honest people " insinuated that the editor had been bought, and others, still more cynical, that he had been bought twice ; but, notwithstanding these uncharitable observations, the article made a deep impression.

The men summoned, from whom the lawyers selected the jury, were in this case found to be of exceptionally good standing, and when they took their seats in the box the defendant, McCauley, could not conceal his uneasiness. The plaintiff's proofs of titles were produced and their case quickly presented. Benham made an able address, confined to the merits of the case. He made no allusion to the newspapers, and treated with disdain the attempt of the defense to affect the decision by the introduction of extraneous matter. On the other hand, the defense was protracted, and a great effort made to work upon the presumed interest and fooling of the jury. The judge charged as usual, pro and con, and the jury retired, followed by several persons employed by Mr. Benham, who saw that no one but the officer in charge had access to their room. Two hours after their retirement they returned and handed in a verdict for the plaintiff.

The blood left McCauley's face. He rose, grasping the handles of his chair, and quitted the room, saying to his attorneys:

"The scoundrel shall not live to enjoy my property. I will defend it."

Hayward, who overheard the remark, smiled; but Benham looked grave. The jury were polled and discharged, after a compliment from the judge. There was no demonstration made by the crowd. It seemed a tame ending; but most of those present did not look upon it as ended, but as adjourned to the streets of the disputed district. As Benham and Hayward, arm in arm, walked down the pavement they were followed a few paces by a man who scrutinized the latter sharply. He was small and slight, with a dark thin face, covered by a thick ink-black stubble, and small piercing black eyes and jet-black straight hair. He was dressed in thread-bare black, with a half-legal look, which he had acquired in half-legal service in the narrow Western State that had the honor to give him birth. He was a lawyer by brevet, not having as yet received a regular commission, though that was not exactly the title bestowed on him where he was best known. He practiced before tribunals in the mines, where the exhibition of the license to practice is not infrequently dispensed with, and had drifted to the city, as thousands drift to cities, restless, eager, dissatisfied. His name was Leson, John Leson, but better known to his familiars on the Mariposa by the name of "Jack." He came to the country, as many another did, to put money in his purse by any means conceivable, saving that of labor.

McCauley called a meeting of his co-defendants—men to whom he had deeded or who now held lots in the estate—and organized for defense. As he still held nine-tenths of the property in his own hands he was forced to bear a like proportion of the expense. A guard was set day and night to give timely notice of the coming of the invaders, arms and ammunition were purchased, and a free lunch by day and night with expensive liquors furnished. All this outlay drained the resources of McCauley, and still the enemy delayed his coming. Men brought in rumors of the advancing foe, and got their drinks and bits of lunch in the character of allied skirmishers ; and returned with fresh rumors, displaying great zeal and intelligence. But still the foe came not. Jack Leson had sought a private interview with McCauley, and had been placed on his staff. He was somewhat reticent, but held and expressed decided opinions on matters of import, and showed a disposition to have matters his own way and take the lead. He would no doubt have distinguished himself, had matters come to the looked-for arbitrament of arms ; but they never came to that, because the Ladrone, acting on the military maxim, never to do what you know the enemy wishes you to do, declined the combat.

He sent his emissaries into the fortified district; indeed, the most active of the lunch-table allied skirmishers were his agents; and when he learned from these devoted adherents that the free lunch was suspended, he knew that the hour to move on the enemy had struck. He accordingly caused to be inserted in the morning paper the following:

"NOTICE.

"TO THE GRANTEES OF M'CAULEY.

" Those who wish their money refunded, or new deeds on moderate terms, will call at the office of Mr. Benham.

"PEDRO HAYWARD."

Leading articles in the papers commended the magnanimous policy of the new proprietor, and urged the McCauley grantees to settle. They needed no urging. Before the end of the week McCauley stood alone, without friends and without resources.

But in his desolation, Leson remained faithful. The two went about in mournful company, laying schemes for the acquisition of fortunes and the demolition of the Ladrone; schemes which only lacked a little money, so hard to get by those who need it, to march forward to a successful termination. And money soon came. A man resembling a ghost, who had been flitting at night about the disputed district during the late troubles, invited them to a consultation in a private room at the Saints' Rest, out of which they issued at a late hour in high spirits and with the longed-for motive power.

One dark rainy night, some time before this person came to the relief of the indigent plotters, a man groped his way with feeble steps up the narrow alley that led to the back door of the iron warehouse. His knock was so weak and low that Solomon did not hear it until its third repetition, and when he opened and the man entered he fell back in fright at his appearance.

"Holy Prophet! Corby!" he exclaimed. "have you come out of the grave? You look like a ghost."

"I feel like one," he answered in a feeble tone, slowly settling down in an armchair. "Bring me a glass of brandy."

"And what on earth," said Solomon, filling and handing him a glass, "brought you to this deplorable condition?"

"Nothing on earth," answered Corby feebly, draining his glass and placing it on the table at his side; "it was something on water did it—sun, and thirst, and hunger. A strong team, Brother, Solomon, as you will find if you ever float on a tropical ocean in an open boat."

"Brother," said Solomon compassionately, "will you have something to eat? I can get from the restaurant anything you like in a moment; the boy is on hand in the next room. What would you like?"

"Nothing," answered Corby; "I supped on raw oysters as I came up from the bay."

"Don't you think then you had better go to bed?"

"No, I want to drink and talk; I am in condition now, since that French brandy, to make my report. If you want to go to bed, I will put it off till to-morrow; but I will drink for hours yet, and would like to talk."

" Then go on," said Solomon, dropping into an armchair and assuming a comfortable listening attitude; " I am eager to hear your story. Will you join me in a cigar?"

" Yes, I feel that I am coming to life again ; and now for my hunt for the widow," he said, as he leaned back in his high soft chair and puffed his Havana, looking the personification of death, with his staring eyes and white emaciated bloodless face.

" Well, as you know, our man Hayward had a month the start, and I must say he used it well."

" Speak of him as Number Twenty-One, Corby, if you please ; it is official and safer. Even an iron house may have ears. It is our rule, you know."

" Very good," he replied, " I'm in favor of the rule, it is a good one. Well, we called at the Custom House, Marcus and I, the day we got to Mazatlan, and wasted time in doing it, for the officer was bought; I soon saw that and turned on my heel. Number Twenty-One had already seen him, effectually. We learned on the landing that he had gone to the south in a coaster; saw him land on his return, and got from an Indian lad who carried the traveling bag of a gentleman who came with him full information.

" He had found the widow in Tepic, bought the land and was going north on the next steamer. I felt outwitted, outraged, and determined to remove him then and there, at all risks. But he was inaccessible, and I saw it would be necessary to lure him out, and we cast about for days to hit on a likely scheme. A cunning Indian in our employ told us one day that he was sending presents to his wife over in Durango. and on this hint I laid a trap and caught him. In brooding over my defeat, before I got him in my power, a whim had seized me to remove him in a special way. and this necessitated our waiting. after we caught him, until the moon went down. The watch got after us. We were compelled to drop him and take to the water. The customguard boat gave chase. Soon I saw they were gaining on us, and I tossed our Indian over."

" Why?" exclaimed Solomon, in surprise.

"To lighten up," replied Corby. "As I heaved him over I saw the expectant shark in the water, and said to myself : 'How queerly things turn out. I am forced to consign my friend to the living tomb specially chosen for my enemy.' It wouldn't have done, you know, to have had him picked up and questioned by the police."

"It was hard on the Indian !" remarked Solomon.

"Oh, I don't know," replied Corby. "It had to be done. I felt a qualm as I laid hold of him, for he was a humble fellow and had served us well ; but he was a Gentile, and we were Saints flying for life."

"True, you were justified," responded Solomon. "Go on with your story."

"Dark came on. The moon sank, and we drifted out to sea. A torrent of rain fell and all about us was as black as night. The next morning it cleared; the mountain tops were still in sight. By nightfall they too had disappeared, and the wind had driven the spray into our boat and spoiled the rain-water.

"The sun rose next day like a ball of fire. The hot air smothered us. The surface of the water was smooth as glass; and for days thereafter, many days, the count of which we lost, we rose and fell on the gentle swell of the ocean, baking to death. A burning thirst assailed us first, followed by a gnawing hunger. Marcus went raving mad, and I threw him down in the bottom of the boat and tied him hand and foot. He had begun to drink salt water ; he wanted to jump into the sea and swim to a palm tree that he thought he saw, and that he said he knew had a spring of cold water at its roots. He saw the spirit of the Indian come out of a shark that was swimming by our side and take a seat in the boat, and talked to it. He said the Indian told him it was cooler in the shark's belly than it was in the boat. When the Indian disappeared another spirit took his seat, followed by another and another, until the wretched craft was crowded with ghosts to whom he chattered in defense of his conduct, until his swollen tongue choked him and he turned over on his face and cursed the Prophet and the Saints."

"What an awful wretch !" exclaimed Solomon. "Did he die ?"

" No."

" And you ; how did you stand it ?"

" Why, to tell the truth, I had my little visions also. I thought my mother took me by the hand and led me down a hill to a spring of cold water ; but when we got near, in full sight of it, though we continued to walk we made no progress. I think I passed a day, from sunrise to sunset, longing for that bubbling water and struggling to reach it. In the night my mother came again, and again we left the cabin hand in hand and walked down the path to the spring. This time we reached it. She took a gourd from a limb overhead, and, kneeling, filled and handed it to me with a gentle smile. She was a mild blue-eyed woman. I see her now. But the water was salt and I pushed it away in disgust, saying it was bitter—it had changed. 'The water is sweet,' she answered, rising and looking me mournfully in the face ; ' it is you that has changed.' Then she vanished. It is always of my mother that I dream."

" Did she appear again?" inquired Solomon.

" Oh, yes ! She came as I lay in the bottom of the boat, nearly gone, knelt by my side, and offered me water that she said was sweet ; but I found it bitter. I pushed it away with a frown, when she rose to her feet, poured the water from the gourd into the sea, and stepped out of the boat. I thought she would sink, and by a tremendous effort raised to a sitting posture and caught at her dress. She had disappeared ; and as I was looking wildly about my eye was arrested by the sight of a ship under sail.

" This brought me to my senses. I waved my handkerchief, and by great good fortune the captain was walking back to the wheel and saw it."

" What ship was it?" inquired Solomon.

" A little Swedish brig, *The Vandal*, bound for this port. She dropped anchor down the bay at sunset this evening."

" And what has become of Marcus?"

" In bed at the Saints' Rest," answered Corby, lighting a fresh cigar. " Marcus is badly demoralized. I am afraid I shall have to look out for a new lieutenant."

CHAPTER XI.

THINKING OF HIS ENEMY, REMINDS THE LADRONE TO LOCK
THE DOOR.

EVERY morning during the absence of Don Manuel and
his party in pursuit of the Grand Ladrone, the family and
servants at San Pablo had assembled in the chapel and offered prayers for their safety. The joy was great at their
triumphant return. A holiday was given by the senora, an
extra issue of provisions and delicacies was made, and the
festivity closed by a dance at night, attended by the peons
of the neighboring estates, and honored for a time by the
presence of the family. The vaqueros who had figured in
the pursuing party, with old Domingo, were the heroes of
the evening ; and one after another were called on to relate
their adventures. Opinions on the conduct of the expedition
were freely expressed. The women thought the ladrones
should have been brought down to San Pablo for trial, where
every one interested could have had a fair chance to see
them, and especially to see the Grand Ladrone ; while the
men were generally disappointed at the prosaic manner in
which the capture had been effected. To surround the fire
and close in on foot was regarded as extremely flat, tending
to deprive the affair almost entirely of interest. The fire
should have been approached by a dash on horseback, and
the ladrones lassoed as they rose from the ground. The
vaqueros could not stand up against public opinion on this
point, but transferred the odium to the Americanos, those in-
novators who, in the pursuit of the practical, were banish-
ing the poetical from life.

The capture was discussed in the hacienda, also, with dif-
fering sentiments. The ladies were of the opinion that Don
Manuel was needlessly exposed in advancing in the line. He
should have remained in the rear, and given orders and su-
perintended the advance. There was no necessity, in fact,

for him to come out of the bushes. The Franciscan broke in at this point :

" I am not a soldier, senora," he said, "but I believe in knighthood. The senor did right to lead the people. How could the Moors have been conquered if the best blood of Castile had hung back when the shout of ' Santiago ! ' went up, and ' Close, Spain ! ' But what am I saying?" he added, suddenly checking himself. " The days of chivalry are past."

" You are right, senor," she answered. " It was our anxiety that spoke."

" The generals," said the senorita, " I am told, nowadays stay in the rear."

" It is true," answered Don Antonio ; " and some of them very far in the rear. . In the days of my great-uncle they were found in the front."

" Was your uncle a general ? " inquired the senorita, with interest. " And did he lead in battle ? "

" My great-uncle was a general and among the bravest. He was called ' Mad Anthony ' because of his impetuous valor. I will present you his life when you learn American."

" I fear I shall never learn it," she sighed, " it is so difficult."

" The speech of the Ladrone to the jury," said Don Manuel, " from its effect on the rough, vindictive men surrounding him, must have been eloquent indeed. I could not understand his words, but his voice was soft and persuasive. When he restored to me the bag of gold dust, with his polished little speech, I was struck dumb with his adroitness and audacity. The heart must have been hard that would have exposed him to the fury of the mob. You named him rightly that night when you called him the ' *Grand Ladrone.*' "

" His escape from the very jaws of death by the mere force of intellect," said the Franciscan, " confirms the appellation. He is indeed a ' grand ladrone.' "

As time passed. Antonio grew despondent over his affairs. The rise in real estate had not come, and his funds were getting low. He could not bring himself to propose to the senorita with an empty purse, and had about resolved to go to the mines, when he received an invitation to dine at San Pablo, to meet Mr. Hayward, a banker from San Francisco. He had brought a letter of introduction from General Pacheco, a friend of Don Manuel, and was cordially received. They found him a pleasant gentleman, easy and fluent in conversation.   He was dressed in the fashion of the day, with his hair and beard closely trimmed.   He made the impression of a cool, careful, business man ; and not one in a thousand would have recalled in the banker the man who went through the terrible ordeal on the banks of the Mariposa.

After the ladies had passed out to the arcade, the gentlemen drew their chairs together over their wine and cigars, and the Ladrone said :

"Gentlemen, I have come down with the purpose of setting up a bank in Monterey, a branch of the house of Hayward & Co.   We do not anticipate much business for the first year or two, but we wish to be on the ground and established when the city begins   to grow.   An experienced cashier will be sent down from our house in the city, who, with a president, will be force sufficient for the little business we anticipate in the beginning.   We wish to secure the services of a president, resident here, who speaks both Spanish and American, to whom we can give our confidence, and who possesses the confidence of the community and some degree of popularity.   General Pacheco desired me to consult with you, senor, and expressed the opinion that you could aid me in the selection of a suitable gentleman."

"I know of one gentleman who fulfills the conditions you have mentioned," replied Don Manuel, "and him I am willing to indorse."

"And who is he?" inquired Don Pedro.

"He faces you," was the answer. "Don Antonio."

Don Pedro, with a bow comprehending both gentlemen, said their house would consider itself fortunate in an alliance with him.   Don Antonio answered with some confusion, for he was taken by surprise, that while he was now idle and would be glad of employment, he had no knowledge of the banking business.   Don Pedro answered :

"The cashier has, and you will soon see to the bottom of

it ; it is not deep. After prudence and rectitude, the rest follow. We propose to our president or manager a good interest and salary. If you are willing to engage with us we will go to town in the morning and arrange all details ; hire, or better buy, a house on the plaza and set the carpenters to work."

It seemed to Don Antonio that this grand and opportune offer had dropped from the skies. The sound of the wedding-bell rang in his ears. The visions of the mines, with their discomforts, dangers and uncertainties, that had been weighing him down, was suddenly lifted and he drew a full breath. He accepted the position in a dignified reply, but his pleasure shone through and was quite perceptible.

They all three rode to the city in the morning, selected and purchased a suitable house on the plaza, and made calls on the governor and several of the principal inhabitants. The purchase of the house in which to open the first bank, the city having so far in its existence managed to get on without one, made a stir, and real estate looked up. Hayward was received with polite consideration, Don Antonio's popularity took a fresh start, and the hacienda of San Pablo rose into a prominence in the public mind it had not enjoyed since its dismemberment.

Hayward left on the following morning for San Francisco. Under the supervision of Don Antonio, a vault was built and such alterations made as were required to fit the building for its new use; it underwent, besides, a general renovation and brightening up.

In due time the cashier came down by sea, bringing with him an iron safe, a set of books and stationery, and a sign on which, in golden letters, was inscribed the legend:

. ANTONIO WAYNE.

BANKER.

He winced a little when he saw his first name transformed thus openly into Spanish, but said nothing, and the sign went up, the doors were thrown open, and Don Antonio launched out on his new career.

One night, soon after this event, Corby called at the warehouse, and drew the attention of Solomon to a notice in the morning paper, commending the new Monterey bank, eulogizing Hayward, and asserting that the Gomez estate had quadrupled in value since it had come into his possession. This was especially distasteful to Corby, by reason of his comparative inability to act. He was still a wreck in effect as in appearance, but his powerful constitution was asserting itself, he was slowly recovering his strength. He looked on Hayward as a condemned criminal in revolt against constituted authority, defying and thwarting the executive officer—him, the elect! His prosperity was very bitter to him ; bitter as the sweet water offered him by his mother at the spring.

"It's a pity you waited for the moon to set," said Solomon, laying the paper on the table, " when you trapped him in Mazatlan ; a great pity."

"I do my work in my own way," retorted Corby with a frown. "So does every man that's good for anything. There's a weak spot in every plot ; it happened to be the moon in that one. If the clouds had come up a little earlier they would have darkened it, but they didn't. We fail, Brother Solomon, because the future is dark, and we are obliged to grope in it, and evil spirits take advantage of our blind-ness and lead us astray."

"Have you heard from the Mariposa yet?" inquired Solomon, wishing to change the subject.

"Not yet."

"You have no doubt of their success, have you?"

"No reasonable doubt," answered Corby. "McCauley doesn't amount to much, but Jack Leson does. I intend to convert that man and swear him into the band ; I can make him useful."

"Corby, I am sorry you couldn't have gone with them to the Mariposa. I would have felt much better satisfied. Leson is a threadbare adventurer. One can never rely on those scamps. Once they get your money in their pockets they drink it up, or gamble it away, or drop it on some fool specu-lation."

"When I divided the money between them, that night at

the Saints' Rest," replied Corby, "I impressed Leson with the policy of doing his duty. I told him plainly that I knew the road to the Mariposa, and would take the liberty of hunting him up in case he didn't report in due time. He understood me ; have no fear of Leson."

"How soon do you think you will be strong enough to get in the saddle?"

"I am mending slowly," answered Corby, impatiently ; "perhaps in a month."

At this moment a knock was heard at the door, and Solomon admitted a man in sordid attire, with a slouch-hat pulled down over his face half-concealing it. He whispered to Corby, who rose and took up his hat, gave a significant nod to Solomon, and followed him out. They walked in silence through alleys and unfrequented streets until they reached the suburb, when they climbed a sand-hill, and, descending, entered an isolated cluster of tents, in the midst of which stood an old adobe, once the residence of a Spaniard, now a quiet house of entertainment devoted to the special refreshment of the Saints. Avoiding the front entrance, which opened into the bar-room and frequented part of the house, the two men passed to the rear, and, tapping at the shutter of a low, detached adobe, were admitted into the habitation of Corby. Several men were seated about a table engaged in conversation, who rose when he entered and stood until he passed alone into an inner room and closed the door. The single window of this apartment was closed with an iron-bound shutter, a sperm-oil lamp was burning on the table, a sage bush smoking in the fireplace, before which sat a tall, well-dressed man, who rose and saluted Corby as he approached.

"I have got that business next thing to accomplished," he said as they took seats. "I will say frankly it is extremely distasteful to me ; but, as you have in some way found out, bankruptcy stares me in the face, necessity forces me to accept your proposition. I arranged this morning to give you an opportunity."

"Very good," replied Corby coolly, rising and producing a decanter of sherry. "Join me in a glass of wine ; walking has weakened me ; I am not well. I am suffering from a late attack of indigestion. Taste that sherry, it is pure and old."

"It is *premier* quality," responded the gentleman, emptying his glass and re-filling it. "It was grown on the hills of Xeres, beyond doubt. Thanks, I will take a cigar ; it is good also, it smells of Havana."

"They are not so very bad," replied Corby, lighting one and leaning back in his rocking chair. "Now I am ready for business. What is the opportunity you offer me ? "

"I will be quite candid with you," he replied, facing him. "Indeed, I may as well, for you seem posted in my affairs."

"Oh ! perfectly," responded Corby, smiling, "I have made your affairs a special study. You would be surprised if I told you all I knew. Go on."

"Then," resumed his companion, with an uneasy manner, "you know that my house has a heavy debt in bank due on Wednesday, which we have no earthly means of meeting."

"Perfectly," replied Corby. "Shall I name the amount ? "

"No," he answered, with a show of irritation.

"Redwood," said Corby, drawing his chair a little nearer to the other, leaning forward and placing his hand on his knee, looking him in the face, "I caught a glimpse of your countenance one day as you were crossing the street and thought yourself unobserved, and read disaster in it. I knew you were the head of a great house. I studied you, then studied the house ; and when I accosted you that rainy night on the plaza I knew you both and made my proposition boldly, giving you time for reflection. You know why I took all that trouble ? "

"Yes."

"Yes ; to bring you here to-night. I knew you would come when your house began to totter, and now you have come let us talk out plain. Your interest is my interest. We are floating in the same boat. Go on."

"You know," resumed Redwood, seemingly relieved, "that I own a ranch down the coast, in San Mateo, on Half Moon Bay."

"Yes ; but unpaid for."

"True ; but I am in possession, and it would take time to oust me. Well, thinking over the situation last night in bed, I determined, when the house fell, to bury myself on the Half Moon ranch and keep out of sight. There is no road leading to it ; the old adobe stands back from a high cliff overlooking the ocean. There is no stock on the pastures, and a Mission Indian is employed as caretaker. Altogether a good lonely place for a broken man. Then the thought occurred to make an effort to raise money on it ; but no banker would loan on unpaid-for land. Then your proposition came to mind ; and I thought of plan after plan for working it out, and rejected them as fast as they were formed, until suddenly one presented itself that I thought would succeed. I resolved to try it, and turned over and went to sleep.

" Well, in pursuance of it I interviewed him this morning in the bank parlor, described the land and requested a small loan on it—a few thousand. 'Come,' I said, 'this is Saturday, and neither of us has any time to talk. I will send a horse to your door in the morning, and we will gallop down the coast and look at the ranch.' He hesitated ; but I said, 'Come ! come ! take a Sunday morning run down to Half Moon Bay, and get a mouthful of fresh air ; as a favor, come.' He consented, and we leave after early breakfast in the morning."

"And to-morrow night will sleep at Half Moon," said Corby.

"We must," replied Redwood. "By the time we get there, and take a run over the ranch, it will be night."

"Sketch the house and surroundings," said Corby, handing him a pencil, and pushing over the table a book, open at the fly-leaf.

"Here," said Redwood, making a rapid tracing, "is the front door leading into the hall, and this the back door ; here to the left are the two bedrooms."

"Which will your guest occupy ?" inquired Corby, interrupting him.

"Which would you wish him to occupy ?'

"The front," answered Corby. "You have marked two windows in it—both iron-barred, of course."

"Of course, like the windows of a jail."

" Is there a lock on the door ?"

" Yes, and a strong one, made to stand a strain."

" Take away the key before he sees there is one, and leave the front door unlocked. Does it creak in opening ? "

" I think it does—yes, it creaks. I remember, it makes some noise."

" Then leave it ajar when you go to bed. And his bed-room door, does it complain in opening ? "

" I daresay it does, but I don't remember."

" Try it, when he is out of the way, and if it does oil the hinges ; but rub the marks of the oiling well off. Now for the back hall door—how does it work ? "

" It has settled, and rubs the floor in opening and shut-ting."

" If you think it will not be noticed, leave it sufficiently ajar for a man to slip through. Your bedroom window—here, this back one—keep your light burning near it until you think he has gone to sleep, then blow it out. Now, where is the cliff ? "

" Here, this jagged line in front, say a hundred yards from the front door."

" How deep down is it ? Do the waves beat against the bottom ? "

" About five hundred feet straight down, and the sea breaks continually against it."

" No tell-tale beach for the sea to throw up its prey on ? "

" Not an inch; not landing for the body of a mouse."

" Good ! Now for the terms. You lost a ship in the China seas some time ago."

" No, not I ! " exclaimed Redwood in astonishment.

" Yes, you did," returned Corby dogmatically. " The trifle has escaped your memory. On Tuesday morning, between ten and eleven, call at the office of the Occidental Insurance Company, and the president will invite you into the back room and pay your loss ; which happens, by a coincidence not so very uncommon, to equal in amount the sum which I have agreed to pay you for the oppor-tunity. If you have occasion, at any time, to account for the sudden possession of this money, refer without hesitation to the president. The case is duly entered on the books, and will stand even judicial investigation. The name of the ship is—is— It has escaped my memory for the moment, but it doesn't matter."

"No; there's nothing in a name," said Redwood.

"If you wish to know it, the president will show it to you."

"I am not at all curious," replied Redwood, smiling. "A rose by any other name would smell as sweet."

"One word more," said Corby, rising. "The payment depends on the happy ending to-morrow night—in death!"

"I will do my part," replied Redwood, as he put on an old overcoat and slouch-hat he had worn in disguise.

"My men will do theirs, you may depend on that," responded Corby, laughing pleasantly. "You will call at the bank Monday evening on your return, and inquire after the health of our interesting friend. You have a good account of your separation to amuse his partner."

"Yes, I have thought it over," said Redwood. "He will have set out very early to reach the bank by the opening hour—wouldn't even wait for breakfast; took a cup of coffee and a cold bite; while I was compelled to lay over several hours, to give instructions to my caretaker."

"You will send him off after supper, of course."

"Yes, to San Bruno."

"By no means," said Corby with decision; "he may run against my men. Send him south; send him to Santa Clara."

"True, I had not thought of that. I will order him to buy and drive up a yearling; that will occupy him all of next day. I would rather he would not be prying about while I am there, anyway."

"Well, good-night," said Corby, walking with him to the outer door. "Shall I send a man with you? There are foot-pads about at this hour."

"Thanks; I have a revolver in my pocket. Good-night."

On returning to the inner room Corby turned the key in the lock, and, going to a corner purposely shaded, opened the door of a concealed closet, in which Marcus lay hidden, and invited him out.

"Well," said Corby, when Marcus had helped himself to

a glass of wine and a cigar and taken a seat before the fire,
" what is your opinion of the Man of Half Moon Bay?"

" Bad ! His voice has a treacherous note in it."

" And what do you think of the plot ?"

" Economical—lacks dash. Two should take the plunge,
not one."

" That would be treachery indeed ! "

" Not so ; the men are Gentiles."

" But what's the use ? Redwood will not betray himself.
We are in one boat ; he can have no motive to play false."

" Many men act without motive," said Marcus sneeringly.
" Men betray themselves and others daily, driven by the
fiend within them to speak. It is not safe, in my opinion, to
spare this Gentile, and there is no reason why it should be
done. What is one life more or less in comparison to the
good cause? Nothing ! a pinch of dust ! "

" You are improving, decidedly," said Corby with a laugh.
" Take another glass of wine."

" Thanks, I believe I will," responded the cynic, pouring
out a glassful, emptying it and puffing his cigar. " Now let
us suppose," he continued, " that your friend of the Half Moon
grows remorseful after a time, what will he do? He will
take to drink ; and some night when the wine is in, his wit
will go out for an airing, and he will unburden himself, in
maudlin confidence, to a supposed friend, a bosom friend who
will expose him, and in a few days the details of the plot will
appear in the morning paper. Then you and I will fall into
the hands of the Vigilantes, or at best take a limited view of
a howling mob through the bars of the city prison."

" You take a gloomy view of the plot, Marcus," said Corby, moving uneasily in his chair and beginning to rock
rapidly.

" Gloomy but true," he continued ; " and again, few men
retain their composure after committing a crime. They are
overanxious to explain, look bewildered, act queerly, excite
suspicion ; are arrested and jailed ; break down and give
themselves away, and at the same time generously give
away their friends in iniquity. Picture to yourself this Half
Moon merchant entering the bank on Monday evening,
racked with remorse and fear, and attempting to play the

innocent with the clear penetrating eye of the Spaniard fixed on him. He will flinch as certain as fate. I tell you, Corby, the man must die."

Disturbed by this presentation of the matter, Corby rose and paced the floor, while his companion returned to his wine and cigar, leaned back in his chair and gazed in the fire, smoking. Presently he resumed his seat, looked thought-fully in the fire, and spoke.

"After what you have said, Marcus, I will not take the responsibility of sparing the life of Redwood. Let him die!"

"Good!" exclaimed his companion, his face lighting up with a gratified smile; "the plot is perfect. Join me in a glass of wine."

About four o'clock in the afternoon of Sunday, heavy rain clouds drifted in from the ocean over Half Moon Bay, obscured the sun, and with a pelting shower drove Red-wood and his companion to the shelter of the house on the cliff. Dismounting at the front door, they hurried into the hall, and, turning to the right, entered the sitting-room and stood before the fire that the Indian had kindled in anticipa-tion of their coming. In a few minutes Redwood excused himself, and left the room to give directions concerning the supper, closed the door after him, crossed the hall and withdrew the key from the lock of the door opposite, put it in his pocket and passed on to the kitchen.

"After you have eaten your supper, Pepito," he said, "I wish you to go down to Santa Clara, and inquire at the post-office for a letter for me; an important one has been misdirected to that place. You can get back in the after-noon to-morrow. If you get the letter and I have left, bring it on to the city; if not, tell the postmaster, if one comes, to forward it to me."

"Yes, senor," replied Pepito. "I will eat my supper on the way, that I may reach the road before it becomes dark."

"Take your dog with you, Pepito; he may bite the strange gentleman."

"I will take him, senor, though he is too good a Christian

to bite your honor's guest. Vicente is a wise dog ; Vicente
bites robbers."

"Still, take him with you ; there are no robbers about at
present for Vicente to bite."

"I will do so gladly, senor. I would be desolate going to
Santa Clara without Vicente; besides, Vicente would not stay
behind, unless one chained him. We never part, he and I."

After supper, which was helped out by provisions brought
down by Redwood, Pepito and Vicente departed for Santa
Clara, and the gentlemen retired to the sitting-room and
passed the evening at cards.

"How does the ranch of the Half Moon impress you,
Hayward?" said Redwood, as they rose to retire to their
sleeping apartments.

"Favorably," he answered; "the grazing is good, and it
seems well watered."

"The ocean view is magnificent," said Redwood, with
enthusiasm; "the lookout over the bay from the edge of
the cliff is unrivaled. I regret the rain prevented you
seeing it."

"I will see it in the morning." replied Hayward, as they
entered the hall; "provided it clears. Let us look out and
see how the weather is." And turning to the left he walked
to the front door. "Halloo!" he exclaimed in surprise; "it
is open! Do you leave your doors ajar at night in this
lonely spot?"

"This is the work of Pepito," answered Redwood. opening the door wide and gazing at the fast falling rain,
"the careless Indian. How dark it is ; as black as Ere-
bus."

"Blacker, if possible," responded Hayward, turning in
and standing by while his host closed and locked the door.
"It is now ten by my watch; at what hour do you breakfast in the morning?"

"At any hour you wish."

"Well, let us say at seven. Good-night."

"Good-night, and pleasant dreams," responded Redwood.
" Pepito will knock at your door and wake you in the morning."

When Hayward entered his room. closing the door, he

took a seat at the table and drew from his pocket a diary,
to look for a date connected with a thought that was passing through his mind at the moment. The oil in the lamp
was nearly exhausted, yielding a feeble light, and as he held
the open book close to it, his glance was arrested by the
phrase, "The so-called Lamb." This was his synonym for
Corby, and this was the page on which he had written the
account of his entrapment in "The Alley of Assassins." His
thoughts now took a turn, he closed the diary and replaced
it in his pocket and thought over that adventure ; of the
total absence of suspicion with which he had followed the
Indian, and of the narrow escape he had made. What had
become of this man who had followed him with such vindictive determination ? Did he land and escape in the marsh,
or drift out to sea? If he went ashore, he doubtless stove
in his boat and sunk her, for she was nowhere found. If he
was carried out by the tide, his boat would have sunk below
the visible horizon before daylight, and been out of sight.
He remembered hearing at the Custom House that the tide
had favored the escape of the assassins. Yes, they had
drifted out to sea, and into the track of vessels passing up
and down the coast. Were they picked up? They had
about an even chance, and again an even chance of getting on a ship going either way. No, more came north ;
for hundreds of vessels never left the harbor for want of
seamen.

The arch-fiend might be in the city now ; might have
been in the city for a month past, shadowing him. Might
have followed him down to the Half Moon that day. Might
be looking through a crack in the shutter at him that moment.

He rose and walked toward the door to lock it. As he did
so, it came to his mind that as he hurried in out of the rain
in the afternoon, and turned to enter the sitting-room, he
chanced to notice a long, old-fashioned iron key on the outside of the room he was then in. The casual sight of it
caused no thought, he had taken it in with a swift glance
that embraced the entire hall ; but the picture of the key as
he was walking to the door rose before his mental vision as
distinct as though he had made it a matter of study and

saw it again with his eyes. He opened the door and felt for it—it was gone.

His soul was now in arms ; the blood rushed to his face. He drew his pistol and stepped into the hall and stood listening. Feeling a current of air on his cheek, he cautiously approached the front door and found it a few inches open. Retracing his steps to his room, he threw his overcoat over his left shoulder, took his hat from the table and put it on ; then standing erect, with his weapon in hand, hanging down at his side, he paused to listen. The blood had left his face. White with determination, his eyes glittered, his features were rigid ; the conviction was borne in on him that he was standing in a trap !

As he turned from the table, the loose sleeve of his overcoat swung near the flickering lamp and extinguished it, leaving the room in darkness. When he had groped his way into the hall he cautiously closed his door, and when he passed out into the night he drew the front door to and left it as he had found it.

He turned south instinctively, bearing to the left to avoid falling over the cliff ; but soon, in the intense darkness, lost consciousness of direction. Whether he was walking toward the precipice or from it he was unable in any way to decide. In this state of uncertainty and bewilderment he stood and thought. Presently he felt his right cheek growing cold. This gave him the clew, and he turned to the left with a confident step and entered the rolling prairie with a light heart.

Meantime, Redwood was sitting in shadow, in a dark corner of his apartment, his thoughts and emotions waging war within him. He was conspiring the death of a guest. True; but who was this man sleeping in the adjoining chamber? The papers, at the time of the Gomez trial, had insinuated that he had been a robber, and even stigmatized him as "a grand ladrone." Corby had whispered to him that he had committed an assassination in Monterey. He had made no denial of the charges in the papers, nor had he proceeded against them in the courts : he was doubtless guilty. The Vigilance Committee were honorable men, and they took life for the public good, in defiance of law, and were sustained by public opinion. If right in several men, why not in one? He clearly had as good a right to sit in judgment as a self-appointed executive committee of three. There could be no shadow of doubt about that. Yes, it was in a manner his duty, a duty he owed to his fellowman, to shut his eyes and permit the men of Corby to throw this objectionable character over the cliff.

It involved no cruelty, no suffering. It was painless and swift—a descent through the soft air, a plunge in the water, and it was over. He had read that the sensation of drowning was pleasant. The house of Hayward & Co. would go on as usual. Its creditors would be duly paid, the business of the great world be undisturbed. It would bring no disaster in its train. What mattered it then? One man of the ten hundred millions crawling over the surface of the globe dying a day sooner or a day later. It mattered nothing.

But if the great house of Redwood fell, on Wednesday, it would matter much. Hundreds would be involved in the ruin, house after house that leaned on it would go down, his name would be dishonored, business paralyzed, causing wide-reaching suffering and sorrow. "The public good demands the extinction of the Grand Ladrone," he said to himself, as he rose to his feet. "Let them toss him over the cliff into the sea. It is foreordained."

He approached the lamp that burned on the window and looked at his watch. It lacked twenty minutes of midnight. He had been sitting in his shirt-sleeves, with his cravat off and shirt open at the throat. He now drew off his boots, and, entering the hall, walked in his stocking feet to the door of Hayward, bent and applied his eye and then his ear to the keyhole. He listened for several minutes, then rose and returned to his bedroom and blew out the light, resuming his seat in the corner.

Ten minutes passed, which seemed to Redwood like ten hours, when Simeon, one of the pre-eminent Saints, pushed open the front door and entered the hall, followed by two lesser lights. He opened the slide of a dark lantern that he carried in his hand, throwing a glare of light down the hall. Then, without a pause, entered the room of Hayward and looked about.

"By the holy Prophet!" he exclaimed in a low tone, turning to his companions and looking them in the face anxiously, "the bird has flown."

"He must be in league with the devil," said one.

"The foul fiend hath given him warning," said the other.

"Come out," said Simeon, entering the hall followed by his men ; "close the bedroom door and push the front one too, to the position it was in when we entered. One of you run to the stable, he may be saddling a horse now ; the other stand here in the hall on watch. I will go to the room of Redwood. If I need you in there I will give the signal."

Closing the door behind him as he stepped in, Simeon cast the light about the apartment until it rested on and illuminated the pale face of Redwood, who stared at the intruder in mute and fearful expectation.

"Is it over?" he inquired at length in a hoarse whisper.

"Yes," answered Simeon, taking a seat by the table and placing his dark lantern on it. "It is over."

"The glare of your lantern is 'ghastly," said Redwood, rising and moving his chair out of the light to the table, and re-seating himself. "I heard no noise."

"None was made," replied Simeon.

"The body is not in the house!" whispered Redwood, apprehensively.

"No," replied Simeon, with a meaning smile, "the body is wet enough by this time."

Redwood shuddered, and rising, lighted the lamp and began to pace the floor. Simeon lighted a cigar, leaned back in his chair, and watched him. Presently he muttered :

"I am sorry."

"Too late," said his confederate, knocking the ash from his cigar.

"Yes, too late!" he replied, halting at the table with his hands clasped behind his back, and looking down at the dark lantern, which shone in his agitated face.

Simeon put the cigar in his mouth, drew from his breast-pocket a flask, took out the stopper, and removing the metallic cup that fitted on the bottom half filled it with liquor.

"Drink," he said, offering it to the distressed merchant; "it will do you good."

Redwood, still staring at the glaring eye of the lantern as though fascinated, automatically reached out his hand, took the cup, and raising it to his lips drained it to the bottom. He then resumed his walk; his step became more rapid and firm, his countenance assumed an expression of composure, his eye brightened, a smile of satisfaction and even of triumph stole over his face. Meantime Simeon lighted a fresh cigar and sat watching him. Presently the rapidity of the walker's pace began to decline, his step became vacillating, he halted by the bedside, stood a few seconds gazing at the bull's-eye of the lantern, then laid down with his head on the pillow and sank into a torpor.

Simeon drew from his vest pocket a small metallic whistle and blew a low note. The door opened and his confederates entered.

"Over the cliff!" he said, rising to his feet and pointing to the prostrate figure of the doomed man.

CHAPTER XII.

PLOT AND COUNTER-PLOT ON THE MARIPOSA.

HUBERT DIGBY, the inhabitant of the pretentious but somewhat circumscribed mansion on the banks of the Mariposa, had been overtaken by the hand of misfortune. He left the mines, where he had been only moderately successful, "to go into the cattle business," as the phrase went. Going into the cattle business meant the buying from the emigrants their worn down and fleshless mules, horses and steers, and grazing them into condition for resale. It was a pretty business and promised enormous profits; but did not keep its promise. He did not enter into the speculation very largely, and one vaquero, Jack Mulcahy, a thin, sprightly and humorous transplant from the garden of St. Patrick, sufficed to round up his stock when occasion required.

One day when Mulcahy was absent on leave a party of several men camped on the river bank and invited Digby down to dine with them. One of the number, who assumed the lead, had light hair and eyebrows, was white-faced and innocent-looking; withal an incessant talker and captivating in his friendly overtures. He knew the State that Digby was from, and talked with affection of it as his own home. They had lately reached California and wished to sell their stock, left at pasture some miles above. Would Digby buy them? No, Digby had all the stock he could manage and did not wish to buy. Then would Digby allow them to fatten on his range? They would pay him well and take the risk of their loss. In fact, they had come to him because they knew they could confide in him. They knew his family at home by reputation, and felt they would be safe in his hands. They had the appearance of men newly arrived in the country, and Digby saw no reason to think otherwise; and very likely their statement was true.

It was arranged that two of them should go up in the

morning and drive down their stock, while the genial one and a companion remained in camp. Digby went up to his house for his brand at their request, heated it in the fire and branded their riding mules, turning the two not needed in the morning out on the range with his own. He passed a pleasant evening at their fire, in that intimacy which persons from the same State were wont to indulge when meeting in this far-off land, much heightened in this case by the actual affection displayed by the white-eyebrowed and guileless chatterer.

But when Digby got up in the morning and looked out, he saw no smoke rising above the clump of trees in the valley ; and, as he went down to the river for water, he passed through the late camp, and found the fire out and the spot deserted. Hurrying back to the house, he mounted and rode out to the ranging ground of his mules, a drove of which constituted the bulk of his wealth. They were gone. Mulcahy, returned from leave, joined hotly in the pursuit, and vowed he would bring back the guilty deceivers, alive or dead. But he never got sight of them, and consequently failed to bring them back in either condition. The neighborhood was aroused, but the best trackers were at fault, and thrown off the trail, so successfully had they doubled or so completely had accident favored their flight.

This blow finished Digby, and forced him out of the cattle business. The land was not his, but the mansion was, and he was obliged, in the reduced state of his finances, to abide in it until he could find some one to purchase and haul it off. He had also his small stock of furniture, his saddles and bridles, branding-iron, and many little things that he wished to dispose of before leaving. Mulcahy was paid off and discharged ; but declined to go until the general breaking up, and remained without wages. He was not without hope that fortune would bring by the Genial Man, against whom he cherished a deadly animosity, and with whom he was eager to foreclose. He had studied his description closely, and felt sure he would recognize him at once.

In this state of things, Digby was seated one evening on his doorstep, musing on the mutability of human affairs, when John Leson and a companion passed by, going down toward the river. Mulcahy, who was standing by, disdained to notice them, having a poor opinion of Leson ; but Digby returned their salute and inquired their destination. Leson answered that they intended passing the night at Allens'. A few words of conversation ensued and they passed on. Leson's companion did not join in the conversation, nor seem to relish the interruption of their journey.

"Who was that man with Leson ?" inquired Digby.

" I never saw him before," answered Mulcahy, " and, if he does not change his company, I do not wish to see him again."

" Why, what have you got against Leson ?"

" His face." answered Mulcahy. " No more, but it is enough."

" He did not make his own face," said Digby.

" No, but he puts the expression to it. Besides, he goes about with a stubble on that does not speak well for his gentility, yet puts on the air of a gentleman, which he is not. He is a bog-trotter—no more."

" There are no bogs here for him to trot over, Jack," said Digby, smiling.

"He will find one to trot into some day, and he will never trot out again," replied Mulcahy. " See the sharp. cold look he throws at you out of the corner of his little black eye. The rope is twisting for him this minute."

"What do you think of his companion, Mulcahy ?"

" I will go up after supper, and take his measure," answered he, " and find out what the two are gallivanting about the country for."

" Do," said Digby, " and bring back his measure in your pocket. And ask Bill Allen if he has made up his mind to take the brown mule."

At dusk, Mulcahy mounted and rode up. He found the stranger in earnest conversation with William Allen, but he stopped abruptly as Mulcahy entered and took a seat. As he did not resume, Allen put a question to him.

"But how do you know he is the same man ? It does not seem likely that it can be."

" We will continue the subject after a while." interposed Leson, in a low tone.

"Why, there is no secret about it, is there?" said Allen. "And if there is, I suppose you are not afraid of Jack Mulcahy. I do not see how he can interfere with you."

"Well, there is no harm in being prudent," answered Leson.

"I will give you to know, Mr. Jack Leson," broke in Mulcahy, threateningly, "that Mr. Mulcahy interferes with no man's business but his own, and will not put up with insinuations. If your talk is honest, go on with it; and if not, you had better shut up. I do not care to hear your palaver."

"Mulcahy," said Allen, "you are too excitable. Leson meant no offense. There is no secret in the thing, and cannot be. If there is, I will have nothing to do with it. What I do, I do open and aboveboard. Now, Mr. McCauley, if you want my help in this matter, answer my question. How do you know this Hayward is the same man?"

"Leson knows he is the same man," answered McCauley, "perfectly well."

"I would know him in a thousand," said Leson, "without the scar. We saw enough of him that night, I should think, to remember him. I have got a pair of eyes, I suppose?"

"You have," said Mulcahy; "such as they are."

"Mulcahy," retorted Leson, "you will carry your impertinence a little too far, if you do not look out."

"Oh, impertinence, is it?" answered Mulcahy, rising. "Be pleased to walk out of the house with me, Mr. Leson, and your elegant black eyes will soon see how far I can carry it."

"This thing must stop right now," said Allen, "or I will turn you all out and go to bed. Sit down, Mulcahy, and hold your tongue and use your ears while we settle this business. As I understand it," turning to McCauley and speaking rapidly to keep the floor from the belligerents, "you want me to sign this paper to the sheriff to appoint Leson a deputy to arrest this man and bring him back for trial. Now, the man has been tried once and ought to have been hanged; but it seems hardly fair to try him again. But if he has robbed McCauley of a million, and he cannot reach him in 'Frisco, why, it is fair, of course, that McCauley should have some satisfaction. My private opinion is, the man ought to hang ; that is, if he is the same man, and really robbed McCauley."

" He did," interposed McCauley. " He forged the deed. The family were drowned, every soul of them. He bought the jury. It was packed on purpose for sale. I did not have a friend on it. He paid them five thousand apiece. One of them got drunk and let it out—my friends have sworn to me that they heard him—but when he got sober he denied it and said he was joking. We can make the man disgorge, if you will help us."

" Leson," said Allen, turning to him, " I will sign this paper, if you will agree before this company to let me hold you responsible if you bring up the wrong man."

" You may shoot me," replied Leson, " if he is not the same man we clapped the brand on that night."

" I will shoot you sure, if it turns out you have been playing a game on me. Here goes for the signature," and he affixed his name to the paper, under the names of the Manleys.

Digby went to San Francisco a few days after this, to endeavor to collect a debt from a person on the eve of returning to the States. After discussing his business with Mr. Benham, his attorney and friend, it occurred to him to inquire concerning the Hayward matter, which had been rehearsed to him by Mulcahy with striking accuracy. Benham informed him of the standing of Hayward, characterized the movement against him as a plot for abduction and blackmail, and requested Digby to call on him and give him warning. Digby flinched at this, as he was disinclined by nature to interfere in the affairs of others ; but Benham insisted, giving him a card of introduction, and he called at the bank. The card was taken up to Hayward's private office, and Digby was presently shown in. Don Pedro rose, greeted him politely, and begged him to be seated. His beard, which he had grown since Digby had seen him, his long hair gone, and his dress, which was in the latest style, so changed him that Digby would have failed to recognize him, but for his voice. He had not spoken long before the mellowed accents, heard in the midnight struggle for life at

Allen's, betrayed the Grand Ladrone. Hayward read the recognition in Digby's face, and said :

" You did not remember me when you entered, Mr. Digby, but you do now."

" I think I do," answered Digby, with embarrassment.

" You know you do," was the reply. " The Grand Ladrone, as the vaqueros of Don Manuel Velasco called that unfortunate man at Allen's, is dead; but his voice and imputed deed haunt the living Hayward. But I will lay the ghost of the Ladrone before I finish with him. I am glad to see you; you stood by the departed Ladrone nobly. If I can do you a service, name it and it is done."

" I come to render you a service, not to ask one," answered Digby. He then gave an account of what took place between the confederates, McCauley and Leson, and William Allen; expressing the opinion that they would succeed in getting a writ and be in the city soon to serve it, and advised Hayward to absent himself.

" No," said he, " I must fight it out, and publicly, as soon as Benham gets the proof against them. But, to come to yourself; how are you getting on in your little house on the Mariposa? Are you making a fortune?"

" No," answered Digby. " Fortune has frowned on me. In fact, in the language of the country, I am next thing to dead broke !"

" Good," said Don Pedro. " I cannot make you collector of the port; but I can give you an equal salary, if you will deign to enter our service—not the service of the Grand Ladrone, who, as a ladrone, never existed, but the service of the house of Hayward. As the collector gets extra fees, so we give extra compensation for special and important service. For instance, a special remuneration of five thousand dollars will be given for settling the business of the bankrupt firm of Leson and McCauley, and you are the man to settle it."

" I?" exclaimed Digby, in astonishment. " How can I settle it?"

" Let us think it over," answered the Ladrone. " Do you know the sheriff of Mariposa County?"

" Very well," answered Digby.

"What sort of a man is he?"

"A very good man. High-tempered and rough, but honest enough."

"Very good, indeed," said the Ladrone. "And now for the way to settle it. See the sheriff and explain the case. These men imposed on him and on the men who asked for my arrest by a false account of the real-estate suit. Benham will show you this."

"He has already done so," said Digby.

"Very well," continued the Ladrone. "Take Mulcahy with you. Let him make his affidavit that they said they would make me disgorge if helped to a warrant. This was conspiracy. Charge it, and ask that a warrant be issued for their arrest. We will meet their warrant with a fresher one. What do you say?"

"If Benham says they are liable for conspiracy and approves of this course, I will undertake it," answered Digby.

"That he will do, and explain to you the plot into which I fell. Go at once. But stay. Cash this check as you pass out of the bank; you must not leave without the sinews of war."

After an interview with Benham, Digby rode night and day to the Mariposa and sought out the sheriff, who informed him that he had sworn in Leson as deputy several days before, and he and his companion had left for the city. Digby laid the case before him, and he sat down at once to issue a warrant for their arrest, but Digby interrupted him.

"Sheriff," he said, "if these men arrest a member of the firm on such a charge it will shake the credit of the bank. I have been thinking they will be willing to approve of any extra expense I may incur to prevent it. You are a man of great push and vigor. If you would be willing to undertake the fatigue of a forced ride to the city, skilled as you are in getting relays and making rapid journeys, we could reach there before the men presented themselves. I am provided with funds and will pay you a thousand down and another thousand if we reach the bank before them. Your presence will be better than a deputy."

The sheriff continued looking at Digby a few moments

after he had ceased speaking, then left his seat, walked to the door, and gave several rapid orders to his men.

"Can you sleep in the saddle, Digby?" he said as he turned back, and without awaiting an answer called to the office boy, "Run over and have the flasks filled with brandy. Digby, send yours over with him. We will be off in thirty minutes. Boy," he called out, "have them put up a lunch for three."

Digby took from the alforja carried by Mulcahy (whom he had picked up in passing his ranch), and handed to the sheriff, a thousand dollars in gold ounce pieces, which he accepted with the remark, "Ther' is no hurry about that." Fresh horses were brought to the door ; the party mounted and left the town on a fast gallop, enveloping the citizens in a cloud of dust as they swept by.

While Digby was enjoying his swift ride with the sheriff, in the warm sun that shone on the Mariposa, Hayward was plodding through the mud and rain, on his way from Half Moon Bay to the city. Beyond the Diablo Mountains on the sea coast there was no dust and no sun, but black clouds drifting in from the ocean, obscuring and drenching the land. In his flight in the midnight rain he had crossed the road without observing it, and after day broke, chanced on a ranch, hired a horse and man, and made his way up the coast. As they rode slowly along his mind was occupied with reflections on the occurrences of the previous day and night. That Redwood was privy to the plot he entertained no doubt ; but he was unable to recall any special word or act that was inconsistent with his innocence. The thought that Pepito was implicated he rejected. as the Mission Indians were proverbial for fidelity. Who then opened the hall door and abstracted the key from the lock ? It was possible Corby had concealed a man in the house in the early evening, but not probable. No ; he felt, though he could give no satisfactory reason to himself for so feeling, that Redwood was guilty. Assuming this ; what was the motive ? He pondered long over the question, and pondered in vain, when the thought occurred to him that his host of last night might be secretly affiliated with the Saints, and had acted under orders issued by their secret council. This would account for the union of Redwood and Corby, and on this his mind settled. The mystery was made clear.

"I think," he said that night at supper with Morales, after relating the late events, "that he is one of them."

"Perhaps," replied Morales ; "but in looking for motives one is often led astray."

"What else could have moved a man in his position to such an alliance ?"

"It may be the house is in trouble," answered Morales, "and Don Solomon may have them in his power financially. But the machinery of the mind is hidden, the lever is not visible, one can only guess."

At this moment a servant entered and handed a note to Morales, which, after reading, he passed over the table to his nephew.

"Is Mr. Benson in his office ?" he inquired, after glancing over it.

"Yes, sir ; at least, in the counting-house."

"Say to him that I will call in a few minutes," said Hayward; and as the messenger left the room he re-read the note aloud: "'Has Mr. Hayward returned from down the coast? Does he know what is keeping Mr. Redwood ?—BENSON.'"

"That looks alarming !" said Morales.

"And mysterious," replied Hayward, putting on his hat and taking up an umbrella. "This has very much the appearance of a plot within a plot."

"Be prudent," said Morales, as he was leaving the room.

"I will state the facts," responded Hayward, "but draw no inference."

"Right; let him draw his own."

When Hayward entered the office of the merchant, Benson met him with a troubled countenance and inquired for his partner. Hayward told his story in a few words and concluded, saying:

"I felt myself in imminent peril and took to my heels."

"Why didn't you warn Redwood?" inquired Benson with emotion.

"Well," replied Hayward, hesitating, "it was a case of devil take the hindmost."

"What had I best do?" inquired Benson, his uneasiness increased by the manner and reply of Hayward.

"If I were you," answered Hayward, "I would send an express to the ranch at once for information. I will confer with you again in the morning if you wish it. Your messenger must be a native to get there in the dark. Goodnight."

Soon after breakfast in the morning a note came down from Benson, saying his messenger had returned, and begging Hayward to ride with him to the ranch. Accordingly they went down together, followed by the two Floridians, Hayward's body-guard, David the pock-marked and William the silent. On their arrival they interrogated Pepito, who gave a connected narrative of events, including his visit to Santa Clara.

"The gentlemen were gone when I got back," he said, "and one horse; the other was left. Vicente barked when he looked in the stable and saw the horse."

They went to Redwood's bedroom. The coat, cravat and boots he had taken off before the entry of Simeon, and his overcoat and hat, were gone.

"The bed has been slept in," said Benson.

"Yes, that is evident," replied Hayward. "Which horse was taken, Pepito?"

"The master's horse, saddle and bridle," he answered; "the one your honor rode is standing in the stable."

"How old are the tracks?"

"He was taken out this morning," answered Pepito· "the tracks in the stable show it ; outside they are washed away by the rain. His hay was all eaten; it would take all night to eat the hay."

"Where do you think he has gone to?"

"I think, your honor, he has gone to Santa Clara, to get that letter."

"It is to me an impenetrable mystery," said Benson. "Let us return to the city. I will send a detective down in the morning ; time now to me is very precious."

On the following day, at the close of bank hours, the paper of Redwood & Co. went to protest, and the house fell. The papers of Thursday announced the flight of the head of the house, "carrying off an enormous sum of money," and the name of Redwood became synonymous with plunder.

CHAPTER XIII.

THE CABIN OF DUTCH CHARLEY.

IN the coast range of mountains, on the right of the trail going west through the Pacheco Pass, and at the entrance of a gorge which ran back from the trail, stood a solitary hostel, the only habitation for many miles on either side. It consisted of a porch, a bar-room and a kitchen. Instead of one host, it had four tall, lounging men. One of this company of landlords was known as Dutch Charley, though an American like his partners. Behind the cabin, and not visible from the trail, the mountains shut in a narrow strip of open grass land, running back into the gorge, nipped short as a sward, and watered by a small rivulet. On the bank of this diminutive stream stood the stump of an enormous tree, broken off by a remote storm. Its top was jagged and rotten, and so high above the ground that a man on horseback could not see into the hollow. The trail, as it approached and left to its right this concealed oasis, at the mouth of which stood the cabin, was a rough mountain mule path.

Digby passed this spot after dark as he rode to Mariposa to see the sheriff. Had he been an hour sooner, he would have seen the conspirators ascend the steps that led up to the porch.

On their arrival at the cabin, where they proposed putting up for the night, McCauley indulged in several copious libations at the bar, alone, as Leson did not join him, and after supper in the kitchen they withdrew to the front apartment, which fulfilled the functions of bar, sitting, smoking and

sleeping room. Dutch Charley sat with them in conversation, the remaining hosts lounging in and out with pipes in
their mouths. All were smoking but Leson, who sat listening, entering now and then into the conversation, and
glancing about.

He soon became restless and dissatisfied. He was of a
suspicious nature and a sharp observer, and he thought he
saw signs which boded him no good. He walked to the door
and looked out. The three landlords were seated on a bench
in the porch: they did not salute or look toward him. Leson
said to himself he had interrupted a private conversation of
which he was the subject—he had lost all thought of McCauley. But for the presence of the men he would have gone
down the steps and disappeared in the darkness. He turned
back into the room and sat down with his head in his hands,
thinking. He was sure they were doomed to death ; it
might come in a few minutes. What could he do? Suddenly a thought struck him ; his face brightened and he
looked up. Dutch Charley was standing at the bar, where
he had just helped himself to a drink, with a burning match
in his hand lighting a fresh pipe. Leson approached him and
said in a low confidential tone:

" I have a great scheme on hand; there is a pot of money
in it. I want the help of you men."

" What's your game ?" inquired Charley.

" Look at this paper," Leson answered, taking the war-
rent of arrest from his breastpocket and unfolding it. " I
am the Leson mentioned here, with authority to arrest Hayward, the richest man in 'Frisco. Read it."

Dutch Charley read it slowly over, and, after finishing it,
said:

" Well, what then ? "

" This," answered Leson. " Hayward robbed that man,"

pointing to McCauley, "of a million by a lawsuit. Instead of carrying him on to Mariposa for trial we will stop here in the mountains and make him disgorge. He will do it to be let off the exposure ; and, if not, you men might persuade him. Put him in a lonely spot in the mountains, on bread and water, and you could soon bring him to terms."

"You bet," said Charley with emphasis. "I say, fellows," he called out to the men on the porch, "come in ; I have struck a lead."

The men entered and gathered about the counter ; the warrant was read aloud by Leson in legal tone, and the entire story gone over by him and McCauley. Leson said he would want two or three of them to go down with him and help make the capture and prevent a rescue on the way back—three would be better, and one might stay and keep the coast clear for their return. This proposal was acceded to, and a thorough discussion of the ways and means took place. The plan settled on before they retired was this.

The landlords were to furnish horses for the party, and such money as might be needed to secure rapid action, Leson having stated that their funds were about exhausted. Deeds were to be drawn up on legal cap in San Francisco, from Hayward to Leson and McCauley for one half the Gomez estate, and to the landlords for the other half. The capture made, the prisoner was to be hurried from the city before his friends could interpose by writ of habeas corpus, or proffer of bail, and carried rapidly across the country, avoiding the regular road, to a secluded hollow in the mountains back of the cabin.

Leson undertook to arrange on the spot the best mode of getting him quickly out of the city. He thought, as at present advised, the arrest should be made at dusk or after, and the horses held up a by-street near at hand. The prisoner was to be gagged and tied on behind Dutch Charley, who made proffer of his oath that all Pandemonium could not take him from him, once in that position. Leson also undertook to produce a notary public of his acquaintance at the time and place desired. The prisoner was to be forced to write a letter to Morales, stating that he had deeded the property, partly for a valuable money consideration and partly to avoid trial and expense, and that no impediment must be thrown in the way of his grantees in their disposal of the property, as his reputation and liberty were at stake; and urging him to buy back the estate, if it could be done on reasonable terms. That, until they disposed of the property and cleared out, he would remain in hiding. Dutch Charley was of opinion that, after the papers were executed, they should cut the Ladrone's throat. But McCauley and Leson protested against bloodshed, and the point was waived.

"I say, Charley," said his companion, as they went back to look after the horses before retiring, "that couple made a narrow escape."

"They did," answered Charley, sententiously. "The devil takes care of his own, every time."

"I notice they beat you on the throat question," said the other, after a pause.

"Not to any great extent," he replied, contemptuously. "I intend to cut all their throats. You don't suppose that I am soft enough to let them carry off half our plunder, do you? Not if I know myself. I have thought the whole thing out. I will bring up extra paper from 'Frisco and make those two innocents deed their half over to me and make their notary take the acknowledgment, and then cut every throat in the party, the notary's included. That is the way to do business. We will have no further use for any of them. And serve them right. Green chaps have no business around where we are. Those two would make no use of their share if they got it, only hoard it up."

"I suppose we will all share in their half," said the other.

"Don't fret yourself about that," answered Dutch Charley, sharply. "I always do the fair thing and the square. thing. I will make a satisfactory divy when we sell out and close the thing up."

"I suppose we will all leave on the steamer if we make the riffle?" inquired his companion.

"Of course we will, and we will not be many days about it, either. There are plenty of speculators in 'Frisco who will jump at the property when they see our deeds on record, and hear the price. We will offer low—we can afford it. Sell out and light out, that is my motto."

The party got off in the following forenoon, leaving one man behind to keep house, and proceeded leisurely on their way, fearing no evil; and several mornings thereafter, before daybreak, the sheriff and Digby halted at the cabin for barley to feed their horses. They lay on the ground and took a short nap, while the horses were eating, and within an hour mounted and pushed on. The next day they reached the city and rode directly to the bank. On being admitted, Digby introduced the sheriff, to whom the Ladrone expressed his thanks and gratification that he had come down in person. "They are here," he said, "and are watched. Leson presented his requisition to the sheriff of the county to-day and had it approved. He did not ask assistance. He has brought with him, besides McCauley, three men who have the appearance of desperadoes, all of whom are keeping close within doors. It is evident they contemplate an abduction, and have no intention of taking me to Mariposa. If I am right in this, they will not make their appearance till after dark.

Leson is a sharp fellow. His requisition does not point at me, the banker, but at one calling himself Hayward. You will find they have no suspicion at the sheriff's office whom he is after."

"I will go at once to the office and get authority for their arrest," said the sheriff. "Of course we will let the bravoes slip through the net; we want no noise. I will carry the two principals out of town quietly and at once. The bravoes will vanish on the first alarm. They will not trouble us."

"Let McCauley vanish also; I fear him not," answered the Ladrone. "With Leson behind the bars, the conspiracy dies. Shut up the arch-conspirator until the next term of court, and then *nolle* the case and turn him loose. Come back as soon as you have seen the sheriff and had your dinner. If they come in your absence I will have them detained in an ante-room."

The city sheriff received his brother of Mariposa very cordially, and gave him the necessary authority for arresting Leson and carrying him beyond his jurisdiction. He furnished him a pair of handcuffs, with which in his hurried departure he had failed to provide himself, and a brace of policemen to assist in the capture. Thus provided, he dined with Digby at a neighboring restaurant, and they all adjourned to a room adjoining Hayward's to await the coming of Leson and his party.

In the meantime the abductors were busy with their preparations. Leson had also procured a pair of handcuffs when he visited the sheriff's office. Straps and a rope were bought to fasten their captive on behind Dutch Charley, and a gag made to prevent an outcry. Provisions were laid in for a cross-country trip, for themselves and horses, and their flasks filled.

At dark their horses were brought to a vacant lot behind

the bank and left in charge of McCauley, who had a delicacy about being seen in active service. Two of the men were instructed to loiter near by, ready if called ; while Leson and Dutch Charley knocked at the porter's door and inquired for Mr. Hayward.

The porter preceded them up the hall stairway and showed them in.

They found the Ladrone in the room alone, writing. He looked up from his paper as they entered and inquired their business. Leson drew up a chair opposite him, placed his hat on the table, and produced from his pocket a paper, which he opened and displayed.

"Mr. Hayward," he said, "I have here a warrant for your arrest, issued by the sheriff of Mariposa, and countersigned by the sheriff of this county. I need not tell you on what charge. The witnesses from Monterey will be brought up and compelled to testify. The case is worked up and ready for trial. Your wealth will avail nothing in the state of feeling on the subject-matter of this case in Mariposa; your experience there will tell you this. I say nothing of the shock an arrest will give the House of Hayward, or of your own fate if taken back to the scene of your exploits. The law even may not be allowed by the people to take its course. All this I merely recall to your attention; you know it as well as I.

"There is one way, and only one, by which you can avert the thunderbolt that hangs over your head. Myself and several other gentlemen have become interested in the property you wrung from McCauley. I have with me two deeds, conveying the property to them. Sign these deeds and acknowledge them before a notary in good faith, and you are free ; refuse, and within thirty minutes you will be on the road to the Mariposa jail."

"How long will it be," answered the Ladrone, "provided I sign these deeds, before I will be called upon to hand over my interest in the House of Hayward as the price of further silence?"

"I am the solitary man you have to fear," answered Leson. "It will be to my interest to keep quiet, and should another move be made against you, I can put it down. Become my friend, and your future will be undisturbed. A little time gained and any act in this shifting population is consigned to oblivion."

"Leson," answered the Ladrone, "I will consign you and your case to oblivion, without the lapse of any time!"

As he spoke he touched a bell, and the sheriff and Digby entered from the adjoining apartment, from which they had overheard the conversation. Leson fixed his eye on the sheriff, and the stubble on his cheeks seemed still blacker in contrast with his white face, from which the blood had fled.

"Leson," said the sheriff, addressing him, "I have here a warrant for your arrest, countersigned by the sheriff of this city. I need not tell so accomplished a lawyer on what charge, but for the benefit of your respectable looking comrade, I will say it is for conspiracy to blackmail. Hold out your hands, if you please;" and he put on the fetters.

Dutch Charley slipped out of the room and flew down the stairway, beckoned his companions as he reached the street, and together they ran to the alley and mounted.

"Get into the saddle, you dog," he said to McCauley, who was hesitating to mount. "I'll shoot that cur through the head," he muttered to the man at his side, as they rode up the alley, "as soon as we get into the sand-hills; it'll be some satisfaction for this cursed slip-up."

But the satisfaction was denied him, for they came to an

obstruction which compelled the party for a moment to ride single file, and McCauley seized the opportunity to wheel his horse and gallop back. Dutch Charley turned in his saddle and drew his pistol, but his companions restrained him, and he rode on in a fearful temper, vowing future vengeance. In the meantime the deserter made his way with breakneck speed down the dark alley until he felt . certain he was beyond the range of the bullets of the dreaded revolver, when he moderated his speed and turned into an alley that led to the eastern suburb. Presently he drew in the rein, and continued at a slow walk, anxious to prolong his ride. He was bent on the performance of a painful but imperative duty: to report to the mysterious and dread Corby the failure of the plot.

He left the scattered habitations and rode into the sand-hills. When he reached their summit he halted and looked down on the lights of the old adobe, the Saints' Rest, that dominated the canvas village in the midst of which it stood. His heart failed him. Neither he nor Leson had been free to communicate with Corby since their arrival in the city, and he was unaware of the alliance they had formed with the landlords, and of the change of purpose from a legal arrest to the plan of abduction. Would Corby believe him ? Would he admit as valid his plea of compulsion ? He was a dangerous man to face with a tale of defeat. But if he shrunk back, the eye and hand of the arch-plotter would be on him soon ; a merciless eye, in that event, and a heavy hand. He had better ride down the sand-hill and alight at the Saints' Rest.

He dismounted in front, hitched his horse, and partook at the bar of several fortifying draughts before going to the rear and tapping on the shutter of the Lion's Den. He was duly admitted, after a careful survey and consultation, and ushered into the interior room, where sat Marcus and Corby smoking, with a bottle of wine on the table between them.

"Where is Leson?" said Corby, sharply, as he noted an air of discomfiture on the face of McCauley.

"Under arrest," he answered humbly.

"What is the meaning of this? Who arrested him?"

"The sheriff of Mariposa."

"What have you bunglers been doing? Explain yourself," said Corby, sternly.

"I think," replied McCauley, turning pale, "that when you hear how it happened you will admit we were not to blame. We did the very best we could; no man could have worked it finer than Mr. Leson. If it hadn't have been for his sharpness I wouldn't have got here to-night—I wouldn't be sitting in this chair alive."

"Go on," said Corby, with a hard expression on his face.

"Leson drew up a petition to the sheriff to appoint him deputy to arrest this land robber; and when we got to the Manley Ranch on the Mariposa we stayed all night and the men signed it—all but the Mexican, who said he wasn't acquainted with the sheriff. They told him that didn't matter; but he said to him it did, and shrugged his shoulders and walked away."

"What asses those Mexicans are," remarked Marcus. "They ought to have punched his head."

"We went on in the morning," continued McCauley, "to the Allens', where the trial took place; above the ford, you know."

"Yes, I know," said Corby.

"One of the Allens was at home, and he signed; but he was rough about it and said he would kill Leson if it didn't turn out to be a square game. There was an Irishman there, dropped in from the Digby ranch, who wanted to fight Leson, and interfered in the business."

" What is his name?" demanded Corby.

" Mulcahy; a most truculent fellow. I shouldn't wonder if he or his master was at the bottom of our troubles; they might have written and warned this man Hayward. Be that as it may, we got the signature and went on to the county town; and the sheriff said he knew the Manleys well, and Allen also, and issued the warrant of arrest and swore Leson in as special deputy to make it.

" Leson laughed when we came out, and said if the sheriff had known who 'the man Hayward' was he wouldn't have been so quick to issue the warrant. We started right back for the city, and one night stopped at a cabin in the Pacheco Pass, on the Diablo. The devils that kept the tavern planned to murder us. Leson found it out, and, to save our lives, laid the business before them, and said they could squeeze the banker when we got him to the mountains on our way back. Three of them came to the city with us to help, and kept us under guard until to-night, when Leson was arrested in the bank and the villains escaped. I slipped away from them in a dark alley, and came directly here to report the first minute I could get free."

" How do you know it was the Mariposa sheriff? Did you see him?"

" No ; but the men said it was."

" All right ; I don't blame you," said Corby mildly, to the great relief of McCauley. " The horse you are riding belongs to the landlords, I suppose?"

" Yes ; a fine horse."

" Go sell him, and put yourself in funds," said Corby, rising. " We are defeated. The affair is at an end. Sorry for you, but it's the way of the world. The poor man goes to the wall every time. Good-by."

"And let me advise you," said Marcus, with a patronizing smile, "to banish the spirit of revenge from your soul, and turn your attention to some other business. Almost anything pays better in the end. Farewell."

"Good-by, gentlemen," replied McCauley, as he left the room. "I am thankful you take the misfortune so kindly."

The suggestions offered him at the termination of the momentous interview made a deep impression on him. He sold the horse the following day, and with the hundred dollars so obtained went on to the Market Street wharf and invested in vegetables, and established a little trade with retail dealers.

"His tale is true, I don't doubt," said Marcus. "We ought to have inquired, however, how they knew they were going to be murdered, as a matter of curiosity."

"Oh, Leson is sharp ; he saw the indications," replied Corby. "Those delectable landlords are not the men to neglect opportunities. Two well dressed men, coming from the mines, would do better to sleep out in the rain and catch cold than put up with them. I'll turn my attention to those scamps, some of these days, if I ever get the time. They have no commission to kill ; they are assassins."

"Your bird will be so shy, Chief Corby," said Marcus, filling his glass and picking out a fresh cigar, "with all this rapid firing at him, that it's my belief you'll never get him."

"I don't intend to try," replied Corby, gazing in the fire.

"What!" exclaimed Marcus in astonishment, "give him up!"

"Yes, give it up as a bad job. There's a spirit wrestling for that man stronger than I am. He has a familiar who wards off every blow aimed at him. He is invulnerable. I will not waste another hour on him."

"Well! upon my word you astonish me!"

"The night after his escape from Half Moon Bay," continued Corby, still gazing in the fire, "I had a dream about him. I dreamed I had him completely in my power. I had a drawn dagger in my hand, and he stood bofore me .bound and defenseless. 'You escaped the cliff,' I said, ' but the dagger, no!' and drew back to strike, when the form of my mother came between us and the dagger dropped from my hand."

CHAPTER XIV.

A MYSTERIOUS FLUSH ON THE PAJARO, WHICH CALLED TO
MIND A SIMILAR EVENT ON THE DIRTY DEVIL.

In the days of the grandfather of Don Manuel Velasco
the hacienda of San Pablo had been dismembered to furnish
portions to the younger children, leaving to Don Manuel's
father, with the old manor house, a moiety of the lands. The
portions thus cut off became united in his father's day in the
hands of his uncle, who, disturbed in his old age by the influx
of the Americans, sold out and removed to Chili.

The purchaser was a young gentleman from the East
named Hurd, of no means himself, but furnished by some
capitalist with the money to make the payment, a cash one,
and to enter largely into the purchase of cattle and horses.
Business was carried on by him with vigor and stir, but not
with profit. He was one of those men who multiply transactions and believe they are building up a fortune when they
are really dissipating one. The day came when a carefully
prepared balance sheet showed this, and the stock was disposed of and the land offered for sale. No bid could be had
for it about Monterey, as real estate was lifeless and the
spirit of speculation had not yet begun to scourge that locality. The agent of the Eastern partner transferred his
efforts to sell to San Francisco. He offered it at the banking
houses, but among them found a listener only at the House
of Hayward. The Ladrone, during an interview with Hurd
and the agent, called in Digby, and the plot was examined
and the price discussed. The agent, anxious to close out the
concern and save something from the wreck, and determined

not to let his only bidder slip through his fingers, offered the
property at a very low cash price ; and Digby was commissioned to go down with him, with discretional power to close
the transaction. On reaching Monterey, Don Antonio was
taken into consultation, the title was examined and a per-
ambulation of the boundaries arranged for. Don Antonio
took Digby out to San Pablo, where they dined and spent
the night. Don Manuel, who knew the boundary monu-
ments, was to be of the party, and the ladies accepted the
invitation of the gentlemen to join and make a picnic
of it.

On a bright balmy morning the party set off in high
spirits, Domingo with the sumpter mules and several servants bringing up the rear. It had been the dream of Don
Manuel's life to reunite this detached land to the old hacienda, and, as they galloped from one landmark to another,
the desire to possess it grew stronger and stronger.

In the afternoon they reached the fuente frio or cold
spring, where the servants were appointed to prepare the
dinner, and found a refreshing entertainment in readiness.
After a rest, turned into a siesta by most of the party, they
strolled about the spot, which was beautiful, before remount-
ing ; and here it was, walking together over a carpet of
bright flowers, that Don Antonio proposed to the Senorita
Dolores, and was accepted, subject to the approval of her
family. The gallop home in the bracing air of the evening
and the rays of the setting sun filled two of the party with
a joy experienced but once in a lifetime. Well for men that
the joys of this life are evanescent ; for, were it otherwise,
the everlasting joys of the life to come would never be
sought for and never attained.

In a few days the transaction was closed, and young
Hurd, his vision of wealth dissipated, returned to the East,

neither wiser nor richer than when he embarked for El
Dorado.

Digby stocked the ranch with cattle from the south, employed vaqueros, and leaving Mulcahy in command, set out
for San Francisco. He was mounted on a'stately Southern
horse, the pick of the herds, and his saddle and accouterments, a present from the Ladrone, were of the finest Mexican workmanship and very costly. As he took the trail for
the north, he presented the appearance of a man who might
very well be suspected of having money about him ; and
more than one tramp during the day cast an eager look at
him as he galloped by.

The robbers who infested this country were fertile in their
devices to waylay and murder the unwary. Coming as they
did from many countries, they brought with them their
varied modes of procedure, which were the more fatal to
the wayfarer as they were unheard of and unsuspected by
him. Many of these fiends held strictly to the one line in
which they were accomplished, and never, however tempt-
ing the opportunity, allowed themselves to be diverted from
it. They seemed to be impelled by an instinct similar to
that which moves the beast of prey, and failing in their well
understood and customary pursuit, would wait in patience,
through want and privation, for the victim to present himself at the accustomed time and place. It does not seem
that it is the love of money that sustains the habitual mur-
derer in his path so much as the lash of the fiend that possesses him and drives him on to final and eternal ruin.
There were men well mounted and well dressed, who rode
singly or in couples. and did their murders from the
saddle. Watching the roads from points of vantage,
they would select a traveler who appeared to them
likely to have money about him, and, mounting and

taking his trail, would pistol him as they rode up. There were low-class men who did their work on foot—ruffians reared in cities who lacked the accomplishment of horseman-ship. There were sneaks who shot from ambush and trem-bled at the touch of the lifeless bodies as they picked their pockets—the pariahs of the craft. Nor were they all equally depraved. Instances occurred in which they displayed a touching regard for one or other of the virtues. One gallant highwayman, awaiting the execution of the sentence of death pronounced against him by a committee of his fellow-citizens, in the brief interval allowed him for preparation en-tertained the jury with an account of his winning the confi-dence of a new arrival, dressed in broadcloth and a white shirt, as he termed it, with an accent of contempt. The stranger boasted of possessing a large sum of money and of the investments he intended making. An investigation into his financial condition, made soon after at the point of a pistol, however, disclosed the fact that, besides his fine cloth-ing, he had little or nothing about him. The robber said that, moved by his excessive innocence, he had made up his mind to " clean him out," yet spare his life : but this glaring want of veracity so shocked him that he ordered the un-principled man on his knees and raised his pistol. He begged for mercy.

" But I remarked to him," said the bravo, " that it would be a mercy to finish him on the spot, as with such a tongue in his head he could not hope to survive over a week or two at furthest. And so his tongue stopped. He has not told another lie since."

It is dangerous to talk of having money at all times and in all places ; for, even when there is no fear of open rob-bery, it tempts the greedy and necessitous to lay plans to secure it. But here on the open road it was madness.

There was the innkeeper who erected a permanent and imposing structure, like the cabin in the Pacheco Pass, who inspired confidence by the stable appearance of things about him. He would inclose with brush a plot of ground and make a feeble effort at a little garden, and, if grass was convenient, he would keep a cow, the presence of which was found to have a peculiarly soothing effect on a suspicious public. Then came the keeper of a migratory tavern or eating-house, consisting of muslin stretched over poles, some-times quite large, comprising a sleeping room and kitchen separated by a canvas screen. An armful of grass was thrown down against the wall here and there for the guest to spread his blanket on, the sight of which determined many a weary man to remain for the night, and a hitching-post or two was planted near the door. These structures could not be said in legal phrase to be attached to the realty, for a train passing by one on its trip up the country would often on its return, in a week or ten days, see the bare poles staring it in the face. The Arab innkeeper, in the interval, had disappeared with his canvas and effects, and gone, no one save himself knew whither.

Many stories were told of the disappearance of travelers in and about these inns of different classes, and prudent travelers were quite shy of them; but the imprudent and thoughtless are in the majority, and these places were resorted to by the hungry and tired, in spite of all that was hinted and known concerning them. They were located at points on the roads remote from settlements, and the ever-changing population was so eager each in pursuit of his own affairs that their acts were seldom investigated, and they pursued their nefarious occupation in comparative security. Now and then, when a clear case was reported against them, the miners would sweep down and, in the phraseology of

the camp, "wipe them out," or arrive to find they had decamped.

If they took a fancy to the horse or mule of a solitary
night guest, or even an article of dress, especially a handsome pistol, it was often sufficient to doom him without the
further expectation of money. They were much influenced
by whim, by their mood at the moment, and by opportunity,
and often deterred by an appearance of resolution or vigilance on the part of the intended victim—a drawn sword
often keeping their own in the scabbard ; and while entirely
free from the restraints of religion, a gloomy superstition
took its place and governed their actions.

At the point where the road or trail from Monterey going
north crossed the headwaters of the Pajaro or Bird River, a
recent structure of canvas had gone up. It was formed of
white muslin tacked on the three sides and over the top of
a rough frame, the front being open. It was oblong in
shape, and divided into two apartments three-fourths of its
way down, by a muslin curtain stretched across to shut off
the kitchen. It stood on the right of the trail and close by
it, and on the right bank of the stream which here flows
east. The large apartment was the dining and sleeping-
room, and contained, in furtherance of these purposes, a
small rustic table adjoining the kitchen, and a layer of dried
grass, which was spread against the south wall and kept in
place by a log. It was sufficient in length for but one person, and quite narrow. The floor, it is perhaps needless to
state, was Mother Earth ; the grass that covered it not yet
worn away, showing but recent occupancy. A hitching
post was planted in the ground on the south side a little in
rear of the front, which was all doorway. Two saddle mules
were picketed on the bank of the stream in front of the
house, nipping grass ; and a dog, ill-favored and apparently

ill-tempered, lay under a tree near by snapping viciously at flies.

The sun was setting. Two men came up from the stream where they had been taking a bath, pending the preparation of supper, and sat down in front of the tent as Digby rode up and dismounted. He had ridden sixty miles since morning and was tired ; his horse also needed rest. The tent was not there when he crossed the stream before, and he had expected to ride ten or twelve miles further on to the next house, an old adobe kept by a Mexican, where he had spent the night as he came down. He was pleased to shorten his ride, and, tying his horse to the post, he took off the saddle and bridle and carried them into the tent, gave him a feed of barley, and ordered supper. He then strolled to the front, and entered into conversation with the travelers seated there. He remarked that their mules were not unsaddled, and inquired if they were going on, or intended spending the night. They answered that they were undecided as yet, that they had thought of riding down several miles until they came to good grass and water, and camping under a tree. Digby assured them that they would have to ride many miles before they found the two combined, and they therefore concluded to stay, and went over to the mules and brought back their saddles and bridles, depositing them in the tent. They were not very talkative, but said they were going to Monterey, and turning the conversation from themselves, spoke of indifferent matters. One of them had a shrewd, observant look, and did not seem quite satisfied with their change of purpose.

Supper was announced, and they all drew up to the little table. It did not justify the time expended in its preparation, but consisted of the usual fare—flat cakes fried in grease, called " flapjacks " from the custom of flapping or turning them over by a toss of the pan ; and fat salt pork and beans, with strong black coffee served in tin cups without milk or sugar. Toward the end of the banquet the observ-ant traveler raised the curtain and stepped into the kitchen for the purpose, or under the pretense, of getting a third pint of coffee, and came back looking more solemn than ever.

After supper Digby sat down in front of the tent to smoke, and invited the travelers to join him. They accepted the ci-gars ; but after lighting them the observer proposed to his companion to lead their mules to water, and they walked off. The cook came through from the kitchen, lighted a cigar proffered him by Digby, and sat down. Presently the men came up from the water leading their mules. They stopped in front of the tent, inquired the amount of the " damage," and saddled and bridled their animals.

" You have changed your mind about staying ?" said Digby.

" Yes," replied the observant traveler, " we have con-cluded to ride to-night and rest to-morrow. The mosquitoes are bad here at the water. I would lie awake all night if I stayed."

The tone in which this was said, while guarded, was sig-nificant, and disturbed Digby. The men mounted and rode off. The cook got up from his seat and walked back to the kitchen, and, after a time, one of the men came forward and told him they were going to bed, and pointed out the grass between the log and canvas as his sleeping-place. He an-swered : " All right ! " The man retired, and perfect still-ness settled down upon the muslin inn. Digby lighted a fresh cigar and smoked on, musing on the propriety of pay-ing his bill and riding on to the adobe, until he caught him-self nodding. He then rose, threw his half-smoked cigar into the road and turned into the tent. He carried his saddle to the bed to use as a pillow, but found the grass raised at the head by a short log. He laid his saddle down, drew his pistol from his belt and stretched out on the bed, not removing his boots or slouched-hat, which was soft and protected his head from the hay. The bed was not uncomfortable, but so narrow that his body pressed against the canvas wall, and the log pillow sloping that way threw his head against it also ; but the muslin yielded, and the position was soft and pleasant. It occurred at once to Digby that he was lying in a trap. He rose to a sitting posture and attempted to push the logs in, but found them staked down. He lay down again, and almost made up his mind to saddle up and ride off ; but he was weary, and the position he was in was very grateful to his senses. His nerves relaxed, and he fell asleep.

The moon went down and darkness took the place of light. The curtain was slowly put aside, and a man in his stocking feet entered the sleeping apartment and stole cautiously to the door. As he passed Digby, who lay facing inward, he cast an anxious and scrutinizing glance at his face, the upper part of which was concealed from view by the hat. The moment the man disappeared Digby rose to his feet. He was not aroused by any noise, for the man made none, but by the presence of danger. It was not his senses that had warned him ; the spirit within him had kept watch. He took up his saddle and walked rapidly out to his horse. He saw the assassin stooping, examining the canvas, which was still bulged out at the spot where he had been sleeping. He held in his hand a bludgeon fit to fell an ox, and the ill-favored dog stood a pace or two behind him with ears erect. When he saw Digby he straightened up and stood speechless, with the club hanging down at his

right side. The dog gave a low fierce growl. Digby threw
the saddle over the horse and cocked his revolver. All this
occurred in a few seconds. They stood within eight paces of
each other, face to face. Not a word passed between them.
The dog advanced a step toward Digby and stopped, the hair
on his neck and back rigid and his teeth gleaming. It was
the nerve of a courageous gentleman against brute force.
The assassin began to back, the dog following his motions.
He halted when he reached the corner of the edifice, and
then Digby quickly accoutered his horse and sprang into the
saddle. As he rode slowly off he turned in his seat and held
his revolver half raised in a menacing attitude. As he descended the river bank, two men came to the front and
looked out. They heard the horse plunge through the water
and bound up the opposite bank, and caught sight in the
dim starlight of a shadowy horseman stretching out over
the plain.

The dog sprang down to the river and stood on the bank
barking ; the men turned into the tent.

"We must pull up stakes and be off the first thing in the
morning," said the assassin.

" Of course," answered the other, who had acted as cook ;
" but what a pity to be obliged to give up this location—a
day's ride from San Pablo. We were sure to catch them
coming up or going down. The last thing Corby said was,
that we should not stir from here until we had bagged two
at least out of the three. He will be furious when he hears
of this flush."

" He will not miss this one so much," answered the assassin. " It was the Monterey banker and the Irishman he
was hottest after. He seems to have a spite against the
Irishman ; he must have crossed him lately. He swore he

would have him, if he had to stab him in the street. If he does there will be a stab back, or I'm mistaken."

"Things are not done so easy here as at the Salt Lake," said the cook. "When a man is spotted there, he goes!"

"Stop that confounded dog's barking," said the assassin, as he lay down on the couch his intended victim had vacated. "I want to get a little sleep."

The cook called the dog into the kitchen, built up the fire and began the preparations for the morning meal. He took up the bucket and went to the river for fresh water, followed by the dog, who stood on the bank gazing over at the misty plain, growling his disapprobation at the conduct of Digby. The cakes baked, and the coffee on to boil, he sat down on the ground and fell asleep, with his head resting on his bent knees. After a time the coals under it gave way, and the coffee-pot tipped, spilling a part of its contents in the fire. The hissing woke him. He replenished the pot, and going into the front room shook the sleeping assassin by the shoulder.

"Get up," he said; "breakfast is ready."

"It is not day yet," he replied, sitting up and staring about him, rubbing his eyes.

"Breakfast is ready," repeated the cook, walking back to the kitchen, followed slowly and yawningly by his companion inquiring the hour.

"I don't know," answered the cook. "Sit down and drink your coffee."

"I'll go see, first," he replied gruffly; "I don't think the night's half gone." And walking to the door he looked across the Pajaro, low down in the heavens, at the pointers in the dipper. They told him the time, very nearly as accurately as a watch. It was a quarter past three.

" Purty time a night to wake a man up," he said, pouring out his coffee. " What do you mean by it?"

" It ain't safe to stay till daylight," answered the cook; " your friend might light down on us with the adobe men at his heels."

" What woke him up bothers me," said the assassin with a puzzled look.

" He saw you go past in his sleep."

" Nonsense !" exclaimed the other, emptying his tin cup and refilling it with coffee. " A man can't see in his sleep."

" Sometimes he kin," replied the cook; " sometimes he kin see deeper into what's goin' on when he's sound asleep than when he's wide awake. I've seed it done. I 'member one night on Dirty Devil River—you know where it is, in the Valley, empties in the Colorow."

" Yes, yes, go on; everybody knows where the Dirty Devil's located."

" Well." continued the cook, helping himself to hot coffee, and laughing as he caught himself stirring it to dissolve imaginary sugar. " Me and a angel named Ike was ordered to remove a feller in them parts that was obnoxious and put on the dead list, and we went and hired to him. We worked hard and done our duty fur three days, and he had no suspicion of us whatsomever; and the third night we fixed on to do the job, and he went to bed, and we done likewise in the room adjinen. So in the middle of the night we slipped out of bed and took our guns and was a movin' cautious into the kitchen, when we heered his bed creak. and we stopped. Then we heered his door shut, which it was open before, and we sot down on our bed and waited.

" ' What waked him?' whispered Ike. the other angel.

" ' Maybe some noise outside,' says I.

" ' But there wasn't none,' says he, ' or we'd a heerd it likewise.'

" ' Maybe,' says I, ' a dream waked him ; but why,' says I, ' did he shet the door?'

" ' 'Twas the dirty devil whispered him to do it,' says Ike, ' him that goes around like a roaren lion a thwarten of us angels.' Ike was great on quoten Scripter.

" ' Do you think he. giv' him notice of our intentions?' says I.

" ' Like es not,' says he ; ' he's none too good fur it !'

" ' Why don't the prophet bind him ?' says I.

" ' 'Cause he's too fur away,' says he ; ' the prophet can't spread out like the devil. He's strong about Lake City, but his power gits weaker and weaker as you git furder away, and the devil keeps a-gitten stronger. Ef we'd a-been nigh the City this man wouldn't a-waked, that's dead sure.'

" So I said I'd heerd say the devil was to be chained some day. And Ike said when the Saints spread over the face of the earth, and the Gentiles was all dead, he'd be chained, and not afore.

" So we kep' a-whisperin' on about the devil and the prophet, till we giv' Number Fifty-Three plenty time to fall asleep ; and Ike said ef I'd carry the candle he'd do the shootin'. So we slipped up to the door, and opened her easy and looked in. The winder was up, and Fifty-Three was non est in wentis."

" Was he ever found ? " inquired the assassin, lighting his pipe by the ingenious method of thrusting it into the fire and withdrawing it crowned with red-hot ashes.

" Never," answered the cook, filling his pipe, or loading it, as he termed the operation. " Ike and me, we tracked him in the mornin', and kept the trail till we got to Cataract

Canyon on the Colorow. There we was throw'd off and couldn't find it ag'in."

" Ef you'd a-follered the Colorow down into the Gentile land of Arizona you'd a-found him," said the assassin.

"I dessay," replied the cook ; "but we didn't."

The cook rolled the blankets into two bundles and filled a small bag with provisions. The men walked to the front ; the assassin drew a match on the sole of his boot and touched it to the canvas ; and the saintly couple walked down to the Pajaro and ascended the stream, sheltered by its banks from the glare shed over the surrounding plain by the burning building. The dog barked with pleasure at the prospect of the ramble before him and received in return a kick from the assassin. The cotton canvas was soon reduced to ashes, but the frame stood smoking, here and there emitting a tongue of flame that served as a guide to the assassins, who had ascended the north bank, and were walking over the plain in the direction of San Francisco, to make report at the Saints Rest in that city of their disastrous failure.

They were many days on the way, and when at length they reached their destination and the cook related the story, ending in the burning and the flitting in the night, the brow of Corby grew dark. He inquired of the cook what he thought of himself. The cook answered that he didn't know but thought it was the devil.

" You men will be of no use here any longer," said Corby, after some thought. " There is a camp of our people on the Yuba where it breaks through into the plain. Go there for the present. You may take a rest for a day or two," he added, as they were leaving the room. " Come to me when you are ready to start. I will send some word up by you."

" Failure on failure," said Marcus, as the men of the Pajaro closed the door. " But amid it all we have our consolations. Within the past month Numbers Eleven and Fifteen have quit the scene—the gay and festive scene, as the poet facetiously terms it."

"This set in which I am specially interested," replied Corby, " seem to sleep with their eyes open. It's my opinion they've got protection of some sort. Solomon, too, has weakened of late. When I told him I had given up his special case, he said : ' All right ; he's a dangerous man ; let him alone.' I think he is beginning to grow lukewarm in the cause. I think Mammon is corrupting the millionaire."

" Let the Ladrone have a rest, by all means," said Marcus. " I drink to his ultimate destruction. Give him rope and in due time he will grow careless and be gathered in. Patience, and shuffle the cards."

CHAPTER XV.

THE proposal of marriage made by Don Antonio was considered in family council at San Pablo. The senora suggested
that the pretendiente should be required to lay before them
proofs of the standing of his family, but the Franciscan
feared this demand would wound his feelings, and the Mexican Minister at Washington was written to for the information. The approval of his father and mother was a sine qua
non ; they would not allow their daughter to enter his family
without it. In due time favorable letters were received, and
Don Manuel informed him they would be happy to welcome
him into the Velasco family. As the senora wished the wedding to take place on the same day of the month on which
her own had been celebrated, and as that period was not far
off, a party set out for San Francisco to purchase the para-
phernalia, composed of Don Manuel, the Franciscan, Don
Antonio and Mulcahy, now become a favorite at San Pablo.
On the third day after their arrival in the city, Don Manuel and the Franciscan crossed over to Contra Costa, intending to ride home through Alameda and make a visit to the
old mission of San Jose. Don Antonio remained to get his
wedding outfit, and Mulcahy to see the town.

In the early days there landed in San Francisco, from the
convict settlement of Sydney, in New South Wales, many
desperate characters who had graduated in crime in England,
and who pursued their avocation with such a high and bloody
hand that the name of " Sydney Duck," by which they were
popularly known, was held in detestation throughout the

land. Pre-eminent among them in evil was a man named Wade ; blood-stained and audacious, he haunted the city of tents by night as its evil genius, and committed murder upon murder. The sun seldom rose in those days without looking down on a fresh tragedy. The vigilance committee was formed, and while it did not overlook the lesser villains, and had abundant material to keep it in motion, a part doubtless innocent, it bent its energies to the tracking and capture of Wade. Hundreds of eyes were looking for him day and night, but they looked in vain ; he seemed to have the receipt of fernseed—he walked invisible.

As Don Antonio returned from the wharf, after seeing his friends embark for Contra Costa, and walked down Montgomery street on his way to his tailor's, he passed a fashionable drinking saloon, in front of which a crowd had been collected by a quarrel between two well-dressed men. The belligerents had been separated, and were surrounded each by a knot of his particular friends, and the whole encompassed by a crowd of idlers, talking and gesticulating. It was lunch time, at which hour the bars were crowded with votaries, and a stream of men, stimulated by the late excitement to frequent libations, passed into the bar and back to the pavement with surprisingly short intervals between drinks. The late encounter was voted a bore, and the opinion freely expressed that the parties had permitted themselves to be separated with altogether too much docility. The conversation turned upon a peculiarly atrocious deed that had been committed during the preceding night, bearing the marks of Wade, and his name, coupled with deadly imprecations, resounded on all sides.

It was at this moment that Don Antonio, with a rapid step, turned into the middle of the street to avoid the crowd, and as he did so a voice called out : "There goes Wayne!"

and a man made a rapid push to overtake him. This call
and movement acted on the crowd like a match struck in a
volume of inflammable gas. The name, imperfectly caught
and perhaps thickly uttered ; the movement in pursuit ; and
the resemblance to Wade in form and height were enough.
A simultaneous rush, like the spring to the stampede of a
herd of wild cattle, was made on him. In a moment he was
the center of a furious throng. The cry of "Wade" caused
men to swarm from the habitations and cross streets like
bees. His hat was knocked from his head, his coat and vest
torn from his back, his watch, chain, and money appropriated, and blows rained down on him, but with small effect,
by reason of the close pack. The mob poured down the street
with Don Antonio in the center, filling it from house wall to
opposite house wall—a living tide, uttering a roar of exultation and rage.

When a man is seized and shaken by a wild beast, the
powers of his mind and faculties of sense are all instantly in
abeyance, save that of observation. He looks up at the
animal standing over and possessing him, with a dreamy
consciousness of his presence and acts ; but feels no pain
and no fear. He is interested in all the details that occur,
but as a looker-on, not personally. Such was the state of
Don Antonio as he was hurried to execution.

The bell at the headquarters of the vigilantes was rung
violently, and numbers hastily responded to the call. At
the head of this improvised force and the guards within the
building, the officers, led by Solomon Stubbs, the Mormon
millionaire, rushed out to the rescue and intercepted the
mob. They were mortified and stung at having been deprived of the honor of his arrest, and demanded the possession of Wade to hang him from the committee window.
The mob were on the way to a favorite sand hill and refused

to surrender their victim, and a struggle immediately ensued. The mob and the vigilantes were "two lions littered in one day," but the vigilantes were the "elder and more terrible," and the mob gave way.

En route to their committee rooms with their captive, followed by the maddened crowd, they were suddenly and successfully charged at a crossing by a band of police, who wrested the prey from their grasp, placed him in a light wagon, and drove him on a fast gallop to the city prison. All this occurred like magic, with such celerity and push that the stupefied crowd woke up to what was being done too late. But the roar that followed the awakening was like the roar of the ocean. They rushed to the prison in thousands and demanded Wayne's surrender with hoarse cries of indignation and rage. But the authorities, who lately had exhibited pusillanimity, and had sunk into contempt, were determined to retrieve their characters and protect their prisoner, so gallantly captured, at any and at all cost.

The baffled crowd after a time withdrew, giving out that they were satisfied to leave the case in the hands of the constituted authorities. But this deceived no one, and the prison was at once converted into a fortress, the doors and windows were barricaded within in a formidable manner, and one hundred staunch men introduced armed to the teeth. In the meantime the vigilantes sent down a committee to complain of the unwarrantable interference of the police, and to demand "their prisoner," under dire threats in case of what they termed a foolhardy refusal. But the men within were strung up to the highest tension, and declared their determination to defend their fortress to the last.

As soon as Don Antonio was safely lodged in prison, Morales and Hayward visited the Vigilance Committee rooms, with Mulcahy, who had been in the tumult and had recognized Don Antonio. The Mormon inquired if they had seen the man, and finding that only Mulcahy— who was unknown to them—had done so, they laughed in their faces and assured them they were mistaken. They then went immediately to the prison, were admitted, and had an interview with the prisoner. Hayward told the chief of police he might draw his check upon the bank in the tens of thousands if he could succeed in getting Wayne out of the city. The chief answered that the prison was closely watched, to frustrate any such attempt, and that his only chance for life was within the walls. He declined more aid, saying that he already had as many men in the prison as he could handle. They returned to the committee rooms and had an interview with the leading men. The Mormon declared that the man was Wade; that he knew him well. Others said the same, and that it was a movement on the part of the " Law and Order Men," to which Morales and Hayward belonged, to cheat justice and triumph over the committee. However, several leading business men who knew Morales well sided with him, and a heated discussion followed, which divided and paralyzed the committee, as far as any attempt on the prison was concerned by them as an organization. Mulcahy informed the Mormon that, if any harm came to Don Antonio through him, he would wring his head off, and that, if any gentleman present would present him with half a cent, he would do it then and there, surrounded as he was by his myrmidons. The millionaire responded that he would hang Mulcahy from the committee window with his Sydney Duck friend. On which several able-bodied men were required to assist his friends in getting Mulcahy into the street.

Hand-bills were struck off and scattered and posted far and wide over the city to allay the excitement, giving the true state of the case, and containing the sworn statements of Don Antonio's friends ; but they were utterly scorned and rejected as a weak device of the enemy.

At ten o'clock at night the rush was made upon the jail. It was surrounded in a few minutes by a vast concourse, estimated at ten thousand. The door and windows were assailed with sledge hammers wielded by powerful arms. The blows were seen to fall thick and fast, but were unheard amid the roar. Men flung their arms up in savage gesticulation, their faces distorted by passion, and showing blood-red in the glare of a hundred torches. An old white-haired gentleman, respectable in dress and appearance, who doubtless came merely to look on, suddenly broke out into a frenzy, and, after raving for a time, ended by calling out at the top of his now hoarse voice—" Blood ! blood ! blood!" Mulcahy, who, with the Ladrone, stood behind and a little above him, disgusted at seeing a gentleman so demean himself, reached forward and crushed his hat down over his eyes. The struggle of the old man to get at him was frantic, but he was wedged in by the crowd and quite helpless. The incident only drew forth a laugh.

Up to this time the assault had proved a failure. The main door, against which their chief efforts had been directed, though battered, was still unbreached. The leader of the mob, speaking from the upper step, restored a degree of quiet. and was heard to announce " that he had called a parley. and demanded the admittance into the jail of a party of men just arrived in the city from Monterey, the residence of the banker Wayne mentioned in the handbills, who could settle the question of identity. That the chief of police" —here he was interrupted by a storm of hisses and anathemas directed at that functionary—" that the chief of police," he continued, " had agreed to let in the deputation, provided the crowd fell back to an indicated distance." He ordered them to fall back and send to the front the party from Monterey, who were in durance on the outskirt. This was accordingly done, and the deputation was admitted. Being led to his cell, Don Antonio recognized several of them, notably a quack doctor, and addressed them by name ; but they looked scared and dubious, and failed to return his salutations. He recalled instances of their acquaintanceship, and entreated them to recognize and save him. But they said they knew him not. They so reported to the mob, when dismissed from the jail with contempt, and were loudly cheered as they slunk away into the darkness.

It was now midnight, and the leader changed his tactics. He was satisfied an entrance could not be forced with sledge hammers. He ordered a lane to be opened in the crowd to the street leading to the plaza, and up it he now marched, followed in double file by the men of action, some forty or fifty in number. He ordered the crowd to keep the lane open and to stand fast, and they obeyed to a man, saving two—Hayward and Mulcahy—who walked along the pavement opposite the leader, giving him all their attention. The column kept the middle of the street. The Ladrone and his companion were dressed in blue blouses and slouched hats. Not a soul was met on the street. They moved with a rapid step, and filed to the right into the plaza to the front of the old adobe Custom House. An ax was produced and the leader swung it in the air and sunk it to the handle in the flagstaff. The Ladrone's heart sank within him. His companion cast a deadly look at the axman.

" A battering ram !" muttered the Ladrone to Mulcahy, who whispered in his ear a few words in reply.

" Good !" said Hayward, with a nod.

The flagstaff fell, scattering the men in front of it. The

axman cut the slim end into handbars, and they were distributed under the main trunk, which a row of men on either·
side raised from the ground, and the procession moved off,
carrying the heavy end foremost. The night was dark. In
advance strode the leader, the Danton of the Avenging
Angels, with a pine-knot torch in his hand. He was a Her-
cules in size and strength, dressed in corduroys and a red
flannel shirt open at the throat, showing his red, hairy
breast. The sleeves were rolled up above the elbows, and the
sinews stood out on his bare arms like whipcords. A blow
from him would have felled an ox, and doubtless, cleaver in
hand, had already brought down scores of them. As he
turned from the plaza into the street, the Ladrone and Mulcahy joined him and walked alongside, the one on his left,
the other on his right.

"Now," said the Ladrone insinuatingly to him as he
stepped up, "we are coming to business."

"Yes," replied the stalwart, with a savage laugh, "the
end is near."

The two men, one on each side of him, quickened their
step and forced the pace, and the column with the battering
ram began to fall to the rear. The street and sidewalks were
paved with pine lumber. A fire a day or two before had
burned several buildings on the right with the sidewalk and
gutter in their front, and at one point nearly to the middle
of the street, exposing to view the sewer, flushed by recent
rain, deep down through which rushed a current of slush and
water. One of the two gentlemen who had so suddenly fra-
ternized with the stalwart, the one on his right, Mulcahy,
locked arms with him as they approached this spot : the light
of the torch flashed back from the waters of the sewer and
the next moment was extinguished. There was a slight,
momentary shuffling of feet in the dark, and all was silent.

The column halted and set down the battering-ram. The torch-bearer, who was bringing up the rear, was called for and came to the front. The commanding figure of the leader in the red shirt had vanished. The couple who a moment before had been walking by his side were gone. A panic seized the bearers of the ram. One of them took the torch and hurried to the cross street a few yards in advance, and looked up and down and called. No answer. He continued on rapidly to the jail, and called out in inquiry to the crowd. He was not there. The man was frightened and excited, and the torch he held disclosed his pale face to all about him. He called aloud in a tremulous tone that their leader had supernaturally disappeared and the devil must have carried him off. He communicated his tremor to those within hearing, and it ran through the entire multitude; the lane closed up and dissolution set in; and when the cathedral clock struck one the mob was dead.

Corby had witnessed the attack from a window in an upper story that commanded a view of the jail. Marcus and Simeon sat near him, having ridden down in his company from the Saints' Rest, the one to give counsel if called on, the other to execute such orders as he might find it necessary to issue. Several retainers, stationed here and there in the crowd, brought in reports from time to time of the condition of affairs, and returned to their posts with such instructions as he found it pertinent to give. A messenger came into the room breathless with haste, to announce the arrival of the Monterey party, and the proposition to admit them to the jail. Corby turned quickly to Simeon.

"Work your way in to Gath," he said sharply, "and tell him I say admit them, but to warn them as they pass in of the danger if they disappoint the people. Hint that the opinion is spreading that they are confederates of the assassin. You," he said, turning to the messenger who had brought the intelligence, " go back and whisper the same to each of the Monterey men, as they are making their way to the jail door. When the honest witnesses come out and report," he said, with a diabolical laugh as the messengers hurried from the room, " the mob will make a savage assault; any little doubt of the identity of the banker and the bandit will vanish."

" I wouldn't have the nerve to risk it," replied Marcus uneasily ; " these men may tell the truth when they come out. Who knows?"

" I know," answered Corby with a sneer. " They'll lie like dogs."

Presently Simeon returned and resumed his stand behind the chair of Corby. The Monterey men ascended the steps. of the jail, and Gath in his red shirt with a torch in his hand was seen bending over and looking them in the face. The door closed on them and a hush of expectation fell upon the mob.

" What was that disturbance I saw a few minutes ago?" inquired Corby of a messenger who entered with a report.

" Some one crushed the hat over the ·face of an old gentleman." answered the messenger.

" What for ?"

" He was yelling for blood," he answered, " and a man in a blouse and slouch hat seemed to disapprove of it."

" What sort of a man was he?" inquired Corby suspiciously.

" He was a slim man," answered the messenger, " and talked with a brogue. He laughed and taunted the old gentleman, who couldn't get at him for the crowd." •

" The Irishman, Mulcahy," said Corby, turning pale with

anger; "I'll take the life of the insolent alien, even if I die in doing it."

"The Irish are no good," said Marcus, puffing his cigar and putting his head out of the window to take an observation ; "you can't make a Saint out of them to save your life."

"They're wedded to their idols," joined in Simeon ; "they laugh at the new light."

"They won't listen to reason," responded Marcus ; "that's what's the matter with them."

"Deaf as adders and blind as bats," replied Simeon, "they won't listen to the new gospel, nor they won't see the new truth. They are foreordained to the bottomless pit. That's my judgment."

"Let the stiff-necked heretics go to perdition," said Corby, irritated by the subject of the conversation, "and look out of the window; there's a stir in the crowd below."

"The door of the jail is opening," said Marcus. "The men of Monterey are coming out. Gath is speaking to them. One has taken his hat off and is addressing the mob. Hear the roar of satisfaction. Holy Prophet, what a din !"

"They rush to the assault !" said Corby. "See the swing of Gath's hammer. What awful power the man has ! Well is he called Goliath, the lion of the Valley !"

"Now," said Simeon in a tone of exultation, "let the Gentile tremble, the slayer of the Saints !"

The group at the window sat looking down on the surging mass of humanity beneath, in the confident hope that each succeeding minute would witness a breach at some point in the fortress and the pouring in of the enraged assailants. But as time passed without this happy consummation Corby became impatient and ordered Simeon down with a message to Gath.

o

" Tell him," he said, " to fire the building forthwith."

" If I can get to him through the press," replied Simeon doubtfully.

" You must get to him," said Corby sternly. " Go ! "

" Simeon has reached him," he said presently. " See, the work has stopped, and Gath is speaking to the people from the steps."

" He has not had time to work his way there," replied Marcus. "What is that movement in the crowd. They seem to be forming a lane ? "

" They are forming a lane," answered Corby. " They are going for combustibles to fire the jail. There go the firemen with Gath at their head. What an imposing figure ! what a leader of men ! the lion of Judah ! the sword of the Prophet ! "

" He does look warlike," responded Marcus, leaning from the window to watch the stalwart, " with his blood-red shirt open at the breast, his gigantic figure, and his flaring torch. His red sleeves are rolled up, I see, ready I take it to operate on the cursed Gentile when he gets at him. What a condition that sinner must be in, hearing the roar of ten thousand voices for his blood. I would very many times rather be sitting at this window smoking than to be in his place."

" The report I had circulated this afternoon," said Corby, "that Hayward was implicated with this wretch in the Monterey murder, did noble work."

" Took the wind completely out of their sails," replied Marcus with a laugh. " It was wisely indefinite and mysterious, and gave the impression that the two were old chums, and were out of the city on that occasion after fresh air. The heading of the printed slip was good. ' The assassin Wade and the Grand Ladrone on the circuit,' took well."

A messenger interrupted the conversation to announce that Gath with his working party were seen to turn into the plaza.

" What are they after? " asked Corby, with a smile.

" No one knows," answered the messenger.

" Follow and find out," said Corby indifferently.

" Gath gave positive orders that no one should follow," said the man.

" He'll turn up presently," said Corby, with a smile. " Go out and keep your eyes open."

" I couldn't get near him," said Simeon, entering at this moment. " The press back of the crowd as the lane was opened made it impossible. I was wedged in tight. He has gone to the plaza."

" Gone of his own motion for combustibles," said Marcus.

" I shouldn't wonder," responded Simeon ; " I saw a pile of pine lumber there as I passed this afternoon."

" Sit down and wait," said Corby ; " he will show up presently. Was the pile a large one? "

" Large enough to fire two jails."

" Good ! now wait."

They sat in silent expectation for ten minutes, when Marcus suddenly rose and thrust his head out of the window.

" What movement is that going on down there? " he said. " The noise is hushed ; the lane is closing up. I believe in my soul the crowd is breaking."

" Not possible !" exclaimed Corby, leaning out of the window and looking down. " What is the matter with them? They seem demented. They are moving off, by Heaven ! "

"Gath is gone!" exclaimed a man, rushing in out of breath.

"Gone where?" said Corby, drawing in his head and turning fiercely on him.

"No one knows," was the answer. "One of his band run down from the plaza and struck a panic in the crowd. Said the Evil Spirit had whisked him off in a jiffy, torch and all; appeared at his side in the form of a bony figure."

"The Irishman!" exclaimed Corby, turning pale with dismay.

"The audacity of that man," said Marcus, throwing his half smoked cigar, with a violent jerk, out of the window on to the heads of the crowd below, "is inconceivable. What kind of death can be gotten up to suit his special case? Burning at the stake is too good for him."

"Well, Marcus," replied Corby, with a sickly attempt at humor, "I will appoint you to catch him. Deal with him as you like. Come, let us ride. We played our cards well, but fate has trumped our winning trick."

As they rode by the cathedral on their way to the Saints' Rest the bell high up in the solitary tower tolled one.

CHAPTER XVI.

FATE OF THE FOUR LANDLORDS.

THE marriage of Don Antonio and Dolores was a brilliant affair. It took place soon after the return of the gentlemen from San Francisco, and Don Pedro and the Senora Catalina, who, with her household, had joined him in San Francisco, were honored guests. He had a private interview with the Franciscan, in which he related the incidents of the Mormon plot, and begged him to vindicate to the family the reputation of the Grand Ladrone, handing him a paper to lay among the presents at the close of the evening as a memento of the night on the Mariposa. When the last guest had departed the Franciscan took Don Manuel by the arm, and. leading him into the library, pointed to a paper lying upon the table among the jewels. As his eye fell upon the superscription he turned pale. The dream of his life was realized. It was a deed from Hayward to the Senorita Dolores for the alienated lands. The silence and charity of Don Manuel at the trial of the Ladrone had received their reward. Silence is golden—Charity above all !

When Mulcahy turned over the keys to Don Antonio he returned to San Francisco and reported to Don Pedro, in whose service he was now regularly enlisted. As there was no special need of him at this time, he was granted a leave of absence, and passed several days very pleasantly in the company of such friends from the mines as came in his way, and enjoyed the pleasure of bearding the Mormon lion in a saloon in the presence of his friends. But as he found no fight in him, he turned contemptuously away and

gave him up, gratified, however, in having put down the
millionaire committeeman who had threatened to suspend
him from a window. But Mulcahy was a man of action, and
these idle pleasures palled upon him. He offered to Digby
to go over to the Mariposa and settle up for him his outstanding affairs, at the same time paying several small bills
that he himself had contracted there in his hours of idleness.
Digby, whose time was occupied with serious matters at the
bank, had not been able to go. He was very well pleased at
this offer, and duly commissioned Mulcahy to wind up his
affairs in that quarter.

Accordingly, Mulcahy set out, well mounted and armed,
and pursued his way leisurely, halting the first night at San
Jose, and reaching the cabin in the Pacheco Pass on the following afternoon. He found but one of the men on the
premises, Dutch Charley with two others having gone
north through the mountains to the neighborhood of Stockton to dispose of some animals they had collected in the
gorge in their nefarious pursuit. He ordered a feed of barley for his horse, took a cold lunch and lay down on the
bench on the porch to take a short siesta. When he awoke,
he called the landlord, to pay him his bill ; but getting no
response, he tightened the girths of his saddle, put the bit
in the mouth of his horse, unhitched him, and looked up and
down the trail. It then occurred to him that the man had
gone back into the gorge, and, mounting, he rode in. When
he reached the lofty jagged stump on the bank of the stream
he halted and looked about him, but saw nothing of the
man. His horse, availing himself of the pause, reached
down and began cropping the short sod. In reaching forward to recover the rein of the bridle, which had fallen on
the animal's neck, he noticed what seemed to him to be a spot
of blood on the stump near its base. Passing his eye up, he

perceived another near its top. His curiosity was now excited, and he determined to investigate the matter. Reining
his horse close up, he drew his feet from the stirrups, rose to
his knees and then to his feet, and stood in the saddle. The
height of his horse, which was a tall one, and his own height
just enabled him to look in. The first object that greeted
his sight was a pair of boots, the feet upward, and nearly on
a level with the break through which he was looking. Rising on his toes he was enabled to look a little further down,
and saw on one of the red leather tops, printed in black ink,
the name—

" EBRIGHT."

The best friend he had in the mines, an old and valued
crony ! He saw, too, in the second that elapsed before he
dropped into the saddle, that other bodies were there. He
drew his revolver, cocked it, and dropped it into the right-
hand pocket of his coat and rode slowly back to the house.
He dismounted, tied his horse, and ascending the steps,
crossed the porch and entered the barroom. The landlord
had returned, and was in the kitchen. Mulcahy rapped on
the counter, and, when the call was answered, ordered a
glass of brandy, bought a bunch of Manilla cigars, and inquired for his bill. Lighting a cigar, he leaned on the counter
and talked pleasantly for a few minutes, meanwhile watching
the man covertly. He paid his bill, bid the man good-even-
ing, lounged down to his horse. mounted, and rode slowly
down the mountain trail.

At noon on the second day following he halted at the
Manley ranch on the Mariposa and took dinner ; after which
he held a consultation with the Manleys and the Mexican.
Ebright was well known along the river. He was of a com-

manding figure and powerful frame, and a successful man, good-humored, friendly, and charitable. It was the latter quality that cost him his life, for he was on his way to the city on an errand for a dying man when he last entered the Pacheco Pass.

"We will get the Allens down to-night," said one of the Manleys, "and they, with four men from over the river, will be enough. Notify them as you go up. We will start at daybreak."

"No," said the Mexican, "wait until you hear by some one coming up that the vultures are all on the roost. They are off on a spree now, and may not be back for a week. Do not go down, ten of you, on one poor chap. Give the fellows a chance."

"He is right," said Mulcahy. "Take them in a bunch. I could have shot the one man myself, and was tempted to do it; but I knew it would flush the covey. I did think of inquiring when his friends would be back; but I weighed it awhile and gave it up. He had no suspicion of the discovery. Be patient and bag the entire gang."

On passing up the river Mulcahy stayed all night with the Allens, and advised them of the proposed expedition to the pass; and two days after a messenger galloped up and summoned them.

On the second day after leaving Manley's in the afternoon the Mariposa party of ten approached the cabin, riding slowly single file along the path, their weapons out of sight, and assuming, as far as they were able, the appearance of innocent travelers. Bill Allen was in the lead, and as he rode up inquired if they could get some barley and something to drink. A man stretched on the bench on the porch answered in the affirmative, and rising, called to two comrades who were playing cards in the bar, who stopped their game and came to the door. As the party one after another came up they quietly dismounted and made fast their horses, and one by one ascended to the porch and entered the barroom. Two men went behind the bar to serve them and the other brought out from the kitchen a bag of barley and weighed out the feeds. Bill Allen, to whom was assigned the lead, bought and distributed several bunches of puros, a strong Mexican cigar cut off square at both ends and popular among seasoned smokers, and began smoking to while away the time until the appearance of the fourth man. The men carried out their portions of barley, fed their horses and returned. Several stopped on the porch to talk with the barley man ; others entered and went up in couples, asking for fresh drinks.

Still the fourth man did not appear. Bill Allen strolled into the kitchen and back, and now noticed an air of uneasiness coming over the men behind the bar. He stepped up to the counter and called for another drink. As he did so he took off his slouch hat and threw it on the counter. This was the preliminary signal, and the conversation in the room ceased.

" Where, you dog ! " he said fiercely, as he took the glass from the man's hand and hurled it back in his face, " is Ebright ? "

The sound of the murdered man's name mingled with the report of revolvers. The barley man dropped on the porch where he had stood talking. The man who had just served Allen fell to the floor with the fragments of the glass that was shattered on his forehead, his face and hair wet with its contents. The third, who had made a rush for life, fell in the kitchen, and in a moment was shrouded in the smoke that poured back through the barroom door. Not a pistol had been drawn by the landlords, the onset had been so sudden and the aim of the men of the Mariposa so true.

Dutch Charley was approaching the house from the rear, and was within a few hundred yards when he heard the fusillade. He instantly turned about and fled up the gorge into the mountains. The Mariposans ransacked the house, then fired it, and withdrew. Dutch Charley witnessed the conflagration from the mountain, and experienced his first remorse. The bodies of the three landlords· were cremated in the burning cabin. In the huge stump on the bank of the little rivulet, the hollow remnant of a mighty pine, a sepulcher that once rose higher into the air and was longer in construction than a pyramid, was found the remains of over .forty men.

Dutch Charley came down into the gorge in the night and unearthed the blood-stained treasure to which he had fallen sole heir. It was in gold coin and dust, in several buckskin belts, in use for carrying considerable sums, which were worn about the body under the clothing. He stripped and buckled them about his waist, and then hunted about for a horse; but the party from the Mariposa had carried them off, loaded with the plunder of the cabin. He crept down in the shade of the forest and looked for some time at the smoking ruins of his habitation, a place that it would be a desecration of the term to call his home. He felt pain at the catastrophe, at the fate of his partners in guilt; but no compunctious visitings of conscience for his crimes, no pity for his victims. But what troubled him the most of all was his loss of courage. His confidence in himself, bred of long impunity, was gone. He felt cowed and frightened. He tried to solve in his mind how the disaster had been brought about. He knew from the volley that had been fired that it was no chance affray. The men had come on purpose, that was clear. While sitting on a rock watching the fire still at work on an upright log that had not yet fallen in, a thought suddenly struck him and he hit the true solution. The comrade who had remained at the cabin during their late absence had casually related, on their return, that he had walked up the trail looking for a stray mule, leaving a tall man sleeping on the bench ; and on his return, finding him gone, had supposed he had ridden off without paying his bill. But that it turned out he had ridden up the gorge, and, on coming down, had dismounted and spent some time smoking and drinking. He said he was a smart, shrewd, jovial fellow, that had gone through the pass before, well-mounted and well-dressed, and no doubt had money. Dutch Charley had responded that he was sorry he had missed his acquaintance, and the subject was dropped, the conversation passing out of his mind. Now it came back.

A vision came over him as he sat in the dark, of a tall, well-mounted man standing up in the saddle and looking into the sepulcher ; of his riding back to the cabin and cajoling his comrade. Presently the burning log fell with a crash into the coals and ashes, sending up ·a shower of sparks and startled him, putting an end to his reverie. He crept back into the mountain, and, after getting at a distance from the ruin, fell into the northern trail and pursued it until daylight, when he laid down in the bushes and slept.

When he awoke he sat awhile collecting his thoughts. He had dreamed that the money about him would bring him to death. Fear had fallen on him. He determined to quit the country. He arranged in his mind to go to Stockton and take a steamer for San Francisco. He had no money with him besides that buckled about his body. It occurred

to him to steal a mule when he descended from the mountain, and sell it when he reached Stockton ; but he lacked
the courage. Yet he felt a superstitious fear of taking off
his belts and using that money, and it so mastered him that
he got up and pursued his journey. But he found himself
sore about the waist. He was carrying no weight to distress
a man of his strength, some twenty odd pounds, but the
location of it next the skin was oppressive, and he felt he
would be unable to endure it as far as Stockton. He turned
into the bushes, stripped, took off the belts and readjusted
them, taking out sufficient to buy a mule and pay his way to
New York, resolving not to take them from his body again
until he reached the end of his journey.

At the first ranch he came to in the valley, he got his
supper, bought a mule, saddle and bridle, and rode on a few
miles, and slept in the prairie under an oak. When he
reached Stockton, he learned that no steamer would leave
until the next day ; so, after getting his dinner, he rode out
of town, afraid to remain over night where his person was
somewhat known. Once outside of the town, he feared to
return ; he was in fact pursued by fear, and resolved to push
on to Sacramento, a long journey, where no one knew him,
and take the steamer from that port. He rode on till night,
taking supper at a tent, but riding on into the plain to sleep.
Thus he continued his journey until he reached Sacramento
one morning about ten o'clock. He made his way at once to
the Fifth street horse market, and put his mule and accouterments in line for sale. He received a hundred dollars for
the outfit, and putting the money in his pocket, walked down
to the river. The steamer *Senator*, he was informed, was
expected in during the night ; and would go down after unloading in the forenoon.

He wandered about the city all afternoon and until past

midnight, restless and uneasy, from one drinking and gambling house to another ; punting a little at a table here and there, but cautiously and with varied success. Toward midnight he entered a room containing but a few tables and but thinly attended. Here he took a drink, lit a fresh cigar, and began to bet. After a few games, thinking he saw certain success, he took out his purse and laid it on a card.

The card did not win. It was not the one he supposed it was, though he felt certain he recognized it by a mark on the back. The instant he perceived he had lost, the dread of having to take off his belts again flashed over him : he snatched the purse from the table, drew his revolver and made quickly for the door. An attempt was made to intercept him, but his old audacity had returned for the moment, and he successfully effected his exit. He walked rapidly down the dark street, turned up at a crossing, and after passing several squares entered a cheap restaurant and lodging house that was still open, sat down at a table and took supper. He secured a bunk and lay down with his clothes on.

He had a restless night, and rose at dawn. He walked the streets, taking a drink here and there at early bars, until he could secure a breakfast ; after which he walked down to the river and boarded the *Senator*, a large and elegant steamer, that had arrived in the night and already commenced to unload. The clerk to whom he applied for a ticket told him that their agent at the office on shore had sold all the tickets the day before, and they could take no more passengers. He offered to pay any price for a passage, but the answer was a peremptory "No!" As he was going down the gangway the clerk called after him :

"If you will help unload, and work your passage, you can go down free."

This was customary when hands were scarce, as the steamers were anxious to get their cargoes ashore and be off without delay. It was also a custom for such passengers to leave
their money belts on deposit with the clerk in his safe, as it
was impossible for them to do the rapid and heavy work
exacted with them on. As Charley stood hesitating, the clerk
guessed the cause, adding—

"If you have a money belt on, bring it to the office and I
will deposit it in the safe."

He turned and walked back up the gangway, his intense
desire to get a passage overcoming his superstitious fear of
taking off his belts. He went into the office with the clerk,
stripped and unbuckled his belts and handed them over.
The clerk threw them on the scales, weighed them, tied
them together with a cord, and attached a tag, on which
he wrote in ink—

"CHARLES CHANDLER.
Gold.
23lbs."

To this he added his name and handed a duplicate tag to
Dutch Charley, who was now transformed into a "roust-
about," and went vigorously to work unloading. The men
were driven by the mate like galley slaves, and by ten o'clock
the cargo was ashore, the passengers aboard, and the *Senator*
steamed away from the landing.

Dutch Charley could not get the attention of the clerk
until the boat got under way. He then entered the office
and the clerk unlocked the safe and handed out the belts.
He strapped them on under his clothing and walked out on
the upper deck. He should have descended to the lower
deck ; for, being a hand, he had no right to remain among

the first class passengers. He knew this perfectly well ; but nevertheless he crossed over and took his seat on the rail on the right hand side. There were very few persons at this time on deck, the passengers being in the cabin stowing away their baggage in their staterooms. Presently the captain, in his uniform and gold-laced cap, came down from the bridge, walked rapidly aft to the wheel, and gave some sharp direction to the steersman. He then stepped quickly over to the rail, near by where Dutch Charley was seated, and looked over the side. A boat that the men had neglected to haul up was dragging through the water and filling from the spray thrown back by the wheel.

" Down there, one of you," he called out in a loud angry tone, " and stand in the stern of that boat until we can haul her up."

Dutch Charley was the only " hand " on the quarter-deck, and, impelled by the savage tone of the captain, he went over the side, climbed down the ladder, and stepped off into the bow of the boat, which was directly under him. This tipped the bow down and exposed the boat to the full action of the wheel, and it began to fill rapidly. The boat swayed so that Dutch Charley made no attempt to reach the stern, as directed, but maintained his position and held on to the boat-rope. The captain, in a rage, throwing a curse at him, called out to a sailor who had run up to " cut the rope." It was too late to pull her up, as she was half full of water, and the only way to save her from going to pieces was to cut her adrift. In a moment the knife flashed from the sailor's belt and the rope was severed. The boat plunged head on and overturned, throwing Dutch Charley into the water. The boat did not sink. but floated bottom up, falling astern. The man sank, but rose to the surface, and, throwing his head back, kept merely his face above water. The boat and he drifted down but a few yards apart, but he was too heavily freighted to make way to it. He must have been a skillful swimmer to have even held his face out of the water as he did.

In the meantime the steamer had forged ahead and left him some distance behind. The engines were reversed and a boat lowered. The clerk called out that the man had eight thousand dollars in gold on his person. The sailors bent to their oars, nearing him rapidly. The passengers crowded the decks and watched the drama with intense interest and anxiety. The boat was almost on him—his face shone above the water, red with the rush of blood. The boatswain rose in the bow, leaned over and was stretching out his arm when Dutch Charley went down never to rise again. His life had hung upon one tick of the clock; but that second, which we all waste by millions, was not vouchsafed him.

Men on board took the bearings of the spot from trees on the shore and avowed their determination to return and dive for the body and the gold.

One evening, soon after the return of the avenging party from the ruin in the mountain pass, Mulcahy dismounted at the door of Allen, to pass the night and hear the news.

"I want my supper, Mr. William Allen," he said, as he entered the door, "and I want the news. I have brought you a message from a friend of yours, who is at the present moment seeing what he can of the county town through the bars of the jail. A melancholy spectacle is your little friend, with a week's black stubble on his pale face."

"Friend of mine!" exclaimed Allen. "What friend?"

"The Hon. John Leson," replied Mulcahy, with a quizzical smile. "He made an effort, with the aid of several devoted friends, to get the wrong man in jail, and got in himself for his pains. The gentleman he was after was the same you wanted to hang here one night. You recall the little circumstance, perhaps ? "

" Very well," replied Allen. " 'Twas a stormy night."

" Quite so," responded Mulcahy, " for the innocent gentleman. 'Twas enough to turn his hair gray, but it didn't. Well, being in town on business and pleasure combined, and knowing Leson was in durance, I called on him to cheer him, carrying in to him, in point of fact, a bottle or two of spiritual refreshment in defiance of law. I would scorn to triumph over a fallen foe."

" And I wouldn't," said Allen, with a frown.

" Yes, you would, William. You don't know yourself. You're a tender-hearted man; and that reminds me, won't you take something before supper?"

After something had been taken and other trivial matters discussed, Mulcahy returned to the captive Leson.

" You see, William," he said, " Leson is innocent of any offense against you. When he got you to sign the petition to the sheriff he thought the Grand Ladrone, as he called him, was guilty, which turns out to be a grand mistake. It was a put-up job by an enemy of his. Now, the sheriff knows it, and the prosecuting attorney knows it, and when his case comes up he intends to nolle the indictment and turn Leson out, free. He asked me to explain the matter to you, for he doesn't want you to shoot at him when he gets out. That seems to be reasonable, doesn't it ? It's an appeal to one's finer feelings, according to my notion."

" It sounds reasonable," replied Allen doubtfully.

" It's all right, William, you can depend upon it," said Mulcahy ; " and now, what about the landlords?"

" Well, we cleaned them out and burned the cabin. We doubled up three. One got away ; he wasn't there."

"Not Dutch Charley, I hope."

"Yes, Dutch Charley."

"What a pity! Why didn't you wait for him? He couldn't have been far off. I'm afraid you were too impatient, William."

"Not a bit of it ; we was cool as cucumbers. I saw the fellows behind the bar was gettin' nervous and there was no time to lose, so I giv' the signal."

"Any of our friends hurt ? "

"Not one. We was too quick for them. 'Twas over in a flash ; they hadn't time to draw. They would have opened on us first if we had waited a minute longer. I saw it was coming and threw my hat on the counter ; and then we blazed away."

"That was the signal ? "

"That was the get-ready signal ; the other followed in a second."

"Did they drop dead?"

"One made a break for the kitchen with three bullets in him. He caught two or three more as he went through the door. That settled him."

"You did very well," moralized Mulcahy, " very well indeed ; but it distresses one to think of the loss of Dutch Charley. It makes the expedition appear so incomplete."

"He'll die in his boots before long," replied Allen hopefully.

"He'll meet his match soon. He'll find his rope short ; it will bring him up with a round turn before his hair gets gray. Let us console ourselves with that reflection, and let him slide. By the way, did you go back to the hollow stump?"

"Yes, and looked in and saw poor Ebright's boots," answered Allen. "We intend to send a party back to bury the dead. The landlords we burned in the cabin; they won't get Christian burial. I was rather opposed to burning them, but the boys insisted on it."

"What objection had you to burning them?"

"For fear they might walk," answered Allen.

"Walk!" exclaimed Mulcahy. "Dead men can't walk."

"Yes they kin," retorted Allen. "And they do sometimes ef they're not put underground. That's to say, if they come to a sudden death."

"But if he is burned to ashes, how can he pull himself together to get on foot? He can't accomplish the feat, William, it's not on the cards; it can't be done."

"I mean his ghost," replied Allen. "You can't burn a ghost, nor kill it in no manner. It can walk, I know, fur I've seen it done."

"When, and where?"

"When I was a boy, I was sent to town one night for a doctor, and had to pass a tumbledown deserted house that a man had been murdered in. So I kept on the other side of the road and hurried by. I thought I saw something glimmer through the fence rails, but couldn't make out what it was, nor didn't stop to try. I was badly skared, but got to town all right and waked the doctor up, and hung about until he got on his horse, hoping, as I was a little chap, he would ask me to git up behind, but he didn't. I ran after him to try to keep up, but when I dropped into a walk to breathe a bit he got out of sight. I cried at first, but when I got sight of the old house I stopped and trembled; then I climbed the fence and took to the fields. But I was afraid to go fur away from the road, fur fear something would

ketch me, and couldn't help lookin' over at the house ;
when all of a sudden a white thing, seemed to me it looked
like a white calf without a head, glid out of the front door,
which was standin' wide open, and tuk after me. I giv' a
yell and took to my heels. When I got home I felt over
the door fur the latch and couldn't find it ; then I felt the
ghost a grabbin' at me, and fell down on the step in a
faint.

CHAPTER XVII.

TRACKED TO THE PINE ARBOR ON THE YUBA.

THE purchase and sale of gold dust being a profitable branch of the banking business, the house in San Francisco determined to enter into it, and dispatched Don Antonio to the northern mines to open up the trade. The dust by weight was of very uncertain value. Although called "dust," it was, in fact, composed almost entirely of small scales, or more or less rounded particles of various size. There was, besides, the lump gold, generally with quartz veins running through it, and the value of this required skill to determine. The variation in the value of the so-called dust arose from the mode of obtaining it.

The gold miner would bring a bucket of earth and gravel from the hole or bank and empty it into a sieve placed over a cradle inclined a little and open at the end, and with several cleats crossing its bottom. His comrade, seated by the cradle, would rock it with the left hand and dip water from the stream at his side with the right, pouring it over the earth. The gold, small gravel, and muddy water passed through the sieve, dropped into the cradle, and was washed down and out, saving the gold, black sand, and very fine gravel, which caught against the cleats. This was scraped out and put into a basin or pan with water and turned about, the gold and black sand sinking to the bottom, and the larger gravel scraped off or allowed to wash over the edge, the basin being slanted, as it was agitated, for that purpose. The separation of the black sand from the gold was effected by carrying on the agitation and washing over, but required skill to get the sand out without pouring over fine light gold with it. Hence the process was never carried to an end, and more or less black sand was put into the bag with the gold, making the ounce vary in value with the greater or less proportion of sand mingled with it. This, and the hazard incurred in transportation to the city, gave rise to the trade in gold dust.

As Don Antonio approached the mountains on his upward journey he came upon a canvas tavern or saloon situated on the open plain, and dismounted for rest and refreshment. The trail he had followed during the day had led him over a vast rolling prairie, destitute of trees and burned brown by the summer heats, waterless and dreary. The streams were dried up and their beds hot as ovens with the reflection from the stones that strewed their sides and bottom. No birds were in the air, no living thing astir upon the ground. He had met no traveler ; his ride had been solitary and depressing. But the rainy season was at hand, on the coming of which the plains would be clothed with beauty and life, and the air cut by myriad wings and vocal with song. Signs of the coming enchanter were already in the air. Clouds began to rise in the mountains, but the plain as yet was unsheltered, and beaten by a burning sun.

Don Antonio sat smoking on a bench in the tent, some half hour after his arrival. when Corby, the Avenging Angel, rode up and dismounted. He walked with a quick step to the counter, and called for brandy and a cigar—nodding to Don Antonio and casting a sharp glance on him as he passed.

"Which way are you going, stranger, up or down?" he said, in a bold, peremptory tone, as he turned from the counter.

"Up," answered Don Antonio, without looking at him.

"There will be a storm in the mountains to-night," interposed the bartender. "You men had better stay where you
are until morning. It is fifteen miles to the next stopping
place, and it is only a pine arbor at that. You cannot keep
dry there in a storm—but suit yourselves and you will suit
me."

A third horseman rode up at this moment and dismounted from a powerful horse. He was of the middle
height, slightly built, dressed in a neat Spanish riding suit
of the best material, and evidently a bred gentleman. He
saluted the company as he entered, called for brandy and a
cigar, and seated himself by Don Antonio, with whom he
exchanged a few civil remarks, keeping his looks directed to
Corby. In a few minutes, finding himself the subject of
scrutiny, Corby, looking the gentleman boldly in the face,
said :

"Do you remain to-night?"

"No," he answered, rising and walking to the door, "I
travel to-night."

Don Antonio walked out at the same time and they
mounted their horses.

"I very seldom ride in company," said the gentleman,
addressing Don Antonio; "but I am not afraid to ride with
you. If agreeable, it will be safer and more pleasant to
travel together?"

"Unless your face and bearing belie you," he answered,
smiling, "you can be trusted ;" and they rode off in company.

"What sort of a house do they keep at the arbor
ahead?" called back Don Antonio to the bartender, who had
come to the door.

"Bad !" he answered.

"What sort of men are they ?"

"Mormons," he replied, as he turned into his tent.

"I dislike to put up with Mormons," said the stranger; "but I do not see how we can well help ourselves to-night. It will be nearly dark when we reach their place, and it is many long miles to the next tent at the upper crossing of the Yuba. Look at those black clouds coming down the mountain. The storm has burst already in the High Sierra. We must stand the Mormons, or stand the pelting of a rough storm."

"It is difficult to make a choice," replied Don Antonio. "By the way," he continued, "I noticed you studying the man with the red beard. Do you know anything of him?"

"I was sure I had seen him before, and was trying to recall where. He is a night owl, and, I suspect, an assassin. It was doubtless in San Francisco and at night. There is an impression on my mind to that effect. Ah!" he added, with animation, "I have it. It was late one night, as I passed the iron warehouse. He was standing in the shadow of the building with Sol. Stubbs. A pretty couple, truly; doubtless bent on evil deeds."

"His avenging angel," muttered Don Antonio, in an anxious tone.

"Have you incurred their enmity?" asked the gentleman, noticing his manner. "Have you reason to suspect yourself on their black list?"

"I have never seen the list," answered Don Antonio; "but I am quite sure my name is on it."

"Ay! ay!" exclaimed the stranger. "Mormons in front of us, Mormons in rear of us. We must stand on the qui vive, with our beards over our shoulders, as the Spaniards say."

Pushing on at a gallop the gentlemen entered the gorge

through which the Yuba issued, and crossing the stream and following its course a couple of miles, turned into the pine forest, and, as dark fell, reached the Mormon Arbor Inn. It stood on the left of the trail, at the base of the mountain, on a flat spot covered with bushes and scrub oak, the whole surrounded by gigantic fir and pine. They rode past the house to the hitching-post a few yards beyond, dismounted, tied their horses and walked back to the door. A man was seated on a bench smoking a pipe, while another was lounging in the doorway. Seating themselves, they entered into conversation. After a few commonplace remarks the lounger passed into the house, and Don Antonio, with the view of reconnoitering the premises, leaving the other two in conversation, walked back on the trail, his movements sheltered from observation by the bushes. Turning into the woods, he took a position under a low scrub oak, from which he had a view of the rear of the building, now lit up by the kitchen fire which burned in the open behind it. A kettle hung over the coals under a tripod, and a man half bent over was stirring the contents with a stick. Another was washing tin plates on a bench close by, and a third lounging. There was no excitement, no sign of plotting or conspiracy. All seemed peaceful and reassuring.

As he stood leaning against the tree, watching the men at the fire, he heard the low, subdued bark of a wolf a few yards to his left, and saw the cook straighten up and look in his direction. In a moment the sound was repeated, and the cook, dropping his stick, walked rapidly toward him. As he neared the tree Don Antonio was under he veered and entered the shade of one close by, whence the bark had issued. A low murmur of question and answer ensued, which seemed to be the exchange of secret passwords, followed by a muttered conversation. One of the voices was sharp and peremptory, and he caught a few words. As they were parting he heard the last sentence :

"If they leave to-night, signal me and we will ambush them at the cut-off."

The cook walked rapidly back to the fire ; and the wolf, as he emerged from his tree and passed to an adjoining one, disclosed the features of the Avenging Angel, Corby.

In a few minutes Don Antonio left the shelter of the oak and walked noiselessly across to the trail and down to the house. As he passed the door, the man he had left in conversation with his friend was going in, in answer to a call from the kitchen. "Come !" said Don Antonio, in a significant tone, without slackening his pace; and, reaching his horse, began to untie him. His friend rose instantly at the summons and was at his side in a moment. "Quick !" he said, as he sprang into the saddle, and giving the horses the spur, they disappeared in the deep gloom of the pine forest. A sharp angry bark saluted their ears as they galloped off, and, turning in their saddles, they saw the men in commotion about the fire and the figure of the Avenging Angel rise from the bushes and rush in.

"We must leave the trail here," said the stranger, as Don Antonio finished a brief recital of what he had heard and seen. "The cut-off he spoke of is the great bend just ahead of us. They can cross the neck on foot and get into ambush long before we can make the detour."

Bending their course to the left, they rode up and along the side of the mountain, putting the endurance of the horses to the test, until their hard breathing warned them to call a halt. They dismounted to further favor them, and as they stood at their heads they distinctly heard far below them the sound of men's feet running across the rocky cut-off.

Resuming their journey, the stranger leading, they fell

into a deer path which gave good footing and made the ascent endurable to man and horse. The mountain was covered with lofty pines which grew, however, apart and allowed
from time to time a view of the stars. As they approached
the summit the sky became overcast, the woods grew dark,
and soon the rain poured down in torrents, the vivid flashes
of lightning illuminating the path only to plunge it into
double darkness. At midnight on the mountain top they
saw before them, disclosed by a friendly flash, a huge hollow
tree into which they rode and dismounted, and there passed
the remainder of the night. At sunrise they descended the
mountain and crossed the Yuba at an Indian ford ; and on
the following day reached their destination—the forks of the
North Fork.

This was a flourishing mining center, and Don Antonio
opened up his operations with vigor. Walking up the bank
of the river a day or two after his arrival, he was hailed by
name from a small pine arbor, and stepping in, discovered
an old acquaintance lying on a bed of leaves on the ground.
He was a young Floridian named Ortega, a descendant of
one of the early Spanish settlers of that State, and had accompanied Hayward in his journey as far as Durango. He
was ill, and had done no work for several weeks. His claim
was poor, but he had some money still in his purse and was
cheerful and hopeful for the future. He was one of those
men who, though never successful, happily never despond.
There are very many of them in the world, and they are its
true philosophers. He had drifted about since his company
had dissolved—which nearly all companies did—on its arrival
in the country ; and finally lodged in the little arbor in which
he lay, not as well off financially, by any means, as he was
when he left the land of flowers.

He declined pecuniary assistance, saying he had enough to

see him through his illness, and had a friend who, since he had been laid up, spent a part of nearly every evening with him and rendered him much assistance. He invited Don Antonio to come up and spend the evening at his camp-fire, saying he felt well enough to get up and sit with him, and promising to do so. Before sundown Ortega got up, dressed, and crept slowly by the aid of a cane out into the open air—the first time for many days.

The day before he was laid up he had noticed that two rough claims adjoining his own up stream, the working places of which were concealed by the rocks from observation, had been temporarily abandoned, the tools lying crossed in the holes. It occurred to him that the men might not have returned and their absence been unnoticed by the neighboring miners; and he made his way to the point from which the tools had been visible. They lay as he had seen them before, and had evidently not been touched since. It was plain they were abandoned, their owners having found claims to suit them better too remote to make it worth while to return for their tools; or, having been killed by Indians or robbers, had laid down the shovel and pick forever. Be that as it may, he had made a rich discovery. The water had been turned from the bed of the stream in the claim above these two, and it had proved very rich. His own had been tested, it is true, and abandoned before he came into possession; but it lay further off. The objection to the abandoned claim was that the water was deep, and hard to wing dam and get at the bottom. Ortega was elated at his good luck, and crept back to his arbor and lay down, his mind filled with golden visions, to await the coming of his expected visitor.

In order to hold a claim after having staked it off, custom required that the miner or his representative should work it at least every third day, and that during a suspension of work for even a day his spade and pick must lie in the hole or at the digging. If he remained away over three days any one who either had no claim or chose to abandon his own could throw out the tools and take possession.

When Don Antonio arrived the camp-fire was burning brightly, and Ortega, lying on his bed of leaves, anxiously expecting him. He congratulated him on his good fortune, and agreed with him in the opinion that, on account of the proximity of the claims to the adjoining rich ones, they could be sold to speculators for a fine price. At this moment the friend of Ortega appeared at the fire. He had light hair and white eyebrows, and a white face ; was thick-set and jovial. In short, he was the Genial Man who had ruined Digby. He did not make a good impression on Don Antonio, who disliked his personal appearance and distrusted his manners ; but the verdant and youthful Floridian immediately informed him of his discovery. He expressed great pleasure at the news and tendered his congratulations, but soon excused himself and took his leave. Don Antonio expressed his surprise to Ortega at his incaution ; but he assured him that "Mohawk" (called after a river of that name, which, however, did *not* flow through Digby's State) was so kind and charitable that it was impossible for him to be guilty of treachery.

Don Antonio was silenced, but not satisfied. He set about the preparation of the necessary stakes and notices to be attached to them, one in the name of Ortega and the other in his own, intending to take it nominally and hold it for him; and, as the night was dark and the ground unknown to him, determined to remain all night in order to mark the ground early in the morning.

At daybreak he went out to take possession, but found

possession already taken. Flaring notices were up on the claims, the old tools were thrown out and bright new ones in. Ortega knew that he had been betrayed and robbed by his white-eyebrowed friend. It afterward came out that, on leaving the arbor that night, he had gone direct to the town, made his preparations, got the use of the names of two acquaintances, and returned, planted his stakes, set his notices, thrown out the old tools and put in the new, and taken possession. But as yet there was no proof of his guilt. He walked up to the fire that night and smiled upon the company. But Don Antonio frowned upon him and Ortega averted his face, and, after showing signs of culpability, he abruptly left and never called again. A notice had been posted that morning in the town offering the claims for sale, and in the afternoon a sale was made to a party of men from Georgia, the leader of whom was a small, withered man who had passed his life in the gold mines of that State; but it turned out that Mohawk had prudently and secretly retained a third interest.

On account of the depth of water in these claims it was resolved at a meeting of the proprietors to build a water-mill to pump it dry. But building a water-mill, a new idea here, on the Feather River tributary, and building one in Georgia were two quite different affairs when it came to the cost. It involved, before they got through with it, so large an expenditure that the assessments on Mohawk's third interest not only swallowed up the money he had received from the Georgians, but also his earnings and accumulations from other sources, which were considerable, and the value of his old claim, which he had been obliged to sell. It was confidently believed that the bottom would be found crossed by seams and crevices as was the claim above, and that a great fortune would be found lodged in them. Mohawk was treated with great consideration as the work progressed, being regarded as a bright, sharp man, a favorite of fortune ; while Ortega, on the contrary, was looked upon as a dull fellow, who had weakly allowed himself to be overreached by his sparkling neighbor.

At length the mill and wing dam were finished ; at great expense, it is true, but they worked admirably ; and it was apparent that when the wheel was set in motion it would soon lay the bed bare and dry. Speculators now sought an interest, and Mohawk could have sold out and retired, with a sum that would have purchased him a farm on his native river; but he held on. He had long since ceased to make any concealment of his unworthy conduct, and quietly enjoyed the reputation for smartness it gave him.

The wheel began its revolutions and a crowd gathered about the "deep claims," as they had come to be called. The bottom was reached and laid bare, and found to be as smooth as the bottom of a wash-bowl, to which, excepting in color, it bore no slight resemblance. Not one grain of gold was found there, and the enterprising Mohawk was beggared. He was in a prominent position in the crowd when the bottom became visible, and was said by a curious but perhaps unveracious observer to have turned green. Public opinion now underwent a change in regard to his character: it said he was a contemptible thief and deserved what he got. Ortega and he left the mines at about the same time : the one to take service with Don Antonio, the other to pursue his benevolent enterprises in fresh fields.

A day or two before Don Antonio left, taking Ortega with him, they were sitting at his fire, discussing the conduct of the Mohawk and his reverse of fortune, when a man who was wearily trudging by sat down and entered into conversation. It was Downey, who had discovered the stream they

were on and in whose honor the town below had been named.
His apparel—slouch hat, red flannel shirt, corduroy pants
and boots into which they were thrust—was all old and tat-
tered. He had a pick on his shoulder and a pan slung at
his back. Several miners who recognized him gathered
about ; and at their solicitation he gave a narrative of his
brilliant though brief career.

He had experienced the extremes of good and ill fortune,
and was a striking type of a numerous class—the improvi-
dent miner. He made no attempt in his narrative to cover
up or make little of the error of his ways ; but expressed the
determined resolution, if fortune smiled on him again, to
make better use of her favors. But fortune had cast him off,
and he was destined to pass the remainder of his days in the
sequestered walks of life. It was rare for fortune to visit any
man in California, and still more rare for her to call on the
same man twice. Small gains were not infrequent, but they
were acquired generally through toil and exposure, danger
to health and life. The one success was trumpeted abroad,
and the thousand failures buried in oblivion. The strength
of youth and the experience of age were alike unavailing to
secure immunity from the perils that lurked by the way.

Early in the Spring, before the snows had left the mountains, Downey, not having before his eyes the fear of death
by Indian or starvation, left Sacramento, and, turning his
face northward, solitary and alone, penetrated nearly to the
summit of the Sierra, and gathered at the forks of the Yuba,
near by where he was then sitting, a fortune estimated at
over two hundred thousand dollars. He had reached there
at a time when the water in the stream was very low, and
here and there a crevice or a round hole worn in the bedrock
was exposed to search. He passed along from crevice to
crevice and hole to hole, scooping out the contents into his

pan and washing them—in the language of the miner, "picking the pockets of the river." He lived on a little hoarded flour, a fish caught now and then, and edible roots. and slept cold and wet.

A California lion had come to his sleeping-place several times at night, prowling about and evincing a strong desire to make a meal of him, but had retired without carrying his half-formed purpose into effect. A movement at those times would have been fatal to him, but he had lain quite still, giving no sign of life ; and this animal will not attack a man unless he moves. He did not evince, he said jocosely, the same prudence subsequently in the city, where he frequently and courageously attacked the Tiger, an animal as fatal to fortune as the lion to life. Indian fires had alarmed him on several occasions, but they were remote and the red man fortunately never struck his trail. Had he done so. Downey feared he would not have evinced the reserve and self-denial of the lion.

Finally one day, after picking several unusually deep pockets, he concluded he had sufficient to support him in ease for a lifetime, and he resolved to beat a retreat while the play was good. He loaded himself with as much gold as he could conveniently carry, hid away among the rocks the remainder, and made his way to the settlements. There he procured mules, and returning, conveyed the treasure in safety to Sacramento.

And now began a waste as rapid in its course as the accumulation. His fortune, acquired in cold and toil and danger in the snow-clad Sierra, could not endure dissipation under a lowland sun, and in ten weeks melted away. Summer friends flocked about him, ate, drank and smoked at his expense, and borrowed, now for this purpose, now for that, but all good, many of them appealing to the tenderest sympathies of our common nature. It was wonderful, the inventive genius displayed in the fabrication of these touching and irresistible appeals, and the amounts by them extracted from the purse of the " best-hearted man on the globe," as he was enthusiastically styled in those weeks of delirium. The Tiger came in for a goodly portion, and the remainder went in various ways, what matter whither ; enough that it was gone. He had entered on his popular and brilliant career of dissipation in the city in the beginning of June, and now in September, at a camp-fire on the scene of his triumph, he sat, penniless and forlorn, relating the story of his folly and defeat.

As he concluded he took a few ineffectual draws at his expired pipe, knocked out the ashes, and, rising to his feet, threw his pan and pick over his ragged shoulder, saying, as he turned to depart :

" Boys, if any of you ever strike it rich, take warning by me."

When Corby and the men of the Pine Arbor ran across the bend, and went into ambush to await the coming of the two travelers, the cook of the Pajaro took a seat in the bushes by his side, and they entered into conversation.

"What frightened them ?" inquired Corby.

'' Who can tell," answered the cook ; " nothing frightened them, nothing happened to frighten anybody. What frightened the sleeping man in our tent on the Pajaro? Some men scent danger in the air, like a dog scents game."

" Did they see you leave the fire when I barked ?"

" No, they were on the bench in front ; they never entered the arbor, and they couldn't see the fire from where they set."

" Who sat out with them, any one ?"

"Dan'el was out when they come, and set talkin' to them

till a minute before they galloped off. I sent fur him to come to the kitchen, and had hardly said two words to him when we heerd the horses' hoofs, and giv' the bark. He kin tell you how they talked and how they acted."

" Call him.—Brother," he said, when Daniel had taken a seat near him. " What were you and the travelers talking about ? "

" I talked with the small one," Daniel answered, " about the storm that was coming up, and how many of us lived here, and how business was."

" What else ? "

" Well, I don't jist remember what ; not about nothin' in particler. He wanted to know how long we had been runnin' the shanty—Pine Arbor, I should say—and if I thought it would leak much, which I told him I didn't think it would, but I didn't know, fur it hadn't been through a rain yit. That's about all I kin think of that passed."

" What did the tall man have to say ? "

" Why, he didn't say nothin'. He got up in a minute and walked out on the trail, and didn't come back till I was goin' in ; then I see him walk quick past the door."

" Which direction did he take when he walked out ? "

" Back on the trail."

" It does beat hell ! " muttered Corby, in a harsh, angry voice. " It's enough to make a Saint swear to see how things turn out. He heard the bark and saw the cook take to the bush. What devil was it prompted him to walk back on the trail ? "

" The same," said the cook, who thought an answer called for, " that helped the man out of the window on Dirty Devil River, and woke the man up in the tent on the Pajaro ; the identical devil."

" It's a trial the Saints are a-passin' through," said Daniel.

" Isn't it about time the travelers were here?" inquired Corby, impatiently.

" It's a long way round the bend," replied the cook ; " but they won't be long now."

" Hark!" exclaimed Corby, rising to his feet and listening intently ; " I think I hear them!"

" It's a lion!" whispered Daniel in an awe-struck tone. "Stand still!"

And they stood still, awaiting the passage of the lion, who passed without molesting them, and the coming of the travelers, who never came.

CHAPTER XVIII.

THE ANNA MARIA.

WHEN Leson was brought up for trial in the county seat of Mariposa, the prosecuting attorney announced to the court that there were no witnesses in attendance and entered a nolle prosequi in his case. He was, therefore, discharged from arrest, and left the town, going first to Stockton ; but, finding business dull in that city, he finally returned to San Francisco and renewed his acquaintance with McCauley, who was on his feet again, engaged in the purchase and sale of small cargoes of grain and potatoes. He had no office but the Market Street wharf, where he bought and resold to larger dealers without handling the cargoes himself. He was doing very well; not making much beyond a living, but his mind was occupied, and he was gradually recovering from his great defeat and fall.

Leson's personal appearance had not improved since his incarceration and residence in the upper town, and his suit of legal black had become more rusty and shining than ever. This was the cause of his being employed, as he lounged about the court, by a suspicious-looking client who wanted some extra professional legal services performed, and their consultation ended by an appointment at a lodging and drinking house near the Old Mission, several miles out of town. He spent the night there, and finding the terms moderate and the prospect of establishing a business among its patrons good, he took up his quarters in the old adobe. It stood back some distance from the road and Mission, in a secluded nook among the sand-hills, and was well adapted for a retreat for the class of persons who frequented it. It had a bar and public sitting-room, and several disconnected apartments, all on the ground floor, which were let out to gentlemen who sought seclusion. One of these, the most shrouded from the public eye, opening on a ravine between two sand-hills, became the personal chamber of " Lawyer Leson," as he soon came to be called. And a very lucrative business of an uncertain kind he quickly established, and a pretty list of acquaintances he made. He was in his element, and much respected and consulted. He had not yet been regularly admitted to the Bar ; but, as his work lay outside the railing, it mattered nothing and did not prevent his admirers giving him the title.

McCauley was invited out often on Sunday, when a dinner of considerable elegance was served in his chamber, with wine and cigars of very fair flavor and quality. Men, at length, were known to drive out from the city, and, alighting at the hotel, to walk around the sand hill and slip into this hidden sanctum, who would have disliked to have their friends see them there. As business grew an air of state was assumed, and partly on this account and partly to avoid awkward meetings of clients, cards were required to be presented at the bar, and men—except some favored clients—were kept waiting and took their turns, as in the ante-room of a cabinet officer. The stubble that had offended Mulcahy was each morning reaped at the shop in the Mission Hotel, and the seedy suit gave place to fitting garments. McCauley began to stand in awe of him, and exerted himself on his Sundays out to entertain him with the news and occurrences that took place on the wharf.

One evening, when dining with Leson, a storm arose and continued into the night with such violence that McCauley, who had walked out, was compelled to remain. Leson pro-

posed to make him a bed on a lounge, and, that settled, they
set in to make a night of it. At about ten o'clock, as they
were still drinking and smoking, a knock came at the door ;
but it was drowned by the noise of wind and rain and their
conversation ; and, receiving no attention, the visitor, impatient of standing in the storm, opened without invitation
and entered. He made a movement to withdraw when he
saw McCauley; but Leson, now a little flushed with wine,
pressed him to remain, and introduced him to his friend as
Mr. Watkins. He was a tall and powerful man, with a
peculiarly stern and threatening expression, heavy eyebrows that met in the middle, and a square jaw. He was
pleasing, however, in his manner, and the sense of repulsion
caused by his appearance soon wore off.

"Well," said McCauley, as soon as the conversation
began to flag, resuming a narrative interrupted by the entrance of the stranger, "the sloop, as I was saying, dropped
anchor at the wharf at four in the afternoon and I stepped
on deck and interviewed the owner. He had aboard a cargo
of first-class potatoes, and I bought the lot, as they lay in the
hold, at a very reasonable price. We went into the cabin to
settle, and I took out my ink horn and paper, and drew up
the bill of sale and a check and pushed them over to him.

" 'Sign that bill of sale,' I said, 'and there's the check
for your money.'

" 'I can't write,' he said. 'Give me the money, and the
cargo is yourn.'

" 'You can get the money at the bank on that check,' I
said, 'and make your mark on the bill.'

" 'You must count the gold down on this table or it's no
go,' he said.

" 'Well,' said I, 'I'll go to the bank and bring the money
down ; but if you knew the danger of keeping such a sum in

your cabin you'd go with me and leave it in the bank until the day you sail.'

"'I don't fear no danger. I kin take keer of it, I reckon. What's the danger?' he asked.

"'Danger of robbers,' I said. 'There's old Wade, the Sydney Duck, prowling the streets and murdering somebody nearly every night. He might drop in on you.'

"'Let him drop,' he answered.

"'If he does,' says I, 'he'll not content himself with killing you, he'll choke your wife and child to stifle their cries.'

"'What do you say to that, Anna Maria ; are you afeerd?' he said, turning to his wife, who stood by listening.

"'Not if you ain't,' she answered. 'The robber won't know we got the money aboard, lest this gentleman goes and tells him, which ain't likely.'

"'Well, Anna Maria, shall we take that wonderful risk?' says he with a laugh.

"'Jist as you say,' says she. 'Bob'll be here to help us if it comes to a fight, which it's not likely.'

"'No, he won't,' says he ; 'Bob's paid off and is goin' to leave as soon as he gits the deck washed off, so you needn't count on his help.'

"'I've always leaned on you for pertection,' says she, 'and I'm not afeerd, Hiram.'

"'All right,' says he; 'come, let's go and git the money.' So we went to the bank and cashed the check, and I went back with him to the sloop, and counted the money out on his table, and got the bill of sale. And, Mr. Leson, I'm going to make a little fortune on that cargo. Potatoes are on the rise."

"What is the name of the owner?" inquired Leson. "Hiram what?"

"Hiram Hanson, from Puntos Arenas ; the sloop's named

The Anna Maria, after his wife. He seems to think a good deal of her and of the little one."

"Why shouldn't he?" said Leson. "A man ought to think well of his wife and children. I should, I'm sure, if I had any."

"I've known men that didn't," replied McCauley; "or, if they did, they had a queer way of showing it."

"If that man Wade should, by any chance, get wind of that money and drop down on the sloop," said Leson, puffing his cigar, "he'll make Hanson wish he'd taken your advice and left his money in the bank. He'll make it a sad night for Hiram, and Anna Maria, and the little one. There's no mercy in that dog."

"He's a cruel brute," said the stranger, "and deserves a thousand deaths. I hear he has left the country."

"It's a wonder they never caught him," said Leson, "with the hot hunt and the heavy rewards."

"Oh, I don't know," replied the stranger, helping himself to a glass of spirits. "The police are a stupid set, and the fellow is sharp. That accounts for it, in my opinion."

"Stupid or not," said McCauley, "the police will get him yet, if he hasn't gone. If he hangs about the city much longer, he's doomed."

"He may be caught in a private trap," replied the stranger, "but hardly in one set by the police. They are too fussy. When they set a trap they cackle, like a hen that's laid an egg. Well," he said, rising, "I must make my way home. You will please notify me, Mr. Leson, when you make the collection. I know where I can place the money to very good advantage, if it comes in time. Good-night, gentlemen; pleasant dreams."

When Mr. Watkins closed the door behind him he turned the corner of the building, crossed the Mission road, and walked down to the bay and up its banks until he halted at the door of a rude hut built of the motley material of a wreck cast by the waves on the beach. He paused to listen. Within, at a table drawn close to the fire, sat a man in rough attire deeply absorbed in the fascinating game of "Dummy." A bottle of spirits placed on the table opposite represented his adversary, to whom he addressed himself in terms of exultation or denunciation as the game went for or against him. A crisis in the play, in which the bottle was getting the better of him, called out a shower of abuse on his opponent, in the midst of which the knock of Watkins was unheard ; but a kick at the door that followed aroused him. He threw the cards on the table, took up a pistol that lay at hand and called out in a surly tone :

"Who the dickens is that?"

"A sea-gull," answered Watkins.

"Come in out of the storm," said the card player, unbarring and opening the door. "What a night !"

"A good bit of weather for our trade. Kegg," replied Watkins, taking off his overcoat and rolling it into a pillow. "I want to get an hour's sleep before your fire. What are you at with the cards?"

"Playin' a little game with Pete. leastwise with the bottle that stands fur him," replied the host. "I don't seem to have no luck sense Pete was took off. That blamed bottle beats me more'n half the time."

"Why don't you cheat?" inquired Watkins.

"Cause 'twould spile the game ef I did. 'Twouldn't seem real no more."

"Pete played the fool hanging about the drinking shops. When a man does a stroke of business he ought to retire to private life at once. If he had gone directly home, as he ought to have done, you would have had him for a partner to-night in place of the bottle; but Pete never had any sense."

"Trouble with Pete was," responded Kegg in a moralizing tone, "that he took too much liquor; didn't know when to stop. Now thur's a time fur all things, a time to git drunk and a time to keep sober, but poor Pete didn't know it; consiquence, they ketched him and hanged him. Which it was done most unlawful, fur they never waited fur to see ef the feller he stuck died or not, which he didn't ; nor they never giv' Pete time fur to say a prayer ef he'd a wanted to say one, which I'm a thinkin' he wouldn't. He was too game fur that, was Pete."

"How much money did he leave?"

"Two hundred and somethin'."

"What have you done with it?"

"Sent it to his mother in the States, along with his gold watch ; the one he found on the street one night a short while afore he was tuck off. It's a fortnite thing he wasn't a wearin' of it when he was ketched."

"What did you write his mother about his death?"

"Why, I writ her he died of the gallopin' consumption, caught a workin' the streets in bad weather, which he was compelled to fur a livin', which he couldn't git nothin' else to do. Purty nigh the truth, wasn't it?"

"Near enough," answered Watkins, stretching himself on the floor with his overcoat under his head. "Now let Pete rest, I am going to sleep. You had better do the same, for you are going out in the storm in little over an hour."

"A job on hand!" exclaimed Kegg.

"Yes, a job on hand."

"On sich a night as this!"

"On such a night."

"I've ben trampin' all day," remonstrated Kegg, "and

don't feel a bit like work.   I was a lookin' for'ard to a good rest."

"There is no rest for the wicked, Kegg," replied Wat-kins ; "console yourself with that reflection and shut up."

About three o'clock in the morning two men descended Market street and walked out on the wharf.   The storm was still at its height.   Sheets of lightning flashed across the bay and lit up the shipping.   The darkness that fell after a flash was so intense that the men halted after a few steps and waited for new light, fearing to step off into the water. They passed several brigs and schooners, and finally groped their way past a sloop that rocked at the wharf with its bow up.   After getting past they halted and faced the stern of the vessel, where, by the glare of the next broad flash of lightning, they read :

"THE ANNA MARIA."

The men boarded the vessel, noiselessly entered the hatch-way and descended.   After an absence of thirty or forty minutes, they again appeared on deck, climbed to the wharf, groped their way along it to the street, and passed through the city to the sand dunes.

At daybreak the wind went down and the storm subsided, but the waters of the bay continued agitated, and the sloop rocked in her berth all morning without sign of life.   At length, McCauley, who was passing to and fro, and each time looked to give a good-morning to the captain, jumped on the deck and called down the open hatchway.   Getting no response, he descended ; but a moment after rushed out and called loudly for the police.   Several of those guardians of the day came aboard and entered the cabin.   Terrible news now flew through the city, and the Market Street wharf was black with people. The knife having been the instrument used in the triple assassination, a mark of the handiwork of Wade, left no doubt in the public mind as to his complicity in the crime. The desire to capture and put him to death was intense and universal. It rose in the minds of several of the vigilance committeemen, those self-constituted guardians of the peace, to a degree of insanity.

Wade, the Sydneyite, had once been in the hands of justice and escaped, and had been seen and was remembered with more or less distinctness by many, among whom was Solomon Stubbs, the Mormon. After the Antonio Wayne fiasco, the chief vigilantes, chagrined at the result, offered large rewards for Wade's capture, and devoted themselvès personally to hunting him down.

Several days after the tragedy at the wharf, this pseudo Saint was standing in a fashionable drinking saloon on Montgomery street, surrounded by some dozen merchant friends and committeemen who had entered for their noon drinks, and talking excitedly. That morning an English merchant ship had entered the port and dropped anchor. The captain, after seeing "all made snug," was rowed to the wharf, and walked to the British consulate to report his arrival. He there fell in with an old friend, also the captain of an Englishman lying in the harbor, who, when their business was finished, invited the newcomer to go with him to a fashionable saloon and take a drink. At the bar at the further end of a long room they observed, as they entered, a group of men with glasses in their hands, engaged in earnest conversation; and, as they approached, Stubbs rushed out and seized the fresh arrival by the throat.

"Wade!" he exclaimed with a shout of triumph. "Villain! you are caught at last!"

"That's not my name," retorted the captain, flushed with

auger, and struggling to free himself ; in vain, for many
hands were now on him, and the crowd about him thickened
every moment.

"Hang him ! hang him !" shouted the wildly excited
throng. "Wade ! Wade ! to the sand-hill ! to the committee
room ! knife him where he stands ! "

"Hear me !" shouted the prisoner, with a voice like a
trumpet in a storm, rising above the tumult that encompassed him. "I am Captain Thomas North, of the British
bark *Alert,* dropped anchor in this harbor only three hours
ago."

"You lie !" shouted the crowd.

• "I can prove it, here and now," continued the prisoner.
"There stands Captain Ben Huddle, of the British ship
Ocean Wave, who knows me well and can swear to me."

"A brother assassin !" shouted a stentorian voice.
"Knife them both where they stand ! "

"Give him a chance," called out a lawyer, pressing his
way into the center. "Hear his witness. Stand back a
little, men, and let him step up. Where is he ? "

"There he stands," said the prisoner, pointing him out in
the crowd.

"Come in, captain, and give your testimony. Make way
for him." The way was given, and Huddle advanced and
stood before his friend, pale and trembling.

"Do you corroborate the statement of the prisoner ? "
questioned the man of law.

"I hardly heard his statement in the noise," replied
Huddle.

"Do you know him to be the master of the *Alert ?* a
British ship now lying in this harbor."

"He told me he was," answered Huddle, shifting his
weight uneasily.

"The scoundrel is prevaricating!" shouted a man on the outskirt of the crowd, flourishing a knife above his head and struggling to make his way in. "Let me get at him!"

"Don't attempt to intimidate the witness," replied the lawyer. "Keep that madman back. Now, Huddle, do you or do you not, of your own knowledge, know whether or not this man is the captain of the *Alert?* Out with the truth. You will be protected."

"Of my own knowledge I can't say. I have never been on the *Alert.*"

"Do you believe he is?"

"I have his word for it," answered Huddle, moistening his dry lips.

"Knock him in the head!" shouted the man with the knife. "He's lying like a dog."

"Keep your mouth shut," retorted the attorney; "mind your own business. Now, Huddle, tell the crowd when you saw the prisoner last and what he was engaged in."

"Three years ago, as near as I can remember," answered Huddle. "He was first officer of the *Flying Cloud.*"

"And where did this meeting take place?"

"In the harbor of Sydney, New South Wales."

"Sydney Ducks!" shouted the crowd. "To the sand-hill! to the sand-hill! Drag them out!"

"Silence!" shouted the lawyer. "Do you think, Huddle, your friend has changed his name to Wade and gone to the bad since then?"

"I wouldn't think it of him," replied Huddle; "but I can't say. I haven't laid eyes on him, until to-day, for years."

"Enough!" called out Stubbs impatiently. "His witness fails him. Down to the committee-rooms with him."

"Run him out to the sand-hill!" shouted the crowd. "Wade! Wade! Run him into the street!"

"One minute!" exclaimed the prisoner, freeing his arm as they were renewing their hold on him, and waving it in appeal. "Ben Huddle, hold up your right hand and swear you know me to be an honest man!"

"I can't," answered the degenerate sea-dog in a low tone, as he turned his back on his friend and pushed his way through the press.

"His own witness condemns him!" Stubbs called aloud. "Clear the track there in front!"

The captain was now taken to the committee room under the grasp of as many as could lay hands on him, Stubbs of course, in the role of captor, having the chief hold of his collar. It was a proud moment for him, escorted by a vast crowd, all eyes bent on him or his captive, now, as it were, a part of himself. He swelled as he passed on and seemed to realize that, after all, there were episodes in life worth living for.

The mob surrounded the committee building and clamored for an immediate trial and execution. But this was superfluous, as the captors were eager for action. The trial began at once, and many witnesses excitedly presented themselves to testify against him, and identified him with great certainty as Wade, the Sydneyite; Stubbs leading off with pride and exultation. But in the meantime the false friend in need, who had so ignominiously deserted the captain in the saloon, had not been altogether delinquent. Before retiring to his ship and shutting himself up in his cabin he had the grace to call at the British consulate and report the condition of affairs.

Soon after, the consul was seen to issue from his office in full uniform, cocked hat and sword, and make his way with a firm step and head erect to face the dread committee and to wrest from their deadly grasp their trembling prey. He sent up his card and was promptly admitted, and at once identified the prisoner as the British captain who had that morning arrived in port and reported at his office with a copy of the ship's manifest; and ended by demanding that he should be delivered up to him by the committee. In reply, the consul was advised that no attention whatever would be paid to his demand, that his testimony would be given its due weight in making up the verdict; but that, if the prisoner should be found guilty, they would forthwith hang him. This cool and unexpected answer excited the indignation of her majesty's commercial agent, who proceeded to indulge in some very uncomplimentary language to the self-appointed keepers of the peace. But he soon perceived he was not advancing the end he had in view, and hurrying from the room, and through the streets to the wharf, he threw himself into a boat and was rapidly rowed to the lower harbor, where lay an English man-of-war.

As soon as the admiral learned the condition of affairs he put on his uniform, and, accompanied by several of his officers and the consul, proceeded in his barge to the wharf, and thence, followed by several captains of British merchantmen and others, marched solemnly to the committee rooms. The official party was admitted, the followers excluded, as the proceedings were secret. The admiral said he had been called on by the consul to interpose on behalf of a British subject whose life was imperiled for no cause, as he was informed and believed; and demanded the surrender of the prisoner. The committee declined to comply with his demand, and avowed their determination to carry out their sentence. This expression gave ground for the belief that the prisoner was already condemned. The admiral now rose

to the height of the occasion. He drew forth his watch and
said :

" If your prisoner is not on my quarter-deck at this hour
to-morrow, I will open fire on the city ; and in doing so I will
endeavor to avoid the demolition of the public buildings and
such great warehouses as belong to merchants not parties
to this controversy."

The conclusion of this brief address was significant, and
told on members of the committee, the firing of whose warehouses by the explosion of bombs would be financial ruin, as
their insurance did not cover acts of war. The admiral
bowed stiffly to the gentlemen of the committee and withdrew. The news spread rapidly over the city. Loud were
the boasts that he dared not execute his threat. It would
involve the countries in war. As if in answer to this, the
man-of-war moved up and cast anchor in a position from
which his guns could bombard the town. Thousands watched
it from the wharves and elsewhere. It lay that evening and
night dark and still, but ominous, on the waters of the bay.

The committee held a protracted meeting, extending
through the night, debating the situation, holding on to
their victim like death, to whom alone they were willing
to surrender him. The mayor and city council boarded the
admiral's ship in a body, to protest against his attitude ; but
he advised them to use such influence and authority as they
might still retain on the vigilantes, who held alike the power
and the fate of the city in their hands. He had announced
to the de facto authorities the contingency on which he
would act. If the British subject, whom it was his duty to
protect or avenge, was not surrendered to him by the hour
named, he would shell the city.

On the following day, as the fatal hour approached, all
eyes were fixed upon the stranger, that lay off, bearding the

awful vigilantes, silent and motionless. Suddenly her drum beat to quarters, her decks swarmed with life and motion and were cleared for action, portholes opened and guns run out. All doubt as to what the Briton proposed to do in the named contingency vanished. The guileless San Franciscan, who up to this moment believed that the spangled banner would shield him against the foreigner in all he might wish to do, was panic-stricken at this ominous demonstration. In a very few minutes the captive, escorted on either hand by a merchant prince, issued from the committee building, was driven to the wharf, rapidly rowed out, and landed on the quarter-deck of the old admiral.

This was a blow from which the vigilantes never fully recovered. The city authorities began to pluck up a little heart and talk with bated breath of putting a termination to the reign of terror. But the leaders in this tragic episode had tasted power and blood, and, drunk with the two combined, were frantic and dangerous to the last.

CHAPTER XIX.

THE WAGES OF SIN.

THE remainder of the day on which McCauley made the ḍiscovery on board the *Anna Maria* was passed by him in great perplexity of mind. The dark and threatening countenance of Watkins haunted him, and his own idle talk in the presence of a stranger, which he feared had pointed the way to the murder, caused him to feel a participation in the guilt. He was questioned and cross-questioned as to the appearance of everything in the cabin when he first entered, his previous payment to the captain, and the hour he had last seen him alive. One of the committee was very particular and close in his questions, and McCauley was tempted to speak of his conversation in presence of Watkins. But he reflected that he had only suspicion against him ; that he was very likely entirely innocent, and that to name him was to doom him. He therefore carried his secret until night, when he walked out to the Old Mission to consult with Leson as to what he should do on this point, when under oath before the coroner's jury in the morning. He found Leson agitated and anxious, and glad of the opportunity to disburden his mind on the subject.

"Watkins—I beg your pardon—Leson," began McCauley, "I am in trouble. I am going before the jury in the morning. Ought I to mention the conversation before your friend Watkins last night?"

"Watkins is not my friend," replied Leson. "He is my client. I own to you it looks bad, and I am troubled about it. If it was certain, I would say, give him up ; but it is far from that—it is only a strong suspicion. Of course, you know what will happen to him if you relate that conversation."

"That is what has kept my tongue tied to-day," said Mc-Cauley. "But the question is, what shall I say if they ask me if I suspect any one? It is a question they regularly put to the principal witness."

"The only thing you can say," replied Leson, "is 'no.' You will swear to a lie, of course; but if you tell the truth, Watkins is a dead man. It is a homicide or a lie, as I look at it, and one must choose the lesser evil."

"It is a very embarrassing position to be in," said Mc-Cauley. "Perhaps they would not hang him, after all, if I did state my suspicion."

"Perhaps not," replied Leson; "but I should dislike excessively to be in his shoes if you tell."

McCauley made no reply, but sat musing, when a knock came to the door and Watkins entered. He was dressed, McCauley immediately noticed, exactly as on the evening before. He saluted the company and took a seat.

"You have heard of the murder on the *Anna Maria*?" said McCauley, addressing him.

"Yes," replied Watkins, "and as soon as I heard it, I thought of your conversation last night. What a strange thing it was that you should have been talking so, maybe at the very hour the deed was being done. It looks as though you, in a manner, foresaw it."

"No one but the man who did it knows at what hour it was done," answered McCauley, looking sharply at him.

"And who did it?" inquired Watkins.

"Who knows?" replied McCauley. "Everybody suspects Wade, of course. He will have a short shrift and a long rope if they catch him, whether he did it or not."

"It will take a long rope," replied Watkins, "for he is a long man."

"You know him, then?" inquired the other.

"I have seen him."

"Where?"

"On his way to jail," said Watkins. "He is a plucky one. The mob howled for him, but he never flinched. If they catch him he will die game."

"The man who kills women and children will be caught," said McCauley.

"I dare say," said Watkins, getting up to go; "and whoever did it, gentlemen, I hope they may get him."

During this conversation Leson said nothing, but listened, and watched Watkins out of the corner of his little black eye. When the door closed on him the two looked inquiringly at each other.

"What do you think now?" asked Leson.

"Oh, I am satisfied," answered McCauley. "He would not have come here to-night, or talked as coolly as he did about it, if he had had a hand in it."

"Maybe not," said Leson dubiously. "At any rate your mind is easy now."

"Quite so," answered McCauley, as he took his leave and trudged back cheerfully over the sandy road to the city.

Leson resumed his writing, interrupted by the visit of McCauley, and was absorbed by his work when he was again disturbed by a knock. Impatient at the interruption, he called out in a sharp tone: "Come in." A gentleman entered, in an overcoat and slouched hat, with the lower part of his face enveloped in a shawl. As he unwrapped this he displayed to the astonished Leson the well-known features of the Grand Ladrone. He removed his hat with a bow and seated himself at the table.

"Leson," he said, "I must beg you to turn the key in the lock. I wish a private and uninterrupted conversation with you."

"Certainly," he answered, complying with the request, and further drew the window curtain close.

"Leson," resumed the Ladrone, "you have doubtless heard of the terrible occurrence on the Market Street wharf last night."

Leson bowed assent.

"The city is thrown," continued Hayward, "into an intense state of excitement again, and it will know no peace until the man Wade and his confederates are taken, tried, and, if found guilty, duly punished by the lawful authorities. I will confide in you and speak with candor. Several firms in the city, our own for one, on the news coming out this morning, had a meeting and resolved to take practical steps to restore law and order. Among other things into which it is not necessary to enter, a sum of ten thousand dollars was subscribed and placed in my hands, to be paid to the individual who will hand over to me the person of Wade. You are the individual, and I am here to arrange the matter with you."

"You are very kind," said Leson, with a sickly smile.

"I am very watchful, if you mean that," replied Hayward, "and have kept close track of you. You have the special ability, and are in a position to effect the purpose. Whether Wade is your client or not, he has not retained you in this hunt. I am beforehand with him. Here is a retainer of two thousand in gold coin." With this he drew from his overcoat pocket a bag of doubloons and emptied them on the table. "Put them away," he continued, "and then we shall be friends."

Leson mechanically gathered up the gold, and opening his table drawer put it in.

"Leson," said Hayward, after the retainer had been accepted and put away, "we can do much together. We will clear the city of the Sydney coves, the scum of England; and, when order is restored, you must come into the city, give up your little office here, and enter on a better field."

After a pause, during which Leson looked dazed, the Ladrone resumed:

"Come, friend," he said, "where is our man?"

Leson rose and produced a bottle and glasses, placed them on the table with a pitcher of water, and invited him to join him in a glass of brandy. Hayward touched his tumbler to Leson's and said, "Success."

"You have lately," he added, after setting down his glass and resuming his seat, "wandered a little from the path. I invite you to return. The door may never be opened to you again. Enter without reserve."

"I will," answered Leson, much agitated, "if you will stand by me."

"I will stand by you," replied the Ladrone, "to the end. Here is my hand."

Leson sat down and commenced making insignificant marks with a pencil on the back of a letter. He was gathering his thoughts. The Ladrone lit a cigar and turned the leaves of a book that lay on the table before him. He was giving him time. Leson threw his pencil on the table and looked up. The Ladrone closed the book. The moment he had been working up to had been reached.

"Here," began Leson, "is the exact situation as it stands. I am morally certain I know the assassin of the *Anna Maria*, but I have no proof. I am equally certain that his name is

Wade, though I know him by another. If you give me time, I will connect the two and hand him over."

" How much time ?" inquired Don Pedro.

" I cannot tell. These things go so much by chance that one must wait sometimes for weeks. Give me two, and I may have to ask another. These birds are shy and must be approached on tiptoe."

" Take as much time as is necessary," said the Ladrone. " I do not wish the bird flushed; but don't let our friends the vigilantes bag him. That would spoil all."

Before a week had passed Leson had assured himself, by cautious questions put to his clients, that Watkins and Wade were one and the same person, and he was ready to effect the capture; but Watkins had disappeared. The pursuit had been unusually active since the affair at the wharf, and had driven him from lair to lair ; and this, with the fear of treachery stimulated by the heavy rewards, induced him to take refuge in the recesses of Mt. Diablo, on the Contra Costa, where he had a secure retreat. It was to his cunning in retiring to this mountain, when hotly pressed, that he owed his long career. Leson made heroic efforts to dis¯ cover his whereabouts, but in vain. His clients did not know, and therefore his cunningest devices to extract it from them failed.

Watkins, when on the point of being surprised one night in the city, had been warned and let out an alley door by a keeper of a low saloon ; and when this person desired to take a larger house and set up a more reputable concern, he applied to him and received the funds for the purpose on his promissory note. This he was paying back in instalments through Leson, as Watkins's connection with him had become known to the chief of police and they dared hold no further personal communication. Watkins, strange to say, though he occasionally expended small sums in dissipation, hoarded money and looked watchfully after his debtors. As it is nearly always by taking advantage of some weakness in him that man is worsted by his brother, so it happened in this case that Leson built on the avarice of Watkins his plan to effect his capture. He informed the keeper of the saloon, who was also landlord of the adobe in which his office was located, and who was in close rapport with the frequenters of his place, that he had collected a considerable sum for Watkins, and, if he would give him notice when he wanted it, he would bring it out from the bank. The landlord told him Watkins had returned, and he expected to see him that night, and would inform him. Accordingly, the next day he advised Leson that Watkins would drop into his office the following forenoon.

At ten in the morning Watkins entered the office and was received with the politeness called for by his late prolonged absence. Leson informed him that he had brought out the money the day before and deposited it in the safe of the Mission Hotel. He handed him a piece of paper on which he had calculated the accrued interest, and added it to the sum pretended to have been received, and suggested to him to go over it and verify the calculation while he walked over to the hotel and got the money.

Watkins took the paper, drew his chair to the table and began to figure, while Leson put on his hat and left the office. It was perhaps a five minutes' walk, the path turning about the base of a sand-hill that hid the hotel from view.

Watkins laid down the pencil and walked to the window. He drew the curtain a little aside, watched Leson as he was turning the base of the hill, and observed, as he was on the point of disappearing, that he turned a quick, anxious look behind. Watkins read the manner and look as a hunted wild animal reads a sign in the forest and immediately left the house. He took a few paces in the direction of the ravine, then turned and walked rapidly toward the city, keeping as close to the road as he could without being seen from it, along the inner base of the first range of low sand-hills along the outer base of which the road skirted. When he reached the break in this ridge, in crossing which he would be exposed to view from the road, he lay down in a clump of sage brush, solitary bunches of which grew sparsely scattered over the undulating and glaring surface of sand.

Leson was not to appear in the transaction, and as he reached the hotel, gave the preconcerted signal and passed into the clerk's office, where he withdrew from the safe a sum of his own that he had brought from the city and deposited the day before. He then returned to his office. He found the Ladrone, Digby and Mulcahy there, and the chief of police with two subordinates, just returned from searching the other rooms of the house.

"The fox has broken cover," said the chief. "He has taken to the sand hills."

"Perhaps to the city," said the Ladrone.

"He has gone," said Leson, "in the direction you would be least likely to follow."

"That is the city," said Mulcahy. "A thousand to one we catch him on the road."

"Go," said Hayward, addressing the chief, "with your men into the hills. We will drive back to the city and have it searched."

The police took to the hills, and the gentlemen returned to the hotel, entered their carriage, throwing back the top to give them an unobstructed view, and set out over the deep, sandy road to the city. As the carriage reached the break in the ridge, the occupants caught sight of a figure turning back and disappearing in a clump of sage from which it had just emerged. All three jumped from the carriage without waiting for it to halt ; and Watkins broke cover and fled.

Men following unlawful paths are aided and urged on to a certain height by their evil genius, and then abandoned. Their courage fails, their nerve gives way, and they go over the precipice. So it was with Watkins. When he reached the sage bush, his hour had struck. Instead of facing a danger, insignificant in comparison with a thousand he had boldly faced before, he lay down and awaited his coming doom ; inert when he should have been in motion, he moved at the exact moment to bring down the thunderbolt. This may be chance ; it is also possible it may be Providence.

In running down a steep sand hill, Watkins floundered and fell forward on his face, and Mulcahy closed with him. A struggle ensued, quickly terminated by the arrival of those in the rear, and he was disarmed, bound, led to the carriage and driven to prison. The court was in session and advanced his case, giving him immediate trial. His guilt and his identity with Wade were clearly proved, and though he had a fair trial, it was brief, all attempts to prolong it unnecessarily being put down. In twenty-four hours after the case was called it was given to the jury, who, without leaving the box, handed in a verdict of guilty in the first degree. Sentence of death was pronounced, and two days thereafter Wade was escorted by the sheriff and his officers, through a dense throng of people, down Market street and out along the wharf to the *Anna Maria*, and hung from her masthead; not in darkness and silence, but in the blaze of a California sun, amid the plaudits of ten thousand men.

A few days thereafter, two men were seen hanging by

short ropes to cranks projecting from adjoining upper windows of a committeeman's warehouse, facing the bay. Who
they were, or wherefore they hung there, were mysteries to
the public. On the same day the celebrated Vigilance Committee adjourned *sine die* and locked up its doors. It went
out, as it came in, suddenly and wrathfully.

   Kegg stood on the summit of a sand hill remote from the
scene and witnessed the drama enacted on the deck of the
Anna Maria. He saw the body of his associate swing to and
fro, struggling. He heard the roar of triumphant vengeance
rise up from the multitude of spectators, and, turning dis-
mayed, retraced his steps to the hut on the beach, built from
the fragments of a wreck. He passed the time until nightfall in digging a hole under the wall opposite the doorway
large enough to admit the passage of his body, and in concealing the traces of it within and without. This accomplished, he cooked and ate his supper, lighted his pipe, and,
arranging his dummy as before, took up and dealt the cards,
dealing to himself the first one, as it gave him a slight advantage over his opponent the bottle. But as he took up
and examined his hand, his mind began to wander. He saw
the body of his comrade swing from the masthead ; he heard
again the shout of exultation. He threw down his cards,
and, turning, gazed in the fire. As was the habit of the
man, he thought aloud, speaking not arrogantly, as he had
done when addressing the dummy, but in a low tone of
monologue.

   " Ef Wat couldn't keep his neck out of the halter," he
began, " wot's goin' to happen to me, as isn't half as downy
a cove as him—no, not the quarter? I'll be scragged ! that's
about the size of it—scragged—and that purty soon, lest I
sees fit fur to draw out whilst the play's good. I'll go to
sea; that's wot I'll do—go to sea. Maybe git beat over the

head with a belayin' pin! Most likely. That wouldn't suit.
No, I won't go to sea. Ef that durned *Malec Adel* had a fit
it out, and not 'lowed herself to be took, I'd a liked to a got
on board of her ; which thur ain't no more pirates afloat in
these waters, more's the pity. No, the sea's no good. I
might go back to my na*tive* land, and keep a bar and a gamblin' den adj'inin', which they haven't got to hangin' men
fur that—as yit ; ef I had plunder enough to start one on, I
would. I might turn a horse trader, or jine the smugglers.
I don't know rightly ef they hang smugglers or not. I think
they do, and, ef they do, it blocks that game. Who's that!"
he called out, starting to his feet as he heard a knock at
the door.

" It's me, Kegg," answered a voice from without.

" Who's me ? " he inquired, turning pale with fear.

" It's me—Hen Gile ; don't you know my voice? "

" Is anybody along with you ? "

" Nary body—all alone by myself."

" Come in, then," said Kegg, unbarring the door. " How
you skeerd a body with sich a queer tap ! "

" Why, my tap wa'n't pertic'lar queer, Kegg."

" 'Twas. Sounded like the tap of a cop. Take a cheer
'longside the fire. I was on the p'int of sendin' a bullet
through the door. Don't tap that way no more, not at my
door."

" All right, friend Kegg. I shall knock quite different
next time. Obleged to you fur not 'tractin' attention to the
shanty by shootin'. It behooves coves fur to keep quiet to-
night."

" Why special to-night ? "

" Cause the cops is out thick, arter Wat's 'complice in
the *Anna Mariar* job."

" He didn't hev no 'complice," said Kegg hoarsely.

THE BLACK LIST. 253

"Hev you seed the paper with the testimony in it?" inquired Gile.

"No."

"Well, a witness said he was hurryin' along Montgomery in the storm that night, and would hev run into a couple of men in the dark ef they hadn't of turned down Market street jist as he got nigh them. He said thur was a bright flash of lightnin', and he seed 'em plain as day. He swore p'intblank to Watkins and described the other feller. Why, the jury found Wat guilty, on the *Anna Mariar* count in the indictment, on his word alone."

"They can't find a man guilty on one man's say so," replied Kegg, looking fixedly in the fire. .

"Well, they did, for Wat told me so himself."

"Where did you see him?" inquired Kegg, glancing sharply at him.

"In the jail," answered Gile. "He sent for me this morning ; told the sheriff he wanted to give me a message for his old mother in England and how they could find me. I was locked in his cell an hour, the jailer standing at the bars of the door outside trying fur to listen ; but we whispered and he heard nothin'. He sent me here .to tell you somethin'; but I'll tell you all he said from the beginnin', ef you keer to hear it."

"Tell it all," responded Kegg.

"'Hen,' he begun a-whisperin', 'I've knowed a many a man play the fool and git hung fur the doin' of it, but I never knowed a wose case than mine. That last play was the meanest card which I ever throwed on the table. Why, two men hed cause of suspicion afore the deed was done, and I knowed it well and seed it plain; but the job come to me in sich a oncommon way it 'peared to me I was fated fur to do it. Seemed to me I couldn't help it. I was kind of drove

by somethin' in me stronger than my will. My judgment
was dead ag'in it. I knowed well I oughtent think of it;
but I sailed in like a drunk man, and made my fust and last
mistake. From that on I seemed to be drove by a blind
devil. What put it in my head to come back from the
mount'in twist as soon as ordinary? What put it in my
head to answer a call of one of them wery two men, and
run into as plain a trap as ever was set? Why didn't I keep
on into the sand hills, as I fust started to do when I run from
Leson's office, and wind round to the wreck and git Kegg to
row me out into the bay in his boat? Why did I squat in
the sage-bush at the gap when the road was clear, and jump
out a second afore the carriage come in sight? Why?
'Cause,' he says, a-puttin' of his mouth close to my ear and
whisperin' low and solemn, ' 'cause somethin' was a-drivin'
of me to my doom.' ' "

"Did he seem game yit?" inquired Kegg gloomily.

"Game! not him; he was all broke up, looked pale and
wild, dazed like. Didn't look no more like old Wat than
nothin'."

"Go on," said Kegg impatiently.

"Well, he said: 'Gile, I done a thing long time ago at
home that I want to make up, as fur es money kin make it
up. Kegg's got the name it's to be sent to. You go to Kegg
to-night arter I'm dead, and take him with you to a certing
mount'in,' which he named, 'to a ravine,' which he p'inted
out to me; 'and when you git thar and come up to the
shanty, Kegg kin walk straight to where the plunder's hid.
You two kin divide a quarter of it atween you fur your
trouble, and the rest send where I told Kegg. Ef you don't,'
he says, a lookin' savage ag'in, ' I'll hant you both.'

" ' We'll do it,' says I.

" ' You better.' says he.

" ' When you git all ready to leave the wreck to-night,'
says he, ' ask Kegg fur. my butcher knife, sneak over the
sand hills to the old adobe, and stick it into Lawyer Leson
to the handle.' ·

" ' Won't it do arter we git back from the mount'in,' says
I, ' and git the money sent safe off ? '

" ' No, it won't,' says he, a frownin'. ' I want to meet him
in hell to-night.' "

Kegg rose with a shudder, mounted a chair, took from a
place of concealment in the rafter a small package of papers
and resumed his seat.

" Here's the name," he said, looking at one of the papers,
" the money's to go to, and if you show me the hut in the
holler I kin find the hid gold. What mount'in is it in ? "

" Monte Diablo."

" I thought es much," responded Kegg, " fur I've put
Wat over the bay offen. We must cross in the night, and
it's time to git ready."

So saying, he rose, crossed to a corner of the hut, and
cleared away the sand with his foot, disclosing the bone
handle of a butcher knife which had been driven down out
of sight into the yielding soil. Stooping, he withdrew the
blade from its hiding place and offered it to Gile.

" Go," he said, " while I bail out the boat, and send the
lawyer down to Wat."

" Not till we get back," he answered, walking to the corner and re-plunging the implement of death into the sand.
" The old Mission is thick with cops to-night."

Within an hour the boat put out from the shore, the sail
was set, and the treasure seekers beat across the bay to the
Contra Costa. At the expiration of a week—during the night
of the following Saturday—they recrossed, their little craft
weighed down with blood-stained gold, which they buried in

the sand in the hut, and over which they spread their blankets and slept. Sunday morning, after breakfast, the comrades dug up the treasure, took out the portion assigned them by Wat, replaced the remainder, and sat down to the table to gamble and drink. All day long, with an interval for dinner, they kept it up; and when night settled on the wreck Gile had lost his last ounce, and, rising, threw down his cards. A heavy rain began to fall, dripping in places through the roof of the hut and sinking into the sand. Kegg buried his winnings and prepared the supper. After the meal, they sat before the fire and conversed, Kegg in good humor, Gile gazing in the fire in a despondent mood.

"I never hed luck run ag'in me all day steady afore," he said.

"'Twas oncommon bad, to' be sure," responded his companion, with a cheerful smile.

"What are you goin' to do with all your money?" asked Gile.

"Why, I've about made my mind up to quit Californy and go back home," answered Kegg.

"Jine meetin' and turn honest, eh!" replied Gile with a sneer.

"No, not ezactly that. You see thur's a openin' in my *native* town fur a saloon, with a little gamblin' hell behind it. I'm thinkin' of openin' up in them two branches of bisness."

"When are you goin'?"

"The fust steamer, after we get Wat's money shipped off."

"We dasn't do that fur a month yit, till things get quiet."

"No."

"I wonder ef Lawyer Leson hasn't got money hid in that

little back office of hisn?" said Gile, after a long pause in the conversation, during which he had sat gazing in the fire.

"Like es not," responded Kegg. "Shouldn't wonder ef he hed a hatful stuck away in his drawers or in the tickin' of his bed."

Gile crossed the floor and, stooping, began to unearth the butcher-knife.

"What are you after?" inquired Kegg in surprise.

"After the lawyer," replied Gile, rising and brushing the sand from the blade.

"Not to-night!" exclaimed Kegg.

"Yes, to-night; there couldn't be a darker nor a better. It's got to be done soon, anyway, so why put off. I'm dead broke, and in the humor fur it this minute. Good-night; I'm a-goin' across the sand hill to stick him."

As he unbarred the door, Kegg urged him to put the deed off, even for a night or two; but he was deaf to his appeal, and stepped out from the light of the doorway into the rain with a ferocious expression on his face.

"When the murder fit takes hold of a feller," philosophized Kegg, as he re-barred the door, "he won't lissen to nothin'; he's like a mad dog, he runs and he bites. That's how Wat come to go to the bad; the fit to shed blood took him, ag'in his judgment, and where's Wat now? That's the question. Gone to hell."

At nine o'clock at night Lawyer Leson sat before the fire in his office in the old adobe, smoking. On the table at his side stood a glass of sweetened brandy and water, in which were submerged some sprigs of mint, which spread a pleasing perfume through the apartment. His table was littered with papers at which he had been at work all day, closing his business at the adobe preparatory to moving to the city under the auspice of the Grand Ladrone. He sat half facing the door, resting, in a pleasant frame of mind. He was growing rich; he had become honest; he was on the point of assuming a place in the ranks of reputable men. A knock at the door disturbed a reverie into which he had fallen, while wreaths of smoke ascended in succession from the cigar to the ceiling. "Come in."

The door opened, and a thin dripping figure came in out of the rain and closed it behind him. Standing against it, he removed his wet hat and made an awkward bow in deprecation of his personal appearance. He was above middle height, with yellow hair worn long behind the ears, a gray eye and a thin Roman nose. He was clothed in light woollen blouse and pantaloons of a dirty yellow, which clung to his body and limbs so closely that it suggested the entire absence of under garments. His boots were muddy, and the water trickled from his person and ran in little streams down the office floor. He felt that his guise demanded an apology, and his bow was in answer to the conscious demand. It was Gile, the agent of the dead robber, sent to execute post-mortem vengeance.

"Are you aware, my man," said Leson, surveying the intruder with an air of offended dignity, "that I only receive by card from the bar?"

"I come about that *Anna Mariar* job," answered Gile, shaking the water from his hat.

"*Anna Maria* job!" echoed Leson in surprise, laying his cigar on the table. "What do you mean?"

"I mean what I seys," he answered. "I was sent fur to talk to you consarnin' in."

"Who sent you?"

"Him that wos run up to her masthead," answered Gile.

"What! Watkins!" exclaimed Leson in amazement.

" Yes, him ; he sent me."

" Why, he's dead, man. What are you talking about ? You must be cracked."

" No, I'm not cracked either," replied Gile coolly. " He told me, the day he was scragged, fur to come to Lawyer Leson, and fur to tell him that he knowed who 'twas thet giv' him away."

Leson turned pale on this announcement, leaned back in his chair, and drew the table drawer in front of him open a few inches ; this brought under view and hand a revolver that lay inside, loaded and already cocked.

" Is that all ? " said Leson after a pause, during which he sharply scrutinized the features of Gile ; " or is there more to come ? "

" No, that's not all," replied Gile, with a conciliatory smile, " thur's lots more to come. He told me likewise fur to say that he didn't look for'ard to a minute's peace in t'other world untell he knowed he'd got wengence ; and he said he'd hant me to everlastin' ef I didn't git it fur him. That's about what he said on that p'int."

" How did he know who gave him away ? " inquired Leson frowning.

" He knowed well the man that done it," answered Gile, with a cold, hard smile. " And likewise I know him ; and I know he done it."

" Do you propose to extort money from the informer ? " asked Leson, hoping the interview might take that turn, and willing to pay any reasonable sum to avoid a personal encounter, which he feared was coming.

" No," answered Gile. " I don't."

" Perhaps you think you are man enough to assassinate him," said Leson, in a tone of defiance, leaning forward and letting his hand drop in the drawer.

"I'm man a-plenty," replied Gile, helping himself to a chew of wet tobacco from his fob pocket. "But I haven't no notion of killin' nobody ; leastwise, jist at present. I never did take no delight in killin' nobody—not me."

"Come to the point," said Leson in a determined tone, his fingers closing on the handle of the pistol, "and stop this beating about the bush. Name your man and say what you want."

"Why, you act as ef 'twas you I'm a aimin' at," replied Gile, with a look of surprise, "which it ain't. It's Kegg I'm goin' fur ; him as went that night with Watkins aboard the *Anna Mariar*."

"Oh !" exclaimed Leson, with a bright smile and a sigh of relief, withdrawing his hand, re-lighting his cigar and leaning back in his chair. "Come up to the fire, friend, and take a seat. Kegg, is it? Well, well ; this puts the matter in a new light. And Kegg was with him on the *Anna Maria ?*"

"He was along with him in that job, and him it was that give him up," said Gile, responding to the invitation to seat himself near the fire, and graciously accepting a glass of brandy and a cigar.

"Your name, if you please ?" said Leson.

"I'm called Gile—in common."

"Now, Gile, tell me what message my old client sent me.'

"He said, ' Show Mr. Leson where the fox is hid and leave him to ketch him and have him hung on the *Anna Mariar*, where they're a-goin' fur to run me up arter dinner.' "

"And where is the fox's hole, Gile?" inquired Leson, in persuasive accents.

"I'm told," replied Gile, evading the question, "they offer big money fur him."

"The reward offered for his apprehension is large."

" Am I to git it? That's the question."

" You are not a lawyer, Gile."

" But I'm an informer, which is more to the p'int."

" True," replied Leson, gazing in the fire a few moments.
" Well, you put me on the track, I will run him down, and
we will divide even. What say you to that?"

"I did think as how I'd a got it all," answered Gile.
" You see, Mr. Leson, it's a dretful mean thing fur to giv' a
comrade up, and a feller ought to be paid high fur it. Can't
hardly be paid too high."

"I have no time to waste," said Leson, consulting his
watch. "Speak up. What do you say? Halves shall
it be?"

"Yes, ef you insist."

"I do. Now, where is he harboring to-night?"

" In a hut down the bay shore, near a old wreck."

"I know where it is," said Leson, turning to his table
and writing rapidly. "Here, take this note to the chief of
police. Light that lantern in the corner and run every step
of the way. Hurry up!"

Several hours later, at about three in the morning, a
party of police surrounded the hut at the wreck and knocked
at the door. Receiving no answer, they opened their dark
lanterns, and were looking about for a heavy stick or stone
to batter their way in, when one at the rear flashed his light
on the head and shoulders of Kegg, crawling out through his
escape. He was ordered back to unbar the door. The party
entered and made search, finding nothing of consequence but
the papers of Watkins, and, retiring, marched their prisoner
over the sand hills to the city.

Presently Gile stole into the hut, carrying the lantern he
had got at the office of Leson. He dug up the bags of
gold and carried them to the boat, floating fastened to the

bank of the inlet near by, stepped in, and pushed out into the bay, keeping close to the shore. He intended to row down to a hiding place he had in view and secrete his treasure. But the oil in his lantern failed and the light went out, leaving him in total darkness. He was a poor oarsman, and, in his confusion, headed the boat from the shore. He changed his direction every few minutes, and thus circled about in the bay until the out-going tide and the river current caught him and hurried him through the Golden Gate into the ocean, agitated by a recent storm. Soon after sunrise an incoming vessel sighted the boat, bottom up, tossing in the troughs of the sea.

CHAPTER XX.

THE LADRONE GOES HUNTING ON THE CONTRA COSTA.

THE main body of the emigrants who passed through Utah on their way to California marched in three columns, aimed at the three main passes over the Sierra Nevada. They pursued their serpentine course in unbroken lines, too strong for attack by Indian or Mormon. Those individual companies who allowed themselves to be allured into short cuts were many of them exterminated by the Saints or Indians, or by both combined; or perished, locked up in the inextricable recesses of the mountains. Though the emigrants as a body were exceedingly well-behaved, there were individuals among them that gave affront, in some instances deadly affront, to the leaders of the Mormon settlements through which they passed. The names of the most defiant and obnoxious were taken down, with a description of their persons, name of the company to which they belonged, the locality and State they came from, and such other particulars as would serve to trace them in California. These men were tried in the secret courts of the community, and those whose acts were deemed sufficiently heinous were condemned to death, their names being entered in a black list. As they went on their way, unconscious of danger, there hung over them a doom that was long after executed, as their condemnation had been pronounced, in the dark.

The Mormons, on account of their vicinity, were early in the gold fields, and when the head of the great emigrating columns reached their destination they were found scattered singly or in companies over the country, occupying the choicest of the already discovered mines. They were regarded with disfavor by the general public, but not molested. When in companies their affiliations were known, and while not boasted of, were not concealed. When singly met, their religious status was unknown and unsuspected, as there was nothing in dress or language to distinguish them. They were neither better nor worse, apparently, than their neighbors ; but, while to all outward appearance free, they were still in bonds in certain matters and to a certain extent, and subject to the orders of their pseudo prophet, the low bred and illiterate heresiarch seated on the waters of the Great Salt Lake.

Like the Old Man of the Mountain, this misleader of men had at his command a ruthless band of fanatical assassins, called, in the impious jargon of the sect, "Avenging Angels"; cowardly, dumb dogs that showed no mercy and ran no risk, doing the bidding of the superior fiend in cold blood, in the hours of confidence and relaxation, at the solitary camp-fire, at the noon siesta, at the dead of night.

The difficulty of executing these sanguinary orders increased with the distance from the source of power. Men immersed in money-getting at the mines were not so easily detached to carry out a sentence as the men in the Salt Valley, and the fear of punishment grew feebler as the power that punished grew more remote. There were men in California who, by reason of their surroundings, it had been reported impossible to reach : and the central junta resolved to send an envoy extraordinary to negotiate their removal, with instructions to use the instrumentality of the San Francisco Vigilance Committee, if possible, to effect the purpose. It was thought the victims might be caught on a visit to the city, or lured there and delivered up.

The eminent ecclesiastic selected for this mission was a

gentleman named Hobson, whose ancestors did not come over with William the Conqueror, or as passengers in the *Mayflower*. They are supposed to have emigrated at a much earlier period with Henghist the Saxon, and were no doubt very respectable people—in their way. As to this person of remote ancestry, he was not pleasing in appearance to the Gentile observer, being somewhat uncouth in manner and having an expression of countenance that, failed to inspire confidence at first sight ; otherwise he was common in look, size and dress, the latter being homely and ill-fitting, and evidently not cut out in Paris or even New York. The rank he held in the Satanic hierarchy to which he belonged was that of bishop. The Right Rev. Hobson, a name—though there is nothing in a name—not calculated of itself to awaken emotions of reverence, certainly inspired the sentiment of fear in the mind of many a thrall among the Latter Day Saints.

This person reached San Francisco by easy stages at a time just subsequent to the bloody drama on the *Anna Maria*, when the Vigilance Committee was on the decline and rapidly reaching the termination of its career.

Stubbs was not well pleased to see his bishop, and would have been glad to have ignored him had he dared to do so. The public thought he had severed his connection with the Salt Lake concern, but it was so only ostensibly. In secret he was still held in the bonds of fear. He found, with the third Napoleon and other weak men, that it is easier to enter into a criminal association than to get out. He, therefore, when Hobson gave him the grips, returned them and entered into secret and unlawful relations with him. After acquiring such social success and such great wealth, his soul revolted at the vulgar companionship and domination of the crafty envoy: and he would have gladly hung him from the committee window but for the dread power that lay back of him, far over the sierra, to call him to account. Hobson explained to him the mission on which he had come and suggested the committe as a means of carrying it out. Stubbs explained to him the altered condition of affairs, and how the power of the committee had been weakened and almost destroyed by the intrigue of a few rich men, led by an audacious adventurer whose agents had not scrupled to attack him and his religion in public and to his face. That one of them, an Irishman, he would be glad to see specially entered on the bishop's black list.

" Never mind the subordinate," said Hobson, whose face grew dark at the recital. " Who is the principal ? If any one is to be marked special, let it be him."

" The principal is a very rich man," answered Stubbs. " A banker called Don Pedro Hayward, though he is not a Spaniard, but from the States."

" One of the accursed States ? " inquired Hobson.

" Very likely, but I do not know from which State ; at any rate, he is personally accursed by the conduct of himself and agents."

" They reviled the Saints, did they ? " inquired Hobson.

" They did through me, publicly and before my friends. One of them, the Irishman, said that ' we were heretics of hell, and spawn of the devil ; and for half a cent he would ride over to Salt Lake and knock the Prophet's head off.' "

" How could you stand such insult ? Why did you not strike him down at once, with the blasphemy in his mouth ? "

" Because it was daylight, and I was taught at the Lake to strike in the dark," answered Stubbs.

" True, quite true," said Hobson quickly. " Well, give me the name of the malignant Irishman. . I will enter it with that of his master in my special list. These will probably suffice. If we strike the shepherd the sheep will scatter. This conspiracy must be broken up. The news of your loss of power will be ill-received at the Lake. How can we get at this Hayward?"

"It will be difficult to accomplish," answered Stubbs. "He seldom, if ever, exposes himself. We have him and his friends already on our local list, and they will be exterminated in due time."

"Where can you point him out to me?" asked Hobson.

"I wish," said Stubbs, with some hesitation, "you could let me out of his case. I am known to be his enemy and cannot work in it to advantage. I will introduce you to Saints in the city who can manage it better."

"So! we grow faint in the service of the Lord, do we, brother? I had heard somewhat of this before."

"It is false, whoever told you," replied Stubbs. "I cannot appear in this special matter without useless and heavy risk : but if you insist, I will."

"I will not insist," the bishop said, with a dark look. "I will ask you to introduce me to our loyal brothers."

"Name the sum of money that you want," said the vigilante, "and you shall have it, and any further sum at any time needed to aid you in the good work. I am ready to do anything to satisfy you and keep my standing."

"Let one of your agents place ten thousand dollars in the bank of this black sheep to-morrow, to the credit of John Shepherd. Here," said the bishop, handing him a slip on which he had written the name, "let him hand the cashier this signature. I accept your voluntary offer, and will draw any further sum that may be absolutely needed. These affairs cannot be conducted without heavy expense. Now, if you please, we will call upon our brethren, and you may rest assured your name will stand upon the book untarnished."

Mulcahy, who was quick and observant, became aware
that the bank was watched, and that he and the Ladrone
were under surveillance. They became very circumspect,
and offered no opportunity to their enemies to take them by
surprise. Mulcahy suspected the vigilante of seeking revenge, but Don Pedro thought it some plan of robbery. As
they called for their usual lunch one morning, they fell in at
the bar with several acquaintances, who were discussing a
projected hunt on the Contra Costa, and were invited to join
the party and accepted.

They were to go over in small sailboats the next day, take
an evening and morning hunt, and return on the following
afternoon. Mulcahy invited the captain and first officer (the
latter bearing the dramatic name of McBeth) of a Scotch
bark to join them; and they took the ship's boat, which carried the four. The sail over the bay was very pleasant and
quickly made, a distance of some fifteen miles, and they
landed at the mouth of a stream that took its rise in the
spurs of the Monte Diablo, distant twenty-five or thirty miles.
After establishing their camp, they went out in different
directions in search of game.

Mulcahy was on the right, next the stream. As they
moved on, they became separated and lost sight of each
other, as bushes were scattered over the surface of the
ground. They had advanced perhaps two miles without
finding game, when Mulcahy, becoming tired of the poor
sport, concluded to try the river, and bent his steps to the
right in hopes of getting a shot at ducks. He crossed a path
that ran up the stream, and, opening the bushes with caution,
got down on his hands and knees, and slowly and silently
crawled to the bank and peered over. He saw no ducks, but
immediately beneath him perceived a body of armed men.

One of them—a man with red hair and beard—was de-

scribing to his companions the personal appearance of two
men, one of whom was to be carried off to Monte Diablo and
the other shot. Mulcahy recognized himself in the gentleman who was to be dispatched, and a queer sensation crept
over him. The other description answered well for the
Ladrone. The work was to be done that evening if their
victims could be found in the bush, or that night at the
camp-fire, after they had fallen asleep. They praised the
liberality of the " Old Man," and declared he should have his
game if it cost half their company. They exhibited and discussed the gag they had prepared for their captive, and they
put it in the mouth of one of the party and tied it behind
his head to see how it worked.

While listening intently to this interesting conversation.
Mulcahy heard a quick step on the path behind him, a man
passed, and in a few moments descended the bank at a point
above and walked down and joined the party. Mulcahy
recognized him as one of two men left behind to care for the
camp and cook the supper. He was evidently expected, and
spoke at once with the leader. He said they had arranged
it so that the parties needed should go out next the river.
He described the party of four, saying the mate was a Scotch
giant, rough as a grizzly bear, and if he got hold of one of
them would squeeze him to death. He advised them, if possible, not to trouble him or the captain. That in case of failure to find them in the afternoon he had arranged their bed
next the river, with the " Old Man's " friends adjoining and
the others further removed. He entered on a description of
the Ladrone and Mulcahy ; but the latter, waiting to hear no
more, cautiously drew himself back and plunged into the
bushes across the path in pursuit of his friends.

Fortunately a shot gave him the direction, and he soon
overtook and gathered them together. They made a circuit

to avoid the gang of ruffians, now out in the bush on the hunt for them, and reaching the shore of the bay next their camp, walked up and joined the two men making their preparations for the company's supper. A high wind was sweeping over the bay, which was already throwing up white caps, and a heavy storm coming in from the ocean. Mulcahy walked up to the man he had seen on the river bank in conference with his confederates and said he thought he had seen him a while before out in the bush ; but the man denied having been out of camp,

" Then," said Mulcahy, " it was a man that resembled you, and I drew up to take a shot at him, as game was scarce, but I thought of my supper and held my hand. It was lucky it was not you, my boy, for you never made a narrower escape in your life." With this, he uttered a little, dry laugh that startled the man, and turned away. McBeth and the captain bailed out their boat and set the mast ; the guns and hunting apparatus and their wraps were thrown in, and they gathered on the shore ready to embark. The wind was increasing in strength momentarily and the waves ran high.

" Captain," said Hayward, " with this wind in our teeth we will spend the night on the bay, if not sent to the bottom by the coming storm. Better take Mulcahy's advice and face it out on land."

" No," said McBeth, interposing. " I left a wife and child at home on the loch above Glasgow—Loch Lomond they call it—and maybe they would miss me if I stayed here all night. I did not come out armed for fight, and I am not a fighting man, Mr. Hayward, anyway, whatever my forefathers were. I will face the danger that I know how to contend with, but will not stand an onset in the dark. I will cross the bay to-night, if I go alone."

"If it were not for the wife and child away on the loch," said the captain, "I would not let you run away with our boat, Mac." This was the permission McBeth was waiting for, and he stepped into the boat.

"One man can never manage her in this sea," added the captain. "It will take one at the rudder and another at the sheet."

"Jump in, then," answered McBeth; "unless you want to lose your boat and your mate, and see the Thane of Cawdor feed the fishes." The captain laughed and stepped in.

"Gentlemen," he said, "we will be back for you early in the morning, unless you conclude to try the water with us.'

"Go one, go all," answered the Ladrone, getting in, and Mulcahy tardily followed. Having matured a scheme for destroying the "Old Man's" band, cook included, he was very reluctant to give it up.

The captain took the rudder, McBeth stood at the sheet, and the other two sat on either side to trim the boat. The company of hunters described by the cook as friendly to the "Old Man," just in from their hunt, came down to the water and called aloud to them as McBeth let out the sheet and they shot into the bay. The howling of the wind drowned their voices, and the storm burst on the little craft in all its fury. The water was lashed until it boiled and poured over the side at every plunge, bringing the boat repeatedly to the verge of sinking. The captain steered admirably and McBeth trimmed the sail with the utmost nicety. They were firm and vigilant. It was evident from their compressed lips and intense watchfulness that they were putting forth all their acquired skill and native powers to ride the storm. It was beautiful to see how perfectly in unison they played their several parts, so adroitly seconding each other that they seemed to move by one and the same impulse. They said, on reaching their ship after a struggle of six hours, that for about an hour in the mid-passage there was scarcely a minute in which they did not expect to go to the bottom.

As they rounded to in the comparatively calm water, and spoke their ship—the *Vandalia*—and a sailor threw them a rope, a young Scotch physician who had come out on her as a passenger appeared on deck and called out in stentorian tones : " All hail, Macbeth ! "

CHAPTER XXI.

THE LADRONE IS CAPTURED AND CARRIED THROUGH THE GOLDEN GATE.

HOBSON had sought the appointment to the mission in which he was engaged with a view to the acquisition of a private fortune. As long as he fulfilled his duty to the sect with zeal and ability the fleecing of a stray Philistine, he knew, would not be strictly inquired into. In thinking over the case of the Ladrone, he frequently suffered an inward pang at the thought that his wealth would perish with him in case he was suddenly removed ; and at last he resolved to have him kidnapped and carried to some safe place of concealment, and there bleed him to death. He could extract perhaps his entire fortune by judicious management, and he might, after accomplishing this result, turn the lion loose with his teeth drawn and claws cut. He was a merciful man, in his own estimation, and brought himself to believe that this course was dictated by charity—that first of virtues. It would save life, attain the end in view, and spoil the Egyptian. It was a happy combination of results, and took a strong hold on a mind that seldom let go a purpose.

There was in this man a certain sense of justice and of

order that impelled him to establish the identity of a doomed Gentile and witness the execution, and not to trust to the word of his instruments, who might impose on him and draw the reward for service either not performed or carelessly and mistakenly done. But to carry this plan out in the city involved great personal risk, and he accordingly cast about for a retreat where the prisoners could be brought before him, examined, and dispatched in safety. His eye had often rested on the Monte Diablo, which could be seen for fifty miles about, lifting its lofty head into the upper air, blue and indistinct in the distance. He crossed the bay with a trusty party and established a camp in the recesses of the mountain. Two men whose names had been inscribed in the black list had been taken in the streets of the city in the night, and brought safely to him, examined, and removed ; and a third unhappy wretch had been taken through mistake and was held in durance. On the night of the day when the band went down from the Diablo to the coast to capture the Ladrone and remove Mulcahy, leaving the " Old Man " alone with the prisoner, he effected his escape. This rendered the Diablo untenable ; the camp was broken up, and Hobson returned to the city.

The last pirate found afloat on the waters of the Pacific coast was a small, rakish, swift - sailing brig, named the *Malec Adel*. She was well adapted to the piratical trade in a small way, and was doing a satisfactory business when she had the misfortune to be captured by a government vessel and brought into San Francisco. She was used by the military for a time as a transport, but finally put up for sale. She attracted a good deal of attention, on account of her rakish appearance and former bad character, and was well known to every one frequenting the harbor.

Hobson took with him a sea-going Saint and gave her a

thorough examination, and, when the sale came off, bid her in. He manned her with a small trusty crew, and dropped down and anchored her in the lower harbor, under the mountain off Sausalito, near the Golden Gate. This was a quiet retired spot, out of the way and free from observation. He now felt for the first time that he was equipped for business. He drew heavily on the vigilantes and on others for greater or less amounts, checked out his balance in bank, and carried his funds in gold to the cabin of the *Malec Adel*. He was far richer than he had ever been before, and felt that he had a colossal fortune almost within his grasp.

He longed for the night to come when he would see the Ladrone ascend the ladder of his piratical craft. Visions of his cabin bunkers filled with gold, and the vessel under way for Europe, floated indistinctly through his mind. His zeal in the service of the Prophet began to decline, and he occupied his thoughts with self and his personal future, in which the care of his numerous dependent families, left behind him in the Salt Valley, did not figure. He bent all his energies to effect this one capture, and planned and consulted with his city adherents almost every night. An attempt and failure would ruin everything; it must be made when all the elements tending to success were present. This caused delay, and several postponements of well-laid plans.

Some time prior to this, Morales and Digby had become alarmed at the condition of business. Speculation was running riot, wealthy men and firms were loading themselves down with real estate and dubious securities. They held a consultation with Hayward, in which they prophesied a collapse, a run upon the banks, and general failure. Morales had been contracting for some time and had the bank in condition to stand any strain that would come upon it. Don Antonio had been fully advised of the situation and had pursued a similar course in Monterey. Morales now urged upon the Ladrone the sale of his real estate, explaining that after the storm burst it would be long before any sales could be effected, and in the meantime the taxes would eat up the property. The Ladrone assented to this view and threw his entire estate into the market on such reasonable terms that he effected the sale of it all for cash, men borrowing money at high rates of interest, four and five per cent a month, to avail themselves of the splendid opportunity. The confident speculators thought he was mad to sacrifice his property, that was rising weekly in price, while a few thinking men heard in it the first mutter of the coming storm.

It was in going out at night to close one of the last of his heavy sales that the Ladrone fell into a trap. The purchaser was a friend of Hobson and deep in the scheme to capture the Ladrone, and had put off closing the transaction several times, alleging his pressing engagements. One rainy evening a note was sent to the Ladrone apologizing for the delay he had caused, saying he found it impossible in the day to get time to attend to it, and inviting him to his rooms at nine that evening, when they would close the sale.

Not the first suspicion crossed the mind of the Ladrone. He was now looking daily for the crash, and was uneasy lest this important sale should be outstanding when it came. He returned an answer by the bearer, as requested, saying he would be at the appointed rooms at nine punctually, and made the deed and papers relating to the business into a bundle, placing it in his breast-pocket. At twenty minutes before nine he set out, and in due time turned into the dark, short by-street in which the rooms were located. It was raining heavily and he was encumbered with an umbrella. He was passing an alley close to his destination when half a dozen men sprang on him and overpowered and gagged him.

As they were doing so he uttered a cry for help. A window was thrown up across the street, and a man called out :

" What's the matter ? "

There was no response, and he could see nothing. The Ladrone, on his back on the pavement, watched him anxiously. He stood, his figure thrown into strong relief by the light behind him, waited a little, then let down the window and retired. They drew a handkerchief over the Ladrone's face and pulled his hat down over his brow to conceal his features and the gag, tied his hands, and hurried him to the nearest wharf through unfrequented streets. Once they were questioned by several men standing at a corner under an awning. They explained that they were taking their friend, who had been overcome, to his ship. They placed him in a boat lying manned and ready, and he was rowed down into the lower harbor to the *Malec Adel,* hurried up the ladder and into the cabin.

At midnight the porter of the bank rapped at Mulcahy's door and informed him that Mr. Hayward had not returned. He said he had gone out about half past eight, not saying where he was going or when he would return. Mulcahy's first impression was that he had been kidnapped and carried over to the Contra Costa. He accordingly rushed down to the wharves, but found them silent and dark, with nothing moving and no lights. He was in a state of distraction at his inability to do anything, and rushed over to and down the long wharf, to counsel with Lacy and McBeth. He hailed the *Vandalia,* which lay near, and Lacy, the captain, came out of the cabin in his night gear and sent a boat for him. McBeth turned out, and a consultation was held.

" They have carried him to the Contra Costa," said Mulcahy.

" They have not," replied McBeth. " They have run him

over the sand hills, or, if they took to water, they have
rowed him down to Sausalito, and carried him up the coast
into the mountains of Marin or Sonoma. See here," he said,
pointing to a map he had before him ; "Mt. St. Helen, in
Sonoma, looks like a spot they might hide in."

"We will scan the bay with the glass at daybreak," said
the captain. "The night is pitch dark. They may not move
from the wharf until light."

As it was plain nothing could be done until day, the
party, after taking a nightcap, retired.

At the break of day they were on deck with the ship's
glasses, and the captain swept the wharves and bay in every
direction ; but no boats were seen to put out. As the sun
rose he directed his glass down the bay toward Sausalito,
and immediately called out :

"The *Malec Adel* is putting out to sea."

"They have got him aboard!" shouted Mulcahy frantically.
"Row me to the revenue cutter," and he rattled down the
ladder into the boat. The men were ordered in to take the
oars, and McBeth called over the side to him to get an order
from the collector of the port, before he went to the cutter,
or he would go on a fool's errand. Mulcahy, chafing at the
delay this would cause, ordered the men to land him on the
wharf, and rushed off to the collector's hotel, had him roused
from sleep, and got an order for the cutter :

"To pursue and overhaul the *Malec Adel* and bring her
back to harbor, if on examining her he saw cause for doing
so. Mr. John Mulcahy, representing the banking house of
Hayward, engaging to make good the damage done the said
brig in interrupting her voyage if the same be found to be
lawful."

Armed with this document, Mulcahy rushed to the wharf,
where he found Lacy and McBeth waiting for him, and they

were rapidly rowed to the cutter. On reading the order the officer in command got her under way as speedily as possible, and dropped down with the tide and a light breeze, passed through the Golden Gate and entered the ocean. Lacy, McBeth and the captain of the cutter raised their glasses and scanned the horizon. The *Malec Adel* was sighted some twelve miles off, hull down and out of sight, all sail set and steering southwest.

"Will we catch her?" asked Mulcahy.

"Doubtful," answered the captain of the cutter, still watching her through his glass. "She is built for speed."

"So are we, are we not?" inquired he.

"Yes, we are," answered the captain. "But, see," he added, handing him the glass, "how her masts rake. If she is well sailed we are as near her now as we will ever get."

This was very disheartening, and Mulcahy walked the deck in great agitation.

"What do you think?" he said, stopping before Lacy.

"I am afraid she is opening the gap," he answered, not taking his eye from the glass.

"The breeze is failing her," said McBeth, a few minutes after. "Her sails are beginning to shake. We will both be becalmed in thirty minutes."

"If a calm falls," said the captain, "I will get out the boats and pull for her. I fear it is our only chance."

"Let every man aboard," said Mulcahy earnestly, "pray that it may fall."

The breeze was from the land and was fast failing the *Malec Adel.* Presently it died out altogether, and her sails flapped and collapsed. She lost headway and came to a stand, rising and falling with the swell of the sea. The Ladrone, who, locked up in the cabin, had been looking back out of the small stern window, watched the cutter giving chase, and had almost given up hope as he perceived her gradually falling astern. But when the wind left the *Malec Adel*, and he saw it still with the cutter and bringing her rapidly up, his hopes rose and he looked about to help himself. One glance around the cabin suggested his plan; it was instantly formed, and he resumed his post at the window to watch the cutter. Suddenly he saw her sails shake in the wind, as the breeze died away from her and retreated to the shore whence it came. It was a land breeze, coming and going by fits and starts.

After a time the Ladrone, who still sat with his eye fixed on the cutter or on her masts, for her hull was invisible, saw two black specks appear and disappear on the intervening water ; then he saw the cutter's sails fill, and the gap between them began to diminish. Presently her hull came in sight. She overtook her boats, picked them up and came on with a strong breeze. Suddenly the Ladrone felt a lurch. The breeze had struck the *Malec Adel* and she filled and lay over to it ; then began to forge through the water. The moment for action had come. The Ladrone sprang to his feet, stripped himself to his drawers, took down a life-preserver from the wall, inflated it and thrust it through the narrow window into the water ; forced the cabin door with a powerful effort, ran out on deck and sprang over the bulwark into the sea.

"Shoot him !" called out Hobson in a rage, as he ran with several men to the stern, drawing their revolvers.

As the Ladrone rose to the surface, a fusillade greeted him from the deck ; but the balls fell harmless.

"Stop her and pick him up !" shouted Hobson. "A thousand dollars to the men that bring him aboard."

"Nonsense," answered the captain. "Hold her steady as she is !" he shouted in a threatening tone to the man at

the helm, who was wavering ; and she was held steady, and
sped like a race-horse on her course.

The Ladrone swam to the life preserver and took it under
his arms. The cutter came by, lowered a boat, picked him
up, and continued the chase. Great excitement prevailed on
the cutter. Every inch of canvas was spread. McBeth, who
took a gloomy view of the situation, suggested that maybe
a reward would help. He had known it to do good in emer-
gencies. Mulcahy took it up, and, after consulting with the
Ladrone, stepped upon a coil of rope, and taking off his hat,
called out : "I am authorized to offer ten thousand dollars to the crew for the capture of the *Malec Adel*."

A great shout met the proposition.

"You are very liberal," said the captain, smiling. "but
the men will never earn the reward. The *Malec Adel* has the
heels of us. She is fast leaving us now."

"The proverb will not hold in this case," said Lacy.
"Our stern chase will prove a short one. She is walking
away."

When the sun set, the hull of the flying vessel had sunk
beneath the horizon; and when he rose again, turning the
ocean between him and the cutter into liquid gold, the *Malec
Adel* had disappeared forever.

CHAPTER XXII.

THE FALLEN SAINTS AND ANGELS ARE CONSUMED BY FIRE.

"MR. JOHN LESON, Broker," was the legend over a set of
chambers in the business part of the city. This gentleman
had relinquished his apartment in the neighborhood of the
Old Mission ; and, under the patronage of Hayward, had
started in a new career, more congenial to his reformed tastes,
while giving free scope to his peculiar talents. In an inner

office he sat with a list on the table before him of the over-due notes of hand that a close examination had disclosed were floating on the market, bearing the signature of Solomon Stubbs, the Mormon Saint and millionaire.

Each note that was well secured by the indorsement of solid men, or by mortgage on lands of triple their face value, was underscored with red ink, and across the face of nearly all of those so marked was written, also in red ink, the word "secured." Mr. Leson was alternately gazing in abstraction at the list and glancing uneasily at the clock on the wall before him, that pointed to eight minutes past 5 P. M., when the inner door opened and a gentleman entered. Leson's face brightened. He turned the list upside down, placed a paper-weight on it and invited his visitor to be seated.

"So you have concluded to take my offer?" he said.

"Yes," responded the visitor. "Sol has requested me to carry it a month, and I could not press the payment. I need a large sum to-morrow, and you can take it. Here is the note, thirty-two thousand five hundred, with interest for thirty days. You really ought to pay half this accrued interest. It is a shame to shave such gilt-edged paper."

"Here is a certified check for the face of the note," said Leson. "You do not think I am buying the paper for amusement, do you? Of course, I will shave it ; that is my business. Put your indorsement on the back, if you please, and hand it over."

The gentleman indorsed the note, and, closely scrutinizing the check, put it carefully away in his pocketbook and left the office. Leson opened the safe and placed the paper in its proper file ; then sat down and penned the following note:

"TO DON PEDRO HAYWARD :

"Sir—The Ashford note is in ; shall I open fire in the morning? JOHN LESON."

He touched the bell and dispatched the note, and sat, during the absence of his messenger, frowning at the table, in which he seemed to see the image of Stubbs. His messenger returned and handed him an answer that ran thus:

" To John Leson, Broker :—Open fire.   Hayward."

On the following morning, at the opening of the great house of Solomon Stubbs & Co., Leson, accompanied by a notary public, presented himself at the desk of the cashier and asked payment for an overdue note which he drew from his portfolio. The amount was large, but a check was drawn and handed over. Another note was then presented with a like demand. The cashier stepped back and whispered with a member of the firm, returned and gave a check for the amount. On the presentation of the third note the gentlemen behind the counter exhibited signs of alarm, when, to their immense relief, Stubbs himself walked in. He ordered a check to be drawn for the amount and was turning away, when Leson handed in his fourth slip. Stubbs flushed with anger and turned on him.

" Am I to understand this to be an attack on my credit ? " he said. " Is this a run on my establishment ? "

" You are at liberty to take it as you like," answered Leson. " This gentleman standing by me is a notary and is prepared to enter protest if you decline payment. I need not tell you what a protest of this note would mean to the house of Solomon Stubbs."

" This note," said Solomon, taking it in his hand, " Mr. Ashford agreed to let run for thirty days."

" That is between you and Ashford," answered Leson. " He has entered nothing on the note but his indorsement. You must pay or go to protest."

" You have more of my paper, I suppose," said Solomon.
" I have," answered Leson. " Several pieces."

Stubbs whispered to the cashier, left the house and walked hurriedly to the Utah bank. He was the president and had a potential voice in the management. Several directors, who were in the bank office when he arrived, saw at once that if Stubbs was not sustained the whole fabric of credit would come to the ground. They at once dispersed to strengthen the deposit in their vaults and Solomon returned to his establishment. He passed Leson and the notary on their way to the bank in a carriage. The checks were paid in gold ; some checks on other banks were offered and declined. They drove to Leson's office, deposited the money in a safe and placed a guard over it. A pause now occurred in the proceedings. This was planned to allow the bank time to re⁻ cruit its resources.

At one o'clock the assault was renewed. Solomon himself took up the notes and checked for them, and at a quarter past two Leson received his last check. The party drove rapidly to the bank, and, just before the hour of closing came, received payment in full and retired to Leson's office.

That evening the city was full of vague rumors of impending trouble. The saloons were crowded and the bars did a rushing business. Men said the house of Solomon Stubbs & Co. had gone to protest, and that his bank had closed its doors and gone into the hands of a receiver. Solomon and his friends went from saloon to saloon denying the reports, and denouncing the originators as enemies to the public peace and security. In due time the crowds thinned out, and San Francisco retired to a troubled slumber.

In the morning, long before the hour of opening, the Utah Bank was besieged by a crowd that blocked the street. A man pushed his way through the press at the hour of opening and wafered to the door a piece of white paper on which was written—"Bank Closed."

A smaller crowd blocked the way in front of the house of Solomon Stubbs & Co. The door was opened, letting out a clerk, and immediately closed after him and locked. He turned and tacked this notice on the door :—"This House Has Made an Assignment."

A run immediately set in on all the banks, but two or three of which survived it. Commercial houses of stability were shaken to their foundations. Before night, credit on the Pacific Coast was dead.

The House of Hayward had no outstanding entanglements and met their depositors with a smiling face. This did not prevent, however, the checking out of nearly the entire deposits. Crowds returned when credit was restored to re-deposit money, but they declined to receive it. Tired of the excitement and danger to person and property, they shipped their treasure to Mazatlan and made preparations for closing their house. To Digby and Mulcahy was resigned the Hayward interest in the Monterey Bank, and they became partners of Don Antonio ; and Mulcahy, subsequently, a connection by his marriage to a cousin of the Senora Dolores. The charity of the new partners was put to a severe test a day or two before they took their departure for Monterey, but they came out triumphant. They had boarded a steamer to see a friend off, and on returning to the wharf met, face to face, the Mohawk—the man with the white eyebrows. The meeting that Mulcahy had longed for and dreamed of had come at last. They stopped and looked at him. Mulcahy put his hands in his pockets as Digby gave his name and drew a long breath.

"Well." he said. "You *are* a cosa de ver, as we Spaniards say—a thing to look at. What are you crying about ?"

"Gentlemen," said the Mohawk, "I am broken down. See my clothing. Look at me. I am ill. I want to get home. I shall die if I do not get off in this boat. I offered to cook in the steerage for my passage. I am a good cook ; Mr. Digby knows it. Will you not tell them so, and get them to take me, for old acquaintance, Mr. Digby ? "

"Well," said Digby, "you are a cool one. For old acquaintance, eh ? "

"Don't hit me now I'm down, Mr. Digby ; do help me," he replied. This was more than Digby could stand.

"Come, Jack," he said, "let's give him a lift."

"All right !" answered Mulcahy. "Come aboard, you spalpeen, and stop your blubbering. We will stow you away with the baggage."

They bought him a ticket in the steerage which insured him passage and coarse food to New York, and, as he was really ill, each handed him a gold five-dollar piece and left him shedding tears of gratitude.

"How we worse than waste ill-feeling on our enemies," moralized Mulcahy, as they descended the gangway. "We ought to be forever pitying, instead of hating them. That is a lesson I got early in life, but I forget it at times."

Hayward and Morales were ready for departure and awaiting a steamer. The bank building, furniture and lot were placed in the hands of Mr. Leson for rent or sale. They were sitting one night in their apartment, over a glass of wine and a cigar, discussing their plans for the future. Don Pedro agreed to retain his interest in the Mazatlan House, but declared his intention of living at Durango.

"In Mazatlan," he said, "you are in the tropics, and on a level with the sea. You are hot ; hotter than Florida a great deal. In Durango we are a mile higher up in the air. I intend to buy back the possessions of my wife's ancestors and restore the ancient glory of the family. I will bring out a colony of poor relations from the pine woods of Florida and people the province with Haywards; fill up the waste places and drive back the Apaches. I will astonish the natives with my improvements."

"You will do great things," said his uncle, laughing.

"I will," said the Ladrone.

Almost as he spoke a cry of "fire" was heard and they ran down into the street. A vacant frame building in the rear was in a blaze, the flames already beginning to beat against the bank. They ran back and, with the aid of the porter, secured such few valuable articles as remained in the apartments, including their papers, and left the building to its fate. A high wind blew from the south. It was about eleven o'clock, and soon after midnight it became evident that the city was doomed.

All was tumult and uproar. Shadowy figures could be seen skulking away from the great illumination down the shady sides of streets, into alleys, loaded with plunder. Others hurriedly advancing for fresh loads with anxious faces, fearful lest the fire might be checked. There was no occasion for fear on that score.

The flames swept down the upper side of the broad main street, leaving the lower untouched. Along the center ran a barricade of every species of goods and groceries, its parapet lined with canned meats, fruits, fish and preserves ; baskets of champagne, claret, brandies and cordials, all opened or in process of being opened and devoured by an army of uninvited guests that thronged this impromptu but highly illuminated table d'hote. Some straddled the table, some sat upon it with their faces some with their backs to the approaching fire ; heads were thrown back, and bottles elevated in the air ; healths were drunk along the line in high good fellowship, or with a show of condescension to fellows beneath them in the crowd on foot.

Between these merry men and the storehouses not yet on fire, from which the plunder they were reveling in had been carried out, was a band of firemen, under the orders of the city authorities, throwing water from their engines upon the advancing flames and on the roofs, in the vain hope of rendering them non-combustible. To these were running the owners of the endangered property with buckets of brandy and champagne, which they served out in pint tin cups to encourage and sustain the men that stood between them and financial ruin. To one who had no personal interest in the property it was quite evident that this stimulant was being thrown away. The fire, with the strong wind in its favor, was too fierce to be checked by human power.

From a building not yet touched a thin, bewildered little man, putting on his jacket, ran out and leaned against the table d'hote, facing and intently watching the advancing flames. After they had seized the house he had issued from and the top was enveloped, he suddenly dashed back and sprang through the open doorway. The revelers who witnessed this uttered a shout of commiseration and suspended the feast, watching—the good revelers—with beating hearts to see him re-issue. But in a minute after he had disappeared the roof fell in with a loud report, sending up a shower of sparks into the midnight sky, and the interest was transferred to the houses further on. All night long the fire raged without intermission and without check, utterly destroying twenty-two blocks—the heart of the city—and many lives, through bewilderment and desperate attempts to rescue money and property.

The great sheet-iron wholesale warehouse of Solomon Stubbs & Co., imported from London, was said to be fire-proof and warranted to be so, provided the doors and windows were kept shut. As the flames approached and enveloped it much interest was expressed to see how it would stand the test. The more so as it was reported that the bankrupt Stubbs and his satellites, with such stuff as they had saved from their financial wreck, had shut themselves up inside, so great was their confidence in its ability to resist the flames if they would keep the apertures closed. The buildings opposite were in full blaze and the warehouse began to warp. The front door opened, and Solomon Stubbs rushed blindly out. Instead of turning up or down the street and joining the crowds that began to cheer him, he dashed straight across and disappeared in the open doorway of a burning building that only waited until he entered to come down with a terrific crash.

A cry of horror went up from the spectators ; then, the curtain having fallen upon this scene, all eyes were turned again upon the sheet-iron building. Those within had closed the door as soon as they had let the bankrupt out ; but in a few moments thereafter the lower doors and windows became so warped, and the heat in their vicinity so great, that all change of exit was at an end, and Angels and Saints rushed to the central portion of the building where the heat was least, and fell or threw themselves upon the floor, gasping for breath, to await their inevitable doom.

At this moment a great shout rose from the multitude, as Corby, chief of the Avenging Angels, appeared on the roof running. He made a desperate leap for a neighboring roof : but whether he reached it or sank into the interven ing chasm could not be seen for the smoke, and was never known.

THE END.